# SPECIAL EXCERPT

The Torquemadan leader removed something from his coat, and Willy heard a hissing sound. The man waved his arm, dispersing a spray, and the werewolves clawed at their eyes and whimpered. He threw the canister at the floor midway to Willy, who heard the metal object rolling in his direction but lost sight of it in the darkness.

A moment later, his eyes filled with tears and his nostrils seemed to catch on fire.

*Tear gas!*

Covering his eyes with his free arm, Willy dropped his flashlight. Coughing, he slid down the wall and kicked out until he heard the metal canister rolling away from him.

"Get him out of here!" the same man said.

Willy heard a staccato of footsteps as the humans rushed by him and retreated down the corridor. He heard claws on the floor and deep panting, like that of a dog. At least one of the werewolves bore down on him, and he couldn't see the damned thing! His fingers found the edge of the door, which he slammed shut. He threw his weight against it just as a heavy body slammed against the other side. Planting his feet, he twisted the feeble lock in the doorknob. On the other side of the door, the werewolf roared in anger. And Willy had shot one of them . . .

*Oh, God, I have to get out of here!*

# THE FRENZY WAR

# THE FRENZY WAR

## The Frenzy Wolves Cycle

Author of the Bram Stoker
Award–Nominated
*Johnny Gruesome*

# GREGORY LAMBERSON

## MEDALLION
P R E S S

Medallion Press, Inc.

Printed in USA

DEDICATED, WITH LOVE, TO MY DAUGHTER,
KAELIN

Published 2012 by Medallion Press, Inc.

The MEDALLION PRESS LOGO
is a registered trademark of Medallion Press, Inc.

Typeset in Adobe Garamond Pro
Printed in the United States of America

ISBN# 9781605424538

10 9 8 7 6 5 4 3 2 1
First Edition

## ACKNOWLEDGMENTS

As always, I'd like to thank my wife, Tamar, for providing the occasional English into Spanish translation and everyone at Medallion Press for their continuing and superlative support. Special thanks to my editor, Lorie Popp Jones, for keeping track of the multitude of characters and timelines that grow increasingly complex as The Frenzy Cycle and The Jake Helman Files progress.

"We have many (rules), but the most critical are these.


'Do not kill man.'


'Do not reveal your true self to man.'


'Do not endanger yourself or your pack.'"


—Angela Domini

to NYPD Captain Anthony Mace

# PROLOGUE

*Luce, Italy*

The iron hammer struck the red-hot silver with all the strength Marcelino Bianchi could muster, fusing together the two halves of the long object lying upon the anvil. Marcelino had labored as a metalworker, a blacksmith, and a silversmith for two decades, and his muscles had become as hewn as the stone face of a mighty cliff. He had learned the trades from his father, who had apprenticed under his own father and now helped Marcelino manage his business. Marcelino had taken his son, Petro, as his apprentice, but he wanted neither his father nor his son to help him now. This was his chance to serve God.

Sweat seared Marcelino's eyes, but still he hammered away at the silver, flattening the blade, reshaping it, making it whole again. He approached his work with the fervor of an acolyte, taking strength and satisfaction from his efforts.

The clanging in his ears, like the tearing of his muscles, inspired him to work harder, to serve those men who served his Lord. Perspiration soaked the long-sleeved shirt he wore beneath his leather apron.

When he finished his task, he seized the weapon's hand-carved handle and drove the great blade into a chest filled with ice, heaving a sigh as steam hissed around him. He found the process purifying and wondered how it would feel to wield the sword in combat.

As she drove through the hilly terrain in her silver Fiat 500, admiring the view of the mountains in the distance ahead, Valeria Rapero engaged in small talk with her passenger, Father Jonas Tudoro.

She thought of the aged priest as a father figure, for he had placed her with a foster family when her parents had died in an automobile crash in Tuscany when she was eight years old and had looked in on her from time to time, monitoring her progress and encouraging her studies. When she turned thirteen, Valeria's foster parents sent her to a private Catholic school, and again Tudoro had checked on her status. His visits became so frequent that he became a mentor to her, and as she neared graduation, he came to her with a proposal.

"The church has need of your services," he said one sunny afternoon on the school grounds. "We've cared for you for nine years. Will you repay us with nine years of service?"

"Of course," she said. "You know I will."

Now, seven years later, after rigorous physical training,

Valeria found herself escorting her mentor to the medieval village of Luce, a ninety-minute drive from Rome. Trees lush with green foliage parted, and the dirt road gave way to a driveway, which led to a three-story stone house that had once been an abbey.

Valeria parked the car and shut off the ignition, and she and Tudoro got out of the two-door compact. A gust of hot, dry wind blew long strands of blonde hair into Valeria's eyes, and she brushed them over one ear. She scanned the bright green yard around the house and saw no sign of children.

A tall man with broad shoulders and a bushy mustache exited the rear of the house, which had a separate roof. A shop, Valeria supposed. The man wore a scorched leather apron, and as he approached them with a wide smile, he removed suede work gloves and stuffed them into the apron's blackened pouch.

"Welcome back, Father." The man's sweat-soaked hair was black, even though he appeared to be middle-aged.

Valeria gazed at the veins in his piston-like arms and felt her own muscles tensing on instinct.

"Thank you, Marcelino." Returning the smile, Tudoro shook the man's hand. "This is Valeria, my protégé."

Marcelino glanced at Valeria, his face registering surprise. Valeria had grown accustomed to such looks. Tudoro was a Catholic priest with gray hair, and she was a young woman not unaware of her attractive appearance. They made an unusual pair whenever they traveled together.

Marcelino offered her a polite bow. "Miss Valeria."

"How do you do?" Valeria spoke in a respectful tone as

she had been taught. Despite Marcelino's powerful-looking physique, Valeria knew she could take him in a fight, but there was no need for her to dress down his ego.

Marcelino gestured to the back of the house. "I'm all ready for you."

Allowing Tudoro to walk beside Marcelino, Valeria brought up the rear, searching the trees for movement. Whenever she accompanied the priest, she acted as his unofficial bodyguard, whether he realized it or not. She would allow nothing to happen to him while he was under her protection.

Marcelino led them into his dark shop, where he closed the wooden door and slid a dead bolt into place.

Valeria eyed the cluttered interior. Chains hung from the wooden beams in the ceiling. Hammers and accessories covered shelves. Silver trays and goblets arranged on a display shelf awaited pickup. A massive anvil dominated the center of the room. She noted a large furnace, a rack filled with precision tools, and an ice chest filled with water. The room felt at least twenty degrees hotter than the outside temperature, and sweat dampened her brow.

Marcelino picked up a narrow box four feet long and set it atop the anvil. Valeria thought the box contained a rifle.

"For your approval," the blacksmith said.

Tudoro looked at Valeria. "Open it."

Valeria felt her eyebrows rising and saw Marcelino's do the same.

Tudoro's eyes twinkled. "Go on. It's yours. Why do you think I brought you along? I'm still quite capable of driving myself."

Valeria moved toward the anvil, the soles of her boots whispering across the floor. With great care, she opened the box, revealing the scabbard and sword within. Using both hands, she removed the sheathed sword. Surprised by its heft, she brought the weapon close to her face, like a cross, and inspected the carvings on its handle: on one side, the head of a man wearing a hood low over his eyes; on the other, the features of a snarling wolf, with two red jewels serving as its eyes. Rotating the sword, she studied the heads in profile, facing in opposite directions.

A shiver of excitement ran through her body. Valeria knew about the swords—she had studied their history—but had never expected to hold, let alone possess, one. Drawing the sword from its scabbard, she wielded it with one hand, not an easy task, and the silver blade gleamed even in the dull light. Only scarred metal a foot above the pommel revealed the sword had once been broken. After setting the scabbard down, she grasped the sword with both hands and resisted the urge to show off her fencing skills in front of Marcelino.

*The Blade of Salvation*, she thought.

"Welcome to the Brotherhood of Torquemada," Tudoro said as Valeria drove away from the blacksmith's house and shop.

Her pulse raced. "I never dreamed it possible."

"Because you're a woman?"

She nodded.

"You've proven yourself more than skilled enough.

You've earned this honor. And the requirements for serving as a knight in this order are different than those of a priest serving the church. Never forget: we're an entity separate from the church despite our obvious relationship to it."

"What will I do now?"

"First, you'll travel to Greece, where you'll join your fellow warriors in our crusade. We've identified several enemy strongholds there. Once you've eliminated them, you'll take the war to America."

*America*, Valeria's mind echoed.

*Piraeus, Greece*

Elias Michalakis paced the cool, shadow-laden living room of the two-story house he had rented for the fall. The first floor served as a garage and storage, with a small back room that Arsen used for his bedroom. Upstairs, two bedrooms flanked the living room, dining room, and kitchen. Elias and Damon shared one room, Otis and Adonia, the group's only female, the other. Galen, their newest recruit, slept on the living room sofa. The landlord had renovated the curved stairway and upstairs in marble before his wife had suffered a stroke and mounting the stairs had become too difficult for her. Such extravagance was wasted on the Wolves.

Elias peered through the sheer curtains at the vast seaport on the Saronic Gulf. Neoclassical mansions covering the hillside gleamed white in the afternoon sunshine. As far as he knew, the only Wolves left in Greece belonged to this cell. They had lost contact with the other cells and had been unable to track down their members. Last night Elias had assigned Otis to stake out a house that might have been rented to a team of agents from the Brotherhood of Torquemada. Otis had failed to return and had not called in, though he knew the importance of protocol. A sick feeling grew in the pit of Elias's stomach. Because Wolves were monogamous and Otis and Adonia had mated, Otis's importance to the group had increased.

*I should never have allowed him to go out on his own*, Elias thought.

"They took him," Adonia said from the sofa. She wore her dark hair short, like the men. "Say it."

Elias knew she was right. "No. It's too soon."

Adonia sprang to her feet. "Bullshit! Those Torquemadan dogs have probably eviscerated him by now." She wore a blue tank top, and the muscles in her slender arms grew taut.

Elias sensed the others in the room tensing. "Calm yourself. Getting angry at me won't help Otis. We have to stay clearheaded until we know what's happened."

Damon took Elias's place at the window, which freed Elias to deal with Adonia's frustration. Damon had helped Elias form the cell. Otis was their first recruit. The three of them had grown as close as brothers.

Adonia's brown irises expanded, blotting out the whites of her eyes. "We're the only ones left. We should be making plans to escape, not continue this futile—"

"Escape to where?" Elias said.

Adonia's teeth elongated as spittle flew from her mouth. "America! Canada! Anywhere but Europe. This continent is *lost*."

Elias took a breath. "And what would we do if we migrated? Hide like rabbits?"

"At least we'd be safe. If we'd left earlier, Otis would still be alive." Adonia caressed her swollen belly. "And my pups would have a father."

Elias measured the woman with a patient stare. He knew she needed to vent.

"Someone's coming," Damon said.

Elias joined his comrade at the window, feeling the others crowding behind him.

"Who is it?" Adonia said.

A dark van stopped in front of the house. Elias tensed his muscles, ready to Change. Then the van's side door slid open, and unseen arms pitched a body to the sidewalk. Elias recognized Otis's black army jacket, if not the figure's discolored features.

"Hurry!" When Elias turned, he saw the others already making for the door, and he ran after them.

Adonia led the charge down the marble stairs, followed by Arsen and Galen, with Damon and Elias bringing up the rear. Their feet scuffled concrete as they raced through the garage, emerging in the sunlight outside as the van drove off.

The five of them huddled around the still figure. Adonia rolled the body over, exposing Otis's dead, swollen features. She cried out and Galen gasped.

Elias turned numb. The van rounded a bend ahead, hidden by trees. Adonia's wail filled Elias with anguish. But something troubled him more than his friend's death: Otis's face had turned a deep shade of purple, while his hands retained their fleshy hue.

As if reading Elias's mind, Damon tugged at Otis's turtleneck. Large sutures circled Otis's neck, and a thick line divided the differing colors like a chasm.

"Oh no," Adonia said between tears.

Elias's pulse quickened. The Torquemadans had cut off Otis's head and sewn it back on. But for what purpose?

Damon unsnapped Otis's jacket, revealing explosives secured to the corpse's chest with wire.

"No!" Elias seized Damon's shoulder, intending to jerk his friend away.

The concussion struck him before he registered the flash of light and the roar deafened his ears, and then wet carnage stung his face.

# PART ONE
# NO-MAN'S-LAND

# CHAPTER ONE

Rhonda Wilson leaned against the back counter, facing her cash register, arms folded as she observed two men browsing opposite sides of Synful Reading. One was a regular, but she had never seen the other man before. She and Jason had just opened the bookstore an hour earlier at 9:00 AM, and Monday was always the slowest day of the week. Jason stood on the sliding ladder, moving older titles spine out on the upper shelves to make room for Tuesday's new releases.

Steam hissed from the radiator, warming her chilled bones. Rhonda looked forward to the holiday season but disliked early December, with its cold wind and rain. At least Gabriel Domini, one of the occult bookstore's owners, allowed her and Jason to keep the heat at a comfortable level. She got so cold in human form.

At eighteen, Rhonda did not know what to do with her

life. She desired to see Europe, and she had taken this job to save money, but she did not know what to do *after* Europe. She had no career goals, and she was mature enough to realize that her interest in writing poetry did not consume her soul to such a degree that it could ever become more than a hobby. She supposed she would attend college down the road when she had an inkling of how she wished to spend the rest of her life.

"You have to set goals for yourself," her mother had told her. "Even if you don't achieve them, you'll find other interests along the way."

Rhonda doubted her mother's wisdom. Right now she liked things as they were. She enjoyed living at home with her parents, the only pup of the litter to have survived childbirth, and she liked working alongside Jason. She liked Jason a lot. They had become close friends the summer after high school graduation because of the time they spent together in the store, and they had just started dating in the fall when most of their friends had gone off to college. Now, with winter coming, she sensed another change on the horizon. She hoped it would be positive.

The customer she recognized—middle-aged, balding, wearing a tan corduroy jacket—approached her and laid a book beside the register. He offered her a polite smile but didn't say anything.

Rhonda glanced at the dust jacket of the hardcover as she rang it up. *The Wolf Is Loose: The True Story of the Manhattan Werewolf,* a true crime book by Carl Rice, author of another true crime book she knew all too well—*Rodrigo*

*Gomez: Tracking the Full Moon Killer.* Seeing the author's new book caused her body to tighten. The store had become unexpectedly successful in the wake of the Manhattan Werewolf slayings two years earlier when the rogue Wolf Janus Farel had caused such a stir, but she wished Gabriel and Raphael Domini did not stock such material.

"They never caught him," the man said. "He's still out there somewhere."

"I know." But Rhonda knew better. According to the leaders of her pack, Angela Domini, the sister of Gabriel and Raphael, had slain Janus and then fled the city. Rhonda collected the man's money and stuck the book and receipt in a plastic bag, which she handed to him. "Have a nice day."

"You too." The man left, and the bells on the door jingled.

*Here I am, a teenage werewolf working in an occult book-store in the Village*, she thought. She did not really consider herself a werewolf—the term carried a negative connotation among her people—but she was a Wolf, and she belonged to the Greater Pack of New York City.

Now she watched her other customer, a tall man wearing a long coat and a knit cap. He seemed determined to examine every book in the store.

Rhonda glimpsed her reflection in the convex mirror mounted high in one corner to help catch shoplifters. She wore her dark hair short, like a boy, but her slender neck and angular shoulders were decidedly feminine. Her mother told her she was too skinny, but she was perfectly happy with her pixie-like body, which was just her human shell after all. Unfortunately, living in the city rarely afforded her the opportunity to assume her Wolf Shape. She wore a navy-blue hoodie over a black T-shirt and tight, faded jeans tucked into short boots.

Jason pressed his feet along the outside of the ladder and slid down it to the scuffed wooden floor like a sailor on a ship. Wearing loose-fitting carpenter's pants and a New York Giants football jersey, he came behind the counter and retrieved the bathroom key, which was secured to a wooden block so it wouldn't get lost.

Rhonda felt his free hand slide around her waist. His touch sent a tremor of excitement through her body, but she swatted his hand away. They stood the same height, and when she looked at him, she saw straight into his brown eyes. She had to admit her heart skipped a beat as he grinned at her. They had not had sex yet. Wolves mated for life, and they agreed they were too young to make that commitment, but they had pleased each other in other ways.

"You want to see a movie tonight?" Jason said.

"What movie?"

"I don't know . . ."

Rhonda smiled. He never had a movie in mind; he just wanted to spend time with her in the dark. "Sure."

She watched him hurry to the back of the store, admiring his butt as he unlocked the office door. They intended to go to Europe together, and she accepted the possibility that they might sleep together then, whenever *then* was. She fantasized about seeing him in his Wolf Form.

The customer turned and exited without saying anything. His abrupt departure caused Rhonda to raise one eyebrow, but she shrugged it off. She had long ago become accustomed to strange behavior from her fellow New Yorkers, especially those humans who frequented Synful Reading. She glanced at the clock beside the register—10:05. Shit, time was crawling.

The bells on the door jingled. The customer who had just left returned, followed by two men garbed in similar long coats. They wore knit caps of different colors, and Rhonda estimated their ages ranged from twenty-five to thirty-five. One had black skin, and he twisted the lock on the door and strode across the store. The fine hair on Rhonda's body prickled. The other men stood before the counter, their eyes locking on her. The black man removed a can of spray paint from his coat pocket and unleashed a hissing black mist at the lens of the security camera mounted on the wall.

"Hey!" Rhonda wanted to scream for Jason.

The man closest to her had a black beard. He reached inside his coat and withdrew a gun unlike any Rhonda had seen in movies or on TV: a pistol with a wooden grip and two barrels, one of them more than a foot long.

She felt her eyes widen as her heart raced. "What do you want? Money?"

*No. They know what we are.*

The bearded man pulled back a spring-loaded mechanism on the gun, cocking it.

Rhonda reached for the alarm button beneath the register. She heard a muffled sound come from the gun—not a shot, really, more of a snap followed by a rush of air. Pain needled her chest, stopping her forward momentum, and when she looked down, she saw a dart protruding between her small breasts. Curling her fingers around the dart, she jerked it out and felt a burning sensation in her chest. The dart slipped from her fingers in slow motion and clattered on the floor. The room rocked back and forth, and the bearded man lowered his gun.

Rhonda's mind clouded, and her body undulated.

Jason emerged from the back of the store. At first he looked puzzled, then concerned.

*Help me, Jason!*

Jason charged forward, and suddenly Rhonda realized that might not be such a good thing after all. The black man and the man who had been in the store first drew identical tranquilizer guns. Jason opened his mouth to scream, but Rhonda could not hear him. He leapt into the air, wild-eyed, just as the men fired their guns. His body twisted in mid-air as the darts penetrated him, and he crashed on the floor between the men.

Rhonda staggered forward to see over the counter's edge.

Jason snarled at the men, his irises expanding so they blotted out the whites of his eyes. Rhonda prayed he would complete his Transformation and tear the men to pieces.

The black man raised a leg to kick Jason, but Jason slashed at the air with one hand, and the man jerked his leg back. The movement caused Jason to topple over, like a table with one leg removed, and he fought to get back on his hands and knees, his face contorted with equal parts rage and pain.

Seeing the darts in his torso, Rhonda realized he had received double the dosage she had of whatever chemical flowed through her veins.

Holstering his gun, the bearded man moved beside the black man and looked down at Jason.

Rhonda slumped over the counter and clawed at its edge to keep from sinking to the floor. She fought to remain alert.

The bearded man drew something from his coat, but it wasn't a gun. It was long and shiny.

*A sword!*

Rhonda opened her mouth to call to Jason, but she had no idea if any sound came out.

Using both hands, the man raised the sword high. Jason looked up, fear evident in his eyes even as his face contorted. The sword sliced the air in a downward swing.

One moment Rhonda saw Jason's transforming countenance, and the next she saw blood gushing out of the stump of his neck as his body lurched forward. Then she blacked out.

Michael moved away from the pool of blood spreading across the dirty wooden floor, then slid his Blade of Salvation into the scabbard fastened to the inside of his coat without bothering to first wipe the blood from it.

Standing at the counter, Myles nodded his approval.

Michael gazed at the head on the floor. It belonged to a creature neither wolf nor human but something in between. He had killed it just in time; in another few moments it would have completed its transformation into something almost unstoppable. "Let's get that bitch out of here. Watch out for the blood."

Henri joined Myles. They holstered their tranq guns

and went behind the counter.

Michael spied a key attached to a wooden block on the floor, where the beast boy had dropped it. He snatched it and hurried to the rear of the store, where he unlocked a door that admitted him into a cramped office. Walking between a safe bolted to the floor and a desk with a computer terminal upon it, he seized a digital recorder deck connected to a security monitor. He unscrewed the connecters, his movements restricted by the blue latex gloves he wore, and pulled the recorder away, leaving cables dangling. On his way out, he pushed the button lock in the doorknob, threw the key and its block on the floor, and shut the door.

His men stood at the front door, supporting the girl monster between them. Her head rolled limp on her neck.

"Let's go." Michael stepped over the headless corpse on the floor and hopped over the crimson pool. Reaching past the female wolf, he unlocked the door and pushed it open.

Eun, the Korean woman he had stationed outside the door as lookout, revealed herself. She caught the door and waved to the white cargo van idling at the curb.

Michael peered outside, looking each way up St. Mark's Place. He saw the usual eccentrics on the sidewalk and civilian traffic but no police. "Go!"

Henri and Myles ran outside into the crisp morning air, dragging the female between them. The van's side door opened, and Valeria crouched in the darkness within it. Henri and Myles shoved the wolf into her arms, and the three of them hauled her into the van and laid her upon the sofa inside it.

Michael crossed the sidewalk without glancing at the pedestrians milling about. Feeling an electric current in the air, he opened the passenger door and got in beside Angelo. A moment later, the side door closed behind him. Then he heard manacles snapping shut and his comrades zipping the unconscious female into the body bag they had brought.

"Move it!" Eun said.

With his steel-grey eyes focused on the traffic ahead, Angelo turned into the street.

"Nice and easy. We don't want to be pulled over." Now Michael glanced at the pedestrians. Those watching the van's departure seemed more confused than alarmed.

"What happened in there?" Valeria said.

Henri answered, his English accented in French. "Michael slew the other beast."

Only Michael's nerves prevented him from gloating.

"That's one for Pedro," Valeria said.

Michael thought of their fallen comrade who had been sent to the United States two years earlier to retrieve the Blade of Salvation that Valeria now carried. He had been slain in Central Park, along with an American priest who served as his contact, by one of the beasts. Pedro had the heart of a true warrior and had been dedicated to their cause. He had died a hero. Now his demise had been avenged.

Angelo turned right onto a one-way street. Two blocks later, he double-parked beside a second van, this one a black GMC Savana.

Michael got out and climbed into the driver's seat of the Savana, started its engine, and unlocked its doors. In his side mirror, he saw Henri, Myles, and Eun jump out and run to the back of the vehicle. Then Angelo moved the white van ahead, giving Michael room to pull out. Valeria joined the others, and the four of them carried the sofa, their captive invisible in the secret compartment within it, to the Savana. They loaded the sofa into the cargo compartment and got in after it.

After the doors slammed shut, Michael turned into the street. Halfway up the block he stopped where Angelo had parked the first van.

Angelo hopped into the passenger seat. "Nice and easy," he said in a sarcastic tone. "We don't want to be pulled over."

Driving forward, Michael tore the false beard from his face as he heard sirens in the distance.

# CHAPTER TWO

**W**illy Diega guided his department issue SUV past the police cruisers parked along St. Mark's Place and double-parked in front of a red Toyota at the corner of the block.

His partner, Karol Williams, shook her head. "How do you expect this guy to get out?"

"If he knows what's good for him? Very carefully."

"That's no way for a police lieutenant to treat the public."

"Tell me that again when the department actually unfreezes the promotions list." Willy had passed his lieutenant's test with flying colors, but the brass had placed all promotions on hold due to budgetary woes. He remained a detective first grade in Homicide South, training detectives new to the unit. Karol was the second detective third grade to serve as his partner since Patty Lane's murder two years earlier.

"What's your big hurry to move up? Are you that anxious to get rid of me?"

In truth, Willy wanted to leave Homicide. He had witnessed enough mayhem during the Manhattan Werewolf case to turn him off being a murder police. But Ken Landry, his lieutenant, had advised him to stay put until his promotion came through. "I'm that anxious to get the pay grade that goes with the promotion. Besides, once I leave Homicide, you can't use being partners as an excuse not to see me."

Karol gave him an exasperated look. "We'll still be in the same department. I don't date cops—ask around."

"I have."

"What did you learn?"

"The guys in your old unit think you're a dyke."

"What if I am?"

"That's cool. We can go watch girls together."

"*That's* why I won't date you. You're a dog, and you're too old for me to teach you new tricks."

"Maybe I could teach you some."

"You never give up, do you?"

"I've got to be true to myself."

"Then how about this: you're my training officer. You're using your position of authority to pressure me into submitting to you."

Willy stared at her for a moment, uncertain what to say. Karol got out of the SUV, and he did the same. Had he taken the game too far? He liked Karol but not enough to risk his career over. Staring across the top of the vehicle at her, he saw her face split into a big smile, her white teeth dazzling against her dark skin. He wagged one finger at her. "You had me going."

"Good. Because if I didn't like you I just might file a complaint, and people would pay attention. You just want what you can't have. Your macho Latin ego can't handle that I'm not interested."

Willy joined her on the sidewalk, and they started forward. "Hey, don't stereotype me." Upon seeing their destination, he stopped in his tracks: *Synful Reading*.

Two police officers stood outside the door, one of them speaking to three civilians. Yellow crime scene tape blocked off the sidewalk, forming a square around the store's entrance and forcing pedestrians into the street.

"Is something wrong?" Karol said.

"Our crime scene figured into an old case of mine."

"Which one?"

"The Manhattan Werewolf."

Karol raised her eyebrows. "How involved?"

"The woman who ran the store witnessed one of the homicides. We considered her a person of interest. She disappeared. We put out an APB for her, but she never turned up. Her brothers own the store now."

"No shit? I'm sure there's no connection."

*I'm not so sure.*

They ducked beneath the tape, and Willy pulled his three-quarter length coat back, allowing the PO stationed at the door to see his gold shield. "Willy Diega and Karol Williams."

The PO recorded their names on his clipboard.

"No press. I don't care how pushy she—*they*—are."

The PO nodded. "CSU is here."

Pulling on his latex gloves, Willy looked over his shoulder at the Crime Scene Unit van pulling up to the curb. "Who are the civilians?"

"The woman says she saw some guys drag a girl out of the store and throw her into a white van that took off. She went inside and found the vic. The two men went in after she came out screaming. We got here two minutes after Dispatch called us. We put out an APB on the van, but no luck so far."

Karol put on her gloves, and Willy opened the door for her and followed her inside the bookstore, where two other POs stood guard. Exotic scents unfamiliar to Willy filled his nostrils, and he wanted to gag: incense. A pool of blood spread across the floor from the gaping neck stump of a headless body. Willy experienced déjà vu. He had seen more than his share of headless corpses on the Manhattan Werewolf case. Glancing at the wall units he saw only books, not messages scrawled in blood. Karol froze in her tracks, the first time Willy had seen her affected by a crime scene, and he stepped around her. The corpse's head lay tilted on one side on the floor. He caught himself sighing with relief. The Manhattan Werewolf's victims' heads had all been missing.

"You guys touch anything?" Willy said.

"Not us," one of the POs said.

Willy pulled on rubber shoe covers and circled the pool of blood to see the victim's face. His heart skipped a beat. The unblinking eyes were completely brown except for their pupils. *Like a dog's*, he thought.

"What the hell?" Karol said beside him.

A sick feeling grew in the pit of Willy's stomach. He circled the corpse and stood straddling it. Sneakers, carpenter's pants, a football jersey—all soaking in blood. Seeing the bulge of a wallet in a back pocket, he bent over and removed it. He parted the leather and examined the photo ID, which showed a handsome boy with curly hair matching that on the head staring back at him.

"Jason Lourdes." Willy did some quick math. "Age eighteen. Queens."

Karol pointed at the corpse's neck stump. "That's the cleanest wound I've ever seen."

"Like it was made by a sword." Willy took out his cell phone and struck auto dial.

"Lieutenant Landry," a voice said after the second ring.

"It's Willy. I'm over at Synful Reading on St. Mark's. The bad news is we got a headless stiff."

"Ah, *shit*," Landry said in a low voice. "What's the good news?"

"The head's right here."

Landry released an audible sigh.

"The vic's only eighteen. Someone cut off his head, possibly with a sword."

"Please tell me that's the worst of it."

"Witnesses say a young woman got snatched too. We have to ID her. I need you to find the contact info for Angela Domini's brothers and get them down here."

"Oh, shit," the PO said behind Willy, who shot him a disapproving look.

"Copy that," Landry said.

Willy read the address on Jason Lourdes's ID, and Landry hung up. Willy looked at Karol. "The Dominis own a funeral home too. At least they did when we shut down the previous investigation."

The bells on the door chimed as Hector Rodriguez from CSU entered with Suzie Quarrel, a member of his team. They wore blue jumpsuits with yellow rubber boots and gloves, and Suzie had dyed her razor-sharp hair purple.

"Somebody call for Rodriguez's Cleaning Service?" Hector's mustache undulated as he spoke. "Oh, *madre*."

"Bag it up," Willy said. "Everyone in the store is forbidden to discuss this with anyone but a superior officer."

"Why are you looking at me?" the PO said.

Willy turned to Karol. "You want to interview the witnesses?"

Sitting at his desk in the K-9 Unit, located at Floyd Bennett Field, where NYPD maintained its Aviation and Emergency Services units, Captain Anthony Mace filled out an online requisition for dog food.

Ever since being removed from Homicide South in the wake of the Manhattan Werewolf killings, which he had been unable to solve to the satisfaction of his superiors, Mace had been relegated to pushing paper in one of the most unglamorous units in the department, his rank largely meaningless, with no chance of escape or promotion. He followed the same routine day after day, scheduling training sessions, assigning new dogs to human partners, and acting like a bottom level administrator in any bureaucracy.

In the span of one case, he had gone from being a celebrity cop with a promising future to a forgotten soldier gathering dust in an office. Now technically part of the transit police, he looked forward to retiring in two years.

His position did have its benefits, though: the phone never rang in the middle of the night; his hours never varied; his wife, Cheryl, didn't worry he might be killed in the line of duty; he didn't agonize about departmental politics, losing the life of a detective under his supervision, or dealing with life-or-death situations; and he was able to spend plenty of time with Cheryl and their daughter, Patty, in their Bay Ridge home. All he had to do was survive the boredom of the next two years without going insane, and he'd be free to pursue other interests while collecting his pension. He daydreamed about that possibility every shift while gazing out his office window.

His cell phone rang, and he checked its display. Willy Diega, one of his former detectives. Pressing the phone against his ear, he settled back in his chair and stared at a framed photo of himself with Cheryl and Patty, taken on Patty's first birthday. "Lieutenant Diega, good to hear from you."

"I'm calling from Synful Reading."

Mace's fingers tightened on the phone. "What's happening there?"

"I caught a DOA related to a likely kidnapping. A teenage boy got decapitated inside the store."

A fear Mace thought he had forgotten resurfaced. "Is his head—?"

"Present and accounted for. But get this: it was cut off. Looks like one blow did it. My guess is the perp used a sword."

The base of Mace's skull turned numb. *The Blade of Salvation.* Almost a year earlier, Willy had told him that both halves of the broken sword had been claimed by some big shot at the Vatican. Closing his eyes, Mace rubbed the bridge of his nose. He had hoped the Wolves would be able to maintain the secret of their existence. "Maybe it's just a coincidence."

"Yeah, and maybe—ah, shit."

"What's wrong?"

"I gotta go. Your wife just showed up."

Pocketing his phone, Willy watched the Manhattan Minute News van prowl the street, its driver searching for a parking space.

*At least they'll have to go around the block*, he thought as he joined Karol and the witnesses.

"This is my partner, Detective Diega," Karol said to the woman and two men.

"Hello," Willy said to them. "Do we have all their information?"

"Yes," Karol said.

"Folks, we're going to release you now. We'll probably need to follow up with you later, maybe even tonight. Don't discuss what you've seen with anyone, especially the press."

"They're not going anywhere just yet," a male voice said behind him.

Turning, Willy saw Detectives Larry Soares and Nick Cato from Missing Persons. The detectives now outnumbered the witnesses.

"We co-own this mess," Soares said.

"That's fine with me. You guys can have the whole bag of shit if you want it. Can we move this conference inside?"

"We'd like to interview these witnesses."

"We'll share the information we have. Let's get them out of here before they describe what they saw to everyone with a TV." Willy turned to the witnesses. "Thank you for your assistance."

They nodded and left.

"The woman saw four adults—three men and a woman—drag a teenage girl into a van," Karol said. "The woman was Asian. One of the men was black. With the driver, that makes five."

Willy saw Cheryl Mace speed walking toward them on the sidewalk, followed by her cameraman, Ryan Costas. "Karol, show them what we've got, okay?"

"You're the boss." Karol led Soares and Cato into the store.

Willy met Cheryl at the crime scene tape. She had been a TV reporter when Willy was first promoted to Homicide, then took a more humane job as an associate producer for an afternoon talk show before she and Mace announced her pregnancy. After her maternity leave, she had returned to active reporting, this time for Manhattan Minute News, a local cable station. She had wasted no time making a name for herself as an aggressive reporter who played by the rules.

"What have you got for me, Willy?"

"A DOA and a probable kidnapping."

Ryan caught up to them, his forehead sweaty.

"DOA," Cheryl said. "You mean a homicide."

"I'm a homicide detective."

She seemed amused by his sarcasm. "Method of murder?"

"That's under investigation."

"Who's the vic?"

"We're not releasing a name until we confirm the deceased's identity and notify the next of kin."

"What's the story with the kidnapping?"

"That's also under investigation."

"Look, we're the first ones here. Give me something to go on the air with before the circus comes to town."

"I've got nothing to share at this time." Willy saw a taxi pull over to the curb and two men he recognized get out: Gabriel and Raphael Domini, the owners of the store. He had interviewed them when their sister, Angela, disappeared during the Manhattan Werewolf investigation.

Cheryl turned to Ryan. "Get some B roll."

As Ryan adjusted the settings on his camera, Willy raised the police tape for Gabriel and Raphael. Both men had dark hair and appeared ashen faced.

"Lieutenant Landry called me," Gabriel said.

"I'm Detective Diega. We spoke two years ago."

"I remember."

Willy recalled that Gabriel had done most of the talking during their previous interview even though he and Raphael were the same age. Angela was the third triplet. He saw Ryan focusing his camera on them. "Let's speak inside."

Gabriel and Raphael gave their names to the PO at the door, which Willy opened for them. Inside, Landry and the Missing Persons detectives stood looking at the head on the floor. Karol shot digital photos while Hector and Suzie set up their equipment.

*The circus is already here*, Willy thought as Gabriel and Raphael stood motionless before the pool of blood. "Watch your step. Is this Jason Lourdes?" He watched the brothers join the MP detectives on the other side of the corpse. Their eyes widened, and their mouths opened in tandem.

Gabriel swallowed. "Yes."

"We have a witness who saw four people drag an unconscious woman out of here and take her away in a van. Any idea who she might have been?"

"I'm technically the manager here," Raphael said in a quiet, intense voice. "The young woman scheduled to work with Jason this morning was Rhonda Wilson. She's eighteen, like him."

Willy gestured to Soares and Cato. "These gentlemen are with Missing Persons. Can you provide them with any photos of Rhonda?"

"Yes, whatever you like."

Willy pointed at the security camera. "Someone spray painted your camera. Is it hooked up to a recorder?"

"There's a digital recorder in the back office," Raphael said.

"Hector, dust that back door and the office for prints before you do anything else."

"We'll take care of that right now," Hector said. He motioned to Suzie, who carried her fingerprinting kit to the back.

Willy turned to the Domini brothers. "Can one of you let us into that office when they're done?"

Raphael looked at Gabriel, who nodded, then followed Suzie. Without prompting from Willy, Karol followed her in turn. Soares elbowed Cato, who joined the party.

"Let's start with the obvious question," Willy said. "Do you have any enemies who would want to kill one of your employees and abduct another one?"

"No, of course not," Gabriel said.

"Did you receive any kind of threats or a ransom note?"

"Nothing. Your call was the first I heard of this."

"Why were two kids allowed to run this store alone?"

"They're both eighteen," Gabriel said. "Jason was just promoted to assistant manager. Most of our staff is made up of college students. This is a small specialty bookstore, not a high volume megastore. My brother and I focus our energy on our primary business."

"The funeral home."

"That's right."

"What about angry ex-employees?"

"We treat our staff well."

"Whatever happened to your sister?"

"She's in Canada."

*He didn't miss a beat.* "Two years ago, I asked you to have her get in touch with me."

"I gave her the message. As I remember, she didn't seem to care. Since the murders stopped, I never pressed the issue."

"Will you tell her about this?" Willy gestured at the body.

"I'll have to do it through the mail because she doesn't have a telephone."

"That's convenient."

"I find it just the opposite. You could always extradite

her, but for what purpose?"

"Our primary concern right now is Rhonda. Do you maintain a list of customers?"

"Just an e-mail list and only of those customers who sign up for it through our website."

"We'll need a copy of that list and the names of any unusual customers you can think of."

"This is an occult bookstore. Many of our customers are eccentric."

"We'll also need a list of your managers and employees dating back two years." Willy's hand radio squawked, and he raised it to his mouth. "Go for Diega. Over."

A male voice came over the radio. "We've got a distraught woman who says she's the mother of the girl who works in there. Two more news crews showed up too. Over."

"Deidre Wilson," Gabriel said. "I called her."

Willy eyed Gabriel. Who told him to call anyone? "Send her in. Over."

"Copy that," the PO said. "Over."

"It's getting crowded in here," Hector said under his breath.

*You can say that again*, Willy thought. "We'll be out of your hair soon."

The bells on the door chimed, and a brunette in her forties entered the store, her features twisted with emotion. She zeroed in on Gabriel, then at the head and body on the floor. She stumbled toward Gabriel, who caught her.

"Where's Rhonda?" Her voice threatened to crack.

"We're trying to figure that out," Gabriel said. "Some

men may have taken her."

She glanced at the body again. "Is that Jason?"

"We haven't told his parents yet."

"Oh, my God! Who did this? *Who*?"

Gabriel looked into her eyes. "We don't know."

Soares stepped forward. "Mrs. Wilson, has anyone contacted you about this?"

"No, no one."

"Has Rhonda said anything about seeing strange people around your home or receiving troubling phone calls?"

"No! She's a normal eighteen-year-old girl. She spends all her time with—with Jason . . ." She broke into sobs.

"What about an ex-boyfriend or someone who was jealous because she wouldn't go out with him?"

Deidre shook her head.

Soares glanced at Willy before returning his gaze to the frantic woman. "You need to be home in case anyone tries to contact you about a ransom. Where do you live?"

"B-Buh-Bensonhurst . . ."

"My partner and I will take you home. We need to stay there with some police officers."

"Gabriel?"

Gabriel made a shushing sound. "It's all right, Deidre. Go with them and cooperate any way you can. I'll send someone to keep you company soon. Does Marshal know?"

She nodded, tears in her eyes. "He's waiting to hear from me. I said I'd call—"

"I'll call him. Don't worry about that."

"Is my baby going to be okay?" Deidre crumpled in his arms.

He held her. "I'm sure she is. You have to be strong for her sake."

Soares called across the store, "Cato, let's go!"

Cato left Suzie, Karol, and Raphael at the office door. He followed Soares and Deidre out the door, and Gabriel watched them leave.

"What kind of girl is Rhonda?" Willy said to Gabriel.

"She's a daydreamer. If I remember correctly, she likes to write poetry."

Karol returned with Raphael.

"The office was raided," Raphael said. "They took the recorder but didn't touch the safe."

Gabriel's expression turned grim.

"I'm afraid your store's going to be closed for a couple of days," Willy said.

"That's not important."

"I don't want to kick you out of your own business, but we need to prevent contamination of evidence."

"I understand. What will you be doing?"

*Gabriel's really used to running things.* "For one thing, we need to notify Jason's parents."

# CHAPTER THREE

Michael pressed his thumb against the button on the remote control, and the chain-link gates hummed as they parted. He drove through the gates and pressed the button again, then entered the compound of dirty brick buildings. The van passed through a short tunnel and emerged into a cratered parking lot. The only vehicles, invisible to the road outside, belonged to him and his companions: vans and SUVs.

The crumbling warehouse in Newark, New Jersey, had come cheap, thanks to the teetering economy. They had paid the landlord under the table and convinced him they only wanted to lock up the lease until they were able to raise the money needed for renovation. The man had been happy to take the cash for property he had been unable to rent.

Michael backed the van up to the concrete loading bay platform and switched off the ignition. "There's no place like home," he said, a joke he doubted his colleagues would grasp. Michael loved American movies and had watched them voraciously, even during his training to become a member of the Brotherhood of Torquemada. He could recite the names of movie stars, the years movies were released, and behind-the-scenes gossip if only he knew someone who shared his interest. But he had no friends beyond his soldiers in arms, and he accepted that such sacrifice was a small price to pay to serve in the Brotherhood. "Everybody out."

Eun opened the side door and hopped out at the same time Michael and Angelo did. They climbed the five concrete steps as Henri, Myles, and Valeria unloaded the sofa from the rear of the van. Michael inserted a key into a box mounted next to the loading bay door and turned it. The metal door ground open, revealing an interior as gray as the sky above. Henri, Angelo, Myles, and Eun pushed the sofa into the bay.

"Do you want me to move the van?" Valeria said.

"No need," Michael said. "This is as good a place as any for it."

She locked the doors and joined the others inside, and Michael twisted the key again and ducked beneath the door as it rattled shut.

Inside, Eun removed the cushions from the sofa and tossed them aside. Their captive lay motionless within the black body bag upon the sofa's interior base. Eun unzipped the bag, exposing the unconscious female, her wrists and ankles chained together.

Eun spat on the floor. "I wish we could kill her now."

Michael removed his coat. "That would defeat the whole purpose of our mission today. We're after intelligence."

Henri pulled off his knit hat, revealing his gleaming head. "Let's put her away while she's still down. I don't want to take any chances."

Angelo, Henri, and Myles lifted their captive from the sofa and carried her in the body bag to the wide metal door that Michael unlocked. Eun and Valeria followed, and Michael brought up the rear. After Valeria flicked on the lights, Michael closed and locked the door.

Inside the warehouse, the men laid their captive across a wide wooden dolly, and Angelo set his large hands on the push handle and walked it forward.

"Are you telling Tudoro we completed the first phase?" Henri said as they crossed the ground floor of the warehouse.

"No," Michael said. "I want complete communication silence. He'll follow the news."

Father Tudoro had been instrumental in recruiting all of the Brotherhood members at early ages. He and the monsignor he answered to were the Brotherhood's primary representatives in the Vatican. Michael knew that perhaps a dozen powerful men controlled the organization in secret. The identities of the others—European socialites who ran in powerful circles, mid-level politicians, and members of the intelligence communities—were kept a secret from the soldiers for security reasons. These high commanders determined the Brotherhood's strategy. If Tudoro died, none of the soldiers could identify the men above them and would have to wait for a new liaison to contact them. At thirty-five,

Michael was the oldest soldier and had earned the right to lead the others into battle.

They boarded a freight elevator and descended to the basement level. Angelo pushed the dolly through the dank lower corridor along gray cinder-block walls. He stopped at an open door, and Henri and Myles helped him carry the female into the room. Michael stood at the one-way viewing window they had installed and watched the men lower the female onto the floor. Then they lifted her out of the body bag and positioned her in one corner on a bed of straw.

Michael glanced at Valeria beside him. "Remove her clothes."

She cocked an eyebrow.

"Animals don't need garments. She's mocking us."

Valeria walked into the cell and whispered to Eun. They kneeled on the floor and used knives to strip the female naked. Then they secured manacles attached to chains bolted into the walls to her ankles and wrists and stood back. Using a key, Henri removed the chains they had attached to her in the bookstore, and Eun fastened a collar around the unconscious girl's neck.

Michael had been surprised when Tudoro had introduced women into the Brotherhood, but Eun had proven herself to be a fierce warrior and Valeria's commitment was unwavering. Looking at Valeria's long black hair, streaked blonde, he had no trouble imagining the curves of her body beneath the coat. He frowned on fraternization within the group but knew that sex provided an important physical and emotional release. As the leader, he felt it would be unseemly for him to indulge in physical pleasure with his subordinates.

The soldiers filed out of the cell, and Angelo slammed the steel door shut with a reverberating clang and slid its iron bolt lock into place.

"What now?" Valeria said.

"We wait for her to wake up," Michael said.

With Karol standing beside him, Willy watched the EMT workers transport Jason Lourdes's bagged body on a gurney to the EMS truck double-parked before the store. The crowd of spectators had swelled, and scattered cameras flashed. He recognized beat reporters, freelance photographers, and news crew members, all of them performing their jobs with detached professionalism.

*They don't have a clue*, he thought. "You want to drive?"

"Sure, why not?" Karol said.

Ducking beneath the crime scene tape, they made their way through the crowd, dodging microphones thrust in their faces. Once they had cleared the gauntlet, Willy said, "I don't need this bag of shit now."

"You think you don't have to work major cases while you're waiting for your promotion to come through?"

"Depending on what this turns out to be, there might not *be* a promotion."

"Why's that?"

"Nothing derails a career like a hot case. Tony Mace was at the top of his game two years ago, all set to move up, and then me and Patty caught Terrence Glenzer's murder. Now Patty's dead and Tony's scooping up K-9 shit."

"You and Patty caught the case. Not Mace. I'm sorry like hell for what happened to her, but being on that case didn't prevent you from getting promoted."

"We don't really know that, do we?"

"You think the department froze all promotions to keep you down?"

"Nah, but with the freeze in place, the brass didn't have to worry about me. They put Tony in charge of that mess, and when he didn't deliver, they sent him to obedience school. And then every one of them took a fall. Me and Landry are the only ones who didn't get hurt, and that's because Tony protected us by keeping us out of things at the end."

Karol circled the car. "You don't think there's a connection between this case and that one, do you?"

Willy looked around the sidewalk, then got into the car and waited for Karol to do the same. "We got a DOA with his head cut off, possibly by a sword. The Manhattan Were-wolf case involved a sword—"

"A *broken* sword."

"The other half of that sword's blade was used to kill a man in Central Park. The perp didn't need both halves to make his point."

"What happened to the pieces?"

"Some bigwig in Rome claimed them."

"So they're not even in the country."

"Angela Domini witnessed the murder of an upstate tribal cop named John Stalk. Tony witnessed that murder too."

"What did he see?"

"He won't say."

"So far, I'm not seeing a pattern."

"That bookstore carried Terrence Glenzer's self-published book about American Indian legends, including several about werewolves. Did I ever tell you what Patty looked like when the Manhattan Werewolf finished with her? What all of the vics looked like? They were torn to pieces. I mean that literally: bones and all."

"I've seen some TV documentaries. So, you think the perp *was* a werewolf?"

He looked into her eyes. "This isn't for any reports, okay? This is between partners. Between *us*. I seen a lot in Homicide but nothing like those DOAs. No fucking human being did those jobs."

Karol raised her hands. "Hey, I don't know what to say. You're going to believe what you're going to believe. But I do know Jason Lourdes wasn't killed by a werewolf. Why would a werewolf use a sword?"

"I don't know. I'm just telling you that case was cursed from day one, and my gut tells me to watch our step on this one, or we'll both be joining Tony at the dog pound."

Riding beside Raphael in the backseat of the same taxi that had brought them to the bookstore, Gabriel found his mind racing in several directions at once, resulting in confusion. Micah, the driver, belonged to the Greater Pack of New York City, so Gabriel felt free to speak his mind.

"A sword," Raphael said. "Not just any sword, either, I bet. The Blade of Salvation."

"We don't know that."

"The hell we don't. The Brotherhood of Torquemada is in this country, and they've found us. Somehow they learned we use the store as a beacon, and they moved on it."

"What matters right now is that Rhonda's missing."

"They'll use her against us. Make her give up our names."

"You keep saying 'they.' The Brotherhood sent only one assassin to face Julian." Julian Fortier, who had used the alias Janus Farel, had terrorized the city two years earlier. A former member of the pack, he had turned rogue after a hunter killed his mate. Gabriel, Raphael, and Angela had been his childhood friends.

"And that assassin was killed, which is why they sent more than one this time. The police said their witness saw four people drag Rhonda to the van. I bet they were all Torque-madans, even the woman. The driver makes at least five."

Gabriel stared out the taxi window at pedestrians and buildings.

"Damn it, we have to *do* something."

Turning to his brother, Gabriel gave him a hard look. "Don't tell me what we need to do. I know what we need to do. I'm the leader of the pack."

Raphael's nostrils flared. "Then what's your plan?"

"Whether we're dealing with Torquemadans or someone else, we have to assume they want Rhonda to identify us."

"And she's just a girl."

*A mistake on our part.* They should have hired only experienced Wolves at the store. "Regardless of how long she resists interrogation, they must know she's a Wolf and that Jason was too; their families are automatically targets. The police are already protecting the Wilsons. That means we have to watch over the Lourdeses."

"The cops have Jason's body. They have his head. Did you see his eyes? He was in mid-Transformation. Even if we take care of these murderers, we could still be exposed. The clock's ticking, Brother."

Karol parked in front of a two-story home in Rosedale covered with unlit Christmas lights. The neighborhood, with its wet green lawns, felt far removed from Manhattan.

Willy had hedged in answering her, but he did see a connection between Jason Lourdes's murder and the Manhattan Werewolf—and he believed the Manhattan Werewolf really was a werewolf.

"Welcome to the burbs, homegirl," he said as they got out of the car.

Karol cocked one eyebrow at him, loaded for bear. "You think I never been to the burbs, esse?"

"It makes me hot when you speak Spanish."

He and Karol mounted the brick-style steps, and he knocked on the front door, which opened a moment later.

A woman with watery eyes and long red hair noted Karol, then shifted her gaze to Willy.

"Mrs. Lourdes?" Willy said.

"No, I'm Sharon King, a friend of the family."

Willy showed Sharon his ID. "Detective Diega and Detective Williams, Manhattan Homicide South."

"Please come in."

Willy and Karol followed Sharon inside.

"Were you expecting us?" Willy said.

"Gabriel called and said you were coming. He asked me to stay with Jennifer."

Willy shot Karol a look as they followed Sharon into an immaculate home. Gabriel had no business interfering with the case. Karol closed the door, and Sharon led them to a sofa in the living room, where a woman with curly black hair and running mascara looked up at them.

"Is it true?" Jennifer Lourdes said.

Willy removed a manila envelope from inside his coat. "We have some photos for you to look at, Mrs. Lourdes." He withdrew the pictures Karol had taken and held them out. "Are you able to tell us if this is Jason?"

Mrs. Lourdes took the photos with shaking hands and looked through them. Tears dropped from her eyes onto the pictures, and she nodded, her face torn with grief.

Sharon sat beside the woman and put one arm around her shoulders.

"We're very sorry for your loss, Mrs. Lourdes," Karol said.

Jennifer sobbed, her chest quivering. "My baby . . ."

Willy sat on her other side. "Is your husband at work?"

"He's on his way home," Sharon said.

*Did Gabriel call the husband too?* Willy held his tongue. "Can you think of anyone who might have wanted to hurt Jason?"

Weeping, Jennifer shook her head.

"He was a good boy," Sharon said. "He never made trouble."

Willy did not want to upset Jennifer by antagonizing her friend, so he made a show of looking straight at his interview subject. "How long were Jason and Rhonda dating?"

Jennifer blew her nose and summoned words between sobs. "They started dating after Raphael hired Rhonda to work at the store."

"Jason had already been working there for a few months, and Raphael promoted him to assistant manager," Sharon said.

Willy raised his eyebrows. "I'm sorry, Mrs.—?"

"King."

"Mrs. King, I know you're trying to be helpful, but I really need to hear from Mrs. Lourdes right now."

Sharon made an indignant expression.

Willy returned his attention to Jennifer. "Forgive me. I have to ask these questions. It looked to me like Jason had a pretty muscular build. Did he lift weights?"

"No."

"I think the detective is asking if Jason used steroids."

Jennifer stared at Sharon, then Karol, then back at Willy. "Jason was a healthy boy. He didn't use drugs."

"Yes, ma'am, I believe you. We need a list of Jason's friends. Is it possible for my partner and me to look in his room?" He didn't want to get a warrant.

Nodding, Jennifer broke into tears again.

"I'll show you his room." Sharon led them up a narrow stairway to a closed door, which she opened.

Willy and Karol entered the bedroom and pulled on

latex gloves. Posters adorned the walls; dirty clothes covered the floor.

"I'll wait downstairs," Sharon said and disappeared.

"Fucking Gabriel Domini," Willy said under his breath.

# CHAPTER FOUR

Rhonda's head rolled from side to side, and her body shivered. She reached down for the blanket, but her hand came away empty, her fingernails brushing her naked thighs. She tried to open her eyelids, but they wouldn't budge. She raised her head, then laid it back down. She inhaled the scents of several different humans: four . . . five . . . six.

The base of her skull pulsed. What happened?

*Jason.*

A man with a beard had shot her with a tranquilizer dart, and two others had shot Jason. The man who had shot her had also decapitated Jason with a sword. Who the hell were they?

*A sword . . .*

A sword made out of silver.

*The Blade of Salvation.*

Rhonda raised herself on her elbow, her eyes finally snapping open, and stared into gloomy near darkness; a single low wattage bulb shined down on her from the high ceiling. She hopped onto the balls of her feet, crouching, and heard the chinking of chain links. Metal manacles gripped her wrists and ankles. She had been lying on straw, some of which now clung to her back and legs.

With slow caution, she stood. The chains were bolted to the floor: four points forming a square. Glancing at a metal door and a mirror set in one cinder-block wall, she seized one chain and pulled it with all her strength, which was not enough to liberate herself. She tried again until her fingers, wrists, elbows, and neck hurt, then released the chain with a frustrated cry.

Panting, Rhonda searched the ceiling but saw only what she decided must be a steam pipe. So where was the steam heat? Cold numbed the soles of her feet.

"Hello?" Her throat felt dry.

Her captives had left three metal buckets against the closest wall. One contained water. She guessed the other two were for her to relieve herself.

*Like an animal.*

Raising her hands to her neck, she touched a leather band, perhaps two inches high, which encircled her neck, tight against her flesh.

*I'm not a dog.*

"Hello!"

She listened to her own breathing. A metallic clanking sound filled the room. Her body continued to tremble, as much from fear as from the cold.

The door swung open, and a figure stood silhouetted across the room.

Discerning feminine curves, Rhonda covered her exposed breasts with one arm and her private area with her free hand.

The woman stepped forward. In the dim light, Rhonda saw she wore black boots, tights, and a sweater and held a tranquilizer gun. As she stepped closer, her features became distinguishable in the gloom: long blonde hair and a hawkish nose that did not diminish her beauty.

"Who are you?" Rhonda said.

"You don't need to know my name. You don't need to know anything about me, except that I control your life."

The woman had a foreign accent. *Italian*, Rhonda thought. "Is Jason dead?"

"The beast at the bookstore? Yes."

*The beast.* Rhonda's eyes filled with tears. "What do you want from me?"

The woman aimed her gun at Rhonda. "For now, a confession."

"I haven't done anything wrong."

"Confess your nature."

Rhonda blinked.

"Tell me what you are, bitch."

"What I am?"

"Your species."

The nightmare became clearer. "I don't know what you're talking about."

"You're a beast. A wolf disguised as a woman."

"Can I have my clothes?"

"Wolves don't need clothes, except for sheep's clothing."

"You're crazy." Rhonda's voice cracked.

The woman holstered her weapon and took from her belt a black object that resembled a remote control. "You're a werewolf. We know this to be true. Your colleague was reverting to his true self when we took off his head. Do you really want to play games you can't win?"

Rhonda steeled her nerves. "There's no such thing as werewolves."

A slight movement of the woman's thumb caused Rhonda's head to fling back and her jaw to fall open, her limbs going rigid and unresponsive at her sides. With her back arched, Rhonda tried to focus on the ceiling pipe as electricity coursed through her body, but the steady vibration prevented her from doing so.

Just when she wondered if the agony would ever end, she fell to her hands and knees and gasped for breath. Even though the charge had stopped, her brain tingled and her muscles continued to shake, a sick feeling spreading through her stomach. She looked at the woman. "Why are you doing this to me?"

"I can increase the voltage. Confess your true nature, or I'll force you to reveal yourself to me."

The sobs emanating from Rhonda's chest sounded more like coughing. Her eyes clouded, and mucus descended from her nose. Electricity seized her body, and she tried to scream.

Mace was laboring over a schedule when he saw Cheryl speaking on the TV. Outside, a Bell JetRanger police helicopter took off, so he raised the volume on the portable television atop his filing cabinet. He recognized the bookstore behind her. She wore a long coat and held a microphone in one hand.

"I'm standing outside the Synful Reading occult bookstore on St. Mark's Place, the scene of a gruesome murder and kidnapping this morning."

Footage of a body bag being carried out of the store on a gurney by two paramedics replaced the image of his wife.

"Police say Jason Lourdes, an employee of the bookstore, was murdered by an unknown assailant."

A high school yearbook photo of a smiling young man with short, curly brown hair filled the screen.

"Lourdes graduated from Rosedale High School in Queens just this summer."

The image switched to another high school yearbook photo, this one of a pretty young woman with short straight hair and a slender neck.

"A witness told police that Rhonda Wilson, a fellow Synful Reading employee and recent high school graduate, was abducted from the scene by four men and a woman who drove away in a white van."

Cheryl's image returned. "Police believe the two incidents are linked, and a search is under way for the van. Anyone with information is encouraged to call . . ."

Mace took out his cell phone and pressed a number. The phone on the other end rang four times, and he was about to hang up when Landry answered in a low voice.

"Tony? It's been a while."

"How are you, Ken?"

"I'm a little busy right now."

"So I hear. I just saw my wife's piece on TV."

"How bad was it?"

"The word *werewolf* didn't come up."

"Today. What about tomorrow? We have to reassure the public that the Manhattan Werewolf isn't back in business."

"How do you plan to do that?"

"Lourdes's head was still at the scene. His body wasn't torn to pieces, and no bloody messages were left on the walls."

Mace knew the owners of Synful Reading were Wolves. It stood to reason some of the employees might belong to their pack as well. "Who's working this?" He had to at least make an effort to protect Willy.

"Diega, as if you didn't know."

"Any luck with the van?"

"We got surveillance footage from a block away. The plates were reported stolen this morning."

"How's Aiello doing?"

"Fine. He's been in charge for two years, you know. But I don't think he realizes how many coincidences we're dealing with here."

"Are you bringing him up to speed?"

"I'm trying. Look, I have to run. We never had this conversation."

The connection went dead.

*Welcome to the sidelines*, Mace thought.

Rhonda fell screaming to the stone floor. Wincing, she took a deep breath. Her teeth rattled inside her skull, and her nausea intensified. "Please stop. Just let me go. Please. I want my mother . . ."

The woman moved closer to her but not too close. She always maintained a safe distance. If only Rhonda could reach her . . .

Electricity tore through her body, sending her limbs flailing at her sides and her face slapping the floor. Was it her imagination, or had the current grown stronger? Her tongue pressed against her teeth, which flexed in their gums. Pushing herself up off the floor, she worked her knees beneath her. Rhonda stared at her hands, her fingers clawing at the floor. She knew she couldn't take much more of this torture in her fragile human form.

*Why should I? She wants to see a monster, I'll show her one.*

She willed the Change.

Willy and Karol walked through the lobby of the Office of Chief Medical Examiner of the City of New York at 520 First Avenue. They had found nothing in Jason Lourdes's bedroom to suggest he was anything but an average teenager. Willy palmed the call button, and when the elevator door opened, he waited for Karol to board it first.

On the fourth floor, an attendant behind a counter directed

them to Autopsy Room D.

"I want some water first," Karol said, stooping over a fountain.

"Don't tell me you're fainthearted," Willy said. "That's a handicap for a murder police."

Karol stood straight and dabbed at the corners of her mouth. "It's the smell more than it is anything I ever see. All those cleaning solutions and chemicals are too much for me."

"You can hold my hand if you want."

Karol gestured to the swinging double doors ahead. "Shall we?"

Willy pushed one door open and followed his partner into the refrigerated autopsy room.

Dr. Byrnes, a white male with a whiter beard, stood near an autopsy table occupied by a nude male body and a detached head. "Good evening, Detectives."

Willy and Karol drew close to the table. Under the overhead lights, Jason's body seemed to glow. The medical examiner had sliced the head's flesh from the base of the neck, along the jaw hinge, past one ear, over the top of the skull, and down to the other side of the neck, dividing the head in two. Then he had tugged the husk of skin from the face like a mask, revealing glistening musculature beneath. The bulbous eyes, minus their lids, seemed to follow Willy.

"The edge of the neck stump lines up perfectly with the head," Byrnes said. "I'm sure DNA testing will prove that they go together like *shama lama ding dong*."

"What did the perp use to decapitate this poor bastard?" Willy said.

"An instrument sharp enough and strong enough to separate the head from the body with a single blow."

"A sword?"

Byrnes shrugged. "Sure, why not? I'll bite."

Willy held his hand out above one of Jason's. The fingers on Jason's hand extended an inch beyond his. "This boy had major piano-playing hands."

"Only if he cut those nails."

Willy leaned close to Jason's head. "How do you explain the coloration of his eyes?"

"I don't. I've never seen anything like it before."

Gripping the remote control, Valeria watched Rhonda writhe on the floor. She told herself this was an animal, a monster, not a human being.

Rhonda slumped over on one side, wincing. Then she looked at Valeria, who gasped: the irises in Rhonda's eyes had expanded, blotting out the whites. The mask of pain on her face reconfigured itself into one of rage, and when Rhonda snarled Valeria glimpsed a mouthful of canine fangs as Rhonda's jaws elongated and her nose stretched into a muzzle.

Valeria removed her thumb from the button on the remote control, and the crackling of electricity stopped. Shifting the remote into her other hand, she drew the tranquilizer gun and aimed it at the figure on the floor.

The creature that had been Rhonda did not seem to care that Valeria had stopped the charge. She got on all fours and growled at Valeria, who took an instinctive step back. Rhonda leapt at her, but the chains snapped her back. As the nude body rolled on the floor, Valeria noted its muscles going spastic from head to toe. In the time it took for Rhonda to rise, black fur spread over her rippling form.

Valeria restrained herself despite the amazement she felt. She had never seen a werewolf before; she had seen only photos and videos. Now she not only stood mere feet from one of the monsters, but she had witnessed its transformation from human form. It was incomprehensible to her that this supernatural beast had appeared to be a skinny human girl just moments ago.

Rhonda's eyes narrowed at Valeria, and spittle flew from her teeth.

Valeria took another step back, then heard footsteps behind her.

"Show no fear," Michael said. "It can't hurt you."

Ignoring him, Valeria watched Rhonda grow a foot taller as her feet stretched into leg extensions. The chains forced the creature to bend over, but Rhonda's eyes remained focused on Valeria. She lunged forward again, and when the chains jerked her back, her jaws parted and she unleashed a howl that caused Valeria to shudder.

# CHAPTER FIVE

When the taxi pulled over to the house in Rosedale, Gabriel leaned forward in the backseat and spoke to the driver. "You don't mind waiting in the car, do you? I'd like you to listen to the news for updates."

Micah shrugged. "Whatever you say. Give Jen and Rodney my condolences."

"I will."

Raphael slid out of the car first and held the door for Gabriel. Gabriel got out and waited for Raphael to close the door, and then they walked to the house together.

"You'd better start traveling with bodyguards," Raphael said.

"I'll consider it." Gabriel knocked on the door.

"If they're staking out the house, they could have us in their sights right now."

Gabriel glanced at the houses around them.

The door swung open and Sharon stood before them. They entered without saying anything.

"Rodney's upstairs with Jennifer," Sharon said. "They're both wrecks."

"Of course they are." Gabriel led the way into the living room, where three grim-faced men sat on the sofa: Tim Riegert, Kyle Chadler, and Samuel Minsky.

"What's the deal, Gabriel?" Tim said.

Gabriel unbuttoned his coat and sat in a chair near the sofa. "We've been discovered; there's no question about it. Members of the Brotherhood of Torquemada may be here in the city. We don't know how many, at least five. They killed Jason and took Rhonda prisoner, and they have their Blade of Salvation with them. The police have Jason's corpse, and there's no covering up anything they learn."

"Fuck," Kyle said.

"What are we doing about it?" Samuel said.

"For the time being, I want you three to stay here." Gabriel looked at Raphael. "Call for relief if you need it, but I want three people guarding this house at all times."

"There are four of us now," Sharon said.

"I want you to go home tonight and get some rest. Come back in the morning and take care of Rodney and Jen so these guys can concentrate on security."

"What about the Wilsons?" Tim said.

Raphael folded his muscular arms. "We couldn't protect them if we wanted to. Cops are swarming all over their house."

Gabriel nodded. "Our enemies won't strike at them

while the police are there, but we'll have to provide security as soon as that situation changes. The Torquemadans must know that the Lourdeses and the Wilsons belong to the pack, and that means they knew who Raphael and I are."

Samuel sat up. "You guys can't go back to your places unprotected."

"I'm meeting Melissa at a safe house later," Gabriel said.

"And I'm staying with my crew," Raphael said. "We're covered."

"What if Rhonda gives us up?" Tim said. "She's just a girl. Who knows what they'll do to her?"

"That's why we need to draw them out as quickly as possible," Gabriel said. "When they strike, we have to be ready. If they come here, make sure you get one of them alive—even if it means leaving in the heat of things."

"There are just three of us, five counting Rodney and Jen. You said there's at least five of them. There could be a lot more."

"Even if these people are Torquemadans, there's only one Blade of Salvation. You can handle them no matter how many there are. Just keep their screaming to a minimum."

Mace pulled into the narrow driveway of his Bay Ridge, Brooklyn home, leaving room for Cheryl to park behind him. The days got darker sooner, and he shivered as he climbed the steps to the front door and unlocked it. Snow would fall soon. He entered the house, passed the French doors for the enclosed porch, and opened the inner door.

Hanging his coat on an upright rack, he ascended the wooden stairs to the second floor, where he and his family lived; they rented the bottom floor to a Mexican family. Inside the long three-bedroom apartment, his German Shepard, Sniper, waited for him, wagging his tail. Mace had inherited the dog from the K-9 unit when the animal had gone blind in one eye.

"Hi, boy." Warmth greeted Mace as he passed the dining room table and set his keys next to the mail. As he passed through the dining room to the living room with the dog at his heels, he saw Patty standing in her playpen with Anna Sanchez, her nanny, kneeling before her.

Patty's eyes lit up. "Dada! Dada! Dada!" She raised her arms, her fingers opening and closing.

Mace scooped up his daughter and rubbed his nose against hers. "Hi, sweetie. How was your day? Did you give Anna a hard time?"

Anna stood beside him. At twenty, she wore clips in her dark hair and a white sweater. She lived downstairs with her parents and two brothers. "No, Captain. She never gives me a hard time. She's a good girl."

"If only she'd embrace potty training."

"Oh, she's too young. All children are different. I know. I taught my brothers. Your dinner's in the oven. Take it out in half an hour."

"Thank you. Have a good night."

"You too." Anna exited and closed the door.

Mace turned on the TV and switched the channel to Manhattan Minute News. "Did you have an interesting day?

Daddy didn't. Daddy never has interesting days at work anymore, but that's a good thing. Let's see what Mommy told Anna to make for dinner." He carried Patty into the narrow kitchen and opened the oven door, with Sniper in tow. "Mm, baked ziti."

Cheryl's voice came from the TV.

"Mama?"

Mace carried the toddler into the living room. "Mama will be home soon. She *did* have an interesting day."

On TV, Cheryl stood outside the Detective Bureau Manhattan. "Police officials have released the following information regarding the murder of eighteen-year-old Jason Lourdes at the Synful Reading bookstore on St. Mark's Place this morning. The murder weapon appears to have been a *sword* . . ."

*And so it begins*, Mace thought.

"Look at all these cars," Karol said as she drove along the residential street in Bensonhurst, Brooklyn. "How many of them do you think are ours?"

Willy studied the parked cars as their headlights illuminated them. "All of them."

She found a parking spot at the end of the long block. Willy got out and waited for her to join him on the sidewalk, and they backtracked to the house they wanted. Willy rang the doorbell, and when a uniformed PO answered the door, he flashed his shield. "Diega and Williams, Manhattan Homicide South."

The PO guided them into the living room, which had been converted into a command station. Soares and Cato, wearing headsets, sat at a table upon which a digital recorder had been hooked up to the main telephone line. Another PO sat in a chair, two detectives on the sofa. Chinese food in containers waited on the coffee table.

"How's it going?" Willy said.

Soares stretched his arms. "We've had a few tips and dispatched patrol units to investigate, but nothing panned out. You?"

"Nada. Can we speak to the father?"

Soares nodded to the PO who had brought Willy and Karol in. The officer went upstairs and returned a minute later, followed by a paunchy, middle-aged man with black hair.

Cato gestured to Willy and Karol. "Mr. Wilson, this is Detective Diega and Detective Wilson from Manhattan Homicide South. They're investigating Jason's murder and would like to ask you some questions."

Marshal Wilson regarded them with sagging eyes. "I already answered these guys' questions three times."

"We're sorry," Karol said. "It's what we do. You never know what piece of seemingly innocuous information could help us with both cases."

Marshal sighed. "All right, let's get this over with."

When Cheryl Mace walked through her living room door, she saw that Tony had already set the table, served dinner, placed Patty in her high chair, and was spoon-feeding their daughter macaroni and cheese.

"Mama! Mama! Mama!"

"Hello, my beautiful baby." She kissed Patty, then her husband.

"How was your day?" Tony said.

"I'm sure you heard the news."

"I've been following your reports."

"That isn't how you heard the news."

"Willy called me."

Cheryl sat at the table. "What did he say?"

Tony just smiled.

"Well, he didn't say anything to me, and I was the first reporter on the scene."

"I'm sure you were."

"I had to wait for Public Affairs to release a statement."

"That's how it works."

She sampled her ziti. *Not bad.* Anna was a good cook, even if her Italian food never quite tasted authentic. "Synful Reading. A decapitation by sword. What do you think?"

Tony wiped Patty's face and turned his attention to his own food. "I have no thoughts on the matter. I'm only a lowly administrator."

Chewing her food, Cheryl studied his eyes. Two years earlier, Tony had told her he had witnessed the Manhattan Werewolf tear an upstate tribal policeman to pieces in the Village. He had gone so far as to call the perp a real werewolf: an actual flesh and blood and fur monster. She had advised him not to make that claim in his report, but he ignored her, and now she was grateful he had a job at all.

At the time, Tony had sent her out of town to stay with her parents, and while she was there, the governor had sent the National Guard into the city . . . and the murders stopped. When she returned home, Tony had lacerations on his face, bite marks on one wrist, and a deep wound in his left shoulder. He told her he had been jumped by a gang. She didn't believe him, but she never pressed the point. The gashes on his forehead healed, leaving light scars that only turned visible when he grew angry, but the injury to his shoulder seemed permanent. He downplayed it, but she knew it caused him pain, and sometimes during thunderstorms his nightmares awoke her.

"Why did Willy call you, if not for insight?"

Tony shrugged. "I couldn't say."

*You mean you won't say.* Cheryl had started seeing Tony after he had apprehended Rodrigo Gomez, the serial killer known as the Full Moon Killer. She had been a reporter on that story and had interviewed Tony as the primary detective several times. When they became involved, he refused to answer any questions related to his job, a policy he continued to follow, other than during the period in which she had worked as a talk show producer.

"Didn't you tell me that someone from the Vatican took both halves of that broken sword?"

He looked at Patty. "Did I say that? I really don't remember."

"Gabriel and Raphael Domini came to the crime scene. What was their sister's name?"

His eyes returned to hers. "Angela."

"Right. Did she ever turn up again?"

Holding her gaze, Tony said, "No. I don't know where she is."

*At least he's telling the truth about that.*

Valeria poured herself a cup of steaming tea. All six members of their party sat at the table in the second-floor office they had converted into a dining room. Other offices served as bedrooms. Valeria and Eun bunked together; Michael and Henri; and Myles and Angelo. They cooked in pairs, and tonight had been Myles's and Angelo's turn: chicken and beef souvlakis and a pasta salad. On the security monitor set upon a counter, the beast continued to rage at her imprisonment.

"She doesn't get tired," Valeria said.

Michael sipped his coffee. "She will. A wounded wolf will run for days without stopping."

"I'm worried about leaving it alone tonight," Henri said. "Maybe one of us should stay behind."

"We need everyone in the field. If it makes you feel better, tranquilize her before we leave. She'll still be out when we return." Michael turned to Valeria. "Are you okay?"

"I'm fine. It's been a big day is all."

Michael wiped his mouth with a napkin. "I suggest we all get a few hours' sleep. It's going to be an even bigger night."

# CHAPTER SIX

Willy and Karol entered the Crime Scene Unit laboratory in the Forensics Division. Detectives in white lab coats sat with their backs to them, hunched over their terminals.

Matt Mostel waved from across the room, then met them in the middle.

"Are Rodriguez and Quarrel gone already?" Willy said.

Mostel, pushing forty, spread his hands apart. "We find sticking to assigned shift times is more productive than working sixteen-hour days."

"What a novel concept."

"Where shall we start: blood samples, hair, or fingerprints?"

"Surprise us."

"In that order, then." Mostel led them over to a digital microscope that had a four-inch LCD screen and a built-in camera. He switched on the screen, which lit up and revealed transparent orange blood cells with a pink hue moving around on a glass slide. "You're looking at a sample of my blood taken an hour ago." He removed the slide and put in another. "Now you're looking at the vic's blood."

The new cells squirmed faster.

"Are you sure you didn't confuse them?" Karol said.

Mostel offered her a patient smile. "He was murdered ten hours ago, but his blood cells are more active than mine."

"Deprive a plant of sunlight and for a short period it grows faster than one that sees the light every day. Then it dies."

Mostel blinked at Karol. "That was a very good analogy. But we don't know yet what the outcome will be for these little buggers."

"They have to die sometime," Willy said.

"I'm sure they will, but I'm more interested in how *busy* they are now. It isn't normal."

He moved on to another microscope and activated its screen.

Willy scrutinized the image. "I see a black line."

"That's a human hair. Take a good look at its thickness." Mostel replaced the slide.

The new image showed a thicker black line.

"Okay, we went from a BIC fine point to a Sharpie marker," Willy said.

"That's the hair of a dog. A Labrador, I believe. It's obviously much coarser." He replaced the slide again. "This one was taken from the head of our victim."

The third hair was thicker than the first and narrower than the second.

"And this one's juuuuuust right," Willy said.

Mostel changed slides again. "We took this one from young Mr. Lourdes's chest."

Willy narrowed his eyes. "They look the same to me."

"That's because they are the same. Hairs removed from the vic's back, neck, arms, chest, stomach, pubis, thighs, calves, and feet are virtually identical in density."

"That doesn't sound right," Karol said.

"It isn't. Androgenic hair should be finer than hair found on a head." Mostel led them over to his workstation, where he sat down and adjusted his monitor so they could see it better. Using a trackball, he brought up the image of a fingerprint. "This is Jason Lourdes's fingerprint on file." A click brought up a longer fingerprint. "And this is the fingerprint of your victim."

"Then our victim isn't Jason Lourdes," Karol said.

"I didn't say that. Watch." Mostel opened up a video file that showed the first fingerprint. In seconds, the fingerprint elongated until it matched the second fingerprint. "I used a simple morphing program to stretch the first fingerprint, which magically became the second one."

"The fingers we saw in the autopsy room were unusually long," Willy said.

"Stretched, I would say," Mostel said.

Willy and Karol traded looks.

"All of this got me thinking. I've never seen blood that behaved like this or fingerprints that change properties as if they're fun house mirrors . . . but I have seen coarse hair like this before."

Willy stared at the man. *Don't you fucking say it.*

"Two years ago—"

Willy threw up his hands. "Oh, man!"

"—during the Manhattan Werewolf murders. We found very similar hairs at several of the homicide sites."

"Shit," Karol said.

Mostel frowned. "I can't make a direct comparison, because the FBI confiscated all our materials related to that case. We weren't even allowed to make copies for our own records. I'm afraid to guess what will happen when I submit my report."

"Maybe the FBI will take over the case," Karol said.

Willy shook his head. "Uh-uh. A couple of Frisbees showed up during that case. They knew about murders from all over the country that were similar to the ones we were investigating. They were only too happy to drop the whole bag of shit in Tony's lap."

Mostel clucked his tongue. "I'm studying evidence that could make me famous, but the department would have my ass if I breathed a word of it to anyone."

"Fame isn't all it's cracked up to be," Willy said, thinking of Mace.

The taxi parked at the brownstone on Roosevelt Avenue in Queens, and Gabriel scanned the shadows for bodyguards. He counted three.

In the front seat, Micah turned to face him. "I'll wait until you get inside."

"That's not necessary. I'm protected here. What's the damage?"

Micah waved him off. "Come on."

"We have to keep up appearances. You've been driving and parking all day, and your records have to seem authentic if you're ever investigated for any reason."

Sighing, Micah rang up his meter. "I'd really rather forget about it . . ."

Gabriel handed him three one hundred dollar bills. "Not to worry. Get some sleep. I may need you tomorrow."

"Sure thing."

Gabriel got out of the taxi, opened the black metal gate, and trotted up the brownstone's stairs. He rang the doorbell and eyed the buildings around him.

The door opened, and a muscular man stood in the light.

"Hello, Arick."

"Come on in." Arick waved to Micah, who drove off.

Gabriel entered the brownstone and hung his coat on a hook as Arick closed and locked the door. Pictures adorned white walls, and polished wooden floors gleamed.

"How many bodyguards are there?"

"Stan's downstairs in the basement, and Marcus is on the second floor."

"And there are three more outside."

Arick sighed. "Raphael called . . ."

"I know." He squeezed his friend's shoulder. "Thank you." He walked up the curved stairs, which squeaked beneath his weight. At the top, he saw Marcus leaning against the wall and nodded to him. Then he opened the door to the master bedroom, and Melissa sat up in the darkness. Two small forms slept in bed with her.

"What's happening?" Melissa said as he switched on the bedside lamp and closed the door. "I know about Jason and Rhonda, but what's really going on?"

Gabriel sat on the edge of the bed beside Damien, one of his sons. Gareth slept on the other side of Melissa. Twins, six years old. "Until we know otherwise, we have to assume they're Torquemadans."

"In America? I didn't think there were even any left in Europe."

He removed his tie, tossed it on the floor, and unbuttoned his shirt. "We always knew we'd have to deal with them eventually."

"Where's Raphael?"

Gabriel nodded at the window. "I bet he and his crew are outside by now."

Melissa smiled. "That's sweet. Do we really need all this protection?"

Turning, he looked deep into her eyes. "I want you and the boys to stay here tomorrow. I also want you ready to leave on a moment's notice."

She rolled her eyes. "Where would we go?"

"To my sister's place in Canada."

"Canada's a big country."

Gabriel shrugged. "It will be a nice trip."

"How long would we stay?"

"Until I decide it's safe to come back."

Willy and Karol sat eating in a Thai restaurant on Twenty-second Street and Broadway.

"Now isn't this better than eating a frozen dinner in your apartment?" Willy said.

"Who says I was going to eat a frozen dinner? I know how to cook. I do it all the time."

Willy aimed his chopsticks in her direction. "After a fifteen-hour day? No way. You were going Lean Cuisine; I know it. This is better."

She gave him half a smile. "Maybe."

"If this case buries our careers, they'll split us up. You'll miss me."

"Maybe." Her smile broadened. "Probably."

"Probably? Definitely. I'd miss you."

"Let's discuss the case."

"We've been talking about it all day. I'm tired of talking about it."

"You think Mostel believes Jason was the Manhattan Werewolf?"

"If he does, he needs to see a shrink."

"You said yourself the Manhattan Werewolf wasn't human."

"He wasn't a teenage werewolf, either."

Karol chewed her food. "Hey, whatever happened to that Colombian girl you were seeing?"

"I don't know. The heat died down."

"And the Dominican woman. What was her name?"

"Lucy. She wanted to be too serious."

"Before that it was the Korean."

"Yung? You're forgetting Karen, the white chick."

"I'm not counting one-night stands."

"Why are you trying to spoil our first date?"

"This isn't a date. It's getting a bite to eat while we work a long shift."

"It could be a date," Willy said under his breath.

"D-O-G."

"Since this isn't a date, I don't have to pay for you, right?"

As Willy entered the squad room for Manhattan Homicide South with Karol, he saw Landry conferring with Sergeant Don Gibbons in Landry's glass-enclosed office. Landry had shed his jacket and rolled up his sleeves and looked weary. Gibbons, who had already passed his retirement eligibility, stood in a crisp uniform. Landry beckoned to the detectives as they hung their coats on the backs of their chairs. Willy gestured for Karol to go first.

"No thanks. I'm not falling for that." She gestured for him to go first.

Smiling, he complied.

"I'm ready to go home," Landry said.

"That makes three of us," Willy said.

"Give me a rundown on your reports before you write them so one of us can actually get out of here."

Willy sat before the desk. "We interviewed the parents of the vic and our missing person and their closest friends.

Jason and Rhonda seem like two normal kids, very together, not troublemakers. Rhonda had no previous boyfriends or jealous would-be suitors. Jason never ran with a gang. The ME and Forensics have some pretty fucked-up shit to report, but that's on them."

Landry sat on the edge of the desk. "I just read Byrnes's report. I'm classifying it. Public Affairs can decide how much to reveal. What have I got to look forward to from Forensics?"

"Aggressive blood cells, mutant hair, and magic fingerprints."

Landry blew air out of his cheeks.

"By the way, Gabriel Domini shows real signs of interfering with this investigation."

"That's an exaggeration," Karol said.

"It's my impression—the *correct* impression. Every kid we interviewed said the same things about Jason and Rhonda. The exact same things. They were coached by someone; I feel it. And Gabriel had a real sway over Deidre Wilson. She didn't care what we had to say, but she hung on his every word."

Rising, Landry slipped into his jacket. "Get some sleep as soon as you finish your reports. I want you rested for tomorrow."

"How rested?"

"As rested as you can be without being late."

Mace awoke at 12:30. Cheryl was sitting in bed beside him, the glow from her laptop reflected in her reading glasses.

"What are you doing?"

"Checking the headlines."

"And?"

"Both papers have Rhonda's face on the cover. The *News* says, 'Police Seek Sword-Wielding Kidnappers.' The *Post* says, 'Ritual Slaying in Occult Bookstore' and 'Police Seek Satanic Kidnappers.'"

Mace rolled away and closed his eyes. "At least there's nothing about the Manhattan Werewolf."

"Well, no one else knows about the Blade of Salvation, do they?"

Mace pretended not to hear her, and then he pretended to be asleep.

# CHAPTER SEVEN

Sitting on the sofa in the living room, Tim zipped through the channels on the wide-screen TV while Samuel stood at the window, peeking around the curtain. Tim had assigned Kyle to watch the backyard from the kitchen.

"Five hundred channels and what do we get? Infomercials and cartoons. What kids stay up until 2:00 AM on a school night?"

"There are different time zones," Samuel said. "They gotta entertain kids all over the country. All over the *world*."

"You telling me they're watching *Scooby-Doo* in China and Nicaragua? In English?"

"How should I know what language they're watching it in?"

Sighing, Tim returned to Manhattan Minute News and Cheryl Mace's report on the murder and kidnapping at Synful Reading. "Doesn't she ever get tired of saying the same thing over and over?"

"You don't seem to get tired of listening to her."

"I'm just waiting for new developments."

"Be glad there aren't any. That's the problem with people today: everyone's watching the cable news networks, waiting for new developments, so the networks have to frame trivial events to seem like new developments."

"This isn't trivial."

"No, it isn't."

"You think Gabriel and Raphael will shut down the store?"

Samuel shrugged. "It's not good for the store to be in the spotlight, but something like this could turn it into a real hot spot for tourists."

"Commerce versus survival of the species. I wonder how Angela's doing."

"I don't know."

"She was hot. I'd have mated with her."

"Sure you would have. And gotten yourself a little closer to Gabriel's inner circle."

"What's wrong with that?"

"Nothing, I guess. Too bad she mated with one of them."

"Yeah. How do you think that happened? I mean, I know we're all the same on the outside, but it isn't natural."

"I check out fine-looking women every day, and I think, 'You could be a Wolf and not even know it.' It's tempting to see if I can bring it out of them. I guess that's how it happens."

Tim yawned. "It must have been an embarrassment to Gabriel, though."

Samuel looked out the window. "I don't think Gabriel can *be* embarrassed."

"What's that supposed to mean?"

"He's too thoughtful, too willing to listen to dissenting voices. He's a peacemaker more than a leader. I wish Raphael was in charge."

Tim sat up. "Gabriel's the eldest. That's all there is to it. Besides, he runs things the way Angus did."

"Angus's way was fine for the previous generation. The world's changed. We need to change with it."

"I don't want to talk politics. Tell me about some of those fine women you check out."

"Not now. I see a van. Turn off the TV and warn Kyle."

Angelo steered the black passenger van along the quiet residential street with Michael sitting beside him. Except for lights flickering in one or two picture windows, the houses in the neighborhood were dark inside, their exteriors illuminated by colorful, flashing Christmas decorations. As they neared their destination, Angelo killed the headlights and slowed down, allowing the van to coast.

"Right on schedule, 0336 hours," Michael said.

Behind them, bodies shifted in the darkness. All the team members wore loose-fitting black garments beneath their long dusters, which were unbuttoned.

Michael unrolled his black mask over his head and affixed his headset. Then he pulled on his night vision goggles, and everyone but Angelo did the same. The world before him turned bright green. Finally, he put on his black leather gloves.

"Open the door," Michael said.

Someone did, allowing cold air to flow inside.

"Now."

One at a time, the Torquemadans jumped out of the moving van and landed on the pavement with precision and in silence. As soon as they settled, they rushed across the Lourdes' lawn.

Michael didn't say anything to Angelo. He didn't need to; they had planned the operation together. He leapt into the air and landed on the street, then took off after the others. Security lights above the house's front door flashed on, illuminating the yard as the van proceeded down the street. Angelo would turn the van around, close the side door, and wait.

The glowing Christmas lights caused distortion in the night vision goggles, and Michael adjusted their filter. He hoped everyone else did the same. He did not intend to break radio silence early.

Two silhouettes crouched at the front door: Myles and Eun. To Michael, they resembled ninjas wearing overcoats. They all did. Myles and Eun attacked separate locks on the door with their lock-picking tools.

Michael followed Henri and Valeria around a maroon SUV and a silver compact parked in the driveway to the side of the house. Henri and Valeria pressed themselves against opposite sides of the door, and Henri removed his own lock-picking tool.

Michael glided past them to the gate of the wooden fence that surrounded the property. Rather than test the gate and risk activating an alarm before they had all assumed their positions, he set his palms on top of the gate and vaulted over it, the Blade bumping against his leg. His boots slapped the concrete louder than he would have preferred, and he hurried to the back door. Like the others, he removed his lock-picking tool and inserted it into the door's keyhole. Hearing a click, he returned the tool to his pocket and listened for sounds inside the house. Then he pressed the Talk button on his headset and whispered, "Is everyone ready?"

"Affirmative," Myles said.

"Affirmative," Valeria said.

"Let's do it."

Valeria held her breath until she heard Michael give the order. Then, exhaling, she opened the door. Henri ran in first, and she followed him and closed the door. To their left, a narrow stairway led to the basement; to their right, three steps went into the kitchen. Based on their intelligence, Michael had to do the same thing out back but alone. Myles and Eun had to pick two locks and enter the override command into the alarm keypad.

With her night vision goggles, Valeria saw Henri open the flimsy door leading into the kitchen, and as she trailed him, she heard the keening of the alarm keypad. The noise would probably awaken the house's inhabitants, but at least a police patrol would not be dispatched in response to an actual alarm.

Henri moved swift and silent, like a shadow, and she did her best to follow suit. She disliked wearing the mask, goggles, and duster, which restricted her senses and movements.

They entered the dining room, then emerged into a great room, where a figure joined them, causing her to jump. She had known Michael would be here, had expected to see him, and yet his sudden appearance had still startled her. The alarm pad in the next room stopped keening.

The three of them continued into the living room, where they saw Myles and Eun standing side by side. Framed photos on an entertainment unit showed Jason Lourdes and his parents at various events and on vacation: just a normal American family. Michael motioned to Myles and Eun, who crept up the stairs. Then he and Henri approached the banister to do the same.

Valeria heard a sound like heavy breathing. Spinning on one heel, she saw three hulking shapes rise before her in unison. She registered their pointy ears and ferocious snouts, and she noticed distinct musculature beneath their fur. The werewolves stood seven feet tall, their gleaming eyes focused on her.

*They can see in the dark*, Valeria thought. "Company!"

When Samuel saw the black passenger van decelerating near the house, Tim notified Kyle, who watched the backyard from the kitchen window. The three of them ran into the basement, where they stripped off their clothes and stood naked, waiting.

When they heard the side door open and saw the male and female assassins enter, Tim nodded to his companions and all three of them Changed. Then they ascended the stairs in dead silence and followed the pair into the great room. The humans joined another male and then a male and a female in the living room. They wore night vision goggles but carried no discernible weapons, though Tim assumed they were armed to the teeth.

The Wolves moved unnoticed along the floor until the first female turned around. Fearing she was seconds from discovering them, Tim reared up on his hind legs, startling her. He knew that Samuel and Kyle did the same behind him. When the woman called out to her comrades, Tim flexed his muscles, showing her just how magnificent a specimen he had become. It was important to keep the element of surprise on their side.

Michael turned at the sound of Valeria's panicked voice and saw three werewolves towering before her, their ears almost touching the ceiling. All three were males, which meant there had to be at least one more creature—a female— somewhere in the house.

*A trap. They were expecting us!*

Using one hand, he eased Valeria out of his way. "Don't let them box us in. They *want* us to go upstairs." He drew the Blade of Salvation from his coat and wielded the heavy weapon in both hands.

The werewolves snarled at the sight of his sword but showed no fear otherwise. Upstairs, he heard the thumping of feet—paws!—and the growling of at least two more beasts.

*Five on five.*

Moving to his right with the stairway behind him, Michael formed a triangle with the werewolves at one point and Valeria at the other. "Take them!"

In response to his command, Valeria and Henri drew swords of their own. Silver swords. Blades of Salvation. He heard Myles and Eun draw their weapons as well.

*Five strong.*

The werewolves looked from human to human, their bestial countenances exhibiting equal parts confusion and rage.

*Surprise!*

Michael charged forward, cocking his Blade over his shoulder and swinging it deep into the first monster's neck. The werewolf howled in agony and sank to his knees. When Michael wrenched his Blade free, blood sprayed out of the gaping neck wound with such force that it splattered the ceiling. He swung his sword again, separating the monster's head from his shoulders. The head rolled across the carpet, followed by gushing blood as the carcass pitched forward.

Inspired by Michael's courage, Valeria charged at the werewolf on the left with Henri behind her while Michael swung at the one on the right.

Both beasts dropped into defensive postures and roared like lions.

Valeria's Blade sank into her target's right shoulder, Henri's into its left arm, severing the claw, which spun through the air. Blood from its open wrist splashed their legs. Valeria jerked her sword free, and she and Henri buried their weapons into wolf flesh, their Blades butting against each other inside the beast's neck.

The werewolf's eyes rolled in its skull, and it opened its jaws to howl but only heaved blood. Its front right claw encircled Henri's Blade, and Valeria worked her weapon through sinew.

Then she turned her body sideways and flung the creature's head at the stairway. Her momentum caused her to sink to her knees in the blood-soaked carpet, and as she used her Blade for leverage to stand, she saw a werewolf crash into Eun above and send her flying down the stairs, the beast atop her.

The second monster Michael attacked nearly knocked the sword out of his hand, and he pirouetted to regain his balance and fend the beast off. He swung the Blade with great chopping motions, driving the beast across the room and away from the others.

*We have to spread out or we're finished.*

As the werewolf roared at him, he sensed the beast's frustration. The Blades were heavy and sharp, their deadly embrace almost impossible to evade. Michael had trained for this purpose for a decade and a half, and he did not intend to show his prey any mercy.

The creature planted its left leg behind it, dropped to its haunches, and seemed to pull itself inward. Then it launched at Michael, who dropped to one knee with his Blade raised in both hands and his head bowed forward.

The werewolf's momentum drove its body into the tip of the Blade, which split it open from chest to groin.

Feeling hot blood paint his back, Michael stood and pivoted on one foot, holding his Blade as a baseball player would a bat. The werewolf rolled across the floor, entangled in its own guts. Michael crossed the soggy floor as the beast managed to work its way up on its claws and knees, and he swung his Blade downward with grim accuracy.

The werewolf sitting atop Eun closed its powerful jaws over her face and snapped them together, shredding her mask. It threw its head to one side, spitting out her goggles, then fastened its fangs over her face again. Eun screamed even as Valeria buried her Blade into the back of the beast's neck. The Korean flailed for the hilt of her own sword, but her frantic movements proved useless.

When Valeria jerked her Blade free, blood splashed her goggles and mask. Blinded, she wiped the lenses of the goggles with one forearm, smearing the crimson. She raised her Blade again and brought it down with less ferocity because she did not wish for her weapon to injure Eun as well. The wounded woman continued to scream in agony.

The werewolf spread its front arms out, geysers of blood spraying out in multiple directions from the violated neck.

Valeria stepped back and kicked the beast, which rolled over. She did not know what sickened her more: the sight of the creature's head barely attached to its neck or Eun's face dangling in strips from her skull. She swung her Blade in a powerful arc that disconnected the werewolf's head.

Eun clapped her hands over her face, which only caused her screams to grow louder.

Valeria heard another scream above her: Myles. The remaining werewolf had clamped its jaws over his left forearm, making it impossible for the man to swing his Blade. The muscular warrior stood with his feet braced on different stairs, using his right hand to beat at the beast. The werewolf released his mauled arm and chomped on it again, and Myles dropped his Blade, which slid down the stairs. He threw his right arm around the monster's head, putting it in a feeble headlock as the creature's teeth split his bone. Myles screamed as his hand and wrist struck the floor, followed by spraying blood. With what must have been the last of his strength, he dove toward Valeria, dragging the beast with him. They rolled down the stairs together, a tangle of human and lupine limbs.

Valeria dropped her Blade, seized Eun's hands, and pushed the wounded woman out of harm's way.

The werewolf crashed upside down against the metal front door, and Henri and Michael fell upon it with their Blades, hacking the howling beast to pieces.

Valeria removed a small first aid kit from her coat and kneeled beside Eun, who continued to scream. She took out a syringe, pulled off its cap, and squirted the clear liquid, checking for air bubbles. Unable to discern such fine details in night vision, she took a chance and drove the needle into Eun's throat, injecting the morphine.

Eun grimaced, groaned, and whimpered, her once beautiful face a tattered and grisly mosaic.

The green glow of her night vision dimmed, and Valeria

realized someone had switched on an overhead light. Tearing the goggles off, she stood. The door, walls, and stairs glistened with blood.

Michael and Henri turned toward her, their clothes drenched and their Blades dripping gore. Myles lay motionless on the floor between two decapitated werewolves. Valeria's comrades removed their goggles.

"Look," Michael said, staring past Valeria.

Spinning around, she gasped. Lying on the bloody carpet, the three werewolves first killed had changed shape: they no longer resembled manlike wolf hybrids but enormous black wolves. Jerking her head back, she saw the remaining two werewolf corpses changing before her eyes: drawing into themselves, assuming more recognizable lupine dimensions.

"Sacred Mary," she said.

Michael retrieved his headset from the floor and spoke into it. "Come get us. Fast."

"Help me," Eun said in a strangled voice.

Valeria helped Eun to her feet. In the light, the woman's face appeared even more ghastly, like a melted crimson candle.

Michael removed a can of lighter fluid and squirted the stairs, walls, carpets, and corpses.

"What about Myles?" Henri said.

"Tonight we honor our dead with fire."

# CHAPTER EIGHT

Awakening to the sound of his cell phone's ring tone, Willy glanced at his alarm clock, which flashed 4:20 at him. He switched on the light and answered the call without checking the display. Only someone from the department would call at this time.

"Diega." He rubbed the sleep from his eyes.

"This is Sergeant Huntley from Night Watch Command," a female voice said. "I'm sorry to disturb you, but I have an urgent call from Detective Faherty from the Arson squad in Queens."

*Arson?* "Yeah, that's okay. Put him through."

He heard a click, then a male voice. "Diega?"

"Speaking."

"Faherty, Arson. We got a house burning in Rosedale. Call it a lost cause. When I entered the address into the system, it spat out your name as the primary on a case involving the owners: Rodney and Jennifer Lourdes, Jason Lourdes's parents."

Willy sat up. "Are they okay?"

"I doubt it very much. We got neighbors all up and down the sidewalk, but no one claiming to be a Lourdes. If they're in there, they're not coming out alive."

*Fuck.* "Is it arson?"

"Too soon to say for sure, but between you and me, I'd say that's a big affirmative."

"I'm on my way."

"You'll be wasting your time. The fire isn't out yet, and even when it is it won't be safe to walk around in there."

"I need to see it. What time should I come?"

"What time does your shift start?"

"At 0800."

"I'll see you then. Grab another couple of hours if you can."

"Yeah, thanks." Closing his phone, Willy climbed back under the covers, but he did not fall back asleep.

An hour later, his phone rang again. "Hello?"

"This is Sergeant Huntley from Night Watch Command again. Detective Faherty from Arson would like to speak to you."

*Déjà vu.* "Put him through."

A click. "Diega, you'd better get over here as fast as you can."

Angelo drove the passenger van through the security gate and into the warehouse parking lot, where he backed it up alongside the cargo van. The occupants had removed their goggles as soon as he drove away from the inferno they had left behind. Eun continued to wail even with the morphine Valeria had given her. Despite their victory, a pall hung over them because of Myles's death.

Michael hopped out of the van first, carrying Myles's sword, and opened the loading bay door. Valeria supported Eun as Henri and Angelo helped them out. Inside the loading bay, they placed Eun on one of two gurneys they had left there, and Angelo and Henri rushed her to the steel door, which Angelo unlocked, and into the gloom.

Michael locked the door behind them. "What can you do for her realistically?"

"I can reduce her pain, and I can sew as much of her face back together as possible, but she'll be disfigured for the rest of her life."

"But she'll live."

"Yes."

Michael slapped her so hard that she cried out. She turned to him, her cheek stinging. It never occurred to her to strike him back.

"You dropped your Blade to pull her away from the stairway."

"I was trying to keep her from getting harmed."

"Don't ever drop your Blade. You risked the life of every other man in that room."

"I'm sorry."

Michael raised the extra sword between them. "Look what happened to Myles. The moment he dropped his Blade, he was a dead man. Now go do what you can for Eun."

Feeling tears form in her eyes, Valeria ran after the gurney.

After awakening at 5:00 AM, Mace dressed in layers of sweats and went for his morning run with his dog, Sniper, a daily ritual. They followed Fourth Avenue up to the Verrazano Bridge, crossed over to Fifth Avenue, ran down to Sixty-eighth Street, then back up to Eighty-first Street. Mace no longer ran for speed or distance but simple cardiovascular. It had taken him a while to grow accustomed to the Brooklyn terrain, but he now loved it, and so did Sniper. The cold air filled his lungs, and he walked back to his house, cooling down, and peeled off the top sweatshirt as they climbed the stairs.

When he emerged from his shower, clad in a terry-cloth robe, Cheryl waited for him with Patty in her arms. "Jim Mint called. He says to call him back. It's important."

Mace grunted. They hadn't spoken since he had been reassigned to the K-9 Unit.

Cheryl set Patty down on their bed and booted up her computer while Mace dialed a number stored in his cell phone.

"This is Jim Mint," a familiar voice said on the other end.

"It's Tony."

"I need to see you this morning. How's 0800?"

Sitting on the edge of the bed, Mace drew a finger across Patty's stomach, eliciting laughter. "I still have a unit to run."

"The dogs will run just fine without you."

Mace pressed his teeth together. "Your office?"

"Make it the Bonaventure. I want to keep this meeting under the radar."

*Of course you do.* "Okay, I'll see you there." Mace shut down his phone and stood.

"The parents of that kid who was decapitated died this morning." Cheryl looked up from her laptop. "Their house burned down. Do you think it was arson?"

*Quite a coincidence*, Tony thought. "I have to leave early."

Cheryl smiled. "For a meeting at One PP?"

"Nope, for a meeting at a secret location. Jim doesn't want anyone to see me going into his office."

"Wear a nice suit anyway."

Willy parked the SUV he had signed out from the Detective Bureau a block away from the fire engines. The sun hadn't risen yet, and Karol yawned in the seat beside him.

"Welcome to the big leagues, where sleep is a rare commodity," he said.

Karol said nothing.

"Are you that tired, or is this getting to you?"

She stared ahead through the windshield. "I've seen plenty of DOAs, but we were in that house yesterday. We spoke to those people."

"It's unusual."

They got out and walked to the smoking house. A dozen neighbors stood on the sidewalk across the street, and Willy spotted Sharon King, the woman who had comforted Jennifer Lourdes. She had tears in her eyes.

They stopped at a RMP car, and Willy spoke to the uniformed PO drinking coffee inside it. "I'm looking for Faherty from Arson."

The PO nodded at the house. "Blond guy dressed like a fireman."

"Thanks."

Willy and Karol moved closer to the house, where they spotted Faherty standing with a pair of firefighters. Ashes covered the neighboring homes, and smoke continued to rise out of molten furniture.

"Diega?" Faherty said.

"Yeah. This is my partner, Detective Williams."

"You made good time."

"Can we go inside?"

"Follow me and watch your step." Faherty led them through the frame where the front door had been.

The house had been reduced to cinder and ash, though the collapsed roof had protected the scorched stairway. Crime Scene Unit detectives photographed several objects on the floor. Karol coughed.

"We expected to find two DOAs. We found six. Only one of them was human." Faherty pointed at the blackened remains on the floor. "I'm not a medical expert, but if you ask me, this one's missing an arm." He jerked a gloved thumb at the ruined stairs. "And it's back there." He stepped sideways. "Now these two look like they were dogs to me."

Willy stared at the long black shapes, charred and headless, on the floor. "They're too big for dogs."

"You ever seen an Irish wolfhound?" Faherty pointed at two smaller shapes. "Their heads were cut off." He nodded at the CSU detectives. "There's three more over there."

"We were here yesterday," Willy said. "There were no dogs, and I'd have noticed five animals that big."

"There's no kennels out back, either. I spoke to a few of the neighbors: the Lourdeses never owned any dogs or any other pets that anyone knows about. But last night one of them—Mr. Santino—says he heard a whole pack of dogs howling somewhere in the neighborhood. So you've got one DOA, who may or may not have been one of the two owners of this house, who lost his or her arm in here, and five dogs— or lions or tigers or bears or whatever the hell they were— with their heads cut off." Using a metal pike, he poked at a blackened metal can. "Arson? You bet your ass."

"Excuse me," Karol said. "I need some air."

Willy and Faherty followed Karol outside, where she sucked in her breath and covered her mouth.

Faherty counted on his fingers. "We got Arson, that's me; Homicide, that's you. And I wouldn't be surprised if we both have to answer to goddamned Animal Control."

Willy raised his hands. "I appreciate you keeping me in the loop, and I want you to continue doing so as long as there's a possibility that this is related to my homicide—"

"But . . ."

"I'm Manhattan Homicide South, emphasis on *Manhattan*. In case you're tone-deaf and can't tell the difference between a Lower East Side accent and one from Long Island, this is Queens."

"How did I know you were going to say something like that?"

Willy handed two business cards to Faherty. "Here's one for you and another for whatever Queens detective catches this case. Stay in touch."

"Yeah, you two have a nice day in the big city."

Rhonda awoke on her bed of straw, her brain feeling syrupy. She remained motionless for a moment, gathering her thoughts. Recalling that she had been in Wolf Form, all she had to do was wiggle her toes to realize she had changed back into her human shape.

*Jason!*

The bastards had murdered him at the store. How she wished she could sink her claws into one of the killers. No matter what happened as a consequence, the desire to tear one of the humans to shreds was greater than any emotion she had ever known. They had shocked her into transforming, then sedated her with their tranquilizer guns. Twice in one day they had pumped her full of their drug.

Now her bladder threatened to explode. Rhonda did not wish to reveal to them that she had regained consciousness any more than she wished to urinate in one of the metal buckets, but she had no choice. Sitting up, she groaned. Her head felt so heavy. She stood, massaging the bridge of her nose and fighting for clarity. Then she staggered to the buckets, her chains clinking, squatted over one, and relieved herself, the sound of her piss striking the bucket's bottom filling the gloom. She gazed at a camera mounted near the ceiling, her humiliation curdling into anger. When she stood again, she saw they had given her no toilet paper.

*Animals.*

Refusing to wipe herself with the dirty straw, she allowed the urine drops to trickle down her legs and air dry.

She heard the metal bolt on the other side of the door slide into the unlocked position, and the door swung open. Three of her captors entered: the man with dark hair who had worn a beard in the store; the woman with blonde-streaked black hair; and the black man who now had a shaved head. They stood facing her with a few feet between them, their tranq guns held ready.

Rhonda swallowed. "What is this, an inquisition?" Maybe she could bait them into identifying themselves as Torquemadans, not that it would alter her circumstances.

"We just wanted to make sure you regained consciousness before we put you under again," the man who no longer had a beard said. "We don't want you slipping into a coma."

He raised his gun, and his comrades did the same.

Rhonda felt her resolve breaking down. "Why are you *doing* this?"

The man fired his weapon, and its dart drilled into Rhonda, above her left breast. Clenching her teeth and wincing, she reached up to grasp the dart, but before her fingers closed around its shaft, she sank to her knees. Jerking the dart out of her flesh and tossing it aside, she glared at the woman and the other man, waiting for them to fire.

They glared back, also waiting.

Then Rhonda pitched forward, embracing the darkness.

# CHAPTER NINE

**M**ace entered the lobby of the Bonaventure Hotel and gave his name to the front desk clerk, who directed him to a conference room on the second floor. He took the wide, carpeted stairs, opened the appropriate door, and froze in the doorway. Two FBI agents sat beside Jim Mint. "Who says there are no more surprises in the world?"

Mint gestured at the empty seat on his right, opposite the FBI agents. "Come in and close the door."

Mace closed the door and walked over to the chair Jim had offered him.

Norton, an attractive woman who still wore her strawberry blonde hair in a ponytail, gave him a too cheerful smile. "Good morning, Captain."

He nodded. "Special Agent Norton." He turned to the bald-headed male FBI agent. "Special Agent Shelly."

"It's Kathy," Norton said.

Shelly wore glasses now. "Congratulations. Most people get us confused. Special Agent Shelly is fine."

"How could I forget? The two of you could have helped me track down the Manhattan Werewolf and didn't." He glanced at Jim. "I'm sorry. I can't discuss that with him in the room, can I?"

"You can discuss anything you want with Jim," Norton said.

Mace sat. "That's a load off my mind."

"Let us know when you're done," Jim said.

"I honestly don't think I've even started. Why am I here?"

"Because your city needs you."

Mace chuckled. "Really? Well, I am a civil servant, which means I live to serve the city. Tell me what I can do for it."

Jim slid two stapled documents across the table and set a pen on them.

Mace picked up and examined the documents. "A non-disclosure agreement? I don't think so." He tossed the paper-work back onto the table.

"Your country needs you too."

"Thus the federales? I love this city. I love this country. But I don't trust the department, and I trust the government even less." He rose. "I hate to pontificate and run, but I think I'll be on my way."

"You know what this is about."

Mace sighed. "I have a pretty good idea."

"Then sit down."

Mace descended into his seat. "What do you want from my life? Haven't you guys done enough to me already?"

Jim nodded at the nondisclosure agreements.

Mace picked up the pen, flipped one document to the signature page, scrawled his name, then did the same with the second copy. Setting the pen down, he sat back.

"I never did anything to you. That was the previous administration."

"You guys are all alike, with your politics and your machinations. Every one of you spends more time covering his ass than doing his job."

"You sound like someone who's bitter because he wasn't invited to the party. Or maybe you were invited, and your invitation was rescinded."

"Did you bring me here for a lecture?"

"Yesterday morning eighteen-year-old Jason Lourdes was decapitated in a bookstore called Synful Reading. I'm sure you know this because your wife reported the news ad nauseam. Synful Reading was once managed by Angela Domini, a person of interest in your Manhattan Werewolf case. As Special Agents Norton and Shelly have been kind enough to explain, they linked your Manhattan Werewolf slayings to a series of serial murders across the country."

Mace glanced at his watch.

"The murders stopped soon after you were taken off the case."

"I guess I was just getting in the way. I thought the murders stopped because the governor sent in the cavalry."

"But the perp was never apprehended, and when the National Guard left, the murders didn't resume here or elsewhere."

"Maybe the perp just needed a slap on the wrist."

Norton folded her hands. "For a man who was obsessed with the case, you never discussed it in public. You could have had your say in Carl Rice's book, but you didn't."

"The guy's a sleaze."

"He made you famous in his previous book, didn't he?"

"He was a sleaze then too."

Jim opened the folder before him and tapped a stapled document. "This is a copy of a report you filed after witnessing John Stalk's murder. The *original* report you filed before the powers that be revised it."

Mace stayed quiet.

Jim slid the report aside, revealing another document. "And this is a transcript of the meeting you had with Deputy Commissioner Dunegan and his aides when they booted you out of Homicide."

*I should have known Dunegan recorded the meeting*, Mace thought.

"The claims in the transcript support those in your report. Do I need to refresh your memory?"

Mace leveled his gaze at Jim. "No."

"The word that appears several times in both documents, without irony, is *werewolf.* While you were on suspension on the day the National Guard rolled into the city, you signed out two objects from Evidence Control: the hilt of a broken sword recovered from Terrence Glenzer's personal safe and the service revolver of Detective Patty Lane, who was murdered by the perp while she was under your direct supervision. Signing out those items while under suspension was a criminal offense."

Mace had always known that signing out those weapons would catch up to him sooner or later. "I returned them that night."

"Yes, you did." Jim flipped to another report. "After signing yourself out of Bellevue's ER, where you were treated for bite wounds and gashes in your forehead." He looked up from the folder. "Your forehead's healed well, by the way." He looked down again. "According to the hospital report, you claimed you were jumped by gang members. A wound in your left shoulder was so severe you attended physical therapy for five months. Since when do gang members bite police detectives?"

"I guess everyone got a little crazy when those guards came marching in."

"Why did you take the items from Evidence Control?"

Mace shrugged. "Maybe I thought I could stop Patty's killer."

"You mean murder him?"

"It wouldn't be murder if he wasn't human."

"Did you have any luck?"

"No."

"It didn't take long for someone to realize you took the items. Dennis Hackley was notified. He ordered an additional round of testing on both objects. Forensics determined that the revolver was fired six times between the time it was initially tested after Detective Lane's murder and before you returned it. In addition, traces of cleaning chemicals were found on the broken sword—chemicals that weren't on it before you signed it out. Hackley was under a lot of pressure and realized he was being forced out. He could have sacrificed you to save himself. Instead he buried the report."

Dennis Hackley, the chief of detectives at the time, had once been Mace's mentor. He had taken over the Manhattan Werewolf case after Mace had been suspended. Mace had no idea his friend had gone to bat for him one more time. After being shit canned by NYPD, Hackley moved to Nebraska, where he took a top spot in a security firm.

"You took the sword and the gun. You checked into an ER with bizarre wounds. You returned the items and apparently used them. And the Manhattan Werewolf vanished, never to be seen again." Jim closed the folder. "I'm impressed. I don't know if I'm looking at a goddamned hero, a goddamned vigilante, or a goddamned monster hunter."

Mace said nothing.

"Hackley didn't bury his findings deep enough. After that monsignor from the Vatican took custody of both halves of the sword, the FBI requested a search for related documents, and guess what turned up?"

Mace raised his eyebrows.

"Here's where we get into national security," Norton said. "We've been investigating these circumstances for years. When we presented you with evidence that your Manhattan Werewolf had perpetrated killings all over the country, we already believed there was something highly unusual about him. Forensics at various crime scenes determined his DNA had qualities unlike any seen before."

"What kind of qualities?"

"The DNA had remarkable healing properties," Shelly

said. "It changed under certain tests . . . adapted . . . survived."

"Adapted how?"

"The DNA was unstable. Its properties changed depending on which tests were performed on it."

Mace had no intention of letting Norton off the hook. "Keeping in mind that I'm a layman in terms of science, exactly how did the properties of the DNA change?"

"It altered its structure," Shelly said, "almost the way a chameleon changes the color of its skin."

"But I'm guessing there were only two or three variables. If you already knew some of this two years ago, why didn't you help me catch my perp?"

"For one thing, our superiors were unresponsive to our theories. For another, we didn't want the responsibility. We were happy to push you in the right direction, and we believe you killed him." He raised one hand. "No need to implicate yourself."

"I wasn't about to."

"Since then we've uncovered evidence—which we can't disclose—that others like your perp exist," Norton said. "Perhaps many others."

Mace turned to Jim.

"Jim already knows everything I've just told you. He's been in the loop since your suspension two years ago. We pushed to have him put in his current position."

"He's a mole for the FBI?"

"We prefer to think of him as an advocate for interdepartmental cooperation."

Jim held Mace's gaze. "I'm a cop, not a fed. But this *shadow species*, for lack of a better term, has me scared. The department won't ever acknowledge these things exist; you know that. But Norton and Shelly know the truth, and they've got the resources to monitor the situation."

"Yes, they're great at monitoring."

"We've classified these individuals as Class L human beings," Shelly said.

"*L* is for . . . ?"

"Lupine."

Mace's body relaxed. *It's finally out.*

"We have no reason to believe these people are a threat," Norton said. "Other than an occasional report of a sighting on an Indian reservation, they've made themselves practically invisible. Your perp was the rare exception. We have to believe the rest only want to live in peace."

*You're batting a thousand*, Mace thought. "If that's the case, then how are they a threat to national security?"

"Knowledge of their existence would cause chaos here and abroad," Shelly said. "Can you imagine the hysteria that would ensue? The prejudices? We want to make contact with them and forge a trusting relationship. We want to protect them for their own good."

"I'm sure the Indians heard a similar sales pitch once upon a time."

"Jason Lourdes had DNA similar to that found in hairs taken at your Manhattan Werewolf homicide sites," Norton said. "We believe he was a Class L human and so were his parents. They're presumed dead, by the way, after their house was burned down early this morning. Six corpses were found in the ruins of the house: only one was human.

Its arm had been chewed off. We're told the other five were 'canine' in nature—huge suckers. Their heads were cut off, just like Jason's."

Mace felt as if he'd been slugged in the stomach. He had seen Janus Farel's hybrid form—half man and half wolf— transform into that of a giant wolf after his death. Someone had killed five Wolves—six, counting Jason—with a sword.

*The Blade of Salvation.*

"We've taken the carcasses into custody and are transporting them to Quantico," Shelly said.

"It sounds like you have all the physical evidence you need to prove these things exist."

"It's easy to extrapolate that Rhonda Wilson and by extension her parents and their siblings are Class Ls too," Norton said. "Possibly Synful Reading's owners and the other employees as well. We know you're familiar with the Dominis. Six of these unique beings may have been killed in twenty-four hours. Clearly, there's an organized force working against them, hell-bent on their genocide."

*The Brotherhood of Torquemada.* "And you want to stop them?"

"Hell, yes," Jim said. "Not just to protect the lives of these Class Ls, as our colleagues call them, but to keep knowledge of their existence a secret from the public."

"Why are you telling me all of this?"

"We have only limited support for our investigation in the FBI," Norton said. "Maybe that will change once those carcasses are autopsied, but right now Shelly and I are the sole agents assigned to this investigation. We've been granted permission to form a joint task force with NYPD—"

"A *secret* joint task force," Shelly said.

"And because of what happened here two years ago," Jim said, "the commissioner's given me permission to devote a small team to the cause. He wants to avoid the panic that happened last time."

Robert Benson had replaced the previous police commissioner after the Manhattan Werewolf fiasco. "How forward thinking of him."

"His motives aren't unselfish. His permission came with several conditions."

"Not the least of which is plausible deniability, I'm sure."

"Naturally. We're still talking about the department after all. The mayor is none too pleased that New York City has become known as the werewolf capital of the world. Every documentary that airs on the Manhattan Werewolf, every book that's published, every video file that's uploaded to the Internet purporting to be genuine footage of a werewolf, is a public embarrassment. The mayor's made it clear to the commissioner that he never wants to see the word *werewolf* mentioned in a headline or news story again."

"So one goal of this secret joint task force is to cover up whatever's going on out there."

"That can't surprise you."

"Where do I come in?"

"You're the only one in this room who's actually seen these things with his own eyes. We can't think of a better person to head up the task force."

Mace blinked twice, then grunted. "I'm not interested."

"You've been sitting on the sidelines long enough."

"I've discovered I like being there."

"This is a chance to redeem your career."

"I have a wife and a daughter who depend on me. I don't want to get back into the game. Fourteen people were killed last time, one of them under my command. I don't want that kind of responsibility again, especially over this insanity. I just want to finish out my two years and retire in peace."

"Bullshit, you do. I'm giving you the chance to hand-pick your own team and make a difference in this extraordinary crisis, with minimal bureaucratic interference—a chance to lead an elite task force."

Mace leaned forward. "I already tried that. Look what happened to me. You guys hung me out to dry." He rose. "I'm sorry, but you'll have to find someone else. Thanks for thinking of me."

His knees shook as he left the room, but he felt good.

*They know I was right.*

# CHAPTER TEN

Willy and Karol entered the squad room and set their coats on their chairs.

"Feels like we were just here, doesn't it?" Willy said.

"We *were* just here."

With a phone pressed against his ear, Landry tapped on the glass front of his office and beckoned them inside. Seeing Captain Bill Aiello sitting in his larger office, also on the phone, Willy opened Landry's door for Karol, followed her into the office, and sat beside her.

Landry hung up. "We don't want a case involving the parents of our vic from yesterday?"

"I don't," Willy said.

"I do," Karol said. "Make me the primary."

Willy glanced at Karol. "*What*?"

"I'll take the case."

Landry sat back in his chair. "Thank you, Karol, but I have a feeling Willy's going to step up to the plate."

"Fine," Willy said. "Whatever you say."

"Brooklyn detectives will work the case, but they're reporting to you."

"Hurrah. Only thing is, we don't even know if the Lourdeses got toasted in that fire. We got one DOA without an arm and five dead dogs without heads. Or five dead wolves."

Landry held his gaze. "Headless dogs?"

"Or wolves. Their heads were cut off just like Jason Lourdes's was. I'm beginning to think we might have more than one sword in play."

"I can't wait to read your report."

"Right." As they exited the office, Willy turned to Karol. "Thanks, partner."

"Hey, I offered to be the primary. There was no way Brooklyn DATF was letting us dump this one on them."

Willy sat at his desk. "Just once I'd like to be the dumper instead of the dumpee." He booted up his computer and opened a report file. "I didn't even take notes at the scene."

"I did."

Cheryl blew into the third-floor office of Manhattan Minute News on West Thirty-second Street and tapped her cameraman on the shoulder. "Don't get too comfortable."

"Discomfort is my middle name."

Turning, she walked backward, keeping Ryan in sight. "I hope the Batmobile's all gassed up."

"Where are we going?"

"Rosedale!"

When she turned around she stood in the office of Colleen Wanglund, her executive producer.

"We already covered Rosedale," Colleen said as she keyed in a story on her computer.

"*I* didn't cover Rosedale."

Colleen's eyes never left her monitor. "I assume that's because you were home asleep. O'Hear covered Brooklyn. He covers the night beat, remember?"

Cheryl set her hands on Colleen's desk and leaned forward. "That was last night. This is today. We need to keep the news fresh, and that fire is part of my story."

"We don't do stories; we do minutes. And there are plenty of minutes right here in Manhattan to go around."

"I saw O'Hear's report. He downplayed the connection between the fire and yesterday's murder—"

"He addressed the connection. What do you expect in a minute?"

"—and he said arson is suspected. We need to follow up and connect some dots."

"So follow up, connect."

"Thank you," Cheryl said on her way out the door.

Gabriel spotted Raphael standing in front of the Domini Funeral Home with Lawrence and Leon, two members of his crew, as Micah slowed to a stop before the East Thirty-third Street business. He also saw Eddie and David standing farther away at opposite ends of the funeral home's boundaries.

"You want me to wait?" Micah said.

"No, that's all right. I'll call if I need you." Gabriel got out and approached his brother as Micah drove off. "Were you out here all night?"

"No, but I did have people here. We need to protect our interests. You heard the news?"

"It's all over the TV." Gabriel opened the front door, which Raphael had unlocked, and they entered the lobby together. "I'm thinking about sending Melissa and the boys to stay with Angela. I need to focus on this crisis, and I need to know they're safe."

"Crisis? We're not talking about some disaster. We're under attack. Six of us have been killed in twenty-four hours, and Rhonda's still missing. We need to call a war council."

They walked along the polished floor. "I agree. Call the delegates in right away. We'll be ready." He entered the office and turned on the lights with Raphael close at his heels.

"How can you be so calm?"

"Losing my cool won't help the situation."

"You need to be fired up if you're going to lead this fight. Show some *passion*."

Gabriel turned to Raphael. "We live every day of our lives repressing our true nature. Today's no different. We're not animals; we're Wolves. I'll lead as I always have, as *my* nature dictates."

Raphael's nostrils flared. "Three of us weren't enough to protect Jen and Rodney. They're dead."

Gabriel clasped his brother's shoulder. "You're right. I underestimated our enemies. I won't make that mistake again."

He waited for Raphael to argue further, but his brother

just glared at him, his chest rising and falling.

Landry read the report filed by Willy and Karol on his monitor. The two detectives sat before him, as they had an hour earlier. Willy stared at the floor while Karol looked straight at Landry, waiting for his reaction.

"We're fucked," Landry said.

"I told you," Willy said.

"Why do we have to be fucked?" Karol said.

Landry drummed his fingers on the desk. "Because this is going to be a big deal, and it's not going to end well, and someone's going to hang for it."

Willy looked at his partner. "'Ask not for whom the bell tolls, it tolls for *thee*.' And me."

"And me," Landry said.

"Let's just dump the whole bag of shit on Brooklyn DATF," Willy said.

Karol looked from Willy to Landry. "Am I missing something? We're murder police. And we caught a murder, probably two."

"Don't forget the animals," Willy said. "Whatever they were."

"We have a duty to investigate this as aggressively as we can, and you two are already acting like we can't solve it. It's only been twenty-four hours."

"Yeah, and our only leads in that time have been six more bodies, toasted like marshmallows, and forensics evidence linking our DOAs to a case that buried some juicy careers." Willy turned to Landry. "When the ax falls, I do *not* want to end up in K-9."

Landry loosened his tie. "What makes you think I'll have any say in the matter? The higher your rank, the greater the fall."

The door opened and Aiello entered, wearing a brown suit and a gold tie. He walked over to a filing cabinet, which he leaned on, and stood taller than anyone in the unit. "Okay, here it is: the FBI's seized all the forensics evidence related to both of your cases."

Willy grinned. "I like the sound of that."

"Oh, you're still on the case," Aiello said. "We just have limited access to that evidence."

"Maybe we should wear blindfolds while we're at it."

"Can we get the evidence back?" Karol said.

"Not a chance," Aiello said. "It's en route to Quantico as we speak. I've been asked to relay to you that no information that CSU or the ME reported can be shared with anyone . . . including me. I'm being shut out. Conduct your investigation. Make your reports. Do the best you can."

"Begging your pardon, Captain," Karol said. "But just how in the hell are we supposed to make our case without forensics?"

"I'm working on it. Be patient. I have to go through channels, and that isn't easy."

A clerk knocked on the door, and Landry waved him inside. The paunchy man handed Landry a report.

"Patrol thinks they found the van used in the abduction yesterday," the clerk said.

Landry looked at the form. "Five blocks from the scene. Thanks."

The clerk exited.

Landry handed the form to Willy. "I suggest you move fast."

Willy and Karol rose in unison.

Mace entered his office on Floyd Bennett Field and tossed his coat aside. Jim Mint and the two FBI agents had stirred up old emotions within him, and he felt his anger at the brass returning. Mint and the feds knew the truth about the Wolves, but the bureaucracy would never allow them to take effective action against the creatures' enemies.

*The Vatican*, Mace reminded himself. He knew exactly who was behind the Brotherhood of Torquemada and had been for centuries. He had made it his business to learn as much about the secret society spawned by the Spanish Inquisition as he could over the last two years. It had become an obsession with him. The Wolves were in danger, and there was nothing he could do to help them, nothing anyone could do to help them. He wished he knew how to reach out to Angela so he could warn her, but he had never heard from her again after they had killed Janus Farel together, and he had feared that trying to find her in Canada would only put her at further risk, the very thing she had gone there to avoid.

Sitting at his desk, he unlocked the bottom metal drawer and took out a DVD that he loaded into his computer. He kept a copy of his files on the Manhattan Werewolf case at home as well. Skimming the records, he copied a name and pasted it into his browser, with no results. Then he located a phone number in the file and entered it into his cell phone.

A female voice answered after the third ring. "Chautauqua Reservation Tribal Police. Marion Morningstar. How may I direct your call?"

"Chief Diondega, please."

"Who's calling?"

"Captain Mace from NYPD."

"One moment."

Mace had called Chief Roy Diondega twice two years earlier, the first time to inquire about John Stalk, one of Diondega's officers who had insinuated himself into the Manhattan Werewolf case, and the second to notify him Stalk had been killed. Stalk had come to New York City from the Indian reservation in Western New York to slay the rogue Wolf, and Mace discovered he was romantically involved with Angela Domini.

From the street outside Angela's apartment below Synful Reading, Mace had witnessed Stalk's savage murder on the fourth-floor fire escape of an abandoned building. The murder had been committed by a creature Mace would never forget: a seven-foot-tall werewolf who used the alias Janus Farel. The monster decapitated Stalk and hurled his head at Mace, then disappeared inside the building.

"Captain Mace," Diondega said. "I never expected to hear your voice again."

Mace had never expected to have a reason to speak to Diondega again, either. "Hello, Chief."

"What can I do for you? All of my officers are accounted for. You got more skinwalker trouble down there?"

Janus Farel had scrawled the Indian word *skinwalker*, which meant werewolf, on the condo wall of Terrence Glenzer, a New York University professor he had killed. Glenzer had come into possession of the Blade of Salvation, a sword used to slay suspected werewolves during the Spanish Inquisition, and Farel wanted the Blade for himself.

"I'm trying to locate Tom Lenape, but I can't find a listing for him." The shaman Lenape had instructed Stalk in the ways of Indian mysticism.

"The medicine man? I don't remember him ever owning a phone."

Picking up the remote control, Mace powered the TV, which he left tuned to Manhattan Minute News. "Is there some other way I can reach him?"

"The only way I can think of is through a medium. Old Tom died from cancer last year."

Cheryl appeared on the TV, standing before the ruins of a burned-down house.

"I'm sorry to hear that. Is there another shaman on the reservation I could speak to?"

"Tom was the only real medicine man we had. The others are what you would call theatrical. What do you need a shaman for?"

"I'm just doing some research, and I'd hoped to speak to someone who shared John Stalk's beliefs."

"Tom believed in the old magic, and he passed that on to John. Now that they're both dead, I guess that magic died with them."

"Thank you, Chief." Mace hung up and raised the volume on the TV.

". . . detectives are reportedly investigating the possibility that Jason Lourdes and his family were executed by drug dealers over a deal gone wrong. This is Cheryl Mace, live in Queens."

*Drug dealers*, Mace thought. NYPD's Office of Public Affairs at work: leak a false lead to the press with just enough insinuation to sell it, and the rumor becomes "news" by default. Leaving the volume raised, he turned his attention to the paperwork that should have been completed that morning.

"Uh-oh," Karol said as she turned down the narrow street.

Willy saw two gleaming white vans and an unmarked SUV parked before, behind, and beside a cargo van, forming a barrier around the vehicle. Hector Rodriguez and Suzie Quarrel stood smoking on the sidewalk across the street, their own van parked farther down the block.

Karol double-parked in the first space she could, and she and Willy got out and walked over to the CSU detectives.

"What's going on?" Willy said.

Hector nodded at the scene across the street. "Federales. They declared jurisdiction and kicked us to the curb like a couple of bad TVs."

Willy saw four men in green jumpsuits scurrying around the cargo van. A man and a woman dressed in black suits crossed the street. Willy recognized the two FBI agents.

"Detectives, I'm afraid you'll have to stand on the sidelines until we've completed our forensics." The woman flashed her FBI identification. "I'm Special Agent Norton, and this—"

"I know who you are," Willy said.

"You do?"

"Two years ago, you jumped ship on an investigation you should have helped. Now you're taking over a case. Why the change of heart?"

"Ah," Norton said. "You worked under Mace."

"My partner was killed by the Manhattan Werewolf. You could have helped us catch the perp, and you didn't."

"You don't know what you're talking about," the man said.

"I wasn't talking to you. I was talking to the lady."

"I'm sorry about your partner," Norton said.

"Thanks."

"We have our job to do, and as soon as we've done it, you can do yours."

"How about we save some time, and you just share whatever you find with us?"

"I can't commit to that right now. Maybe later. We've already been in touch with Captain Aiello." Norton glanced at Suzie and turned around. Her partner followed her back to the vans.

"She remind you of anyone?" Hector said.

"Yeah," Willy said. "Only Patty was rougher around the edges."

"And Patty wasn't gay," Suzie said.

"What do you want us to do?" Hector said.

"What she said: wait, then do your job. Give us a call when you get in there. Come on, Karol."

As they returned to their car, Karol said, "You think those feds will leave anything for Hector and Suzie to find?"

"Not a chance."

"For someone who doesn't want this case, you sure seem territorial."

"They're not here to work the case. They're here to cover up any substantial evidence they find. Our job just got even harder."

Rhonda turned her head from side to side, the ceiling coming into focus. The pattern of corrosion in the pipes appeared different, and she knew they had moved her to a different room. Something had been attached to her face from her nose to under her chin, and straps encircled the back of her head.

*A muzzle!*

Flat on her back, she felt cold metal against her skin. She tried to sit up, but pressure on her chest held her in place. She attempted to raise her arms, then her knees, but they would not budge. Raising her head, she looked over her naked body. Four thick leather straps, each one four inches wide, secured her to a stainless steel table. Smaller straps held her wrists and ankles. She tried to press her shoulders against the strap closest to her head, but she could not move. A frustrated growl escaped her throat as she allowed her head to bang down on the metal surface. Being strapped to a table was far worse than being chained in a cell. What the hell did they have planned for her now?

*Dissection?*

She wanted out. The desire to Change welled up inside her, but rationality won out: she would not be any less trapped in Wolf Form.

The door opened and her three captors returned. This time, their tranq guns remained holstered. The black man carried a leather pouch, though. The woman closed the door and joined the two men at the table. The Caucasian male— the leader, she had concluded—circled the table. She heard a clicking sound, and then the end of the table on which her head rested rose without noise so that her body faced the Torquemadans at an angle.

*Some sort of hydraulic mechanism*, she thought. Her eyes darted to each of her captors. They regarded her with what looked like revulsion. Her frightened breathing sounded louder within the confines of the muzzle.

The leader nodded to the black man, who set his pouch down on a small table. Peeling back Velcro straps, he revealed a set of gleaming scalpels.

Rhonda's heart pounded in her chest.

Removing a scalpel, the black man nodded at the woman.

"A demonstration." He approached Rhonda, who focused on the scalpel. "Call me Henri. I want you to know who I am. I want you to have a name to curse as I take you apart."

Rhonda wanted to scream.

Henri looked her body up and down, as if searching for a sensitive spot. He tapped the scalpel in the palm of his free hand. Then he brought his arm up, the scalpel reflecting light even in the gloom.

Rhonda pressed the back of her head against the slab as the blade slashed down, opening her torso in an angle that ran from above one breast to below the other. Blood spurted out at the man's face and chest, and his features assumed a rapturous expression.

Rhonda found her scream.

# CHAPTER ELEVEN

Two and a half dozen men and women, representing different neighborhoods from the boroughs of New York City, sat in the Domini Funeral Home's viewing room. They wore dark suits and black dresses, as if in mourning, and sat on folding chairs with padded cushions.

Gabriel walked to the front of the room, a closed casket on the pedestal behind him, followed by Raphael, with Lawrence and Leon standing along the walls like sentries. Gabriel raised his hands and the whispering voices faded out. He measured the faces staring back at him and saw many emotions but mostly apprehension.

"Thank you for coming on such short notice," he said. "We've obviously got a situation on our hands that can't wait."

Bennett Jones, a grocer from Staten Island, rose. "This is all your fault. You should have closed down Synful Reading after your sister left the country. It was foolish to leave it open. Now look what it's gotten us."

Some of the Wolves muttered their agreement, and Gabriel felt Raphael's anger rising.

"Would I ever tell you what to do with your business? Synful Reading's been in my family for forty years. It's an institution in that neighborhood."

"That's the problem. It's too well known, especially after that so-called reporter wrote his book about the Berserker." Bennett returned to his seat.

The Berserker was a term the Greater Pack had used to describe Janus Farel before they learned his true identity, Julian Fortier.

Gabriel kept his tone even. "I won't argue this point. You may be right."

Saphire Kuda, a gypsy who ran a flower shop in Washington Heights, stood. "I just want to know one thing: Are these killers Torquemadans?"

Gabriel saw bodies tightening before him. "For now, we have to assume so. They killed Jason Lourdes and abducted Rhonda Wilson, then killed Rodney and Jen Lourdes, Tim Riegert, Kyle Chadler, and Samuel Minsky."

"And burned down Rodney and Jen's house," a gray-haired man named George Allen said without standing. Allen, who represented the Upper East Side, had been an advisor to Angus Domini, Gabriel's father, when Angus had led the pack before Gabriel.

"Every Wolf who's been executed so far has been decapitated. The police have determined that a sword killed

Jason. After seeing the body, I concur. Five decapitated Wolves in one location suggest at least five swords."

Murmurs became gasps.

Anne Wong from Prospect Park half rose. "Five Blades of Salvation?"

"In all likelihood, yes. But not necessarily. Any sword could do the job if it was strong enough, and if its wielder knew that decapitation is the easiest way to kill us. But the methodical nature of the attack, coming less than a day after Jason was killed, indicates a team of individuals with combat training and knowledge of our society. I fear the worst."

The voices in the room rose once more, and Gabriel raised his hands in a placating gesture. "These assassins aren't our only problem. Raphael and I saw Jason's corpse. He had begun to Change when he was killed. His face had just started to alter its shape. My sources confirm the corpse—and the five carcasses of the others—were sent to Quantico, the FBI's headquarters in Virginia. There's no way for us to recover the remains as we have in the past or to destroy them. Just as we have to assume our enemies are Torquemadans, we have to assume the government of this country is becoming aware of our existence."

Eyes widened and jaws opened.

*There, it's out*, Gabriel thought.

Joe Sevin, a tall black Wolf with salt-and-pepper hair, stood. "If the Torquemadans left Jason's head behind when they took Rhonda—"

"Then they didn't care if they exposed us or not. They may even desire that exposure to cause such a panic in this city that it's harder for us to mount an offense against them."

"What about Rhonda?" Anne said, rising all the way.

Joe settled into his seat.

"Again, all we can do right now is speculate. They didn't kill her; they took her prisoner, which means they have a use for her."

"To torture her until she gives us all up," Manny Moses, a white-haired lawyer from Long Island said, jumping to his feet. "That girl will be the end of us."

"I have faith in Rhonda," Gabriel said. "But finding her *is* a priority."

"Two years ago, we worried about the Berserker exposing us. Now, *this.*"

Cecilia Perez, a pediatrician from the Bronx, stood up at the same time as Patrick Reily, a housepainter from Astoria. Patrick motioned for Cecilia to speak first.

"If the Torquemadans identified Rhonda and Jason just because they worked at the bookstore, then they also must know you and Raphael are Wolves. This funeral home is probably under observation."

"You're probably right. That's why we had you all come here dressed as if you're attending a service."

"They could still follow us when we leave . . ."

"They could, but there are thirty of you."

"It was reckless of you to summon us here like this."

"I didn't want to take a chance on exposing a safe location."

"So you took a chance on exposing us instead. Thanks a lot." Cecilia sat with her jaw clenched.

"They must suspect every one of your workers is one

of us," Patrick said. "And then there are mutual contacts among us: shared doctors, lawyers, dentists . . . Every connection puts each member of the Greater Pack in danger. And if the Torquemadans don't have the resources to make those connections, the FBI will."

*He's right*, Gabriel thought.

Before he could comment, Eddie appeared at the back of the room.

"What is it?" Raphael said.

"Someone's here to see Gabriel," Eddie said. "One of us. But a stranger."

Gabriel glanced at Raphael, who raised his eyebrows. "I'll be right back."

Heads turned as Gabriel followed Eddie out of the chamber.

"What's his name?" Gabriel said as he and Eddie crossed the corridor.

"He wouldn't give it to me. He said you're the only one he'll speak to."

Rounding the corner, Gabriel saw through the glass front doors a tall man standing beside David outside. As he and Eddie neared the door, David turned in their direction and the stranger did the same. Gabriel had never seen him before.

"Let him in," Gabriel said, stopping outside the office.

David opened the door, and the strange Wolf entered the lobby. He had short, curly black hair, and Gabriel sensed kinship with him because of something in his eyes: the burden of leadership.

"I'm Gabriel. Who are you?"

The Wolf stood before Gabriel. "My name is Elias Michalakis."

Valeria watched as Henri used a rag to wipe the blood away from Rhonda's torso. Rhonda's head quivered, her eyes wild, and sweat trickled down her face like teardrops. Valeria feared the young woman was about to transform again. Then she blinked at Rhonda's body. Her flesh was smooth and undamaged, with no sign of the deep gash Henri had inflicted. Valeria had read about the beasts' healing powers in reports, but seeing them in action caused her to feel awe. Why had God granted such abilities to these unholy monsters?

"You see?" Henri said.

Valeria nodded.

Michael moved closer to Rhonda. "We don't want you to talk. If we did, we wouldn't have muzzled you. For now, we just want you to know that we mean what we say. We don't make idle threats."

He held out one hand, and Rhonda lowered her eyes to see it. Henri withdrew a second scalpel and set its handle in Michael's open palm. The two men stood on either side of their prisoner, scalpels raised.

Rhonda locked her pleading eyes on Valeria, who swallowed.

Michael pressed the blade of his scalpel against Rhonda's throat. "This very fine precision instrument has a blade sharp enough to cut off your head."

Rhonda's gaze shifted to Michael, who said, "We know that decapitation is the best way to deal with your kind."

Rhonda's breathing quickened, her naked breasts rising and falling, and deep, whistling breaths filled the cone of her muzzle.

"But killing you isn't what we have in mind. You're far too valuable a specimen for that. The beauty of having a captive with remarkable healing prowess is that no matter how badly we torture you, you won't die on us."

Michael drew the scalpel across Rhonda's throat. A narrow red line appeared in her flesh, and blood poured out like a waterfall. Rhonda's eyes bulged in their sockets as blood flowed down between her breasts.

Valeria felt nauseous. She knew that Rhonda was not a human being, but she *looked* human enough, and the gaping neck wound made Valeria taste vomit. But she fought back the sickness in her stomach. It would be unacceptable for Michael to witness such squeamish behavior.

*She's just an animal*, she told herself. *Worse: she's a demon.*

Valeria's body turned rigid when she saw the irises of Rhonda's eyes expand, blotting out their whites.

"Here we go," Henri said.

Rhonda's body tensed, her veins pressing against her flesh, which rippled. Her fingers and feet extended, and as her muscles went spastic, black fur spread over her body. Within the confines of her muzzle, she issued a pathetic-sounding howl. She strained against her bonds, attempting to free herself, but the wire woven into the leather straps held her in place.

Michael glanced over his shoulder at Valeria, who drew her tranq gun, then nodded at Henri. The two men leapt at Rhonda, slashing her with their scalpels.

"I'm the last member of my cell," Elias told the assembled Wolves. He stood between Gabriel and Raphael. "The Torquemadans wiped out the rest in a sneak attack. They abducted a member of my team, killed him by cutting off his head, surgically reattached his head, then dropped his corpse off at our doorstep with a bomb wired into his sternum. The resulting explosion killed the rest of my team and left me badly wounded. One of our party was female. She was pregnant."

Gabriel studied the expressions of the Wolves, shifting between shock and outrage. With their population dwindling, a pregnant female represented a grave loss.

Manny rose. "You said you're the last member of your cell. What about other cells?"

Elias's face remained deadly serious. "In Europe? I know of none. The packs there were brought to the brink of extinction decades ago, thanks to the Torquemadans. We lost contact with each other one by one. If any Wolves survive there now, they do so without the benefit of Wolf society, and they're hiding like animals."

"How is it possible?" Anne said. "This war was fought in secret. How could so many be dead?"

"The process of our genocide in Europe took centuries. The Inquisition, of course. The first and second world wars didn't help, and neither did decreased fertility. We took a good number of them with us, though."

"How many are left?"

"There have always been just six Blades, so there have always been six assassins to wield them and six apprentices to take their place. In the past, there's also been a small support network assigned to facilitate travel, lodging, weaponry, and medical aid. I believe we successfully eliminated much of their support. That's why they're taking such bold steps now; they're like cornered rats. There can't be more than a dozen active members of the Brotherhood left. Maybe only half a dozen, one for each Blade."

The Wolves murmured in dismay.

"A *dozen*?" Raphael said.

Gabriel cast a disapproving look in his brother's direction.

"How could a dozen humans pose such a threat to us?" Anne said. "There are thousands of Wolves in the US, almost two thousand here in New York."

Elias offered Anne a smile that suggested he held little regard for her math skills. "But they have the Blades of Salvation."

Anne threw up her hands and sat, Manny right behind her.

"We don't share your religious beliefs or your superstitions," Gabriel said in a diplomatic tone.

"Then how do you explain six Wolves murdered in one twenty-four-hour period?" Elias said.

"It just takes a sharp enough sword or ammunition powerful enough to destroy a Wolf's head."

Elias looked out at the crowd. "You must believe in the Wolf gods . . ."

"Our ancestors *were* gods. But the time of the gods has passed."

Elias turned to Gabriel. "I've heard of your strange beliefs. I can't accept them, but I can tolerate them. We need the strength of unity. My people are gone. As far as I know, our kind only exists in North America now, at least with any semblance of organization. And we need organization to track down these killers. I'm here to help you, but as long as I live, so do the beliefs of the European Wolves."

"Help us how?" Patrick said, rising.

"You need my knowledge and experience. I know these Torquemadans well."

Saphire stood up on the other side of the aisle. "If there's no more than twelve, why do we need your help? All we have to do is locate them."

"They're moving fast, trying to kill as many of you as they can before you can find them. They operate in secrecy, but their goal is also to expose you, to draw other humans into this war. To some degree, they have already succeeded."

"Like Janus Farel," Gabriel said.

Elias raised his eyebrows, then nodded. "We found Janus in a drug den, destroying himself in the fashion of human addicts. He voluntarily entered such a pitiful state after a hunter killed his mate here in the US. We took him into our cell, cleansed him, and trained him to fight the Torquemadans alongside us."

"Julian was my childhood friend. Did you send him back here?"

"No. He returned on his own after we expelled him. Our method of warfare was to strike at the Torquemadans in a manner that suggested human terrorists. Janus wanted to reveal his true nature to the world, to elicit fear in mankind."

"He was a true terrorist."

"An *extremist*."

"And yet the first person he killed in New York was Terrence Glenzer, a man who possessed a Blade of Salvation."

"*Half* of a Blade. I admit I provided him with that information."

"Two years ago, his actions nearly exposed us. You set that plan in motion."

"No. Janus killed many humans in other states before he came here. I merely directed him to kill Glenzer and retrieve the Blade so it wouldn't fall into the Torquemadans' hands. Then he disappeared."

"We killed him before his plan to instigate a war between the species could succeed."

"But he came close. I saw the reports on TV: National Guards swarmed this city. Tell me, who killed him?"

Gabriel hesitated.

"Our sister," Raphael said.

*Damn it*, Gabriel thought.

"One female against Janus? I'm impressed. And skeptical. Where is she now?"

"That isn't important," Gabriel said.

"I have no interest in avenging Janus. I loved him like a brother, but brothers follow different paths." He glanced at Raphael. "As I said, his methods were too extreme for me to accept."

"And what methods do you propose now?" Raphael said.

"First, you need to adopt a buddy system: two families

in every household, watching each other's backs. If the Torquemadans know who all of you are, that will cut the number of potential targets for them in half. Second, you need to create a plan for searching the city and its boroughs. We have to sniff them out."

"We already have such a system in place, easy to implement," Gabriel said.

"But only in Manhattan," Raphael said. "The outer boroughs are too large. Plus, there's New Jersey."

"Then start with Manhattan and work your way out. It will take longer, but it's the only way. The Torquemadans operate as my cell did—in absolute secrecy, leaving no paper trail behind."

Raphael glanced at Gabriel.

Gabriel looked out at the faces of those waiting for his answers, then turned to his brother. "Do as he says."

Sitting in a booth with high wooden backs in the rear of Gracie's pub, Mace sipped his scotch and waited. A crowd had formed for happy hour, and the bartender, a pretty blonde who knew how to smile for a tip, played a selection of recent pop hits.

Jim Mint made his way through the animated bodies and sat opposite Mace. "Sorry I'm late."

"Could you have found a dive with less light?" Mace said.

"I'm just being discreet. This joint's a little too trendy for cops."

"You said I could handpick my own team. Here's the

list." Mace slid a napkin across the nicked table.

Jim scanned the names on it. "Most of these are no problem, but Aiello's never going to let you have Landry. That's his right-hand man. Be reasonable."

"I was reasonable last time. This time I'm going to do things the right way—my way. Don't dangle terms in front of my nose like a carrot and then jerk them away. If you want me to do this, Landry's part of the package. Otherwise, find yourself another boy, and try convincing *him* what he's up against."

"This task force is supposed to be a discreet operation. How can it be if a captain is screaming at the higher-ups because you pilfered his looey?"

Mace stood. "I'll see you around. Or maybe I won't." He pushed his drink aside. "Get this, will you? It's the least you can do."

Jim motioned with both hands. "Sit down."

With his eyes locked on Jim's, Mace returned to his seat.

"All right, you can have Landry." Jim took out a business card and offered it to Mace. "Here's your new address. Get this thing up and running."

# CHAPTER TWELVE

Rhonda heaved a deep sigh, her vision coming back into focus. Her throat, limbs, midsection—even her breasts—throbbed where the Torquemadans had violated her flesh with their scalpels. The wounds had healed when she Changed into human form, but the pain lingered. Sweat burned her eyes, and tears rolled down her lower jaw, along the edge of the muzzle, and clung to her brutalized skin like raindrops after a storm.

*How much time did they spend torturing me?* No human being could have endured such abuse.

She thirsted for water.

*No, I want blood. I want meat!*

The leader reached for her head, and she flinched. He unbuckled the straps around her head and removed the muzzle, which he discarded. She breathed in fresh air.

The two men had barely broken a sweat going to work on her, and the female Torquemadan had just watched the whole assault.

"Last night we killed five of your people in their hybrid form," the leader said. "I use *people* in the most limited sense of the word. You're animals. Worse than animals—demons. Two of those we exterminated were Jason Lourdes's parents."

Fresh tears obscured Rhonda's vision when she thought she had none left. Mr. and Mrs. Lourdes had treated her like family.

*Maybe he's lying*, she thought.

"We killed them the same way we did Jason. One member of our party died in combat, and another was wounded."

*Good. I'm glad. I only wish they'd killed more of you.*

"We can kill your parents just as easily. We know who they are. We know where they live."

*No!* Rhonda pressed against the restraints, even though she knew it would do no good.

"We also know that Gabriel Domini is your leader and his brother, Raphael, serves as his right hand."

"I don't know what you're talking about," Rhonda said, gasping.

"Now, I want to know how many werewolves occupy New York City. I mean, Manhattan and the surrounding boroughs. I also want to know the first and last names of every werewolf you know. Think back to your childhood, which wasn't so long ago, and tell me every single person you and your parents socialized with. When possible, provide an address, even a general location."

"There's no such thing as werewolves," Rhonda said.

The man gestured around the room. "This is not a fantasy, not a dream. You're here, and so are we. You've revealed your true nature to us. There's no escape, either physically or psychologically. Tell us what we want to know, or we'll kill your parents."

"Fuck you." It felt good to say the words.

The man smiled at her. He scooped up the muzzle and placed it over her face again.

Before he could secure the straps, she willed the Change and snapped her jaws at him. The Transformation took too long, and her Wolf jaws were not fully extended when they snapped shut, so she only caught his nose instead of his entire face.

The man screamed, blood fountaining out of the gaping hole where his proboscis had been. He fell back, still screaming, his face awash in his own blood.

As Rhonda felt her fur spreading over her body, she chewed on the nose, savoring its foul taste.

*Let them try to reattach it.*

She heard a pop and felt pain between her breasts, nothing compared to the pain she had just endured. Turning her head, she saw the woman holding the tranq gun, which she had discharged. Rhonda spat what remained of the nose at the woman, who stepped aside to avoid the gnarled and bloody flesh. Out of the corner of her left eye, Rhonda saw the black man reach behind him and draw a sword from the scabbard strapped to his back.

*The Blade of Salvation . . .*

With a fiery look in his eyes and his teeth clenched, the man ran straight at her, cocking the sword behind his head.

"No!" the man without a nose said.

Rhonda bowed her head forward, trying to protect her throat with her snout. But the black man did not swing the blade at her neck; instead he buried it in the joint of her right arm with a great thwack. Rhonda watched in disbelief as her claw and the lower half of her arm fell to the floor, and the remaining stump of her arm, liberated from the leather strap, sprang upward, pumping blood. Then the sedative took effect and she lost consciousness.

Mace felt awkward reentering his old stomping ground, the Detective Bureau Manhattan on East Twenty-first Street. None of the POs loitering outside seemed to recognize him. Or maybe they knew his identity and just didn't care about Captain K-9.

*Not anymore,* he thought as he pressed the elevator button.

On the fourth floor he walked along the hallway, the walls painted lime green on top and brown on the bottom, to the open double doors of Manhattan Homicide South. Listening to his rubber-soled shoes squeak on the floor tiles, he experienced a rush of familiarity. The squad room had not changed; the desks were arranged the same way they had been when he had served here. Sergeant Don Gibbons sat at the desk used by Ken Landry during the day. As a lieutenant, Mace had occupied that office for three years.

Landry stood in the office of Captain Bill Aiello, speaking

to the tall man. Mace had occupied the captain's office for a far shorter period of time, when the Manhattan Werewolf had preyed upon the city. Landry and Aiello appeared to be deep in conversation, the office door closed.

Willy Diega sat at his old desk, speaking on the phone, his jacket off and his tie loose around his neck. Also on the phone, a black woman who wore her short hair tight to her scalp sat at the desk opposite him. Willy had mentioned Karol Williams to Mace, who had never met her. As Mace approached Willy, the detective looked up at him, his eyes registering surprise. Willy raised one finger, indicating he would be off the phone in a moment.

Gibbons exited his office and walked over. "Anthony, how are you?"

Mace shook the older man's hand. "Good to see you, Don. Why haven't you retired yet?"

"Believe it or not, I just put my papers in. Six more weeks, my friend."

"Good for you. Fishing in Florida?"

"You know it. How about you?"

"I've still got two years left. I don't plan to hang around like you did."

"That's understandable," Gibbons said in a low voice. "What brings you here?"

Mace watched Willy hang up. "I need to speak to Willy actually."

"Oh." Gibbons sounded surprised. "Well, it was nice seeing you." He clasped Mace's hand. "Say hello to Cheryl for me."

"I will."

As Gibbons returned to his office, Willy stood. "What's up, Tone?"

Mace nodded in the direction of the interview rooms. "In private."

Willy shrugged. "Sure."

Mace followed Willy into an available interview room. Willy remained standing, so Mace did too.

"Before you ask, I can't share information with you about any active investigations." Willy dropped his voice to a whisper. "The feds are crawling all over this."

Mace suppressed a smile. "The brass is putting me in charge of a task force that will take over your current cases. I'm taking you with me."

Willy folded his arms and spoke in a skeptical tone. "Tony Mace back from the dead? How did you pull that off?"

"They came to me. Apparently they consider me an expert."

"That's awesome. I'm happy for you. And I'm happy you're taking over the case, because I don't want it. And I don't want to serve on your task force."

"I'm not looking for volunteers. This is a done deal."

Willy snorted. "I didn't join the force to fight . . . you know." He made a comical howling sound.

"I'm not going to discuss the task force's objective here."

"That's fine with me. I don't need to know anything, because I'm staying put."

"I've arranged for your promotion to go through. Starting tomorrow, you'll be a lieutenant."

"Huh. You're full of surprises tonight. The freeze is department wide."

"I made it one condition of my taking this assignment."

"You've really learned to play the game, haven't you?"

"I always knew how to play it. I just got waylaid. This is no game, though."

"I earned that promotion. I shouldn't have to accept a transfer to get it."

"This is how the world works. I need you, just like I need Landry."

"What about what I need? I still have nightmares, don't you? No promotion is going to change that."

*I have worse nightmares than you do*, Mace thought. "You *are* coming with me. So is Williams."

Willy aimed a finger at Mace's heart. "Uh-uh. No way. You leave her out of this."

"You're partners, and she's already familiar with the crime scenes and the evidence. She's in the mix, whether you like it or not."

"Oh yeah? We'll see about that." Willy headed for the door, which opened before he reached it.

Karol walked in. "Where do you come off speaking for me?"

Willy glanced at the mirrored viewing window. "What, are you spying on me?"

Landry entered behind Karol, then Aiello brought up the rear and closed the door.

"This concerns me too." Karol faced Mace. "I want in on this operation, Captain. Thank you for the opportunity."

Willy raised his hands to the ceiling. "Opportunity? Jesus, why does everyone put their careers ahead of their lives? *Mira*, this is a *dangerous* assignment. You're not ready for it."

He turned to Aiello. "She's too green."

"It isn't my call, Diega." Aiello glanced at Mace.

"I'm sorry, Bill. I hate to deplete your resources like this, but I know who I need."

Aiello spoke in a tight voice. "What can I say? We all serve the machine." He looked at Landry and the detectives. "If you'll excuse me, I understand this is a classified operation."

The room quieted until Aiello closed the door behind him.

"This is bullshit," Willy said.

"Get it off your chest now, *Lieutenant*," Mace said with an edge in his voice.

"Congratulations, Willy," Landry said.

"Thanks. Did you get a promotion too?"

"No such luck."

"See what playing nice gets you?"

Landry shrugged. "I go where I'm needed."

"Aren't you the good soldier?"

"Watch it. You're not a lieutenant until tomorrow."

"So put me on report." Willy pointed at Karol. "You know she isn't ready for this, but you didn't say anything?"

"First of all, I disagree. Williams has proven herself capable."

"Thank you," Karol said.

"Secondly, even if I did agree with you, my opinion wouldn't matter. I got drafted just like you."

Everyone in the room turned to Mace.

"Let's go get something to drink," he said.

Gabriel led Elias into the foyer of the safe house, followed by Raphael. Arick, who had opened the door, closed it now and turned the locks.

"Arick, this is Elias," Gabriel said. "He'll be staying here indefinitely."

Gabriel watched Arick size up Elias. Although his reaction to the visiting alpha was cool, he offered his hand, which Elias shook.

"Leave us now," Gabriel said.

Arick appeared to be hurt by Gabriel's order. "I'll be in the basement." He walked to a door in the hall, opened it, and descended the creaking stairs on the other side.

"The spare room is upstairs to the left of the bathroom," Gabriel said. "It's yours as long as you need it."

"Thank you," Elias said.

Several suitcases and boxes had been stacked beside the curved stairway.

"Daddy!"

A staccato of footsteps on the hardwood floor preceded the blurred appearance of two boys who ran to Gabriel. Kneeling, he embraced the twins.

"You're home!" Damien said.

"Mama says we're going on a trip!" Gareth said.

"That's right," Gabriel said.

"Will you come with us?" Damien said.

"No, not right now. Maybe I'll join you later."

Gareth pointed at Elias. "Who's that?"

Gabriel stood. "This is my friend Elias. He's going to keep me company while you're away, so I don't get lonely."

Gareth moved forward, extending one hand. "Pleased to meet you."

With an amused look in his eyes, Elias shook the tiny hand. "Pleased to meet *you*."

Damien stood rigid, and Gabriel nodded at him. With slow steps, the boy joined his brother and held out a stiff hand. "Pleased to meet you."

Elias shook Damien's hand. "Pleased to meet *you*, my friend."

Gabriel smiled. "They're so different."

Melissa appeared in the doorway leading to the dining room, the sleeves of her shirt rolled up and the top buttons loose. She wore jeans, her hair pulled back. On seeing Elias, she stopped.

"Hello," Elias said.

"Hello."

"This is Elias Michalakis," Gabriel said. "He's visiting from Greece."

"I've never met any of our people from Greece," Melissa said.

"We're a rare breed," Eias said.

"Elias will be staying here while you're gone," Gabriel said.

"I see." Melissa's voice conveyed true understanding. "Boys, finish your dinner."

"But I want to—"

"*Now.*" She cut Damien off.

Frowning, both boys disappeared into the kitchen.

"I'll see to my room now," Elias said.

"Let us know if you need anything," Melissa said.

"I will. Thank you." Elias climbed the stairs.

Gabriel felt tension radiating from Melissa.

"I'd better go. There's a lot of organizing to do." Raphael moved to Melissa, kissed her cheek, and left.

Melissa raised her gaze upstairs, then fastened it on Gabriel. "That man is a killer. I smell it all over him."

"We need killers now," Gabriel said.

"Why's he here?"

"He came to warn us about the Torquemadans, too late."

"Then he should go back where he came from."

"The Torquemadans have killed his people there and in most of Europe, it seems. He has nowhere to go, so we can't turn him away. Besides, he has information that's useful to us. We need him."

"I don't like it."

Gabriel took her in his arms. "I knew you wouldn't."

"Don't trust him."

"I'll try not to."

She leaned her head against his chest. "I'm not looking forward to this trip."

"You'll feel better knowing the boys are safe."

"But I'll worry about you."

Gabriel stroked her hair.

# CHAPTER THIRTEEN

Mace led his party through the Irish pub to the back corner, where a black woman wearing a leather jacket sat nursing a mug of golden beer, a half-full pitcher on the table before her.

"Hello, Candice," he said, standing beside her.

Candice raised bloodshot eyes to Mace. "Captain."

Mace sat beside her, Landry beside him, then Karol and Willy.

"De-*tec*-tive *Smalls*," Willy said, filling an empty mug.

"Detective Willy." Candice nodded to Landry. "Hello, Lieutenant."

"Candice," Landry said.

Willy gestured to Karol. "My partner, Karol Williams."

Candice raised her mug to Karol in a toast. "Williams."

"Karol," she said as Willy filled her mug.

Mace looked around the table. "Candice is joining us from DATR."

"Kramer's just thrilled about that," Candice said.

Rod Kramer, the head of the Digital Audio Transmission Recording, and Candice had monitored radio transmissions when Patty Lane had gone undercover at a nightclub called Carfax Abbey II to lure the Manhattan Werewolf into a trap. Instead, Janus Farel had killed her in a department issue vehicle during a high-speed chase through the Village.

"Are you thrilled?" Willy said.

Candice shrugged. "I'll finally get my promotion to detective sergeant, right?"

Willy rolled his eyes.

"Am I the only person at this table not getting a promotion out of this?" Karol said.

"I'm not," Landry said.

Raising one hand, Mace motioned to the server on the floor, indicating they wanted another pitcher. "If we do what the bosses want, we'll all be in a better place than where we are now."

Making a skeptical face, Landry poured the last of the beer into his mug. "And if we screw up, we'll wind up in far worse positions."

Willy rapped his knuckles on the tabletop. "Okay, Captain. What exactly is our mission?"

"I'll explain in a minute. First, I want a drink. Then I'm going to tell you how I killed the Manhattan Werewolf."

Silence hung over the table for a moment.

"I fucking knew it," Willy said.

Mace sipped his beer, savoring the flavor.

"I hope you're not about to put us all in an awkward position by confessing to a murder," Karol said.

The music and voices around them were loud, so Mace did not worry that someone might overhear them. "First of all, it was technically self-defense. Secondly, murder describes the homicide of a human being, and what I killed wasn't human."

All the eyes of his audience remained riveted on him.

"Then what was it?"

Mace glanced at each cop in turn. "Except for Karol, every one of us sitting here heard Janus Farel, the perp in the Manhattan Werewolf case, kill Patty Lane. Willy and I even saw Patty's remains. He tore her to pieces, her car too, and left his clothes behind in tatters. No one in Astor Place reported seeing a naked man running around. But several witnesses in the subway station reported seeing what they described as a giant black dog run onto the lower platform, where it tore off the head of a police dog that pursued it, and disappeared into a tunnel."

Landry looked around at his companions, his gaze settling on Karol. "We logged reports from other witnesses who saw the dog run past different stations as it headed uptown on the tracks. Only they called it a wolf."

"How do New Yorkers know the difference between a big black dog and a wolf?" Karol said.

"Some of them even called it a werewolf," Willy said.

"Now wait a minute. I saw the photo that was released of the perp, and he didn't look like a dog, a wolf, or a werewolf to me."

"That was a screen capture from the surveillance video shot from a camera hidden in Patty's car," Candice said. "During the attack, he was visible for only a few seconds, and then his back blocked the camera. We heard fabric tearing, snarls like an animal would make, and Patty's screams." She swallowed. "Then we heard worse sounds."

"Since Willy was Patty's partner, I pulled him out of the field," Mace said. "But I allowed him to help me and Landry at the squad room. The key to the case seemed to be a man named John Stalk."

"That upstate Indian cop," Willy said.

"He was a tribal policeman from the Chautuaqua reservation," Landry said.

"We brought Stalk in for questioning," Mace said. "He wouldn't cop to it, but I knew he believed in the skinwalker legends of his people. His rifle was also loaded with silver bullets."

"But we let him go," Landry said.

"Two FBI agents came to the squad room. I can't tell you what they said, because they classified what they shared with me, and revealing that information would be a treasonable offense."

"We saw those same two feds today," Willy said.

Karol nodded. "They locked down the van that was used to abduct Rhonda Wilson before our people could even check it out."

"They might not have wanted anything to do with the Manhatttan Werewolf, but they're running roughshod over the Lourdes and Wilson cases."

"Agents Norton and Shelly are part of this task force," Mace said.

"*What?*" Willy sounded as disgusted as he did surprised.

"I'll get to them in a minute. Stalk was staying with Angela Domini, the woman who managed the Synful Reading bookstore for her father, Angus Domini."

Karol glanced at Willy. "Gabriel and Raphael Domini's sister."

"Angus died a day earlier," Mace said. "His body was cremated at—"

"The Domini Funeral Home," Willy said.

"I went looking for Stalk at Angela's apartment below the bookstore. No one answered. I was about to leave when I heard screams from somewhere above . . . and howls. I ran into the street and looked up. On the fourth-floor fire escape of an abandoned building across the street, I saw something tearing Stalk apart. It was human in shape but covered with black fur. Fuck me if its head didn't look like a wolf's."

"Four stories is pretty high up," Karol said. "The perp could have been wearing a costume."

"The *perp* burrowed into Stalk's stomach with its muzzle, licked the blood off its fingers, and threw Stalk's head at me like a watermelon. Then it disappeared into the building. There must have been a dozen witnesses."

"I took some of those reports," Willy said.

"So did I," Landry said.

Mace felt everyone's attention on him. "I reported what I saw to Commissioner Dunegan and his cronies. That's when they suspended me. They also changed my report before they buried it."

Karol folded her arms. "You expect us to believe the Manhattan Werewolf really was a werewolf?"

"I believe it," Willy said.

"So do I," Candice said. "I always have. It feels good to say."

Landry turned to Karol. "The evidence is there. A preponderance of it. It's just too hard to believe."

"Actually, the evidence *isn't* there," Mace said. "The brass either buried it or destroyed it, or the FBI confiscated it. All that remains are a trail of unexplained dismembered and decapitated bodies, some YouTube clips, a lot of urban legends, and several ruined careers."

Landry turned back to Mace. "I'm sorry. You never said why . . . I assumed they wanted someone to blame for what happened to Patty."

Willy took a swig of beer and set his mug down hard. "I want to hear how you did the monster."

Mace gathered his thoughts, weighing how much to reveal. "I was out running along the FDR the morning the National Guard came to town. I saw the perp watching me, but he disappeared before I could get to him. Thanks to the media, he knew who I was. I believed he was following me, that it was me or him. But before I could get to him, he pulled a disappearing act. I sent my wife out of town right away."

"I don't blame you," Candice said.

"Angela Domini went off the grid, but she reached out

to me, and I met with her."

Landry raised his eyebrows. "There was an APB out on her . . ."

"She was afraid the Manhattan Werewolf would kill her, but she was unwilling to turn herself in. She told me the name of the werewolf and where he lived. He was using the name Janus Farel, but his real name was Julian Fortier."

"You said he wasn't human," Karol said.

"He was a wolf in human's clothing," Mace said. "I signed out two items from Evidence Control: the revolver Patty had the night she was killed and the Blade of Salvation."

Willy shook his head. "That damned broken sword Terrence Glenzer had . . ."

"Why did you sign out that evidence?" Karol said.

"Because I intended to kill Janus Farel. Angela told me the Blade would kill him—or at least that Janus believed it would, which was enough."

"How did she know that?"

Willy frowned. "She ran an occult bookstore."

"Why did you take Patty's revolver?" Landry said.

"I needed a gun because they made me turn mine in, and I thought it would be poetic justice to use hers."

"Was it?" Candice asked.

"Not exactly." Mace's heart beat faster as he relived the events he had tried to block from his mind for two years. "I broke into Janus's house, a brownstone in the Village he'd inherited from his family. I searched the premises during a thunderstorm. There was no electricity, so I had to rely on my cell phone and the lightning for illumination. The floors were covered with dog shit. In the basement, there was a torture chamber filled with human skeletons. And I found a closet full of skulls . . ."

"The heads he took from his victims," Willy said.

"Many more than we knew about. I was scared out of my mind. Janus came home, and I tried to hide, but he found me. He was naked and looked human enough. But his eyes *changed*, turning completely dark."

"Jesus," Landry said.

"I emptied Patty's revolver into him at point-blank range."

"You mean you *executed* your perp?" Karol said. "What was your evidence that he was a werewolf? That a naked man's eyes got dark during a storm?"

"Did I say I killed him then?" Mace supposed it was a good thing to present his account to a nonbeliever, to see just how crazy his story sounded to an objective listener. "I saw the bullet holes in his chest and one in his head. No one could have survived that. But Janus opened his eyes and smiled at me. And then he changed . . . into a seven-foot-tall werewolf, the same monster that I saw kill Stalk. He chased me and we fought. I took the Blade out of my coat, but he bit a chunk out of my shoulder. I watched him eat my flesh. He would have killed me, but Angela showed up. She saved my life. They fought, and when he was about to kill her, it was my turn to save her life. I picked up the Blade and drove it into his heart, and that was the end of him."

"I hope he didn't change back into a human," Willy said. "Because that would make it hard for you to dodge a murder charge."

"No, he changed into a wolf. A giant black wolf. There

was nothing remotely human about him."

"Angela Domini saw this too?" Landry said.

Mace nodded.

"Where is she?"

"She went to Canada."

"There goes your alibi if you ever need it," Willy said.

"I don't need an alibi. As far as I know, there's nobody left. Angela called her brothers and told them to dispose of the body at the funeral home. Then she took me to the ER, and after I signed myself out, I drove her to a car rental agency. That was the last I saw of her."

"So Gabriel and Raphael Domini destroyed evidence related to several homicides, not to mention an earth-shattering scientific find," Landry said.

"I don't know for sure if they did or not. She never mentioned me to them. She told them she killed Janus."

"What I want to know," Karol said, "is how this Angela Domini saved your life from a supposed werewolf."

Mace met Karol's gaze. "She was a werewolf too."

Four pairs of eyes blinked at him in unison.

"They call themselves Wolves. They're shape-shifters who have lived here and on other continents for centuries, their existence predating Cro-Magnon man. When the Europeans invaded the continent, the Wolves adopted the forms of those men. They've been living among us ever since."

"Begging your pardon, Captain," Karol said. "But that sounds like bull to me."

Willy never looked at his partner as she spoke but continued to stare at Mace. "Either you've had too much to drink, or I haven't had enough."

"I know what I heard Janus Farel do to Patty," Candice said. "He wasn't human. And like you said, witnesses saw this wolf man or werewolf or whatever he was. But what you're telling us now . . . an entire race?"

"They're peaceful," Mace said. "They're also endangered. All they want is to be left alone."

"Janus Farel had a strange way of showing it," Landry said.

"He was a renegade," Mace said. "For reasons Angela didn't know, he broke with his society. His goal was to expose their species and start a war between us and them."

Karol leaned forward. "If she was part of a secret species of werewolves, then Gabriel and Raphael—"

"—are our links to that society."

"And Jason Lourdes and Rhonda Wilson—"

"Probably belong to the same species and society. Why don't you and Willy tell everyone about the bodies found in the Lourdes' home?"

"You mean the *ruins* of the Lourdes' home," Willy said. "Six bodies, only one of them human. The rest were canine . . . and decapitated."

"Like Jason," Karol said.

"I'm willing to bet two of those canine carcasses belonged to Jason's parents," Mace said.

"Even accepting that Janus Farel was some kind of monster, this is more than a little hard to believe," Landry said.

"Really? Maybe for someone who hasn't spent two years contrasting werewolf legends to what happened here. Except for Karol, I'm sure we've all read Terrence Glenzer's book."

"*Transmogrification in Native American Mythology,*"

Willy said. "I read it twice."

"Janus made believers of us when he killed Patty. The other murders, from Glenzer to civilians to cops, just made that belief irrefutable."

"And the bosses covered everything up," Candice said.

"They tried to save their careers. It didn't work. None of them even live in the state anymore."

"But the forensics . . . the eyewitnesses . . . the photos and videos . . ."

"Buried, discredited, and ridiculed. As far as the world is concerned, the Manhattan Werewolf retired when the National Guard came in."

"I'm not saying I believe you," Karol said. "In fact, I'm telling you all right now that I don't. But just for the sake of argument, you say these creatures want peace."

"For the sake of argument, let's consider them human beings with highly unusual DNA. Our own government calls them Class L humans."

"You believe they're victims in whatever's going on?"

"They *are* victims. Someone's declared war on them."

"Who?" Landry said.

"The Brotherhood of Torquemada."

Understanding settled over Landry's face. "The ones who fashioned the Blade of Salvation in the first place."

"An order of self-proclaimed knights who served Torquemada during the Spanish Inquisition, executing witches and werewolves for him. Glenzer wrote about them, but I've spent so much time doing my own research the last two years that I could teach a college class on that period in European history. When the Inquisition fell out of favor, the knights formed a secret society—the Brotherhood of Torquemada—and continued their war against the Wolves."

"And you believe they still exist?" Landry said.

"Glenzer came into possession of one half of a broken Blade of Salvation. I believe he contacted the Brotherhood and tried to sell his half of the sword to them. He discovered who they were from his own research, or maybe they contacted him. The night that chopper crashed in Central Park—chasing a *wolf*—two men who weren't cops were also killed. One was a priest named Francis Hagen. I spoke to him shortly before he was killed. He admitted that Glenzer had arranged to give the Blade to a monsignor in the Vatican, and this monsignor had contacted Hagen to assist in the transfer of ownership.

"The other man killed was Pedro Fillipe, a Dominican who was conveniently raised in Italy after his parents died in a hurricane. Fillipe arrived in the US the same day Glenzer was murdered. I think he was sent here to retrieve the Blade for the Brotherhood. In Central Park, Hagen was torn to pieces, but Fillipe was killed with the blade of a broken sword—the other half of the Blade of Salvation."

"You believe this mysterious monsignor belongs to the Brotherhood?" Willy said.

Mace nodded.

"And Janus Farel already had one half of the Blade?"

"More likely, Fillipe brought it with him to kill Janus."

"The Vatican claimed both halves of the sword," Landry said. "I remember them saying it was some sort of—"

"—religious artifact."

"The Vatican. Shit."

"I'm Catholic," Willy said. "Are you telling me that my church has its own army of werewolf killers? Because that sounds pretty cool."

"Not necessarily. This monsignor that Hagen told me about may have only been acting on the Brotherhood's behalf."

"Or maybe he's funneling cash to them," Landry said.

"That's a savvy speculation, Ken."

"The church is one of the biggest corporations in the world; it just isn't classified as such. And the Vatican is its home office. Depending on his clearance level, a monsignor working there could divert funds to another entity."

"A *secret* entity. Torquemada had six Blades fashioned. Six knights did his dirty work for him, and each knight had an apprentice. So conceivably, twelve men formed the Brotherhood, and twelve may exist today."

"You still haven't told us our objective," Willy said.

"As I said, Norton and Shelly are working this with us. Who knows how long the FBI's been sitting on evidence that these Wolves exist. Norton and Shelly told me they know the Wolves are peaceful. They supposedly want to make contact with them, possibly study them. Whatever their motivation, they want to prevent a panic. Our job is to do just that. We need to make sure no one else discovers the Wolves' existence and makes it public."

"That cock-and-bull story about Jason Lourdes and his family being killed because they crossed drug dealers . . ." Landry's voice trailed off.

"Are we just a mop-up crew?" Candice said.

"No. Our objective is also to stop the Brotherhood from assassinating these Wolves, by any means necessary."

"That sounds specific and vague at the same time."

"The feds and the brass don't want these men to stand trial for obvious reasons. If we take them alive, the FBI will make sure no one ever hears from them again. And if we can't capture them alive, the FBI will take custody of their bodies. Either way, we'll never get famous for this investigation. We're sworn to secrecy."

"National security?" Candice said.

Mace nodded.

Willy finished his beer. "We're a secret task force hunting a secret brotherhood that's targeted a secret species in a secret war. None of us had better change jobs, because that will look whack on our résumés."

"I'll lay out the operation tomorrow morning, but I wanted to have this get-together without our colleagues to make a few points. First, we don't have to worry about interference from the brass. But on the flip side of that coin, we're on our own, so don't expect any backup from the department. The only other people assigned to this task force are Hector Rodriguez and Suzie Quarrel, and they don't know any of this. They'll continue to work from their department. If any of us reveals the nature of this task force to anyone, the bosses will deny it, and I promise their wrath will be swift and thorough.

"Second, you're not to trust our federal partners. We have to involve them, but they're here to keep tabs on us while pretending to share information. Be careful with your e-mails, phone calls, even conversations with each other at our new home. I've just told you more than I've told them. We don't know what secrets *they're* keeping."

"Where's home, Tony?" Landry said.

"Chinatown." Mace passed out a business card to each person. "The city maintains an empty office suite in a walk-up on Mott Street. It was a social services office before the layoffs."

"Chinatown?" Willy said. "Parking's going to be a bitch, T."

"The Oh-Five precinct is two blocks away on Elizabeth. You can park there. We'll meet at base camp tomorrow morning at 0900. That will give everyone time to go to the motor pool and sign out your vehicles. The good news is you can hang on to them until this assignment winds down."

"What's the bad news?" Candice said.

"Because we're such a small unit, we're going to be on call 24/7."

Willy blew air out of his cheeks. "Overtime?"

"Unlimited."

"Dress code?"

"Office casual."

Willy raised his mug. "Let's go catch some werewolf killers."

One by one, the others touched their mugs to his, Karol last.

*Everyone makes it home*, Mace thought.

# CHAPTER FOURTEEN

illy drove uptown with Karol beside him in his Accord.

"I can't buy into any of this," she said.

"That's fine. You don't have to. Maybe it's better for your state of mind if you don't. We're after the people who killed Jason Lourdes and abducted Rhonda Wilson. You don't have to believe that Jason was a werewolf—and Rhonda might be too—to know that the perps are bad guys."

"They also killed five animals," Karol said. "*Whatever* they were."

"Disregard the victims and focus on the perps."

"You seem to have come around to this assignment."

Willy shrugged. "We're soldiers, and the generals tell us where to go. I'd rather be working under Tony than Aiello on something like this. Tone's already shown that he watches the backs of his people. He's not afraid to throw himself on his sword, so to speak."

"How can you follow someone who believes in fairy tales?"

"I guess because I believe in them too. But if you can't, you should get out now. You should anyway."

"Back to that. Are you afraid I can't pull my weight? Or do you think I'll be a liability because I don't share your willing suspension of disbelief?"

Willy stopped at Karol's building on Pelham Parkway. A pair of lanky teenage boys stood on the stoop, chatting in a casual manner. Shifting the car into Park, he faced her. "Let me show you something." Taking out his wallet, he removed a photo of a woman with red hair. "That's Patty."

Karol studied the photo, then looked up at Willy. "I've asked you about her a lot of times, and you've never shared anything."

He stuck the photo back into his wallet. "Some wounds run too deep." He looked ahead at the passing traffic. "Every day we live with the fear that this could be the day we catch a bullet. Even if it's just a quiet voice in the back of our head, it's still there."

"I try not to think about it. Live for today, not tomorrow."

"Yeah, well, it's not that easy. Not when you've lost a partner. I don't just worry about myself; I worry about you too."

"Look at me."

He did.

"You don't have to worry about me. I can take care of myself."

"That's what Patty thought, and she was one tough lady."

"So am I. I didn't make it into Homicide by being soft."

"See, that's what I'm talking about. Patty was pretty new to the unit too. Because she was a woman, she knew she had to be tougher than the men around her, and she was. Tougher than me, that's for sure. That made her take unnecessary risks. She always wanted to be the first one out of the car and the first one through the door. Not to get the collar but to prove she deserved to be a murder police."

"Then that's one difference between us. I don't need to prove myself to anyone. I don't feel I have to be tougher than the guys, either."

"It was the luck of the draw. Patty answered the phone, so it became her case. And there was no telling her what to do on her first big case. Me and Mace were in a surveillance vehicle when Janus Farel killed her. We had to listen to the sounds of him tearing her apart. It was the worst thing I've ever heard. Patty's car crashed into the Astor Place cube, and when we got there the whole area was pandemonium. Cars honking, traffic jammed, people running around like in one of those Japanese giant monster flicks. We had to leave our vehicle and run to the crime scene. Tony got there first. The driver's side door was on the ground. Patty's remains were inside. Blood was everywhere. I'll never forget that sight as long as I live."

Karol touched his hand. "I'm sorry."

"I was pissed when Tony pulled me off the case until I realized he was enabling me to work it from inside the squad. Then he got suspended and I was shut out. All I wanted was to get out of Homicide when I scored high enough for a promotion, but then the freeze came down. I was the next man in line, so Aiello and Landry put me in charge of training. That kind of responsibility was the last thing I wanted."

"You still could have asked for a transfer."

"That isn't how it works. As a lieutenant, I would have been transferred to another unit. If I wanted it to be a good one, I had to stay put and not look like a flake. That's what it all comes down to: covering your ass and playing the game. It's a fucked-up system."

"Well, I'm glad you're my trainer."

Willy drew in his breath. "I don't want anything to happen to you."

"I promise not to take any big risks."

"I care about you too much. I cared about Patty too but in a different way."

"Different how?"

"We were partners . . ."

"We're partners."

He felt himself groping for words. "Yeah, I know. I just see you another way is all."

The headlights of passing cars illuminated her brown eyes. A moment hung between them. Then Karol leaned forward, her lips stopping short of his.

"This better not be a play . . ."

"It isn't."

Before she could change her mind, he closed the distance between them and kissed her.

When Mace entered the second-floor apartment of his house, he found Cheryl sitting on the sofa, her ankles crossed on the coffee table with her laptop resting on her thighs, Sniper lying on the floor below. She had changed into black capris and a loose-fitting shirt, and she pecked at her keyboard while Manhattan Minute News played on TV with the volume low. An empty wineglass and a half-full bottle of Merlot stood on the glass table. She looked up at him, the TV images reflected in her glasses. Sitting beside her, Mace massaged her feet, and she laid her head back with a tired moan.

"How's Patty?" Mace said.

"Sound asleep . . . finally. How was your day?"

"I'm not in the doghouse anymore."

She raised her head. "So I gathered. What can you tell me?"

"Nothing. My assignment is a secret."

"There are no secrets between husbands and their wives if they want to stay husbands and wives."

"What happened to that professional understanding we had?"

"That was when you were in the doghouse and your secrets couldn't interest me."

Sitting back, Mace pulled her legs across his and nodded at the laptop. "What are you doing?"

"Reviewing old stories on the Manhattan Werewolf." Her gaze held his.

"You could always just read Carl Rice's book on the

subject," Mace said.

Reaching beside her, Cheryl raised a copy of *The Wolf Is Loose: The True Story of the Manhattan Werewolf.*

"You didn't," Mace said.

"Technically, Manhattan Minute News did."

"It's still money in Rice's pocket."

"He thinks the Manhattan Werewolf is still out there."

"He is, isn't he? Unless he turned into a pumpkin."

"Where will you be based?"

"At an undisclosed location."

"What's your rank?"

"I'm still a captain."

"How many people will be calling you that?"

Mace smiled.

"Landry? Diega?"

He held his smile.

"What will happen if I ask Public Information what you're doing?"

"They'll tell you I'm doing deep background research on some unclosed homicide cases."

"Which could mean anything. How convenient."

Mace spread his hands apart in a gesture of exaggerated helplessness.

Cheryl aimed a finger in his direction. "I'm coming after you."

"I hear you're pretty tough."

Her voice turned serious. "How is this a good idea? What do you stand to gain if no one knows what you're up to?"

"If I produce results, then I'll wind up somewhere better than I was."

"I thought you were looking forward to retiring."

He rubbed Sniper's head with one foot. "I am. I'd just like to go out with a little respect."

"What happens if they fuck you over?"

"Then it will be business as usual."

Willy stood in Karol's living room, surveying framed photos of Karol and her family. He didn't wish to be nosey but found it difficult to shut down his detective's habits.

The bathroom door opened, and Karol stood half silhouetted within the dingy light. As she stepped closer, he saw that she wore a satin nighty that clung to the curves of her small frame. Heat rose from his body, his gaze drawn to the light reflected in her dark eyes. She clicked off the lamp providing most of the illumination, then turned her back to him and entered the bedroom. Studying the slope of her slender neck and her firm ass, he followed her into the darkness.

Striking a match, Karol lit a medium-sized candle, its flickering flame highlighting her defined cheekbones in soft golden light. Willy gazed at her reflection in the mirror of her bureau, and when Karol looked at his reflection in return, she caressed her neck with one hand.

"Are you sure you want to do this?" she said.

He nodded. "Oh, I'm very sure."

"You'd better keep this between us."

"Who would I tell?"

"I mean it. I won't be known as a department slut. I've worked too hard to gain respect."

"You're my partner. I wouldn't do anything to hurt you."

"This will change our partnership."

He knew she was right. "Now that my promotion's come through, we won't be partners for long."

She circled her bed, her eyes never leaving his. Then, with slow movements, she crawled across the blankets like a jungle cat and lay on her back.

Willy stepped out of his shoes and unbuttoned his shirt, then slid out of his slacks. He stood before Karol in a muscle shirt and boxer shorts.

She giggled. "Take those off, please."

Breaking into a grin, Willy shed his undergarments and made a show of flexing his muscles.

Spreading her legs, Karol scraped the insides of her thighs with the tips of her fingernails.

Willy felt his smile fading, his desire for Karol overtaking him. With his erection stabbing the cold air, he climbed onto the bed and crossed it on his knees. Lying over Karol, he kissed her and tasted her tongue. She raised her knees, squeezing her legs against his hips and rocking against him. He felt her hands sliding over his back, her fingertips pressing against his flesh. He ran his own fingers over her head, his kisses matching hers in their hunger.

Karol nipped at his lower lip, and he pulled the straps of her nighty over her shoulders and forced it down to her waist, freeing her dark breasts. Karol hiked the nighty over her hips, allowing him access to the wetness between her legs. Groping for his hard organ, he pressed it against her slick spot and felt resistance. Pulling his mouth away from hers, he looked into her eyes with rising surprise. Her lips parted, revealing her white teeth.

Then Karol wrapped her arms around him, almost pinning his arms, and thrust herself against him, biting his shoulder as she took him inside her.

Rhonda regained consciousness with the pain of her teeth digging into the inside of her mouth. Opening her eyes, she focused on stone.

*I'm lying facedown*, she thought, turning her head so that her teeth released their hold on her torn, bleeding mouth. She bowed her head, taking the pressure off her nose and putting it on her forehead. A whimper escaped her lips as images cascaded through her brain: Jason's head rolling across the floor of Synful Reading . . . peering at the leader of the Torquemadans, the bald-headed black man named Henri, and the woman with the blonde-streaked black hair . . . the men slashing her flesh with their scalpels . . .

Spreading her legs apart, she heard chain links clinking. They had moved her back to her cell. Saliva pooled on her tongue, and her scalp tingled.

*What form am I in?*

Throwing her left hand beside her shoulder, she turned her head to the right to gaze at her other hand and saw only straw on the floor. Swallowing, she brought her arm perpendicular with her other shoulder and glimpsed something white and gauzy with a red flower at its center. Tears blurred her vision even as she focused on the blood-soaked bandage wrapped around the stump of her human arm. The memory of Henri swinging the sword at her came roaring back.

*They took my arm!*

Rhonda trembled, and her tortured gasps produced bubbles of snot in her nostrils. She did not wish to give them the satisfaction of knowing how much they had hurt her, but each convulsive heave of her muscles produced a shuddering weep, until at last she threw back her head and unleashed a wail. "Bastards . . ."

She heard the familiar sound of the bolt sliding into place on the other side of the steel door, followed by the sound of the door swinging open, then footsteps. Closing her legs together, she looked over her shoulder at her tormentors. The woman gripped a tranq gun, but the leader, a bloody bandage covering his nose, was unarmed, his expression flat. Henri was nowhere to be seen. Curling her lips into a snarl, Rhonda tasted her own blood.

"The bitch is angry," the leader said. "Like a wounded animal."

Rhonda directed her glare at the woman, who said nothing. "Don't talk about me like I'm not here."

"Do you think you're in a position to give orders?" the leader said. "Henri may not be here, but I can hack off your other arm just as well as he could."

Rhonda sucked on the cuts inside her mouth to keep from answering.

The leader gestured at her. "We bandaged your stump. Healing powers or no, you were bleeding profusely, and I didn't want to take a chance on losing you."

*I wouldn't have died*, Rhonda thought. "What time is it?"

"You don't need to know that. Remove the bandage."

Studying each of their faces, she had no doubt they would continue to maim her if she resisted their instructions.

*Give an inch, and they'll take a foot*, she told herself.

The monsters waited.

*I have to save my strength. Appear to be broken. I can't avenge Jason if I'm dead.*

Using her elbow for balance, Rhonda sat up and swung her legs beneath her, protecting her private parts from their eyes. Raising the stump of her arm, she had no choice but to gaze at their brutal handiwork. With her remaining hand, she peeled back the adhesive tape that held the bandage to her and unwound it to the end, then discarded the bloody bandage and stared at the purplish flesh which tapered to a red seal. She closed her eyes, shutting out the image.

"Unbelievable," the woman said.

"If only my wound could do the same," the leader said. "Will your hand grow back?"

"You'll just have to wait and see," Rhonda said.

"If you live that long."

"Aren't you supposed to promise to let me go if I tell you what you want to know?"

The woman looked at her leader, waiting for his answer.

"Human beings don't make promises to animals. I'm sure you have no expectation that we'll allow you to survive this ordeal. The best you can hope for is that we'll show you mercy when we put you down like a dog."

She refused to let her voice crack. "It's too late for that."

"You could provide us with the names we want, and as soon as we verify the identities of the creatures you point us toward, we'd put you out of your misery. Or you can persist as you have, and we'll make your remaining life hell. You'll pray that whatever manner of god you believe in ends your suffering."

Rhonda stood erect, naked and proud. "My people don't worship any gods but our ancestors. You can threaten me all you want . . . torture me . . . kill me. But I promise you, nothing you do to me will compare to what's going to happen to you." She glanced at the woman. "*All* of you."

The woman swallowed, and Rhonda smelled her fear.

"My people do worship a god," the leader said. "The one true God. My companions and I will gladly lay our lives down for Him. You're descended from demons, not gods. The grandchildren of jackals are still jackals. There are all kinds of torture: physical, psychological, emotional, spiritual. The pain you feel in your arm now is nothing compared to what you'll experience when your parents are dead."

With rage blinding her judgment, Rhonda charged at the man, the chains snapping her back. "*You leave my parents alone!*"

The leader offered her a sympathetic smile. "I'm afraid it's too late for that."

Changing, Rhonda howled in anguish.

# CHAPTER FIFTEEN

**M**arshal Wilson exited the upstairs bathroom of his Bensonhurst home and joined his wife in their bedroom. They had both lived in Brooklyn their entire lives, and he felt comfortable living near the Eighteenth Avenue elevated train tracks. He closed the door, cutting off the muted sounds of the television downstairs. The last day and a half had been the worst he had ever endured.

From the bed, Deidre looked at him with tired eyes. She seemed to have aged years since their ordeal had started. "When are they going to leave?"

Marshal sat on the edge of the bed. "I don't know. They said they'd have to reduce their numbers after the first forty-eight hours, but after what happened to Rodney and Jennifer . . ."

"I want them to leave. We're prisoners in our own home. I want to help with the grid search. They're wasting our time. There isn't going to be any ransom call."

"You know what Gabriel said. We have to maintain appearances."

"I don't give a damn about appearances. I don't give a damn about what these police think we should be doing, and I don't give a damn about the pack's need for secrecy. My daughter's missing, and I want to be involved in the search for her."

Looking at her, he tried not to sound angry. "*Our* daughter."

Tears filled her eyes. "I feel so helpless . . ."

Marshal took her into his arms, and she wilted against him. "I know. I feel the same way."

"Five Wolves down, plus Jason. Six in all. Do you think she's all right?"

He stroked the back of her head. "I do. She has to be. We're going to bring her home. And the people who took her are going to pay."

"Why her? She's never done anything to anyone."

Marshal had asked himself the same thing over and over. "She was just in the wrong place at the wrong time. They knew about the store."

"She was so happy working there. Poor Jason . . ."

He felt her convulsing against him, and he wanted to offer her more convincing reassurance. They had nothing to cling to but fading hope.

"When she's home and this is all over, I want us to leave the city. Let's get a house somewhere in the country in another state."

He knew that even if Rhonda did come home, she would never leave New York City. She loved Manhattan and hoped to move there one day. "Whatever you say."

They held on to each other, their desperate need for contact interrupted by shouts from below.

Soares threw his cards on the table. "I'm hungry."

"You just ate a sandwich," Cato said.

"I'm bored. I get hungry when I'm bored." Standing, he stretched his arms.

Cato glanced at his phone. "It's 11:40. Our relief will be here in twenty minutes. Let's go someplace decent to eat after we get off."

Yawning, Soares covered his mouth. "Sounds good. I gotta take a leak."

Soares went down the hall to the narrow bathroom and closed the door. In his four years with Missing Persons, he had spent a lot of time in the homes of distraught families, waiting for the phone to ring. He had a few happy endings to tell his own kids but not many. Considering the Lourdes kid had been decapitated, he wasn't holding his breath for a good outcome regarding Rhonda Wilson. Her parents spent most of their time upstairs, and he preferred it that way. He felt bad for them but had learned not to grow close to the family members of case subjects.

After relieving himself, he washed his hands and returned to the living room, where he saw Cato setting his phone down, a perplexed expression on his face. "'Sup, yo?"

"That was Liaguno. From now on, we're to notify a new task force of any developments in this case."

Soares sat across the table from his partner. "What task force?"

"I dunno. Something connected to Homicide. Tony Mace is heading it."

"Where'd they dig that guy up?"

"Last I heard, he was running the motor pool or something."

"A van just parked out front," said PO Lewis, the uniform stationed at the front window.

Soares looked for a reaction in Cato's eyes. They both rose from their seats and headed over to the window.

Before they reached it, Lewis spun in their direction. "Holy shit, get out!"

Angelo steered the van beneath the elevated train tracks, then made a right-hand turn when he reached the long metal stairways descending from the station above. Dozens of men and women loitered outside, many of them smoking outside bars. As the busy street receded behind the vehicle, houses and residential buildings came into view, most of their windows dark and the night quiet. Making a left turn onto a side street, Angelo searched the houses for street numbers. Then he saw the empty police cruiser parked at the curb ahead.

"We're here," he said. "All set?"

"I'm ready," Henri said in the back.

Pulling ahead of the cruiser, Angelo slowed to a stop.

He saw no police officers outside, just a silhouette peering around the curtain of the picture window to his right. Then he unbuckled his seat belt and climbed into the back. "Be fast." He opened the sliding door. "There's someone at the window."

"Not for long," Henri said.

In the dim illumination provided by the dome light in the ceiling, Angelo watched Henri get down on one knee and raise the rocket-propelled grenade launcher to his shoulder, the rocket at the end of the weapon protruding outside the van.

The silhouette in the window grew darker, almost solid.

"He sees us," Angelo said.

"And I see him." Henri squeezed the trigger of the anti-tank weapon. The soft explosion that followed sounded no louder than a standard gun, and white smoke filled the back of the van.

Angelo turned his head in time to see the upstairs of the house disintegrate in an orange and yellow fireball, the accompanying roar radiating outward as debris rained down on the van. The blast demolished the first floor of the house, which seemed to fold in upon itself before dark smoke cascaded out. The ground shook, triggering high-pitched car alarms all around the block.

Henri tossed the RPG launcher down on the van's floor, and Angelo shut the door. Angelo climbed up front, shifted the van into gear, and stepped on the gas. The van shot forward as flaming boards pierced the murky smoke ahead and unseen projectiles dented the top of the van. The smoke dissipated, and in the rearview mirror Angelo saw bright flames leaping out of the smoky ruins of the house.

The cell phone's piercing ring caused Mace to stir in the darkness. Rolling over, he blinked at the digital alarm clock as he clicked on the bedside lamp: midnight. Beside him, Cheryl pulled a pillow over her head. For a moment, Mace felt like he was back in their Manhattan apartment. He picked up his phone and squinted at its display, which flashed Detective Bureau at him. It had been a long time since he had seen that identification. "This is Mace."

"Captain, this is Sergeant Biro at Detective Bureau Brooklyn," a male voice said.

*Brooklyn . . .*

"I have instructions to notify you with any developments in the Rhonda Wilson abduction."

Mace blinked sleep out of his eyes. "Go ahead, Sergeant. You've got my attention."

"The Wilsons' home in Bensonhurst is in flames, and neighbors reported hearing an explosion. Two detectives from Missing Persons and one uniform were present. There doesn't seem to have been any survivors."

Mace felt the blood draining from his head. *Three cops killed.* He took a pen from the end table drawer and pressed it against the notepad by the lamp. "Give me the address."

The war had begun.

# PART TWO
# THE FRENZY WAR

# CHAPTER SIXTEEN

After they made love for the second time, Karol slipped out of bed.

Admiring her nude body, Willy folded one arm behind his head. "Where are you going?"

Karol stopped for a moment, an odd expression on her face. "To the bathroom."

He nodded at her closed hand. "With your cell phone?"

"I just wanted to check my messages without waking you. We did get kind of busy as soon as we came in."

Propping himself up on one elbow, he felt the gold medallion around his neck slide along his chest. "I'm ready to get busy again."

She set her phone on the bureau. "We're going to be exhausted tomorrow. I don't want Mace to think he made a mistake bringing me on board."

"*Mira*, you kept me waiting a long time. Now I've got you right where I want you. I don't plan to let you go."

Positioning one knee on the bed, Karol looked down at him, faint light shining through the windows highlighting her body. She drew her fingers along the inside of her breasts down to her flat stomach. "You want this?"

Beneath the blanket, Willy spread his legs. "I'd show you how much if it wasn't so damned cold."

Karol descended onto him like a bird and pecked at his swollen lips. Sliding his hands around her waist, he pulled her closer. She slid her tongue into his mouth, then pulled it out, teasing him. Using one foot, he pushed away the blanket separating them and felt her heat against his skin. She rubbed herself against him, and he readied himself for entry.

A cell phone rang, and he glanced at her bureau.

"That's yours," she said, rolling off him.

"Give me my pants?"

"Get them yourself." She strode past his pants on the floor, took an electric-blue robe from her closet, and put it on.

Hopping out of bed, Willy snatched up his pants, removed his cell phone from its holder, and pressed it against his ear. "Diega."

"It's Ken. The Wilsons' Bensonhurst home was obliterated. Tony's on his way to the scene. Soares, Cato, and a PO were inside. No survivors."

Willy stood straight. "Damn. W—I'll be right there."

"Negative. Tony says he can handle whatever needs doing. He just wanted everyone to know."

"I'll call Karol. You worry about Candice."

"Thanks. I'll see you later."

"Yeah." Willy shut down his phone.

"What's going on?" Karol said.

"Somebody roasted Rhonda's house. Her parents, Soares and Cato, a PO—no one made it out alive."

"My God," she said, lowering her voice. "We're going, right?"

"Tony says no. He wants us rested for tomorrow." Climbing back into bed and under the covers, he raised the blanket for her.

She got in beside him, and they held each other without speaking.

Mace lived two miles away from the Wilsons' neighborhood, and he parked a block from the fire scene. Three fire engines, several squad cars, and a pair of ambulances occupied the street, and multiple news crews recorded the inferno, which had spread to the houses on each side of the Wilson home. Uniformed officers held the crowd back while firefighters hosed the houses.

As Mace showed his ID to a PO and ducked beneath the safety tape, he felt the heat from the flames on his face. White-hot embers rose to the sky on thick, billowy smoke. Standing between two fire trucks with his hands in his coat pockets, he watched the ruins of the middle house smolder. He spotted some Brooklyn DATF detectives and several clean-cut men in suits.

*FBI? Homeland Security?*

He wondered if they would discover the charred carcasses of decapitated Wolves inside the wreckage.

"This is a hell of a first day, isn't it?" Norton said behind him.

Turning, he saw Shelly beside Norton. "Yeah, so much for getting a jump on things," Mace said. He surveyed the walking suits. "Yours?"

"Some of them," Norton said. "There are a lot of agencies here. The preliminary suspicion is that an RPG was used to blow up the house. We're checking satellite surveillance."

*Jesus*, Mace thought. "What a game changer."

"You can say that again," Shelly said. "Every antiterrorism unit with jurisdiction will be working overtime on this."

"So will every cop in the city, with three men down. So much for our secret war."

"Why did you come alone?"

"There's nothing for my people to do here. I'd rather let them get some rest."

"After you met with them without us."

*Are you following me?* "I have a relationship with most of those people. They needed certain reassurances."

"We're part of this team too. From now on, we want to be included in every briefing, even if it's over drinks."

He saw no point in angering them. "Fair enough."

"I don't think there's anything any of us can do here. Why don't we all go home and get some sleep?"

"That sounds like a good idea."

As they approached the crime scene tape, Mace saw reporters and cameramen bunching together, forming a gauntlet. He recognized several of the faces but not all of them.

"Captain Mace!"

Ducking beneath the yellow tape, Mace raised it for Norton and Shelly.

"Why are you back in the field, Captain?"

"Does the NYPD believe that drug lords destroyed this house?"

Steeling himself, Mace faced the reporters. "I have no comment."

Gabriel shook his sleeping wife's shoulder.

Melissa woke with a start, blinking at him in the glare of the bedside lamp. "What is it?"

"Marshal and Deidre were killed."

Sucking in her breath, Melissa sat up.

"The Torquemadans blew up their house, taking three police with them. Things are going from bad to worse fast."

"I don't want to leave."

"You have to think of the children. You have to protect them."

"*You* should be protecting them."

Gabriel caressed her cheek. "You know I wish I could."

She glanced at the alarm clock—1:30 AM. "Can't we leave in the morning?"

"No. Take a quick shower while I pack the car."

She kissed him, and he watched her go into the bathroom and close the door. Then he walked downstairs and helped Arick load the luggage into Melissa's maroon

Subaru. Members of the security detail stood on the sidewalk, scanning the trees and buildings.

When Arick closed the hatchback, Gabriel clasped his shoulder. "I'm trusting you with my family. Don't let me down."

"I won't, but I wish I was staying here. I don't like the rumblings of dissent I'm hearing."

He didn't ask what rumblings Arick meant. "I'll be fine. Don't worry about me."

"Can you tell me where I'm going at least?"

"Just get to the Canadian border. Melissa will take it from there."

Arick smiled. "You'll never change."

Melissa appeared in the doorway, carrying Damien. To Gabriel's surprise, Elias appeared behind them, carrying Gareth. Gabriel opened the rear passenger door and held out his hands. Melissa passed the sleeping boy into his arms. He considered allowing him to sleep but decided instead to shake him awake. "Damien . . ."

Damien opened his eyes.

"You and your brother are leaving with your mother and Arick now. I want you to do what your mother says. Do you understand?"

Rubbing his eyes, Damien nodded.

"And take care of your brother. You're the oldest." Gabriel kissed him on the forehead, then set the boy on the booster seat inside the car and fastened a seat belt around him. Damien went limp almost immediately. Turning back, Gabriel took Gareth into his arms. The boy, already half awake, blinked at him.

"Are you ready for your trip?"

Gareth nodded without much enthusiasm.

"Behave."

"I will."

Gabriel kissed him and seated him next to Damien. Closing the door, he shook Arick's hand.

"May I come straight back?" Arick said.

"No, but I hope to see you soon."

Arick nodded, glanced at Elias, them circled the car and got in behind the steering wheel.

Melissa moved before Gabriel, her eyes shiny even in the streetlight. "The boys and I can make the trip alone. Arick should stay here with you."

He cupped her face. "It's better this way. I'll worry less."

"But I won't."

He kissed her lips, then held her.

Melissa looked into his eyes. "Settle this fast. I want us back together as soon as possible."

"I intend to."

They kissed again, then Gabriel opened the front passenger door for her and she got in. He closed the door, and Arick drove off. The vehicle grew smaller, then disappeared into the city.

"I never married," Elias said beside him. "I have no children."

Gabriel glanced at his companion. "Then what are you fighting for?"

Elias seemed to consider the question. "For our species, but I value my own life as well."

Offering him a slight smile, Gabriel returned to the safe house.

Mace found Cheryl sitting in the living room with Manhattan Minute News playing on TV.

"What are you doing up?" He already knew the answer.

"You just missed yourself," she said. "'No comment.' I bet it felt good to say that again."

"It didn't feel good under the circumstances."

"The story made the other local channels as well. They actually interrupted infomercials for the news. Are we under attack by terrorists? Or is it still drug dealers?"

He pulled off his tie. "No comment."

"*Tony* . . ."

"I'm going to bed."

Cheryl followed him. "'Captain Mace,'" she said in a low voice. "'Why are you back in the field, Captain?'"

In the bedroom, he peeled away his clothes.

"'Does the NYPD believe that drug lords destroyed this house?'"

Mace climbed under the covers. "Good night."

She got in beside him and pressed her body against his for warmth. "Did you know the men who were killed?"

He searched his memory. "I don't think so."

She didn't say anything else.

# CHAPTER SEVENTEEN

Willy opened his eyes just after 5:30 AM, with Karol sleeping half on top of him. It had been a good night for him beyond the sex. He knew that Karol's concerns about their working partnership were valid, but now that his promotion had come through, he would be transferred out of Homicide soon enough. Then they wouldn't have to worry about potential conflict—as long as they both survived the insane assignment Mace had thrust upon them. Gazing at her sleeping features, he promised himself he would not allow Karol to put herself in danger.

Sliding out from beneath the covers, he shivered. In the bathroom, he noted scented soaps with pastel colors. He gargled with mouthwash, then returned to the bedroom and slipped into his slacks, taking care to be quiet.

Karol's eyes fluttered open anyway. "Running out the back door?"

He zipped his fly. "You've only got one door."

She raised herself up on one elbow, supporting her head with her palm. "What's your hurry?"

"I need to go to my place to change my clothes. It wouldn't look good if I reported for duty wearing the same threads I had on yesterday, would it?"

"Why not? Everyone knows you're a dog."

Willy sat on the edge of the bed and pulled on his socks. "I'm no dog. And if I was, I'm not now."

"Are you trying to convince me or yourself?"

"I don't need any convincing." He stood. "You want to come with me? I'll wait for you to shower. Then you can wait for me to shower at my place and we can get some breakfast."

"I don't think I'm ready to go home with you."

"Oh, but I can come all the way over here?"

Karol laid her head back on her pillow. "That's right."

"Okay, whatever you say." Leaning across the bed, he kissed her. "I'll see you at our new HQ."

"Later . . . Lieutenant."

Grinning, he picked up his shirt and left the bedroom.

Rhonda awoke in human form on the straw-covered floor. She had been unable to sleep for hours, worried about her parents, but had finally managed to drift into a restless state of unconsciousness. She had no way of knowing the time of day. The tranquilizers had induced so much sleep that she no longer trusted her internal clock.

She studied the stump of her arm. The flesh at the end

had healed without leaving a seam, but the arm did not appear to have grown any, leading her to believe it might not. At least it wasn't chained. Standing, she swatted loose straw off her buttocks, then walked over to the metal buckets and, ignoring the camera, relieved herself. When she had finished, she stood facing the camera and stared at its lens, clenching her remaining hand into a fist. She wanted to know what had happened to her parents. She *needed* to know.

Before long, she heard the bolt sliding and saw the door open. Henri entered, accompanied by a man with blond hair, who carried a wooden crate which he set on the floor between them and her.

Henri gestured at the man beside him. "This is Myles. He planned the attack that killed your parents last night."

*No!* Rhonda's body turned numb, and she sank to her knees. First Jason, now her parents! The tears came again. *I'm all alone . . .*

"Your home is nothing but ashes," Myles said.

She felt as if she had been kicked in the stomach.

Opening the crate, Henri lifted a live chicken out and set it on the floor, where the bird strutted and clucked. "Your breakfast."

Rhonda blinked at the brown and red chicken. Was Henri joking?

"Other than Michael's nose, you haven't eaten since we brought you here. We'll provide you with nourishment, but we sure as hell won't cook for you."

Wiping her tears on her forearm, Rhonda glared at Myles. "I'll kill you. I'll kill every one of you."

Myles glanced at Henri, who grunted.

"That's the spirit," Henri said. "I want you alive and kicking, so we can go at it again. I wonder what I'll cut off next."

Before Rhonda could summon a response, Henri jerked his head toward Myles and they left the room, closing the door with a shuddering echo. As she heard the bolt sliding into place, Rhonda lowered her gaze to the chicken. Henri had called the animal her breakfast, so she knew it was morning. Helping her get her bearings, at least with respect to the time of day, had been his first mistake. Identifying his leader by name had been the second.

*Michael.*

She still did not know the name of the woman with the black hair streaked with blonde and the hawkish nose. Was it just the four of them?

Rising, she moved toward the chicken, which turned away from her. Before it could escape her reach, she grabbed under its body. The chicken flapped its wings and kicked its feet, and Rhonda cradled it to her body. She wanted to stroke its feathers and put its mind at ease, but she had only one hand.

"Poor little chicken, we're both prisoners. We should stick together."

But she knew that was not possible. Her empty belly ached, and she required sustenance. Her muscles burned from Changing so many times in such a short period of time. She had never killed an animal before.

*I'm not an animal.*

But she could be.

Willing the Change once more, she sank her canine fangs into the chicken's quivering body and tasted hot blood.

Mace took a taxi to the Detective Bureau Manhattan and collected the first receipt for his expense account. He reported to the motor pool and signed out a black Jeep Cherokee, then made the drive to Chinatown. Parking his vehicle in the NYPD's lot at the Fifth Precinct headquarters on Elizabeth Street, he spotted Landry getting out of a white Cavalier. He tapped his horn and got out.

"Great minds drive alike," Landry said.

They left the lot together.

"That was quite a story you told us last night."

Mace stuffed his hands into his coat pockets. "Like Candice said, it felt good to get it off my chest."

"Does Cheryl know?"

"She knows I saw what killed Stalk and what I reported. She knows I got screwed over. And she knows that when she came home, I had stitches in my forehead and half my shoulder was missing. But I never told her about Janus."

They entered the throng of people swarming through Chinatown, the wind carrying the smell of fish.

"Is there any chance we can requisition more detectives?" Landry said.

"I don't think so. Jim Mint wants as few people as possible to know about this operation. And to be honest, I don't want anyone on board who I can't trust. It's bad enough we have to work with Shelly and Norton, and I have my doubts about Williams."

"She's good police."

"That doesn't mean she's suited for this assignment. Even Shelly and Norton are believers. She's the only outsider."

"She and Diega make a good team."

"Believe me, that's the main reason I included her."

On Mott Street, they faced a four-story brick building with a fire escape. It reminded Mace of the building where Janus Farel had killed John Stalk. Shelly and Norton stood outside the front doors, sipping coffee from large cups, and Mace and Landry crossed the street and joined them.

"Good morning," Norton said, her disposition cheery.

"This is Lieutenant Landry," Mace said.

"Ken," Landry said, shaking their hands.

"Shall we?" Norton said.

Mace glanced at his watch. "It's early yet. I'd prefer to wait for the others so we can all go up together. Let's wait for them in the lobby."

"Whatever you say."

Mace entered the foyer, and the others clustered around him while he read a number from the card Jim Mint had given him and punched it into the keypad on the wall. The alarm system whined, and he led them into the narrow lobby with no furniture or directory.

"The city went all out with the accommodations," Shelly said.

Willy, Karol, and Candice filed in.

Willy eyed Shelly and Norton. "Looks like the gang's all here."

They rode an elevator to the fourth floor, where Mace used a key card to unlock the gray metal door facing them. He entered a space filled with sunlight filtered through wide, dirty windows and flipped a switch. Fluorescent lights in the ceiling turned a small reception area with brick walls ugly. Passing a vacant desk, he walked through a doorway with no door into the main area, where half a dozen cubicles led to two glass-faced offices and a conference room. Computer monitors and large pots with dead plants and trees served as the only décor.

"Lovely," Candice said, vapor billowing from her mouth.

Willy switched on more lights.

"It's freezing in here," Karol said.

Willy tapped an ancient-looking fan with a metal cover. "Look at this. If the heating's just as modern, you can tell why."

Shelly walked over to the windows and pressed one hand against the radiator. "It's cold, all right. NYPD spares no expense as usual."

"The FBI's more than welcome to provide us with alternative space," Mace said. He took out his cell phone, located a number, and pressed it.

After the third ring, Jim Mint answered.

"Our base camp leaves a lot to be desired."

"What, no hot tub?"

"No *hot*, period. Get someone over here to fix the heat, or we're going to have to start burning the furniture."

"Okay, okay. I already have IT coming over to secure your computers on an independent server. Anything else?"

Mace looked at his team members. "What else?"

"I see a refrigerator but no water cooler," Landry said.

"There's no coffeemaker, either," Candice said.

"You get that?" Mace said.

"Yeah, yeah, I'm writing it down."

"We'll need assorted office supplies too: pens, pads, staplers, tape, a city map, pushpins . . ."

"I'll get you everything you need to get started. You can requisition everything else later."

"I want three TVs and a cable hookup for each one."

"You planning to catch up on The History Channel?"

"No, just the news. Judging by the way this place was stripped bare, be sure to make toilet tissue and paper towels a priority."

"I hope you're this thorough running down your case."

"I promise we will be." Mace closed down his phone. "Okay, let's get set up. I'll take whichever office is smallest. Ken and Candice, you'll be working together, so you share the larger office. The rest of you, pick your cubicles. Let's meet in the conference room in ten minutes."

With Elias sitting beside him in the backseat, Gabriel peered out the window of Micah's taxi at the city. Every parked car, every doorway, every window, and every rooftop posed a threat. How many Wolves had Raphael assigned to secure the small piece of the neighborhood? Too many, he feared.

"Maybe we should have come separately for your safety," Gabriel said.

"That would only amount to wasted energy. They already know who *you* are, and they already know who *I* am."

"Maybe you should just stay at the safe house, then."

"I'll move in the shadows when I can strike out against our enemies, but I won't hide in a hole like some fox."

Micah pulled the taxi over to the curb, and Gabriel saw Lawrence and Leon standing guard outside the funeral home, which meant Eddie and David had to be nearby.

Micah pressed a button on the meter and looked over his shoulder. "You want me to wait?"

Gabriel paid him. "No. The less time you spend here, the better. As a precaution, I'll find another way back to the safe house."

"Whatever you say. Have a good day."

Gabriel observed Lawrence and Leon scanning the buildings across the street. He pulled the car door handle and stepped out, his nostrils filling with crisp Manhattan air. Sensing Elias behind him, he crossed the sidewalk and heard Micah drive off. Neither Lawrence nor Leon opened the door for him, which would have meant lowering their guard for the sake of his vanity.

"Good morning," Gabriel said without expecting a reply. He opened the door for Elias and followed him inside, where they wiped their shoes on the mat. Because the door was unlocked, Gabriel knew Raphael had come in early. Removing his black leather gloves, he opened the office door.

Raphael looked up from the monitor on his desk, and Gabriel saw images of firefighters battling an inferno. Raphael wore a New York Rangers hockey shirt and blue jeans.

"I take it you're not working today," Gabriel said as Elias came in behind him, allowing the door to close.

Raphael sat back in his chair. "Of course not. Neither should you. We need to close down until this is over, maybe for good."

Gabriel hung his camel hair coat on the rack and sat at his desk, turning his chair to face Raphael. He wore a dark suit as usual and gestured to the chair at the third desk. "Have a seat, Elias."

Elias sat without saying a word.

"I sent Melissa and the boys away as soon as I received word about last night's attack. Arick went with them."

"I know. You should have kept him here."

"I have you to advise me. Why do I need Arick?"

Raphael's expression turned sullen. "You said they wouldn't attack that house with police inside it. You said you wouldn't underestimate them again."

"Are you finished?"

Raphael seemed to take a deep breath. "Yes."

"Have the families doubled up with each other?"

"Most of them."

"Have you deployed our available people to search the grid?"

Raphael nodded.

"We still don't know if Rhonda's given us up. The next attack should tell us. If she hasn't, then there are only three likely targets: your home, mine, and here. Since you and I have evacuated our homes, this is the most likely spot."

Raphael's body seemed to relax. "Are we calling another war council?"

"No. Assuming Rhonda hasn't given up the names of other Wolves, the Torquemadans must be watching us here. If the same Wolves come here more than once, they'll identify our people and follow them. For the moment, we're the only targets. Call each delegate, and order him to contact his constituents by phone. We'll provide text message updates as necessary."

"They'll want to be involved in the decision making."

"Why should they be? I'm the alpha, and we're at war. Between adapting to new living arrangements and searching the grid for our enemies, they have enough to do."

"What if the delegates ask why you sent your family away?"

"Right now you and I are the primary targets, so I fear for my family's safety. Any Wolf who shares my fears about his own family may do the same. But everyone must be made aware that a sudden exodus of our children will not go unnoticed by the authorities, and I have reason to believe we face a far greater threat than the Torquemadans on the horizon."

# CHAPTER EIGHTEEN

**S**itting at the middle of the long conference table while Landry plugged in a portable space heater he had found, Mace opened his briefcase and took out a notepad and some pens. "Arm yourselves."

Candice tore off a page for herself and another for Landry and slid the pad to Shelly. Landry took his seat between Mace and Candice as the FBI agent pushed the notepad beyond Norton to Karol. Shelly and Norton each produced an electronic writing tablet to use instead.

"We're obviously working under less than ideal circumstances," Mace said. "But we'll straighten those issues out. This is a joint NYPD and FBI task force. Our objective is to identify and apprehend the perps behind the abduction of Rhonda Wilson, the murder of Jason Lourdes, the murder of an unidentified male at the Lourdes' home, as well as five canines, and the murders last night of Marshal and Deidre Wilson, Detectives Cato and Soares, and PO Lewis. These murders are being treated as the work of drug dealers, organized crime members, and terrorists."

"Next thing you know, it'll be Martians," Willy said.

"We need to operate under the radar. As far as the department is concerned, we barely exist. Seeing as how New York City is the law enforcement mecca of the world, we have to run our investigation without tripping over any other agencies or tipping them off about what we're up to. As much as possible, we need this operation to be clandestine."

Norton leaned forward in her seat. "Captain, I just want to clarify to everyone here that Special Agent Norton and I are here to offer support only. You're calling the shots."

*Cover that ass fast, lady*, Mace thought. "So noted."

Shelly opened his briefcase. "As to the clandestine nature of this task force, I have nondisclosure agreements for everyone to sign before we proceed." He handed one copy of the agreement to everyone but Mace. "This stipulates that you may not discuss the details of this operation or any discoveries made by it, even in general terms, with anyone other than your superior officers, except in a court of law. If you violate these terms, you will be subject to severe penalties, including but not limited to termination and prosecution."

Willy flipped through the pages of the agreement. "This sounds like bullshit to me. Are we serving together or not?"

Shelly's voice remained a monotone. "Everyone sitting here realizes this is an extraordinary situation in which we find ourselves, with implications reaching far beyond this city's safety. The government has a clear mandate regarding national security, and these agreements pertain to that mandate."

"Well, I notice we each got only one copy. That seems a little shady to me."

"Captain Mace is in charge of this task force. He was given authority to choose his own team. If you want to serve on the team, you need to sign the agreement. It's that simple."

Willy glanced at Mace.

"I already signed one."

Blowing air out of his nostrils, Willy picked up his pen, signed and dated the agreement, and tossed it across the table to Shelly.

One by one, the other men and women signed their agreements and returned them to Shelly, who placed them in his briefcase.

"We're obviously a small unit," Mace said. "Landry will man base camp in the day, Smalls at night. Congratulations on that promotion, Smalls."

"Thank you, Captain."

"I'll cover a swing shift except when one of them takes a day off. Lieutenant Diega, Detective Wilson, and Special Agents Shelly and Norton will work the field. I don't intend to be landlocked, though."

Landry smiled. "Day shift? Night shift? We're all going to be working long days, Tony. We should get some cots in here."

"Good idea. We're all on call 24/7, and if the last two attacks are any indication, these assassins are a night crew. Every unit and agency investigating the three attacks will copy us on any developments as they occur, but as far as they're concerned, we're just doing deep background research. We're to share nothing with them and obviously nothing with the press. No one knows we're here, and I want to keep it that way." He took a moment to gather his thoughts. "The department and the FBI only acknowledge the existence of people with unusual DNA who have been classified as Class L humans."

"Preliminary reports confirm that a RPG was used to destroy the Wilsons' house last night," Norton said. "Most likely, it was fired from inside a van or from the back of a truck. The scattered remains of five people were discovered."

"Human people?" Willy said.

"Yes."

Mace focused on the female FBI agent. "Has Quantico made any determinations regarding the corpses and carcasses?"

"Nothing conclusive," Norton said.

*I bet.* "Did they at least narrow down what type of animals they were?"

"Nothing conclusive."

"The perps call themselves the Brotherhood of Torquemada, which is a secret society descended from the Spanish Inquisition."

"How do you know *that*?" Norton said.

"You and Mint put me in charge because of my expertise in certain areas. This is one of those areas."

"We know the history of the Blade of Salvation," Shelly said, "and our research shows this Brotherhood of Torquemada once existed, but you're making quite a leap."

"The existence of a modern Brotherhood of Torquemada is the least fantastic aspect of this case. If you accept the existence of—"

"Class L humans . . ."

"—and you accept a connection between them and the Blade of Salvation, then it's only logical to assume the Torquemadans are the perps."

"Why?"

"Because the Torquemadans used swords. Blades of Salvation, to be precise. And Jason Lourdes and those five canines were all decapitated by swords. So there's reason to believe at least five Torquemadans are on US soil. Historically, there were six members in the brotherhood at all times, with six apprentices waiting in the wings to take their places. It's possible that unidentified corpse with the missing arm was one of them. If we can identify him and trace his movements, we may be able to track down the others."

"Unfortunately, his remains were burned to a crisp, so we don't have prints to work with, just DNA and dental records."

"Two years ago, Pedro Fillipe was killed in Central Park with the other half of the Blade that we found in Terrence Glenzer's safe. I think he brought that half of the sword with him to kill the Manhattan Werewolf. If I'm right, he was a member of the Brotherhood."

Pushing his glasses up on his nose, Shelly consulted his tablet. "Fillipe was Dominican, but he came from Rome."

"Both halves of that sword went to a monsignor in Rome. Now, I doubt our assassins traveled here together, but I'm willing to bet they're all from overseas." Mace looked at Shelly. "Use your resources to search for Europeans and

Dominicans coming here over the last two weeks. Whether they came alone or not, I'm sure they didn't come with families or children."

"Have you ever heard of looking for a needle in a haystack?"

"I know it's a long shot, but how many big cases have been solved by innocuous detective work?"

As Shelly entered information into his tablet, Mace turned to Norton. "Fillipe was killed with a priest named Francis Hagen. I believe he was staying at Hagen's church in Queens. It's possible that our assassins are all staying at a church, near one, or in separate churches. Make up a list of every Catholic church in the five boroughs. If possible, learn which priests were close associates of Hagen's and concentrate on them."

"That's a lot of legwork," Norton said. "I'm going to need more shoes."

"Make sure they're comfortable." Mace turned to Landry. "I know you and Candice have your hands full getting this place up and running, but I want you to go through your old research on the Blade of Salvation and follow up with this monsignor. Let's see if he paid for any airfare to the United States."

Landry nodded as he scribbled on his sheet of paper.

"Candice, the initial reports on the attack on the Lourdes house say that the alarm was shut off. I want to know if the wires were cut, if the alarm company's computer was hacked, or if someone who works there might have given out that information."

"What about us?" Karol said.

"Gabriel Domini and Raphael Domini are the key to this little war. Synful Reading is closed, but the Domini Funeral Home is still open, and that's where Gabriel and Raphael work together. If the Brotherhood goes after them there, they can take them both out at the same time. I want the two of you to stake out that crematorium."

"They've both seen me and Karol," Willy said. "They'll make us."

"Assuming Gabriel and Raphael are Class L humans, they'll make anyone who's watching them."

"What if they leave?"

"If they leave together, follow them. If they leave separately, follow Gabriel. And if they don't leave at all, stay put. If necessary, we'll relieve you. That funeral home has to be the next target. We may get a chance to end this quickly."

"What do you want us to do if we see a bunch of guys in robes carrying swords?"

"Call us for backup, and if you can, don't go in until we arrive."

"There's an elephant in the room," Karol said. "Let's say these Class L humans turn furry and grow fangs. What are we supposed to do if we run into them?"

"Our job is to bring in these Brotherhood members, and in so doing, protect the Class Ls. Do not engage the Class Ls."

Willy looked out the glass partition at the office space. "I don't see any cells or interview rooms. What are we doing with these fanatics if we apprehend them?"

"Dead or alive, we turn them over to the FBI. No collar,

no paperwork, as if nothing ever happened."

"With three of our own dead, I got no problem with that."

Norton opened her briefcase. "There's one more formality to take care of before we begin." She took out a pair of scissors and a handful of paper envelopes. "I need a hair sample from each one of you."

Willy snorted. "Drug testing? Really?"

"Class L testing," Shelly said. "We have to make sure everyone in this group is what he says he is."

"Did you two have to give anyone a hair sample?"

"Yes," Norton said. "But if it will make you feel better, we'll provide additional samples."

"I'll go first," Mace said.

Cheryl entered the offices of Manhattan Minute News with Ryan trailing her. They had spent the morning in Bensonhurst, interviewing neighbors of the Wilsons on camera. Ryan carried his equipment down the hall to the editing suites, where he would assemble the interviews into a one-minute segment that would play in rotation on the cable channel throughout the day.

She sat at her desk and opened her e-mail. Dozens of messages materialized on the screen, and she skimmed their subject lines, searching only for urgent items. A fresh message from Colleen appeared: See me now.

Cheryl looked up from her monitor at the glass-faced office. Inside, Colleen juggled a landline and a cell phone while facing her monitor. Cheryl made her way to the office door, rapped on the glass, and entered as Colleen hung up the landline and concentrated on her cell phone.

On the wall-mounted TV, she saw a press conference in full swing at One Police Plaza. Craig Lindberg, the Commissioner of Public Information, stood at the podium addressing the reporters. "It's certainly not impossible, or even likely, that a major illegal narcotics organization could lay its hands on this type of ordinance, but at this time we're also investigating the possibility of terrorist activity."

Colleen set her cell phone down.

"What's on your mind, chief?" Cheryl said.

The producer arched one eyebrow. "I've been on the phone all morning because of you. Or, rather, because of one of your fans." She held out an envelope. "This came today."

Cheryl took the envelope in both hands and stared at the return address: Rodrigo Gomez, c/o Sing Sing Penitentiary, Ossining, New York.

*The Full Moon Killer*, she thought with an involuntary shudder.

Cheryl had met Tony while covering the serial killer's murder spree. The attention the case brought helped both their careers, especially Tony's, after he arrested Gomez for the murders of five women. Carl Rice, a tabloid reporter, sensationalized the case in a true crime book called *Rodrigo Gomez: Tracking the Full Moon Killer*, which became a surprise best seller and a cable TV movie, assuring Tony's fame while she moved on to the next story. Unlike Tony, Cheryl had read Rice's book, a poorly written but suspenseful story with a heroic protagonist and a twisted villain.

She had also watched the TV movie, which was filmed in Toronto and starred a former soap opera actor as Tony

Mace. Cheryl liked to tease Tony that his TV counterpart was taller than him. A former sitcom star portrayed Cheryl, and in TV movie fashion, the fictional Tony and Cheryl got together during the manhunt, when in reality Tony had waited until after the media frenzy surrounding the case had died down before asking Cheryl out on a date.

Tony was also featured in Rice's follow-up book, *The Wolf Is Loose: The True Story of the Manhattan Werewolf*, which was even more sensational. This one suffered for not having an ending, though Rice did his best to use the lack of resolution to terrify his readers. Cheryl was pleased not to be represented in its pages. The book was also a best seller, but no TV movie was produced, leaving Cheryl to wonder what had become of her former soap star husband and her sitcom star alter ego.

Rodrigo Gomez's letter read:

---

Greetings from Sing Sing.

Our cable doesn't carry Manhattan Minute News, but I do follow your stories online. I so enjoy the reporting of Cheryl Mace, formerly Cheryl Chimera. We go way back. (Don't we, Cheryl?)

I'm writing you with good news!

After seven years of incarceration in this hellhole, I've finally decided to tell my story to the world. The whole story, the real story, not just the crumbs I fed to Carl Rice. And I want you to be my conduit. On four conditions:

1. Cheryl Mace must conduct the interview.

2. The interview must be broadcast live, with no commercial interruptions.

3. There will be no preinterview.

4. Get your lawyers working on this now. My offer's good for twenty-four hours from your receipt of this letter. I'll consent to do a one-hour interview within forty-eight hours. After that, I approach another outlet.

I look forward to chatting with Mrs. Mace.

Sincerely,
Rodrigo Gomez

Cheryl lowered the letter, feeling a mixture of dread and excitement.

Colleen stood. "I've already been in touch with the warden there, and our legal department has too. If you're on board with this, we can make it happen: a one-hour live interview tomorrow at 8:00 PM, preceded by a special on Gomez's crimes and followed by a panel discussion on your interview. We'll repeat the whole block around the clock and on the weekend too. Say the word, and we'll get started on promotion."

Cheryl folded the letter and stuck it back into the envelope. "Of course I'm on board. How could I say no to what you just described?"

"I like that you're such a team player, but don't you need to discuss this with Tony first?"

Cheryl considered the question. Tony would have

definite concerns about her safety and would probably disapprove of the idea for a number of other reasons. Under ordinary circumstances, she would discuss such an unusual proposition with him, but he hadn't discussed his new assignment at NYPD with *her.*

"No. Let's do this. It will be good for all of us."

# CHAPTER NINETEEN

Mace entered the Golden Fleece restaurant a little after noon. He spotted Lou Graham sitting with his back to him and suppressed a smile. Circling the table, he looked down at the chief of detectives, who wore a light gray suit and sipped ice water. The man seemed deep in thought.

"Hello, Lou."

The COD looked up, his smile warm but strained at the same time. "Tony, it's good to see you."

They shook hands and Mace sat.

"I wish it was under different circumstances."

"You could have looked me up anytime."

Lou nodded. "You're right. I'm sorry. I meant to see how you were doing. Then I replaced Hackley, and before I knew it, two years passed. Ah, hell, who am I kidding? We both know the score. I didn't know what to say, and I knew the bosses wouldn't let me reinstate you, and now I don't know what to say again."

A server filled Mace's glass with ice water.

"Don't sweat it. I never expected anyone to go out on a limb for me."

"Well, I'm sorry all the same. You know what they say: out of sight, out of mind."

"And now we're sitting face-to-face."

"Congratulations on digging yourself out. I've never seen that happen before."

"I didn't do anything but say yes. They came to me." Mace opened the menu.

"I almost wish they hadn't."

"What's got you down?"

"You're not in a good position, and now neither am I."

"We've known each other a long time. Speak your mind."

"A decapitation, a kidnapping, five dead animals, and an act of terrorism. And the worst thing is Jim Mint pulling you out of mothballs and putting you in charge of a covert operation."

"I'm sorry my reemergence has caused you such distress."

"It's *why* they chose you that has me worried. You've been the central figure in two major cases. Rodrigo Gomez is in prison. The Manhattan Werewolf was never caught, and whoever he is, he buried a lot of careers."

"Are you worried about your career?"

Lou leaned forward. "Who isn't? This may be Jim Mint's operation, but I'm technically responsible for you and your actions now. Who's to say I won't follow in the footsteps of Hackley, Chu, Stokes, and Dunegan?"

"We all move where the chess masters put us. No one can control collateral damage."

The server returned, and they placed their orders.

"Did you know Terry Wright?" Lou said after the server had left.

Mace tried to place the name. "I don't think so."

"He worked vice for ten years, made a big name for himself mopping up Times Square. He retired to Tampa and never even came back to visit as far as I know. Anyway, back in the day, when crack was doing a major number on the city, the bosses called Terry and his crew in and offered them an assignment not so different from the one you have now. They told them to clean up Forty-second Street . . . by any means necessary. 'Leave no stone unturned, no body in plain sight, no paperwork to be filed.' They had a mandate to bury bad guys and answer to no one. Terry told me they were game: they set up shop above a bar on Forty-fourth Street and selected their targets—an actual hit list. Just when they were about to pull the trigger, one of the higher-ups pulled the plug instead."

Mace sipped his water. "What happened?"

"Some people would call it progress. The city planners got together with some developers and mapped out the fu-ture: theme restaurants and megaplexes and trademarked cartoon characters. When the money came through, the big boys decided that a real cleansing of Forty Deuce could backfire and damage their investment. Otherwise, who knows what would have happened? It was a different time then. Fingerprints were still stored in metal filing cabinets, not on hard drives and in clouds. There were no video cameras at major intersections, no satellites studying us from afar, no twenty-four-hour news cycles, no real Internet. In other words, Terry's gang might have pulled it off."

Mace smiled. "Thanks for the vote of confidence."

"It would have been a long shot even before your perps blew up that house. Now you've got cops hunting cop killers, feds hunting terrorists, every news organization hunting a major story, and you and your people expect to conduct a covert operation. The opportunity for this to blow up in all our faces is astronomical. I hope you'll exercise caution."

Mace hoped his expression did not betray his thoughts or emotions. "I've been sitting on my ass on Floyd Bennett Field for two years. Now that I'm off it, I have no intention of exercising caution, and I have every intention of getting results."

Valeria sat in the chair beside Eun's bed and looked down at the wounded woman, who opened her eyes and blinked, her head wrapped in bandages like a mummy.

"How do you feel?"

"Hurts," Eun said in a whispery voice.

"I can give you more morphine."

Eun shook her head, which caused her to wince. "Later."

Valeria touched her comrade's arm. "There's no reason for you to be in pain. We can manage it with drugs."

Eun swallowed. "Face?"

Valeria had dreaded this question but knew it was

inevitable. "You need plastic surgery. I did what I could, but you know I'm no doctor."

Eun closed her eyes, and tears pooled in her lashes. Valeria knew the salt in the tears would cause Eun additional pain if they soaked through the bandage and reached her wounds, so she dabbed at her eyes with cotton balls.

Eun opened her eyes again, and her lips curled, revealing her teeth. "Fight."

Valeria managed a smile. "*Sleep.*"

Eun sighed, and Valeria rose and exited the room. Closing the door behind her, she shivered. The warehouse was cold, the expense of heating it too great, so they turned on space heaters in the rooms they used and wore their coats everywhere else. She carried handfuls of tissues in her cargo pants to blow her nose. In the dining area, she served herself stew from a pot and joined Michael and Henri at the picnic table.

"Where's Angelo?" she said, tearing a piece of Italian bread from a loaf.

"Staking out the funeral home," Michael said. "An old friend of ours showed up at their doorstep: Elias Michalakis."

"We killed him."

"Apparently not."

Valeria suppressed her astonishment. From the back window of a fleeing van, she had seen the explosion which tore the werewolf cell asunder. "Have you made a decision about the funeral home yet?"

"Let's see how the day goes. Circumstances will dictate our next move."

"I think we should take a day to rest."

Michael sipped his juice. "We need to keep hitting the beasts hard. A different method each night to throw them off guard. Now that Michalakis has joined them, they have intel on our ways."

"If the bitch doesn't talk and we hit the Dominis tonight, we won't have a target tomorrow. The effect will be the same."

"Except that every day we remain here increases the chances of the authorities storming in. We need to take advantage of every night."

Valeria dipped her bread in the stew. "Maybe we should relocate."

"No. We're safer here than moving."

"We're only four strong now."

"We were four strong last night, and it took only two of us to kill two of them and three police."

"We need reinforcements."

Michael's expression turned to one of annoyance. "I contacted Tudoro. He arrives tomorrow. Maybe he'll have our apprentices with him; maybe he won't. I'd like to have one more victory to report when he gets here."

Valeria felt a sense of relief. The priest Tudoro was a reassuring presence in her life. He would assess the situation and advise Michael as to the best path to follow.

"How's Eun?" Henri said.

"She's in pain but refusing morphine. She needs real medical attention. Surely Father Tudoro can put us in touch with—"

"Tudoro will make a decision about Eun when he gets here," Michael said in an even tone.

"I think we should all leave. Separate, then reunite at another target zone and take the beasts there by surprise, just as we did here. That will give us time to make sure our apprentices are ready for combat." Valeria glanced at Henri, who sat watching the confrontation in silence.

"Your job is to follow my orders. If you can't do that, return to Rome. You don't *have* an apprentice."

"You know I'm committed to our mission. I just think the casualties we've suffered have been too great."

"I disagree. We've only—"

A shrill scream interrupted them.

Henri rose first. "Eun!"

They ran out of the dining room, their boots stomping the wooden floor. Valeria brought up the rear as Henri threw open the door to the medical room and they charged inside. Valeria froze in her steps.

Eun stood at the sink across the room from her bed, the bandage that had been wrapped around her head strewn over her shoulders. She stood with her back to them, and Valeria saw her disfigured countenance reflected in the mirror. Eun whipped her head around, facing them with her grisly features. Valeria had sewn several flaps of Eun's tattered face together, fashioning a patchwork broken up by sections of exposed and glistening gristle. Eun resembled an autopsied cadaver that had been reassembled by someone with no knowledge of the human face. Tears streamed down her cheeks as she yowled, her eyes wide with horror and rage.

"Get her back in bed," Valeria said.

Michael and Henri charged at their petite companion,

who flailed at them.

"No!" Eun said, her voice a screech.

The men wrapped their arms around her and thrust her onto the bed. Valeria jerked a drawer open, withdrew a syringe and a bottle of clear liquid, and filled the syringe.

Eun threw her head from side to side, like a woman possessed. "No! No! No!"

"Hold her still," Valeria said.

Michael locked Eun's right arm into a rigid position, and Valeria inserted the needle of the syringe into a vein and pressed the plunger, injecting the sedative.

"Noooo . . ." Eun turned quiet and her body relaxed. Her breasts rose and fell, and the rest of her body grew still. Staring at the ceiling, she closed her eyes.

Willy and Karol sat in the front seat of the Jeep Cherokee Willy had signed out from the motor pool. Across the street and one quarter of the way down the block, two men stood like sentries outside the Domini Funeral Home. Willy recorded them on a HD camera while Karol took still photos beside him.

"There's two more," Willy said.

"Where?"

"On this side of the street at each end of the block."

Karol looked behind them, then straight ahead. "What kind of funeral home needs security?"

"One run by werewolves worried about werewolf hunters?"

"I feel like the only nonalcoholic at an AA meeting.

You people could have started a support group, you know; you didn't have to form a covert task force to work through your delusions."

"We'll see who's deluded when the fur starts to fly. So far, this war has been one-sided. What happens when the persecuted strike back? We may not be a secret for long."

"Class L humans." Karol clucked her tongue.

"According to what Tony said, they should be Class H wolves."

"How long are we going to sit here? The next full moon isn't for two more weeks."

"You've been spoiled driving around with me. Murder police don't normally do stakeouts. Make yourself comfortable."

"They're going to make us. People don't usually leave their cars running when they park them."

Willy shut off the engine. "Does that make you happy? Now we'll freeze to death."

"Those four guys are handling it okay, and they're outside."

"They're werewolves, though. They probably have fur on the inside of their bodies keeping them warm."

"Look at them. Do you really think they could be werewolves?"

"Sitting here looking at them in the daylight? No way. Ask me again when the sun goes down."

"Think about it: If creatures like Tony described have existed since before we did, how come there's never been any proof?"

"Who says there hasn't been any? Torquemada executed hundreds of people as werewolves during the Inquisition."

"He also executed people for being witches."

"And Wiccans exist."

"Wicca's a religion. The people who practice it don't fly around on broomsticks. What frightens me is that the brass and the feds are buying into this."

"They aren't buying anything—they're the ones doing the selling. But that doesn't mean they believe in what we're doing. It just means they're covering their asses. Get used to it, and don't trust any bosses on this except Tony."

"You sure have a lot of faith in him considering he spent the last two years supervising dogs because of how he handled his last big case."

"The fact that he *kept* his job after everything that happened says a lot."

"I'm ready for some coffee. How about you?"

"It will only make us have to take a leak sooner, but what the hell."

"Back in a flash."

Watching Karol get out of the SUV and head up the sidewalk toward a coffee shop, Willy decided she looked good in jeans.

When Mace reentered the base camp, he saw Shelly and Norton at their desks, working their cell phones and gazing at their monitors. A few feet away, a pair of legs dressed in navy-blue work slacks protruded from beneath a desk. In the conference room, a man with slicked hair attached a cable to the computer. Landry and Candice had left their office door open, and Landry rose from his desk with a coffee mug in hand.

"I see the place is becoming functional," Mace said.

"There's no place like home. The computers are wired to a secure server, but we don't have landlines yet. The TVs are in, but we can't get cable until tomorrow. How did it go with Graham?"

"We have the full support of the COD, unless anything goes wrong. Any developments here?"

Landry nodded at Shelly and Norton. "They're going to be busy for a while." He made a conspiratorial wink. "I dug up the Evidence Control records on the Blade of Salvation. Both halves were sent to a Monsignor Delacarte at the Vatican. I tried reaching him, but apparently he's in the hospital. I spoke to his secretary, who claimed to know nothing about the sword. He said he'd look into it, but since Rome is six hours ahead of us, I doubt we'll hear anything before tomorrow."

"Good work."

Candice joined them. "I didn't get anywhere with the alarm company, so I'm going to head over there and see what I can rustle up in person."

Mace watched Candice put on her coat and leave. "Anything from Willy and Karol?"

Landry took out his cell phone, pressed the screen a couple of times, and showed Mace an image of a man standing outside a building. "There's a couple of guys standing watch outside the funeral home. Otherwise, no activity."

Mace's phone vibrated, and he checked its display: Sing Sing Correctional Facility. *Rodrigo Gomez.* "Excuse me," he said to Landry, then entered his office and closed the door. The room felt alien to him. "This is Mace," he said into the phone as he sat in a worn office chair.

"Captain, this is Warden Strand at Sing Sing."

Mace remembered the warden, a tall, thin man with a negligible mustache. "What can I do for you?" He opened the pencil drawer of his desk and found nothing but nicotine gum wrappers.

"I'm calling you regarding Rodrigo Gomez."

"I gathered. Has something happened?"

"Nothing serious. You were his arresting officer, so I wanted to make you aware that he's doing a live television interview from here tomorrow night."

Mace closed the drawer. "Oh? With what network?"

"Manhattan Minute News. Your wife is doing the interview."

Mace sat straight. "What kind of security will you have?"

"I assure you your wife will be perfectly safe."

"I assume I can be there?"

"Of course."

"Thank you for calling, Warden. I'll see you tomorrow."

# CHAPTER TWENTY

"I'm not crazy about that passageway," Willy said, noting the narrow pedestrian tunnel that descended below the funeral home.

"You see them all over Brooklyn," Karol said. "They usually lead into courtyards."

Willy stretched his arms and yawned.

"It's only 5:30, and it's already dark outside," Karol said.

"It'll be Christmas before we know it. I wonder what you'll get me."

"Don't get personal on the city's dime."

"I hear you. During company hours, you want things between us to be the way they were before last night, right?"

"Copy that, Lieutenant."

"In that case, when are you going to sleep with me?"

She smiled. "When pigs fly, hell freezes over, and I see a

living, breathing werewolf."

"*Mira*, I hope none of those things happen. I need to stretch my legs. You ready for dinner?"

"There's not much else to do but eat."

"I can think of a few things, but we'd have to abandon our post to do them. What do you want?"

"Surprise me."

"Okay. I'm going to circle around the block and check out the other side."

"Try not to get lost."

"I'll leave a trail of bread crumbs just in case." Willy started the SUV's engine, giving Karol a blast of heat. "I want that heat on when I get back." Climbing outside, he inhaled cold air. Careful to avoid looking in the direction of the funeral home so as not to make eye contact with the guards outside, he walked in the opposite direction, waited for the light to change, and crossed Thirty-third Street, merging with the rush hour pedestrian traffic.

As Willy rounded the next corner, he noticed a man with a red ski jacket leaning against a bank wall with both hands stuffed into his pockets. The man stood perhaps twenty feet from the mouth of an alley that Willy estimated ran into the passageway on the other side of the block. Staring straight ahead, Willy registered a woman with blonde hair pulled back in a ponytail standing an equal distance away from the alley ahead. Like the man, she seemed to stare off into space. Willy knew better.

Reaching the alley, he stooped on one knee, untied the

shoelace of his sneaker, and tied it again. From the corner of one eye, he glanced down the alley and saw a number of exits from the buildings on either side illuminated by lights above them, as well as green metal Dumpsters. A graffiti-covered brick wall divided the opposite side of the block from this one. Standing, he resumed his walk, cutting across the street at a diagonal angle between passing cars so as not to pass the female.

*Who knows what they smell*, he thought. He entered a bodega and joined a line at the food counter. Glancing out the front window, he took out his cell phone. Before he could call Karol, the phone issued a salsa-flavored ring tone, and he saw his partner was calling him. He pressed the phone against his ear. "I was just about to call you."

"You're missing the changing of the guard."

"Really?" He lowered his voice. "There are two more lawn fairies on this side of the tracks."

"Hurry home, honey."

"I miss you, mama." He closed down his cell phone.

When Willy exited the bodega with his bag of food, his gaze passed over the woman standing watch across the street. She stared straight at him. Pretending not to notice her intense glare, he looked away and walked in the opposite direction.

Reaching Second Avenue, Willy crossed the street and headed back toward Twenty-eighth Street. He crossed that and made his way toward the SUV, noting the two new sentries stationed on opposite sides of the funeral home. Seeing

Karol seated behind the vehicle's steering wheel, he climbed into the passenger side. "Where did the other guys go?"

"Two were replaced. Two just left."

"One of the two on the other side was a female."

"Does that make her a bitch?"

"She definitely noticed me."

"That makes her a slut."

"That little recessed passageway leads into a courtyard divided by a brick wall maybe eight feet tall. The alley on the far side is wide enough for a garbage truck, and there was a metal gate as wide as a regular door in the wall. The Dominis must take their garbage through that gate to one of the Dumpsters in the alley. The sentries who just left could have circled that way and gone in through the gate."

"Too bad our computers weren't online before we came out here. We could have come armed with a little intel."

Willy took two clear plastic containers filled with food out of the paper bag.

"What's that?" Karol said.

"*Arroz con habichuelas y pollo.*"

"Chicken and rice and beans?"

"You know your Spanish food. That's good. Maybe you can cook it sometime."

"Now that you're back, do you want to call Landry, or should I?"

Willy handed her the containers and plastic forks. "Let me do it. Keep it lieutenant to lieutenant and all."

Mace saw Cheryl waiting at the bar as soon as he entered Maz Mescal on East Eighty-sixth Street. Before moving to Brooklyn, they had frequented the Mexican restaurant often when they had lived in the neighborhood. She sat on a stool with her legs crossed, sipping a margarita.

When she saw him, she sucked on her stirrer. "Why, Captain Mace, whatever brings you here?"

"The tortillas," Mace said. "Shall we?"

Cheryl slid off the stool, and Mace took her arm and guided her to the dining area, where a host seated them.

"It's been a long time since we ate here," Cheryl said.

"It's been a long time since we ate anywhere alone."

"What's the occasion?"

"Maybe I'm feeling nostalgic. Or maybe what I have to say couldn't wait until I got home."

Her expression cooled. "You heard."

"Warden Strand thought it appropriate to notify me."

"Since you were the arresting officer."

He smiled. "You're good at this."

"I'll be perfectly safe, my love."

"I know you will be, because you're not doing that interview."

A server set a bowl of tortilla chips and some sauces before them. "May I get you a drink, sir?"

"I'll have what she's having."

"Very good." The man walked away.

"This really isn't the time for you to start behaving like

a Neanderthal," Cheryl said.

"Not a Neanderthal," Mace said. "Just a concerned husband and father."

"You never interfered with my career before."

"You never tried to interview a serial killer who had an ax to grind against me before. At least, not as far as I know."

Cheryl leaned forward. "I never had the opportunity before—and it's a rare and exceptional opportunity. I've pretty much been filing sound bites since I started this job last year. This is the first chance I've had to make a significant splash, and in case you haven't noticed, I'm not getting any younger."

"In case you've forgotten, Gomez murdered five women."

"How could I forget? I lived that story for two months."

"I called Colleen on my way over here—"

"You did *what*?"

"As the arresting officer, it's appropriate for me to make certain inquiries about my convicted felon."

"You're dangerously close to stepping over the line, mister."

"Here's a news bulletin for you, Mrs. Mace: when my family's concerned, I hop, skip, and jump over that line like it isn't even there. We have a beautiful little girl at home who needs her mother."

"That little girl needs her father too, and I didn't stand in your way when you accepted your current mysterious assignment, which, I might add, you've told me nothing about."

"Colleen told me that Gomez requested you do the interview."

"He insisted on it."

"Why do you think that is?"

"Oh, I don't know. Maybe because I spent even more time on camera covering the Full Moon Killer than you did?"

"Or maybe he sees this as the perfect opportunity to strike back at me by hurting you."

"You're being ridiculous. Security will be through the roof; the station's legal team is making sure of it."

The server returned with Mace's drink. "Are you ready to order?"

"Yes. I'll have the number seven, and my wife will have the number nine." They always ordered the same thing.

Cheryl raised one finger. "Just a moment. I think I'll have the number four instead tonight."

"Yes, ma'am." The server departed.

"You're not doing that interview," Mace said in a blunt tone.

"The hell I'm not."

"We'll see about that."

"What are you going to do, arrest me?"

"You're being stubborn."

"And you're being unreasonable, not that it will do you any good. This isn't 1950."

"If you're determined to go through with this, I'm going to be there."

"As the arresting officer? How quaint. Here's a news bulletin for you, Captain: I don't care. What's a little more quality time between a husband and wife?"

Mace searched for a retort but came up empty-handed.

"Now, why don't you tell me all about your first day on your new job?"

The ring tone of Willy's cell phone sounded at quarter after seven. Checking the display, he answered. "What is it, Lieutenant?"

"Start calling me Ken now that we have the same rank," Landry said.

"Maybe once I start feeling like a lieutenant."

"I'm knocking off for the night."

"Aren't you the fortunate soul?"

"Candice is holding down the fort. Any idea how long you and Williams are staying at it?"

"At least until 2100 hours. We've had a little activity here but nothing major. Two lookouts replaced the two out front, and I spotted two more in the back."

"Do you want me to have Shelly and Norton cover the rear?"

"No, thank you." He glanced at Karol. "We've got it under control."

"Tony's having dinner with Cheryl, but he's coming back. Call me if you need anything."

"You got it."

"If you two pull a late night, adjust your schedule accordingly tomorrow. Just keep me posted."

"Copy that." Willy set his phone down. "Landry says if we stay up all night we can come in late tomorrow. Guess what we're doing?"

Karol smiled. "Surprise me."

Willy raised his eyebrows. It was the first time all day Karol had flirted back with him.

"Heads-up," she said.

Willy looked out his window as a taxi parked at to the curb outside the funeral home. The lobby lights in the building went dark, and Gabriel, Raphael, and a third man exited the building. "The Domini boys. Who's that with them?"

"I have no idea," Karol said. She raised her camera and took several shots as Raphael locked the door and shook hands with the other men. Then Gabriel and the unidentified man got in the taxi, which drove off. Raphael walked in the opposite direction, passing the lookout stationed on that side without saying anything to him. "Our orders were to follow Gabriel if they both left."

"Yeah." Willy started the engine and pulled out of the parking space, his head darting in both directions, searching for the opportunity to make a U-turn. "Hold it."

"What?"

"Raphael's coming back."

Karol looked out the windshield. "What the hell?"

Raphael returned to the funeral home and unlocked the door.

"Maybe he forgot something," she said.

The two lookouts followed Raphael, who opened the door and went inside.

"Uh-huh," Willy said with a skeptical voice.

Raphael punched a code into an alarm pad and turned on the lobby lights. Then he and the lookouts retreated from view. A moment later, the lobby lights turned dark again.

Willy backed into the parking space. "If you ask me, Raphael's keeping secrets from Gabriel. Maybe he's running a late night card game: werewolf poker or something."

They sat in silence, waiting. Ten minutes passed.

"They're not coming out," Willy said. "And they left that front door unlocked."

"Not exactly the actions of werewolves hiding from their slayers," Karol said.

"More like the spider inviting the fly to be supper."

"What should we do?"

"Sit tight and see who shows up to be supper."

# CHAPTER TWENTY-ONE

**M**ace walked the two blocks from the Fifth Precinct parking lot to the building on Mott Street in cold darkness. Manhole covers spewed steam into the frigid air. The rest of his dinner with Cheryl had been strained, and she took a cab home to Brooklyn.

The memory of his last interview with Rodrigo Gomez burned strong in his mind. The Full Moon Killer had confessed feeling kinship with the Manhattan Werewolf, and Angela Domini had confirmed to Mace that Gomez was a repressed Wolf, even though Gomez didn't know it at the time. Gomez had thanked Mace for arresting him, for the good of society. It had been a striking change from when Mace had arrested the serial killer and testified against him in court. Who knew what other metamorphosis had occurred within Gomez's brain and body over the last two years? If he had come to understand his true nature and had learned how to transform into a Wolf hybrid, conventional security could not protect Cheryl from him.

Mace used his key to unlock the front door of the building, punched a code into the alarm pad for the second door, and crossed the narrow lobby to the elevator, glancing at one of two security cameras that covered the lobby. He boarded the elevator, which rose, and wondered where this investigation could lead. If his team located the cell of Torquemadans and took them alive, were they signing the men's death warrants by turning them over to the government? He understood the need for a covert task force, but no matter how he rolled the term around in his mind, it equated to a secret police force. He wanted to protect the Wolves as much as possible, but he did not like the idea of being the equivalent of the KGB.

*I have to control the situation*, he thought as he exited the elevator. His key card admitted him to the squad room, and he made his way into the office area.

Shelly and Norton sat facing each other, slouched in their seats.

"There he is," Norton said with a tired smile.

"You know, you two don't have to wear suits," Mace said.

"Actually, we do," Norton said with a hint of resignation. "But you don't."

Mace shrugged. "It's a hard habit to shake."

"I'd have no trouble doing it," Norton said.

Candice came out of the office, her coffee mug in hand.

"Long day, Detective Sergeant?"

Candice made a noncommittal expression. "Not really. I shouldn't start feeling it until after nine."

"Well, you're not scheduled to start until four tomorrow. Even if you come in early, I don't want to see you before noon."

She smiled. "Oh, you're going to deny me all that OT at my new pay grade?"

"Yes. How did everyone do today?"

Norton tapped a stack of papers. "I've got a long list of all the Catholic churches in New York City, nearby New Jersey, and surrounding areas of New York within a one-hundred-mile radius, with contact information for each."

"And I've generated a list of seventeen hundred single males from other countries who have entered the US alone over the last three weeks, either by plane or boat," Shelly said. "I hope to cut that list down to two hundred tomorrow by using certain determining criteria. I assume you want me to trace their travel and hotel records to further eliminate those we show are nowhere near New York City."

"You read my mind." Mace looked at Norton. "I want you to start knocking on church doors."

"It's against bureau protocol for a special agent to conduct a potentially dangerous investigation alone," Norton said.

Mace knew that Norton wanted to keep an eye on things in the office. "That's fine. You and Shelly work on the list of foreigners together tomorrow. When you're finished, the two of you can go church hunting."

"Whatever you say."

"I got nowhere with the alarm company," Candice said.

"They swear none of their people with access to the Lourdes' alarm code would violate company policy by sharing them."

"Which means they're either lying or wrong," Mace said. "Or their system was hacked."

"They claim their security's airtight."

"There's no such thing," Shelly said. "A sophisticated cyber terrorist can break into any corporate system on earth. Even the bureau's mainframes have been hacked."

"Keep at it, Candice," Mace said. "It's too soon to let them off the hook." He looked at the feds. "You two should go home or wherever it is government types go after work. I don't know yet what time Willy and Karol are knocking off, so I'd like to know the two of you will be on hand in the morning if Landry needs you."

"We were just waiting for you to get back," Norton said.

"I know it must be strange working with such a small unit."

"Not for us. It's usually only the two of us, wherever the bureau sends us. It's sort of a luxury to be part of a team working out of the same space." She stood. "Let's go, partner."

Shelly rose as well.

"Good night," Candice said in a sweet tone Mace knew to be insincere.

"Good night," the special agents said, making their way out front.

Mace watched them leave. When he turned to Candice, she rolled her eyes without saying anything. He walked her back to her office. "Is Night Watch Command set on the protocol?"

"Yes: you, me, and Landry will take turns catching any

calls after 0100 hours. Whoever receives the call will tell them who else to call. You're up first."

"My wife will appreciate that."

"We received a memo about her interview tomorrow. You must be excited."

She spoke in such a monotone that Mace wanted to laugh. "I plan to be there."

"In that case, your wife must be excited."

"We're equally excited." Mace went into his office and unlocked his briefcase. The first item he took out was a framed photograph of himself with Cheryl and Patty, which he set on his desk. The second was a framed photo of Detective Patty Lane.

At 9:20 PM, Willy's cell phone went off, and he checked the display. "Fearless leader," he said to Karol, pressing the phone against his ear. "Go ahead, Captain."

"Put me on speaker," Mace said.

"Copy that." Setting the phone on speakerphone, he set it in the hands-free cradle beneath the dashboard. "We're all ears."

"I'm getting ready to leave, and I just wanted to check on your status."

"Oh, we're good. No complaints. We've been burning a lot of gas staying warm, though. Raphael and his boys haven't shown their faces since they went back inside two hours ago."

"Maybe they're spending the night."

"Like they're hitting the mattresses, goombah style? That doesn't make sense. Why station lookouts outside during business hours unless you know you're a likely target, and if that's the case, why wait inside for a RPG to take your asses out? I gotta figure they think someone's out there watching them, and I don't mean us. That unlocked door is an open invitation to the unwelcome wagon."

"Do you see anyone else out there?"

"Negative. But I also gotta figure that assassins who carry swords are closet ninjas."

"Do you need relief? Me and Candice could take over."

"Oh no you don't. We haven't had OT in months, and now that I'm a looey I need to upgrade my wardrobe. As long as we feel it's worthwhile, we'll hang tight. If our spidey sense tells us we're wasting our time, I'll have patrol increase their drive-bys just to be safe and we'll go home. We'll use Karol's vehicle tomorrow. If this is going to be an ongoing stakeout, maybe Landry can find us an interior site? It is December."

"I'll mention it to him. You two have a safe night."

"Thanks."

"Good night, Captain," Karol said.

"Good night," Mace said.

Hearing Mace hang up, Willy blew air out of his cheeks. "Why don't you get some sleep? There's no point in us both staying awake."

"You'll get no argument from me. Give me an hour and a half, then I'll spell you."

"You got it."

Karol reclined her seat, and Willy switched on the radio and located a slow jazz station.

Valeria awakened with a start, her alarm clock beeping nearby. Moonlight shone through the wide window in the room she occupied, and for a moment she felt disoriented, unsure of her location. Then she saw the empty cot beside her that Eun had slept in before suffering her injuries. Fumbling in the darkness, she switched off the alarm, her senses confused by the erratic sleeping schedule.

She got out of bed, flipped on the overhead light, which cast dingy light over her concrete and metal surroundings, and dressed in her loose-fitting combat outfit. Sitting on the edge of the cot, she pulled on her rubber-soled boots. When she stood, she secured her gun belt around her waist and strapped its holster around her leg. Realizing the importance of layered clothing in winter, she slipped on a down vest and snapped it up. She took her duster from its hook and then picked up her Blade of Salvation from where it leaned in the corner and slid it into the long pocket she had sewn inside the duster. Opening the door, she flipped off the light and stepped into the cold corridor, leaving the space heater running in her room.

As Valeria neared the dining room, she resisted the urge to rub her arms in response to the shivers rippling through her body. She opened the door and saw Michael and Henri packing gear into black bags on the table. Each man had suited up for combat.

"I made espresso," Henri said.

"No, thanks." She never drank anything before a mission. "It's easier for you guys to relieve yourselves on the fly than it is for me."

Michael picked up one of the bags. "Are you ready?"

Nodding, Valeria put on her duster.

"Let's go."

Henri picked up the other bag, and the three of them exited the dining room and rode the freight elevator down to the ground floor. In the loading bay, Henri pressed the garage door button and the door rattled open, providing them with a view of the parking lot.

"Let's take an SUV tonight," Michael said.

Willy snapped awake. He had not intended to fall asleep. Karol slept with her head on his arm, one hand on his leg.

*11:10 PM*, he thought. *Shit!*

The funeral home remained dark, and no one moved on the sidewalk. He gave Karol a gentle shake.

She sat up, blinking.

"I dozed off."

Karol gave him a disapproving look. "You should have woken me if you were too tired to stay awake."

"I didn't mean for it to happen. You wore me down last night."

"We have no way of knowing if Raphael's gang left or if anyone else went inside."

"We could always knock on the front door and see if it's locked now."

"That would be great for our cover."

"I'm going to walk around the block and see if those lookouts are still out back. Sit tight."

Switching off the overhead dome light, he opened the door and got out, breathing cold air. With his hands stuffed into his coat pockets, he walked to the corner and crossed against the light. Traffic was sparse, with few pedestrians in sight. He cursed himself again.

*First night on the new job and I screwed up.*

As soon as he could no longer see his SUV or the funeral home, he broke into a jog. He slowed to a walk before he reached the next corner and crossed the street. Turning right, he saw the bodega, closed now, and no sign of the lookouts.

*They must have gone inside.*

Approaching the dark bodega, he looked across Thirty-second Street. A black SUV occupied the alley, facing him, its headlights turned off. Willy's heartbeat quickened. Crossing the street, he took out his cell phone. The SUV was empty. When he reached the mouth of the alley, he looked from side to side. No civilians. Raising his cell phone before his face, he photographed the SUV's license plate. Then he called Karol.

"Talk to me," she said.

"No lookouts and there's a black SUV parked in the alley." He read the license plate number to her. "Call it into Candice, will you?"

"Copy that."

Willy closed the cell phone and slid it into its holder. No sooner had he removed his hand from the device than it vibrated. He pulled the phone free and saw Karol's name on the display.

*What the hell?* She couldn't have run the license plate so fast. He answered the phone.

"We've got company," Karol said. "A man wearing a long coat just crossed the street. He's going down the steps to that passageway."

*Damn it.* "Tell Candice we need backup. I'm going in."

# CHAPTER TWENTY-TWO

**H**enri steered the stolen SUV across Thirty-second Street. Three people scanned the stoops of apartment buildings and closed shops for signs of life.

"No sentries," Michael said beside him.

Valeria sat quiet in the back.

"Make the call," Henri said.

"I want a better look first," Michael said.

Henri slowed to a stop as the SUV passed the mouth to the alley. He looked over his shoulder at Valeria, who raised her night vision goggles to her eyes.

"The alley's clear," she said. "Fire escapes . . . windows . . . rooftops. I don't see anyone."

"Take no prisoners," Michael said.

Casting a final glance around the area, Henri backed the SUV into the alley. He looked behind him, focusing on the commercial Dumpster against the alley wall. Approximately fifty feet from the street, the SUV came to a stop just shy of the Dumpster, and Henri killed the engine.

They sat in darkness, waiting and watching.

After several minutes, Michael pressed a button on his headset. "Angelo?"

Henri heard a faint sound: Angelo's voice coming from the speaker in Michael's ear.

"We've arrived. Stand by." Michael turned to Henri. "We'll signal you."

Henri nodded, then watched Michael and Valeria get out of the SUV. In his rearview mirror, he saw them creep toward the Dumpster. Valeria hunched over and clasped her hands, giving a boost to Michael, who scrambled on top of the Dumpster without making any noise. Michael grabbed Valeria's hands and lifted her until they were face-to-face, then she set one foot on the Dumpster, followed by the other. They turned to the wall, setting their hands upon its concrete top.

A moment later, they disappeared.

Valeria landed on the garbage-strewn pavement like a cat, her gloved fingertips brushing the ground for balance. At the same time, Michael landed beside her. They faced a brick courtyard illuminated by three lights mounted on the walls around them. Without saying a word, they scanned the shadowy terrain. The green glow of Valeria's night vision goggles made everything in sight appear alien. Michael nodded to her, and she pressed a button on her headset.

"Come on in."

"*Oui.*"

Michael moved to his left, making room for Henri, so Valeria moved to her right. She heard the SUV door close, then the sound of Henri climbing onto the Dumpster. A moment later, he dropped between them and secured his night vision goggles. The three of them rose in unison and strode forward over discarded cartons and cans and bottles.

Hearing a sudden sound to her right, Valeria spun in that direction, drawing her tranq gun as she crouched to fire it. A pair of rats scurried behind a garbage can. Exhaling, she stood erect, holstered her weapon, and faced her comrades. She could not read their expressions behind their goggles.

Michael jerked his head toward their objective, and they moved to a steel door set in the side of the building on their right.

Michael pressed the switch on his headset. "We're ready."

Valeria heard Angelo's reply over the speaker in her headset: "It's about time. I'm on my way."

Henri drew a crowbar from beneath his coat.

As the man in the long black duster descended into the passageway between the funeral home, Karol slid down the SUV's passenger seat, peering over the dashboard. She wished that Willy had not hung up, and she tried calling him back, but he didn't answer.

*"Tell Candice we need backup. I'm going in."*

She pressed auto dial for the task force headquarters.

Candice answered midway through the third ring. "Detective Sergeant Smalls."

"It's Williams. Our suspected lookouts are gone, and there's an SUV parked in the back alley. A Caucasian male wearing a long black coat just entered the passageway beneath the funeral home. This could be it. Willy's going in alone from the rear to monitor the situation, and we need backup."

"Copy that. I'm putting out the call now. Wait for us to report to the scene."

"Negative. I'm going in after my partner."

"That's an order, Detective."

"I can't hear you, Sarge. You're breaking up. I'll try not to engage until backup arrives." Karol closed her cell phone and slid it into its holder. When she got out, she locked the doors manually to avoid the chirp-chirp caused by the remote. A gust of wind blew garbage along the sidewalk, and a man in a peacoat zigzagged toward her in a drunken manner at the end of the block. She wanted to run around the block to the alley but feared she would reach Willy too late, so she crossed the street, resisting the urge to draw her weapon in public. She saw her reflection in the funeral home's glass front doors and tensed up as a taxi passed behind her.

Veering to her right, Karol stared down into the darkness of the passageway, then pressed her back against the wall beside the steps, listening. Across the street and down the block she saw a uniformed doorman smoking a cigarette. She raised her gaze above the lit windows to the darkened sky, then took out her phone and tried Willy again to no avail.

Seeing no other choice, she stepped before the opening to the passageway, set her hand on the butt of her Glock, and descended into the waiting darkness.

Mace had not fallen asleep yet when his cell phone rang. He knew from Cheryl's lack of movement that she was awake too, pretending to sleep. He picked up the phone and saw Smalls on the display. He did not turn on the light. "Mace."

"We've got possible activity at the funeral home: an SUV parked in the back alley and one Caucasian male entering a passageway near the front entrance. Willy's investigating the alley, and Williams told me she was backing him up before she turned off her phone."

*Damn it*, Mace thought, getting out of bed. "Call everyone in."

"Even Shelly and Norton?"

"Everyone."

"Copy that. I'm locking up now. Do you want me to call in uniforms?"

"Negative. I'll see you there." Hanging up, he took a pair of slacks out of the closet and pulled them on.

The light on Cheryl's side of the bed came on, and she sat up. "Trouble in the big city?"

Buckling his belt, he took a fresh shirt from the closet. "Too soon to tell."

"Please be careful."

He ignored the ache in his shoulder. "I always am."

As he hurried out of the house, he was glad that Patty prevented Cheryl from following him. Driving along Fourth Avenue, he waited until he was five minutes away from home before he set his magnetic strobe on the SUV's roof and flipped the siren switch.

Valeria watched Henri wedge the crowbar's end between the edge of the steel door and its frame. They stood in silence, waiting for Angelo, who appeared at the opening of the passageway that ran between the funeral home and its neighboring building.

Angelo had already secured his goggles over his face. He turned to the wall closest to him, with his back to them, and spread his legs. Steam rose as he hosed the bricks with his urine. Then he zipped his pants and joined his comrades. "Sorry," Angelo said to Valeria.

She ignored him. What did she care if he relieved himself? He had been spending most of the day standing in the cold and wandering the shops along Twenty-eighth Street within sight of the funeral home.

Michael nodded to Henri, who leaned against the crowbar, pressing his hands against its shaft with all his strength, a grimace on his face. The door sprang open, a piece of metal skidding across the ground, and Michael caught the door before it could slam against the brick wall. Darkness yawned before them.

Henri returned his crowbar to his belt and entered.

Valeria watched him turn from left to right, surveying the interior. He reached inside his duster and drew his Blade of Salvation free of its scabbard. Without facing them, he beckoned them forward with his free hand, which then grasped the handle of his sword.

Michael entered next, followed by Valeria. Michael drew his Blade, and she did the same. They stood in a service corridor with linoleum tiles, a pair of locked doors to their right. Angelo entered behind Valeria, leaving the door ajar. Valeria waited until he drew his Blade, then turned back to Henri and Michael. Michael gestured with his sword, and Henri moved forward, pressing his back against the wall as he rounded the corner ahead. They walked in single file about ten feet apart, giving themselves room to swing their swords if necessary.

Henri reached another door at the end of the corridor. He grasped the knob and pulled the door toward him, hopping back at the same time, poised to strike with his Blade. Valeria followed him and Michael into a space with two stainless steel doors—perfect squares—recessed side by side within a ceramic brick wall. Because of the intensity of the green night vision on the wall, she assumed the ceramic bricks were white.

*Ovens*, she thought. *Crematories.*

Michael motioned to her and moved to the crematory on the left, leaving the one on the right for her. Releasing her grip on her Blade with one hand, Valeria stood before the crematory door, threw its latch, and jerked its handle down. She swung the door open, revealing the empty man-sized slab resting on tracks inside the oven. Michael pulled the slab out like a drawer, inspecting the space beneath the tracks, and she did the same. Then she closed the door at the same time Michael did.

They entered another narrow corridor, where Henri opened a door and peeked inside. Leaving the door open, he proceeded down the corridor to yet another door. Michael glanced inside the room, and then Valeria did the same. She saw a wide stainless steel table with drain holes drilled into it, a double sink, and a counter covered with jars of cotton balls and chemicals.

*An embalming room.*

Grateful no cadaver lay upon the table, she moved on. The next door was wider and manufactured of stainless steel, with a matching lever handle. Michael had left it open, allowing frigid air to spill into the corridor. Valeria peered inside the refrigeration room at eight empty gurneys. Considering how many werewolves had been killed the last few days, the Dominis weren't doing much business. She moved on, leaving the refrigeration room door open for Angelo, and a moment later she heard him close it.

Henri led them through a door into a carpeted area that opened into three chambers. A wider corridor with wooden walls intersected with another corridor ahead, and Valeria knew they had entered the funeral home proper. Henri opened a wide wooden door and entered the first of the three chambers.

Valeria followed Michael into the chamber, where

pedestals displayed a dozen different models of caskets. The four of them fanned out, circling the caskets, making sure no beasts hid inside them or behind the pedestals. The night vision goggles made it impossible to discern the different colors used for the caskets and their lining, but she noticed different styles and engravings in their construction.

When Henri exited the display room, he looked from side to side, as if trying to decide which way to go next. Then he turned motionless. Michael joined him and froze as well, and when Valeria stood beside them, what she saw chilled her: down the corridor, shapes skulked toward them. Valeria counted four, each beast traveling on all fours close to the floor. They made no noise, their snouts open to reveal jutting fangs, their eyes bright green in the night vision, their ears pinned back in an aggressive manner.

"Attack formation," Michael said.

Angelo moved close to the wall on his right, and Valeria positioned herself halfway between him and Henri on her left. She assumed Michael had distanced himself from Henri as well.

When the four beasts reached the end of the corridor, fifteen feet away from Valeria and her comrades, they rose on their hind legs, which seemed to change proportions in relation to their trunks. Growling, the beasts opened and closed their front claws, which retained the arrangement of human fingers despite their extended length. In Valeria's estimation, these monsters differed from those they had slain in the Lourdes' home: they showed no fear of the Blades or those who wielded them. Two of the monsters moved to her right, two to her left.

*They're trying to box us in*, Valeria thought. The animals showed cunning.

But the Inquisitors had their own strategy and closed their ranks. Valeria moved forward, focusing on the werewolves who faced her and Angelo. She stood with her back to Michael, and Angelo with his to Henri. She heard Michael's Blade scrape against its scabbard and knew he had sheathed it.

"Val, switch to your gun," Michael said.

Sliding her Blade into its scabbard, she drew her tranq gun and aimed it at the beasts, shifting her gaze from one to the other. She knew she would have time to fire only one dart before the creatures sprang on her.

Snarling, the werewolves pressed closer.

With his Glock drawn, Willy peered inside the SUV parked in the alley: empty. Setting both hands on the Dumpster behind the vehicle, he swung his legs onto the metal lid, pushed himself forward, and leaned over the top of the wall, staring at the courtyard below. He vaulted over the wall and landed in loose garbage. With his back against the brick wall, he held his Glock in both hands and scanned the courtyard. Then he moved forward, facing the passageway that led to the front of the funeral home, and stopped at a metal exit for the Dominis' business and saw it had been left ajar.

Willy knew Karol had probably just finished calling Candice for backup. He also knew that backup would not arrive for some time but Karol would arrive at the scene momentarily. He could not decide whether to go in on his own or wait for her.

*Fuck it. I'm a lieutenant now.*

Besides, going alone meant less risk to Karol. He swung the door open and took out his flashlight, which he activated. A circle of light, not unlike a full moon in the sky, appeared on the wall. Raising his Glock, he stepped inside and looked around, swinging the flashlight in each direction.

*Some kind of service corridor.*

He followed the corridor, his flashlight beaming off the floor, walls, and ceiling. Opening a door, he shone the flashlight along white porcelain bricks and stainless steel squares and knew he had entered the Dominis' crematorium. He crossed the room to another door and opened it.

Somewhere ahead, a man screamed.

With the hair on the back of his neck standing on end, Willy sprinted forward. He passed a number of doors before reaching a final door at the end of the corridor. Then he heard it: the snarling of animals. Snarls like he had heard when Patty was murdered, only multiplied.

*Oh, Jesus Christ. It's all true.*

He seized the doorknob, but his hand froze. Then he flung the door open and aimed the flashlight at an unbelievable tableau.

The snarling of the werewolves grew louder, and Valeria heard the scrabble of claws behind her.

Henri cried out and fell to the floor with one of the beasts clutching the wrist of his sword hand between its powerful jaws. He screamed, and at the same time Valeria heard the clanging of metal as his sword fell somewhere behind her. She also heard Michael fire his tranq gun, producing a startled yelp from the beast remaining behind her, then draw his Blade.

"Shoot it!" Angelo said.

She aimed her tranq gun at the beast gnawing on Henri's arm, then raised it to fire at the two creatures advancing on her.

They stopped in their tracks at the same time.

"Save Henri!"

She dropped her aim again, but Henri had managed to pull his own tranq gun from its holster. He pressed it against the breast of the creature and squeezed the trigger, the sound of the shot muffled by fur. The beast's entire body seemed to flinch, but it refused to release its hold on his arm.

Valeria fired at the closest beast, the tranq dart sinking into its chest. The creature yelped with a spastic flinch and jerked it out. Holstering her gun, she drew her Blade once more, which allowed Angelo to sheathe his sword and draw his tranq gun, which he fired at the other beast.

Brandishing her Blade, Valeria prepared to aim a blow at the neck of the werewolf chewing on Henri's arm, but the beast pulled Henri so that the screaming man blocked her path. Not yet unconscious, the other beasts moved slower. Angelo drew his Blade again and extended it before him, holding the two monsters at bay. Just as Valeria wondered how Michael was managing with the only werewolf that had not been tranquilized, the creature leapt over Henri, landing beside the two dazed creatures.

*Three on three*, Valeria thought.

Then light flared in her goggles, and she heard a man's voice. "Police!"

# CHAPTER TWENTY-THREE

Willy clamped his Maglite on top of the Glock's barrel so he could hold the weapon with both hands and aim within the light. The moving circle revealed only glimpses of the figures tangling inside.

A man wearing night vision goggles turned toward him, looking almost inhuman. Then the light passed over the head and shoulders of a pair of furry and ferocious-looking creatures that snapped their heads in his direction, their eyes a solid shade and their teeth almost as long as human fingers.

*Werewolves.*

Willy recoiled, and his heart skipped a beat. His first instinct was to shoot the creatures on sight, and he had to remind himself that he was tasked with protecting them from their human antagonists. At this moment, that objective seemed insane. The monsters darted out of the light, and he heard snarls coming from every direction before him. His flashlight exposed the legs and arms of other people and monsters, their blurred motion preventing him from getting a count. Another tight-lipped face with goggles came into view and ducked away, the corner of a long coat swooping through the beam like a bat.

On the floor, a man thrashed around, his arm pinned between the jaws of a powerful-looking beast. A sword sliced the moon circle, its silver blade reflecting light at Willy, and severed the man's forearm. He screamed and rolled away from the werewolf as blood gushed out of his new stump, painting the floor.

Moving his flashlight in a circle, Willy caught a man sheathing his sword inside his coat and picking up another sword from the floor. Before he could decide what to do, the man disappeared into the blackness.

*They're all too fast!* He was tempted to unload his gun into the darkness.

The wounded man continued to scream.

"Get him up!" a male voice said.

Two pairs of gloved hands hoisted the screaming man to his feet, and the werewolf spat out the remainder of the arm, the fingers on the hand twitching. The creature tried to rise but pitched forward with a wet-sounding sigh and stopped moving.

*What caused that?*

The man who had picked up the sword darted into the light again, plucked the severed limb off the floor, and disappeared.

Whipping the flashlight around, Willy glimpsed a woman and another man supporting the screaming victim between them while holding the three standing werewolves at bay.

"Stop or I'll shoot!"

The werewolves advanced on the humans, and Willy squeezed the trigger. The deafening gunshot caused the most aggressive werewolf to flinch with a startled howl, and a bloody hole appeared in his long torso.

The Torquemadan leader removed something from his coat, and Willy heard a hissing sound. The man waved his arm, dispersing a spray, and the werewolves clawed at their eyes and whimpered. He threw the canister at the floor midway to Willy, who heard the metal object rolling in his direction but lost sight of it in the darkness.

A moment later, his eyes filled with tears and his nostrils seemed to catch on fire.

*Tear gas!*

Covering his eyes with his free arm, Willy dropped his flashlight. Coughing, he slid down the wall and kicked out until he heard the metal canister rolling away from him.

"Get him out of here!" the same man said.

Willy heard a staccato of footsteps as the humans rushed by him and retreated down the corridor. He heard claws on the floor and deep panting, like that of a dog. At least one of the werewolves bore down on him, and he couldn't see the damned thing! His fingers found the edge of the door, which he slammed shut. He threw his weight against it just as a heavy body slammed against the other side. Planting his feet, he twisted the feeble lock in the doorknob. On the other side of the door, the werewolf roared in anger. And Willy had shot one of them . . .

*Oh, God, I have to get out of here!*

His eyes and throat burned. Holding his breath, he snatched the flashlight and staggered blindly down the hall, then opened his eyes again and gasped for breath. Nothing eased his pain, but at least when he aimed his flashlight he could see where he was going, and he ran through an open door.

*Where the hell is Karol?*

Praying she had not run smack-dab into the Torquemadans, he took out his cell phone, but even with the aid of the flashlight he couldn't discern the details of the phone through the tears in his eyes. He drove himself forward through the crematorium, confident that a left turn would bring him to the door he had entered in the first place. His brain felt like it was boiling in the tear gas.

Feeling fresh air on his face, Willy slammed into a closet door, rebounded off it, and staggered outside, where he filled his lungs with fresh air. Coughing, he fell to his hands and knees and turned his head in time to glimpse two of the Torquemadans hauling their wounded comrade, a black man, over the top of the wall. The wounded man was black. Staggering to his feet, Willy raised his Glock, but the Torquemadans vanished. He ran forward but stopped when he heard something growling nearby.

Wiping the tears from his eyes, he lifted his gaze to two black shapes perched on the railing of a fire escape ten feet above him and realized they must be the sentries he had seen posted outside earlier. Taking a step back, he swallowed.

The werewolves leapt from the fire escape and landed on the ground before him. They rose like men and snarled at him like beasts, their eyes blazing with hatred and spittle flying from their jaws. As frightening as the creatures inside had been, these two, fully illuminated by the lights mounted on the surrounding walls, seemed far more ferocious. A similar monster had torn Patty apart.

Willy aimed his Glock. Maybe a head shot would take one of them out before the other one could tear into him.

On the other side of the wall, the SUV peeled out.

The werewolves turned at the sound and glanced at each other. The one on Willy's right dropped to all fours, sprinted to the wall, and leapt over it in a great bound. The remaining creature stepped toward Willy, whose gun shook in his hands. A powerful figure landed in the space separating him from the monster and roared at the advancing creature. Another werewolf.

The newcomer rocked back on its haunches, ready to spring into action. The werewolf stalking Willy roared back and tried to dart around the smaller wolf to get at him. But the newcomer issued a barking command and feinted left, blocking its way. The two werewolves faced off against each other, and Willy debated whether to take the shot while he had it. Then the predatory werewolf turned, ran for the wall, and jumped over it. The remaining werewolf rose and faced Willy, who continued to back up. Even though slighter than the two wolves that had just departed, the creature stood taller than him.

But not for long: the wolf's legs had three segments

rather than two, and the bottom extensions drew in upon themselves, becoming shorter and human. Its body absorbed the black fur as if sucking it inside the skin, and the lupine head assumed human dimensions.

*Oh, God, no!*

Willy experienced a wave of nausea as the werewolf reverted into a naked human female with glistening black skin.

With her breasts rising and falling and vapor billowing from her mouth, Karol nodded at the entrance to the passageway. "Since I saved your life, how about getting my clothes for me?"

Michael climbed into the front seat of the SUV, tossed Henri's severed and bloody forearm into the passenger seat beside him, and tore off his night vision goggles. As he watched Angelo and Valeria load Henri into the backseat, he found himself wishing they had brought a van after all.

Angelo sat in the back on the passenger side, with Henri's head in his lap. He pulled off his goggles as Michael keyed the ignition, stepped on the gas, and roared out of the alley.

Valeria tossed her goggles aside and unbuckled her belt, which she pulled free of her belt loops. "Jesus, why did you cut off his hand?" She tightened the belt around Henri's stump, forming a tourniquet.

Michael raced into the street, and Angelo supported Valeria as she tended to Henri.

"Because otherwise we would have had to leave him

there," Michael said. "That beast wasn't letting go."

Valeria took Henri's goggles off and looked down at her comrade. His dome was covered with sweat, and his eyes lost focus. "He's in shock," she said.

Angelo stared out the rear window. "We've got company."

Michael glanced in the rearview mirror. One of the beasts was galloping after them on all fours in the middle of the street! It kept pace with the SUV, then gained on it, then disappeared. An instant later, a thud shook the SUV as something slammed onto its roof. Michael saw Valeria gaze at the ceiling wide eyed, and he stomped on the brake. The werewolf rolled over the SUV's windshield and hood into the street. As soon as it got to its feet, Michael stepped on the gas, launching the SUV forward. The vehicle's headlights illuminated the creature, which shielded its eyes. Then the SUV slammed into the werewolf, spinning sideways through the air like a Frisbee, to Michael's left and into a car parked at the curb, triggering an alarm.

As Michael sped forward, he saw the dazed werewolf roll over, get up, and slink back toward the alley. He wished he could have turned around and gone after it.

"Drastic measures," Valeria said with disgust as she returned her attention to Henri.

Michael felt himself growing hot. "Of course. It would have been fine if that cop—if that's really what he was—hadn't shown up. We had everything under control."

"Bullshit. Henri would have lost his arm either way."

"Then why are you giving me shit for what I did? We couldn't leave him behind, and we couldn't leave his *hand* behind. I did what I had to. Now you do what *you* have to—keep him alive and let me drive."

Willy stood gaping at Karol. "I don't believe this."

She folded her arms over her breasts, hiding her large nipples. "I'm cold. Get my clothes."

"I *fucked* you—"

Karol strode past him. "Do you want a medal or a chest to pin it on?"

Taking out his cell phone, he followed her into the dark passageway. "You took the DNA test . . ."

"I was in human form when they took the sample, so my DNA was human too. If I'd been in Wolf Form, my DNA would have read as a Wolf's, and if I'd been in mid-Transformation—like Jason Lourdes was—it would have looked like a combination of the two."

Willy called the squad room.

"Smalls," Candice said. "What is it, Willy?"

"I guess you could say I engaged the enemy. There were four of them; one is seriously hurt. They got away in an SUV, last seen heading west on Twenty-seventh Street." He read her the license plate number.

"I'll put out an APB now," Candice said.

Willy hung up. "You're one of them. You're one of Gabriel Domini's fucking werewolves!"

Karol stopped where she had left her clothes piled up and dressed. "Boy, there's no getting one over on you, is there?"

"You're spying on the operation."

Karol pulled her clothes on. "It's not as shady as you make it sound. We have to protect ourselves. That means infiltrating human society at all levels. I worked my way into Homicide, but I didn't tell Mace to choose me for the task force. When he did, I couldn't ignore a golden opportunity to help my kind."

"Those two *wolves* almost killed me."

"You're right. It's a good thing I came along when I did."

"Couldn't you have just howled at them to back off without getting all furry? They must know you."

"I could have, but I would have been in no shape to protect you if they weren't willing to reason."

"You're a mole. You're a werewolf *and* a mole."

"I have the same objective as a Wolf as I do as a woman: to preserve my species. My interests aren't at odds with the department's or with those of the task force. We want the same thing: to stop the Torquemadans."

"Does that mean you're going to tell Tony about this?"

She zipped up her coat. "No. Are you?"

Willy considered her question. "Jesus, I don't know. Why the hell couldn't you have told me all this before?"

"Because I couldn't trust you then. I don't know if I can trust you now."

"But you exposed yourself to save my ass."

"Let me explain something to you. You were my first and you'll be my last. Wolves are monogamous, and we mate for life. I tried to dissuade you, but you kept coming after me, like the dog you are. I didn't ask you to do that.

It's bad enough being in an interracial relationship. It's a lot harder being in an interspecies one. I gave in to your charms, and now I'm stuck with you. I couldn't very well let Leon tear you to shreds."

"Leon?"

"Never mind. Let's go out front. It isn't exactly safe here."

"There are still three werewolves inside."

"No, there aren't." Karol walked through the passageway toward Twenty-eighth Street.

"How do you know?"

"Trust me on this point. All we want is to be left alone. They're not sticking around to answer questions."

"You were in on their plan."

"No, I wasn't. I answer to Gabriel. I have no idea why Raphael and his crew decided to spring a trap on the Torquemadans without his say-so, and he would have told me if he knew about their plan. If you hadn't walked in on them, maybe those Wolves would have killed those murderers, and the purpose of our task force would be moot."

"Or maybe the Torquemadans would have killed your people."

"Maybe." She climbed the steps onto the sidewalk.

Joining her, Willy just blinked.

Karol sniffed him and frowned. "Tear gas. Delightful. You can't tell anyone my secret. My life is in your hands."

Willy studied her. "I don't know *what* to say about any of this. I still can't believe I fucked you."

"And you'd better stop saying that, because your life is in *my* hands too. We're forbidden from mating with your species and sharing information of any kind. If Gabriel, Raphael, or anyone else finds out, they'll put it to a pack vote, and the outcome will almost certainly be an order for your death and possibly mine. Any number of Wolves would be only too happy to do the deed."

"That's some peaceful, loving people you have."

"Rules, baby. We're all part of one system or another, and self-preservation is the name of the game."

"You're feeding information to Gabriel. That makes you a traitor to the department. If I look the other way . . ."

"I'm no traitor. I'm a cop. I've served this city for six years, putting my life on the line every day. I protect the people here—human and Wolf—and I'd never do anything to put another cop in harm's way. But this is a war, and my people are already endangered. I have to do everything in my power to stop these Inquisitors."

Headlights appeared in the distance: two vehicles.

"I saved your life, Willy. Are you willing to throw mine away?"

"I can't believe I fucked you."

Karol slapped him hard enough to leave a stinging sensation in his cheek, which he rubbed. Then she kissed him, pushing her tongue against his. He did not resist her.

"My life is at stake," she said.

# CHAPTER TWENTY-FOUR

"All units, this is an all points bulletin for a black SUV heading west on Thirty-second Street, license plate CYT 5166." The voice over the police band radio came out a squawk.

"That's us," Michael said. "Looks like we're taking the train." He turned right.

Valeria looked at him, aghast. "What about Henri? He can't take a train."

Michael sped toward Thirty-third Street, then turned left. "If he isn't dead, he will be soon. There's nothing we can do for him. He stays here."

Valeria felt her eyes widening. "We can't do that!"

"You've done all you can for him." He pulled into a parking space and switched off the engine, then looked behind him at Henri, who had turned still and quiet.

A police car crossed the intersection ahead, moving downtown.

"He's right," Angelo said. "We have to go."

Michael detached the police band radio. "Angelo, bring his Blade." He opened his door and got out.

Valeria felt tears in her eyes. "Angelo . . ."

Angelo got out on the passenger side and hid Henri's Blade inside his duster. "We have to get out of here." He closed his door.

Valeria caressed Henri's head. "Farewell, my friend."

He did not respond.

She got out of the vehicle and closed her door. Michael and Angelo were already walking up the street, taking turns glancing over their shoulders. At the intersection, bright lights, numerous pedestrians, and heavier traffic distinguished the neighborhood from the one they had just left.

"I'll go first," Michael said. "You two come down a few minutes later. Pretend to be a couple. We'll travel in separate cars."

Angelo put an arm around Valeria's shoulders, comforting her. They watched Michael cross the street and descend the stairs to the PATH station.

"That's two men down, plus Eun out of action," Valeria said. "Not a very successful campaign."

"We've inflicted our share of casualties," Angelo said. "Let's go."

Angelo guided Valeria across the street, but all she felt was her Blade against her. Slipping her hand inside her pocket, she felt around for the remote control, then pressed the button on the detonator.

When Mace arrived at the Domini Funeral Home, he saw Candice speaking with Willy and Karol. Mace parked at the curb before the funeral home and got out. Crossing the sidewalk to his subordinates, he noted Willy's and Karol's nervous expressions and Candice's look of incredulity. His senses told him that the call had not been a false alarm.

"You were right, Tone," Willy said. "I saw them. I fucking saw them! Three inside, two more outside."

"Class Ls," Mace said.

"They were *huge*. And four Torquemadans, dressed to the hilt in combat gear and carrying swords. They all got away, but one of those assassins was hurt bad. Fucking *Class L* had its teeth in the guy's forearm, and one of his own players hacked off the arm and took it with him."

Mace glanced at Karol. "What did you see?"

"I was at my post when Willy called and said he was going in through the back alley. When I reached the courtyard through this passageway"—she gestured at the narrow tunnel running below the building—"he was alone. But there's blood all over the ground and wall, and it leads through the funeral home to where Willy says the fight occurred."

His instincts told Mace that Karol had seen more than she was admitting. He turned back to Willy. "Tell me everything."

"When I saw that SUV parked in the alley, I recorded its license plate number, then I climbed over the wall into the courtyard. The door to the funeral home was busted open, so I went inside. I had probable cause. Then I heard screaming . . ."

Mace listened intently to Willy's story. It felt good knowing that someone else truly believed what he had been through.

". . . and two more Class Ls jumped off the fire escape and landed right in front of me. They stood there, snarling and showing me their gums. Then they both took off over the wall. I guess they wanted the Torquemadans more than they wanted me."

"Good thing," Candice said.

"Probable cause or no, you had no business going in there alone," Mace said. "No unnecessary risks, remember? Everyone comes out of this alive."

"I know. You're right. It was a bad call on my part. I fired that shot . . ."

"No reports."

Willy nodded, a look of relief on his face. Mace realized Willy hadn't looked at Karol once since his arrival.

"Raphael and his boys were in there. I didn't see them when they went in, and we never saw them come out."

"You were awake the whole time?"

Willy frowned. "I told Karol to catch some Z's, and I nodded off by accident. I'm sorry. But the front door's still unlocked, and the alarm is off. There were five of them in there at one point, and there were five Class Ls."

A police cruiser pulled over, and Mace saw Landry park behind it.

"I called Hector and Suzie," Candice said.

The cruiser's passenger window slid down, and a female PO looked out. "Everything okay here?"

Candice flashed her shield. "Everything's fine."

The woman nodded. "Have a good night."

The cruiser drove off, and Landry joined the quartet. "What did I miss? I heard the APB."

"Willy and Karol will fill you in. Candice, call Gabriel Domini and get him over here. Tell him there appears to have been a break-in and an altercation and the alarm is off. I want him to answer questions."

"What about Raphael?"

"Tell Gabriel we think it would be prudent for him to come alone."

An SUV pulled over, and Shelly and Norton got out.

"What happened?" Shelly said.

"Diega and Williams were just about to run the incident down for Landry," Mace said. "I don't want anyone going inside until Gabriel Domini arrives."

"This way for the ten-cent tour," Willy said, leading the group into the passageway.

Mace watched another SUV park down the block. *Hector and Suzie*, he thought.

Candice got off her cell phone. "Gabriel's on his way."

Hector and Suzie walked up the sidewalk.

"Yo, these task force hours are crazy," Hector said. "We got a stiff?"

"Just some blood samples," Mace said. "Maybe some fur too. If we're lucky, fingerprints. You can start in the back courtyard, but don't go inside until the owner gets here."

"Got it. Let's gear up, Suzie Q."

The CSU detectives returned to their SUV.

"There's nothing like conducting a secret investigation in public," Candice said.

Ten minutes after Hector and Suzie disappeared down the passageway with their equipment, a yellow taxi arrived. Mace watched Gabriel Domini pay the driver and get out.

Gabriel wore a long camel hair coat. As he approached Mace and Candice, a look of recognition spread across his features, and he motioned with one gloved hand. "Captain Mace."

*He remembers me two years later.* Mace gestured to Candice. "This is Detective Sergeant Smalls."

"I called you, Mr. Domini," Candice said. "The front door was left unlocked, and the alarm wasn't set."

"That's impossible. My brother and I left here together earlier. I'm positive we locked up."

"Yes, but your brother returned a short while later with some other men," Mace said.

Gabriel raised his eyebrows. "How do you know that?"

"We have your business under surveillance."

"Why? Am I suspect in some crime? Surely you don't think me or my brother had something to do with Jason's murder and Rhonda's abduction?"

"Quite the opposite: we believe that whoever killed Jason and kidnapped Rhonda wanted to get at you."

"But why? I'm of no importance."

"Nevertheless, we believe the break-in here tonight and the attack on Synful Reading are connected."

"Why did you ask me to come here alone?"

"Because when your brother returned, he left the door open. He practically invited someone to go into your establishment after hours. And our detectives never saw him and his friends leave."

"Did the intruders go in through the front door?"

"No, they broke in through the courtyard door. Maybe they saw him leave the door open and sensed a trap."

"Or maybe they *didn't* see him leave the door open and believed the back door was the best way in."

"Either way, the building's still open, and your brother is long gone. There's blood in the alley and inside."

"You suspect my brother was harmed?"

Mace gave Gabriel a long look. How much could he reveal without revealing too much? "No. One of the intruders lost an arm in the melé."

"My God." Gabriel gestured at the door. "Can I see if anything's been stolen?"

"Sure, but let's go this way." Mace gestured at the passageway.

"It's dark," Gabriel said.

*He sees perfectly well in the dark*, Mace thought. "We'll use my flashlight. I never leave home without it. Candice, do you mind holding down the fort here?"

"I don't mind, Captain."

Mace took out his flashlight and entered the narrow passageway, followed by Gabriel. It stretched perhaps sixty feet, and their footsteps echoed in the darkness, the flash beam bouncing off the walls. They emerged into the courtyard, where Hector and Suzie scraped blood samples off the ground and wall. The CSU detectives wore bright yellow latex gloves. Willy, Landry, Shelly, and Norton stared at Gabriel, but Karol barely glanced at him.

"Familiar faces," Gabriel said. "Hello."

"Mr. Domini," Landry said.

"How's it going?" Willy said.

Mace gestured to Shelly and Norton. "This is Special Agent Shelly and Special Agent Norton."

"Hello," Norton said.

"Federal agents?" Gabriel said.

"It's not unusual in kidnapping cases," Shelly said.

Karol pointed at the open door. "You can see where they broke the door, probably with a crowbar. The blood is self-evident. It leads over the wall to where Willy saw their SUV."

Mace turned to Willy. "Why don't you walk us through what happened?"

"You got it," Willy said.

"Stay off our blood," Hector said without looking up.

Willy motioned to the open door. "I climbed over the wall and found the door ajar. It was obvious someone had forced it open, so I entered the premises." He stepped inside the corridor, illuminated by fluorescent lights.

Mace gestured for Gabriel to follow Willy, then followed him. He heard Landry, Norton and Shelly, and Williams behind him. The group followed Willy down the corridor, stepping around the blood spatters on the floor.

"I made my way down the hall and turned here . . ."

The blood continued, smeared with footprints. Switching on lights, Willy led them through the crematorium, down another hall, and into the funeral parlor, where great pools of blood had soaked into the carpet, which had also been torn by what appeared to be long claw marks. The party of seven stared at the blood.

"The lights were off when I came in here," Willy said. "I only had my flashlight to see. There was a struggle going on, and I counted eight figures involved."

"What did they look like?" Gabriel said.

"That's classified at the moment," Mace said. "I notice you don't have any cameras back here."

"Only on the front doors. We've never had any need for additional security before."

"I'd like to see the footage for tonight," Mace said.

"Of course. Whatever you say, Captain."

Mace faced his team. "Willy, Karol, Ken—go home. Norton, Shelly—hang tight until I'm finished with Mr. Domini. Ken, tell Candice I want her to stick around until Hector and Suzie finish."

Circumventing the blood, Gabriel turned on the wall sconces for the long corridor ahead. "This way."

# CHAPTER TWENTY-FIVE

Gabriel switched on the office lights and admitted Mace, who glanced at three desks. A monitor and digital recording desk rested upon a filing cabinet. The monitor showed the front foyer.

"The recorder is off," Mace said.

Gabriel glanced at the recorder, his body stiffening. "That's odd."

Gabriel switched on the machine and pressed a button. The monitor turned black, then sped through images in reverse: four men left the building, and two entered it. Gabriel pressed another button, and the footage played at regular speed in proper sequence: Gabriel and Raphael exited the building, locked up, and parted company. "See? There we go."

The screen turned black, and Gabriel adjusted the controls. "It must be malfunctioning."

"Detective Diega and Detective Williams saw your brother return right after you left. He didn't turn the alarm back on. He must have shut off the recorder, but first he erased the footage of him and his crew coming back."

Gabriel faced Mace. "For what possible reason?"

"Because he set a trap for the Brotherhood of Torquemada."

Was there a flicker of recognition in Gabriel's eyes?

"The Brotherhood of what?"

"Let's not play games. You know exactly what I'm talking about, and I know you're the leader of the pack. Why don't we go someplace quiet to talk, where we won't be distracted by all this police procedure?"

Gabriel's face showed little emotion. "I don't think it's in my best interest to go anywhere with you."

"Why not? I'm sure you have people watching you. There's a diner a few blocks away. We can go there."

"Shouldn't I have a lawyer with me or something?"

"A werewolf with a vampire?"

"This conversation is beginning to make me uncomfortable."

"Not so uncomfortable that you'll do anything drastic, I hope. I only want to help you."

Gabriel's nostrils flared. "All right. Let's go. How many chances will I get to eat dinner with a police captain?"

*How many chances will I have to eat dinner with a werewolf?* Mace thought.

Mace and Gabriel exited through the front of the funeral

home, where Candice stood waiting on the sidewalk.

Using his remote control, Mace unlocked the doors to his SUV. "Hop in," he said to Gabriel. "I'll be right with you."

Gabriel circled the SUV and climbed into the passenger side.

Mace joined Candice and spoke in a low voice. "Have Patrol conduct visible surveillance here the rest of the night. Shelly and Norton can go home."

"Aye, aye."

Mace slid behind the wheel of his SUV, keyed the ignition, and pulled into the street. "How's Angela?"

"My sister's in Canada."

"That doesn't answer my question."

Gabriel turned to him. "Is your interest personal?"

"In a manner of speaking: she saved my life. I guess I saved hers too. And then I killed Janus Farel."

Gabriel was silent.

"Angela told me where to find him. She said she wanted a human to kill him. She told me all about your people. I broke into Janus's brownstone—the one he owned under his real name, Julian Fortier—and he almost tore me to pieces. That's when Angela showed up. After I drove the broken Blade of Salvation into his heart, she fixed me up. I was with her when she called you and told you to come get the carcass. Then she took me to the ER, and I took her to the car rental agency. I knew she was going to Canada before you did."

"I don't know what my sister told you—"

"I saw Janus in Wolf Form when he killed John Stalk

and when he tried to kill me. Angela was a Wolf when she came to my rescue. She turned into a human before my very eyes. I know this city is crawling with werewolves and you're their leader."

Gabriel stared hard at Mace. "Who else shares your beliefs?"

"Let's save some conversation for dinner."

Willy pulled over to the Fifth Precinct parking lot and stared straight ahead.

"Do you plan to never speak to me again?" Karol said. "That's how boys act in elementary school."

"I don't know if I should talk or howl."

"You're a dog. Maybe you should bark."

He turned to her, mouth open to speak, only to see her smile. He felt his anger dissipating and did his best to summon it back. "Don't do that. This is serious shit."

"You're right; it's my life."

"You're Gabriel's plant—"

"Gabriel didn't enlist me for this assignment. Mace did."

"And if I don't tell Tony, I'm an accomplice."

"Maybe I should just leave the task force? Or resign altogether?"

"That would make things a hell of a lot easier."

"I can't do that. You may hold my life in your hands, but this isn't just about *my* life. It's about the lives of my people. Innocent people, like Jason Lourdes and Rhonda Wilson and their parents. I have to do everything I can to stop these murders."

Willy took a deep breath. "Wolves, not people."

"Good night," she said in an icy tone.

Willy watched her get out of the SUV and enter the lot. Bowing his head, he sighed. Then he drove away.

Mace and Gabriel sat opposite each other in a booth located at the back of the diner, which was only one quarter full, sipping watery coffee. Framed photos of movie stars covered the walls.

"You have kids, right?" Mace said.

"Two sons." Taking out his wallet, Gabriel removed photos of two boys and laid them side by side on the table for Mace to see. "Gareth and Damien."

"Good-looking boys. Twins?"

Gabriel put the photos back in his wallet. "Yes. How about you?"

Mace took out his wallet and set a photo on the table. "One daughter, Patty, named after the policewoman Janus Farel murdered."

Gabriel studied the photo. "She's beautiful. How old?"

"Almost two. Yours?"

"Six. I remember when they were two. It was a fun age."

"I ordered increased patrols around your apartment and your brother's, but as far as we can tell, neither one of you has been home since this started. Neither have your wife and children."

Holding Mace's gaze, Gabriel offered a slight smile. "You haven't convinced me that I should confide in you.

How do I know that you're not recording this conversation?"

Mace reached inside his jacket and took out an envelope from which he removed a stapled document that he offered to Gabriel, who skimmed it.

"That's a copy of a nondisclosure agreement I signed. It was prepared by the higher-ups who authorized the task force I'm running—the task force charged with stopping the Brotherhood of Torquemada. It forbids me from divulging any facts related to this case to anyone not in the task force or to whom the task force answers. If I'm wearing a wire, I've already hanged myself for treason."

Gabriel handed the document back. "Why would you take such a risk for me?"

"Like I said, Angela saved my life. Even though I did the same for her, I feel like I still owe her. Also, I took an oath to serve and protect. I know the NYPD didn't have your kind in mind when they drew up that oath, but I see you as human. I believe what Angela told me, that you're a peaceful people who only want to be left alone, that Janus was a rogue. You deserve protection as much as the rest of us do. The Brotherhood of Torquemada is a terrorist organization, plain and simple, and they've killed three cops. The department wants them stopped, and the feds want your existence kept a secret. Their interests—my interests—intersect with yours."

Gabriel drummed his fingers on the table. "My sister told you too much. We have rules against that, punishable by death."

"She helped me stop Janus . . . your Berserker. I couldn't

have killed him without her. Surely she deserves special consideration?"

"Angela's always been a rebel. She's broken rules before."

"Like mating with a human?"

"I'm used to making allowances for her."

"If you're already an endangered species, maybe you need to lessen the severity of your laws."

Gabriel showed Mace the palms of his hands, his fingers spread out. "Despite our similarities, our species really are different. In my society, we vote on important developments, but we don't legislate." He closed his hands into fists. "Our laws are instinctive. After centuries of hiding from your kind, our sense of self-preservation is inbred. Angela has always operated against those instincts."

"And Raphael? It seems to me he's playing his own game, one that poses as great a threat to your survival as Janus's did. One of my men saw your Wolves in action. Two of them almost killed him. I want to keep your people safe, but I need to keep mine alive."

"The burden of leadership. My brother has always been loyal to me, but this is a stressful time. You mentioned feds. How bad is it?"

"I can't say for sure. At the start of this, those two FBI agents and a high-ranking police official asked me to head up this task force. I was led to believe that individuals within the bureau suspect the packs exist. I don't know how many. The agents are part of my team, but if I had to guess, I'd say they pushed NYPD into this arrangement. All the evidence gathered so far has been sent to Quantico. As we speak, those carcasses are being dissected and DNA is being analyzed and compared. Whatever methods you've employed to cover up your existence in the past won't fly in Virginia. We may be able to stop the Brotherhood, but what happens when the government gets involved?"

"One thing at a time. How many people are in your task force?"

"There are nine of us."

"How much do they know?"

"Everything to varying degrees."

"If you arrest the Torquemadans, there will be a trial. Our existence could still be made public."

"My superiors don't want that. If we take the Torquemadans alive, we're turning them over to the FBI."

"Who will keep their imprisonment a secret and torture them. In which case, your government will learn the history of my people, and we'll still be in danger."

"I was told the government wants to observe you and possibly make peaceful contact with you."

"Do you believe that?"

Mace considered the question. "No."

"What will they do, propose a treaty with us? Confine us to reservations? Allow us to sell tax-free cigarettes to feed our families? Or will they pursue a more explicit form of genocide?"

"I don't know. But they know you're in New York. Any of you who stay here do so at your own risk."

"I've already sent my wife and children away until this is over."

"Maybe you should consider not bringing them home."

"My wife is a strong-willed woman—like yours."

Mace disliked people knowing anything about his personal life, but Cheryl's relative fame as a local celebrity made that unavoidable.

"I read about her interview tomorrow night."

"Rodrigo Gomez is one of you."

Gabriel's face seemed to tighten. "I really must have a talk with my sister."

"I brought Gomez in. I had a personal reason for pressing her on the point."

"I remember when you arrested him. It was a relief to us. My father was grooming me to succeed him while Gomez terrorized the city. You did us a favor. Then that book came out, and we got nervous all over again."

"Carl Rice has been an ongoing irritation to me."

"He made you famous, didn't he? I saw the movie. You looked taller on TV."

"I get that a lot."

"We can't keep enough copies of *The Wolf Is Loose* in stock at Synful Reading."

"That's unfortunate."

"At least they haven't turned that into a movie yet."

"I understand the rights have been optioned."

"Do you see any money from that?"

"No. I refused to cooperate with Rice on either book. I'm just a figment of his imagination."

"I wonder what he'll write next."

"You have to help me help you."

"What would you like me to do?"

"Angela found Janus Farel. You can help me locate these

Torquemadans before anyone else gets killed."

"Julian walked into Synful Reading while Angela was working—just like you did. She had his scent."

"After tonight, Raphael and his crew have the scents of four of the Torquemadans."

"If you're right, I'm sure he has his own plans for them."

"Then you've got to rein him in. Let him track them down, but allow me and my people to handle the confrontation for your own good."

"If you arrest any of the Torquemadans, you have no way of guaranteeing they won't stand trial. You have no idea what your superiors will do with them, no matter what they say now."

"Trust me, the last thing the authorities want is to cause any more panic than there's already been. Keeping these guys out of the public eye is a priority."

"Your plan makes sense, but I can't promise anything."

Mace took out a business card. "You can reach me here at any hour. Where are you staying?"

Gabriel pocketed the card. "Someplace safe."

"I can provide you with additional security."

"The fewer people who know my location, the safer I'll be."

A deafening sound from outside, like a giant toilet flushing, overwhelmed the conversations in the diner, and Mace noticed the water in his glass rippling. Patrons exchanged terrified glances, and by the time the sound faded, a chorus of car alarms had commenced. Gabriel closed his hands into fists again.

# CHAPTER TWENTY-SIX

**M**ace ran out of the diner onto East Thirty-fifth Street, followed by Gabriel. He saw people running in the direction of the PATH train station two blocks away. Turning, he sprinted in the opposite direction and climbed into his SUV. Before he had turned the ignition, Gabriel opened the door and got in beside him.

"This isn't a ride along," Mace said as he affixed his strobe light to the vehicle's roof.

"I'll only follow you on foot if you tell me to get out."

Mace activated the siren. "Strap yourself in."

Gabriel buckled his seat belt, and Mace pulled into the street. In the distance, orange flames rose high from a parking space and black smoke obscured the view of skyscrapers. Transit police exited the PATH station, and a squad car stopped in the middle of the intersection. People ran from the scene as well as to it.

Mace double-parked. "You stay here."

As soon as he got out, he smelled burning smoke. Running through the intersection, he flashed his ID at the two POs who had just gotten out of their patrol car. "Keep everyone back!" he said over the screaming car alarms.

The flames and smoke rose from a vehicle in a parking space. He ran close enough to the inferno to feel the heat from the flames on his face. The roof had been blown off the SUV, and the doors and hubcaps lay smoldering in the street, blood and oil mixed on the pavement, burned flesh and clothing spread out like frosting on a cake. The stench of burning skin filled his nostrils, and he gagged. Backing up, he glimpsed something lying on the ground underneath the SUV on the opposite side of the street. Covering his mouth and nose with one hand, he crouched and saw a human hand and forearm with black skin. The end of the forearm looked as if it had been cut from the rest of the arm.

He took out his phone and called Candice. "I'm at the PATH station. It looks like someone blew up an SUV. I'm willing to bet it was our sword-wielding terrorists. Their man probably died, and they knew they'd been spotted, so they blew up the vehicle with him inside it so we couldn't identify the corpse. Only problem is, the severed arm didn't get burned, so we can lift fingerprints. Get Hector and Suzie over here right away."

Willy unlocked the door to his apartment and went inside. He tossed his unopened mail and keys on the table and peeled off his leather jacket. Then he set his Glock on the table too. *Christ, what a long and unbelievable day.* He just wanted to take a shower and crawl into bed. Instead, he turned on his computer and the television, which he switched to Manhattan Minute News with the volume off. His door buzzed.

*Who the hell?*

Probably neighborhood kids, running around late at night. He pressed a button on the intercom. "Yeah?"

"It's me," a female said.

*Karol.* But he had just seen her. "What do you want?"

"To talk."

Sighing, he buzzed her in. Then he wondered if he should be admitting a werewolf into his apartment after midnight. He grabbed his Glock and clipped its holster to his belt again. Then he sniffed his underarms and frowned. He hurried into the bathroom, slapped some cologne onto his face, and returned to his door, which he opened. Karol stood there. His heart jumped in his chest, and he flinched. He felt his cheeks grow hot.

Karol smiled. "Did I scare you?"

"I'm a little on edge. Aren't you?"

Moving forward, she slid her hands up his chest and around his neck and kissed him on the mouth. He raised his hands to push her back, then clasped her sides, and finally set them around her waist. She bit his lower lip, then rubbed his crotch, arousing him. Allowing their mouths to separate, she looked into his eyes and then walked around him. He closed the door, and when he turned around he saw her drop her coat on the floor and untuck her shirt from her jeans. She had no trouble finding the bedroom.

Swallowing, he followed her and stood in the doorway, where he flipped the light switch.

Wearing an orange bra, she kicked off her shoes and unzipped her jeans, which she squirmed out of. As she stepped free of the denim, he saw that her thong matched her bra. "Take your clothes off."

"I don't know if I want to."

She dropped her gaze to between his legs. "Yes, you do."

"I don't know what you are . . ."

Karol strode toward him. Her hands slid along the sides of his ribs, fingernails scratching him. "You know what I am. You know *who* I am. Are you man enough to handle me? Show me. Everyone's got an animal inside them. Let me see yours."

This time he kissed her hard. She dug her fingers into him, and he pulled her against him. Then he pushed her onto the bed and took his shirt off. Propping herself up on her elbows, she raised one knee, watching him as he removed his jeans and his boxers. Staring at his erection, she made a little grunt and smiled. She took off her bra and slid out of her thong, and he climbed on top of her, pushing himself against her moist opening.

Rolling over, she raised herself on her hands and knees and looked over her shoulder at him. "Like this," she said in a husky voice.

Willy mounted her from behind, thrusting himself hard into her, locking his hands on her hips so she could not crawl away. She snarled at him, a moan escaping from between her clenched teeth. As he pounded away, he felt himself snarling as well.

Spreading her fingers wide, Karol slid her hands forward, pressing her breasts against the mattress and arching her back. "Bite my neck. Please . . ."

Leaning forward, he clamped his jaws over the back of her neck and felt her shudder. He wrapped one arm around her waist, controlling the lower half of her body. A long, low moan escaped from her lips, transforming into something more animal than human. Sweat soaked his brow, and as he continued to thrust, driven on by her musky scent, he prayed she would maintain enough control to stay in her human form.

*Please, God, don't let her change!* He released his bite on her. "Don't stop!"

Fastening his teeth on her flesh once more, he plowed her forward. She cried out, then laughed. He did not stop.

*Do it. Do it!*

At last she howled, and he unleashed himself.

A dozen official vehicles blocked off the intersection, and Mace imagined many more idled beyond his line of sight. Firefighters had already extinguished the blaze, and the wreckage of the SUV smoldered. The fire engine remained parked nearby, the firemen awaiting instructions. Standing downwind from the smoke, Mace and Candice watched

Hector and Suzie package the hand in a plastic bag.

"There's newspeople all over the neighborhood," Candice said.

"Just keep them far away."

She hurried off.

"How many bodies?" Mace said.

"Oh, only one," Hector said. "Unless there's bodies clinging to the buildings like Spider-Man, and we just don't see them."

Mace saw Shelly and Norton approaching with half a dozen other officials in suits. "Make sure you've got those prints."

"They're in my pocket," Hector said without looking up.

The cavalry arrived.

"Captain, I'm Michael Kelly with Homeland Security . . ."

". . . Derek Clendening with the bureau . . ."

". . . Emil Novak, NYPD Counterterrorism squad . . ."

Mace faced the men. "Who's taking charge of the crime scene?"

The men exchanged apprehensive glances.

"I am," they said in unison.

Norton and Shelly stayed quiet.

"Just make sure you copy me with your findings. I wasn't the first officer on the scene. Two of the uniforms back there were."

"We need to send the evidence to Quantico," Norton said.

"Of course you do." Mace turned and walked away. As many as one hundred onlookers watched from the sidewalks, and he saw cameramen training their cameras on him. When he reached his SUV, he saw that Gabriel had disappeared. Then his gaze locked on the PATH station across the street. Turning, he zeroed in on Candice and waved her over to him.

"Is something wrong?" she said.

"Get your hands on the security camera footage inside that station, going back four hours. I don't care if all these federal agencies get them too, but I want copies immediately. Requisition the appropriate corresponding footage at other stations from the Transit Authority. Make sure Ken knows to expect them. I want him to concentrate on the footage as soon as we get it."

"Yes, sir."

The Port Authority Trans-Hudson service used tunnels only in Lower Manhattan, Hoboken, and downtown Jersey City.

*Jersey*, Mace thought.

# CHAPTER TWENTY-SEVEN

**E**un awoke with her face on fire.

*Where the hell is my medication?*

Sitting up, she groaned. The clock on the bedside table read 1:03 AM. She had a vague recollection of Valeria telling her there was a mission tonight.

*Did they leave me alone?*

She pulled back the blanket. Valeria had dressed her in flannel pajamas. Swinging her legs over the edge of the bed, she stepped into the slippers on the floor and stood. After staggering past the electric heater to the bathroom, she relieved herself and faced the mirror. Although her face remained wrapped in a bandage like a mummy, in her mind's eye she saw only the hideous countenance she had seen earlier. No amount of plastic surgery would ever restore her beauty, and she doubted she could ever look anything other than disfigured. She had pledged her life to Father Tudoro and the Brotherhood; she accepted that she could be killed at any moment for their cause. But she had never anticipated that the price she would pay for battling monsters was that she would become one herself.

Eun wanted to leave this place, to return home . . . but she didn't really have a home. Orphaned at age four, she had been placed with a foster family in Isernia, Italy, by Tudoro, then enrolled in boarding school. After Tudoro enlisted her in the Brotherhood, she had gone off the grid, living first in the Brotherhood's training barracks, which relocated on a semiannual basis, and then in a series of apartments under assumed names. She had followed Michael into battle in Naples, then Finland, then Greece, and now the United States. She had devoted her adult life to exterminating the beasts. She believed in the cause.

*What do I have to show for my sacrifice?*

She wished she had been able to accompany her comrades on their current mission. The satisfaction of slaying some beasts would have made her feel better.

Hunger pained her stomach. She left the medical room and made her way to the dining room, where she gazed at the monitor on the wall. In her cell, the bitch they had captured slept on her side. As far as Eun knew, the beast still had not provided Michael with the information they sought. She turned to where Myles's Blade had been mounted on the wall.

Sticking to the shadows, Gabriel walked along the tree-lined street to the safe house. As he neared the low gate, two figures separated from the darkness, as he knew they would, and surrounded him.

"Gabriel!" David said. "We were worried."

"Raphael's waiting inside," Eddie said.

"Thanks." Gabriel walked up the steps and opened the front door.

Raphael and Elias sat on the living room sofa.

Raphael jumped up at the sight Gabriel. "Where the hell were you?"

Gabriel studied his brother. "I was answering for the mess you created."

Raphael's jaws tightened, but he did not avert his eyes from Gabriel's. "I took action. I'm not ashamed of it."

"You were seen entering by the police and not leaving. And then you were seen by the police in Wolf Form."

Raphael's nostrils flared. "We'd have prevented him from speaking, but Karol Williams protected him. You should have warned me that she was staking out the funeral home. You must have known."

Gabriel did not care to admit what he did or did not know. "*You were seen*. If you were going to carry out some rogue operation behind my back, you should have taken better care to protect our secrets."

"I laid the trap. Everything went according to plan. We'd have feasted on those Torquemadan dogs if that cop hadn't walked in on us. He ruined everything."

"There are police in the real world. We deal with them all the time. That's why Karol does what she does."

"Make her tell me the identity of the Hispanic man who saw us. I'll silence him forever."

"Have you become stupid as well as reckless? The police are after the Torquemadans. We're the victims. Kill one of them, and they'll be after us as well."

"They will be anyway."

"I don't think so."

"You've played this too close to your vest. I'm entitled to know: What do the police know?"

"Not just the police—the FBI. And you're only entitled to know what I think you should know. Right now that isn't much. As an advisor, a confidant, and a brother, you've betrayed me."

"How could protecting our people be a betrayal to you?"

"You don't strike at anyone unless it's on my orders."

"We're at war. We need leadership, not speeches. Action!"

Gabriel looked at Elias. "Someone's lit a fire under my brother."

Elias said nothing.

"No one's done anything to me," Raphael said. "If you won't do what's necessary, then I will. These Torquemadans have to be found and killed. I came close tonight, and now I have their scent."

"Leave them to the police."

Raphael scrunched up his face in disgust. "Why?"

"Because the police can take care of the Torquemadans

without exposing us more than you already have."

Raphael's entire body seemed to tighten. "What happens if the Torquemadans are taken alive and they stand trial? What's the risk of exposure to us then?"

"He's right," Elias said. "At this point, it's best if we handle this situation ourselves."

Gabriel offered Elias a tight smile. "Perhaps you should actually become a member of this pack before you challenge my leadership of it."

Elias did not answer, but he did not lower his eyes, either.

"How will the police even locate the Torquemadans?" Raphael said.

"You track them down, then give me their location. I'll pass it on to Karol, who can feed it to someone we can trust."

"A human, you mean? You're talking about violating one of our key laws."

"A human we can *use*, then."

Raphael gave him a hard look. "You're playing a dangerous game. I won't be a part of it."

Gabriel felt cornered. "You'll do as I say. I'm the leader of the pack."

Raphael shook his head. "I can't. I have to do what I think is right for the pack. I'm sorry. Me and my crew will take care of the Torquemadans."

"If you disobey me, there will be repercussions."

"So be it."

Stung by the betrayal, Gabriel watched Raphael leave. Then he turned to Elias, who sat looking at him. "Go with him. He'll need your counsel."

Elias rose. "I'll get my things."

As the Greek werewolf climbed the stairs, Gabriel slid onto the sofa. With Melissa and the boys out of the country, Arick watching after them, and now Raphael dissenting, he felt utterly alone.

Awakening to the grinding sound of the metal door opening, Rhonda sat upright, raising both knees and covering her breasts with her arms. The stub of her right arm ached, and she instinctively moved her elbow joint.

*My arm is growing back*, she thought. But would her hand grow back fully developed, with working fingers?

A figure entered the cell, someone she had not seen before: a short female with shoulder-length black hair. Her neck and face were wrapped in bandages, with openings for her eyes and mouth. She wore a black combat outfit and brandished a sword. If she hadn't felt in such danger, Rhonda might have laughed. For now, the woman aimed the tip of her sword at the floor.

"Stand up, you bitch," she said in a hoarse voice.

Rhonda obeyed, straw falling from her flesh. She did not bother to cover her private parts, and the woman looked her over from head to toe. Rhonda saw Asian eyes between the bandages.

The woman raised the tip of her sword at Rhonda like an extension of her arm. With her free hand, she pointed at her face. "One of your kind did this to me. One of you killed Myles."

"Good," Rhonda said in an even tone. "You'll all be dead before this is over."

"We're prepared to die. Are you?" The woman took a step to her left.

Rhonda took a slight step back. "Yes. Just not now."

The woman continued moving to her left, and Rhonda stepped back, keeping her movements subtle.

*Come a little closer*, she thought.

"What makes you think you have any say in the matter? You're our prisoner, nothing but a chained animal."

"And what are you, except disfigured for life? I bet whoever tore your face off thought it tasted good going down."

The woman drew her sword into swinging position. "Maybe I'll wear yours after I flay you alive."

Inching away, Rhonda threw back her shoulders. "I think I'll eat the rest of you."

The woman's upper lip curled, which caused her to wince. She seemed to take satisfaction in the pain. "Why aren't you afraid of me? You're in your human guise. I could kill you easily."

"You must think so, or you wouldn't be here by yourself. Where's everyone else? Did they leave you alone?"

"I don't need them. I don't need anyone."

"That's good, because with whatever's under those bandages, I don't see any intimacy in your future."

Unleashing a defiant war cry, the woman swung the sword over her head.

Rhonda raised both hands to catch the blade, but the woman dropped to a crouch and swung the sword into her left leg instead. Rhonda screamed and went down on her knee.

The woman wrenched the sword out of her thigh, producing a fountain of blood, and leapt away, drawing her sword once more.

Whimpering with tears in her eyes, Rhonda rocked back and forth in pain. She raised her head and looked at her attacker. "You're the bitch," she said through growing teeth.

Within the space in the bandage, the woman's almond-shaped eyes widened, and Rhonda knew that her irises had expanded. She expected the woman to flee, but instead she charged at her, raising the sword above her head.

Rhonda had only an instant to decide her next move: jump out of harm's way or will the Change.

*Change. Change.*

Leaping forward, Rhonda transformed into a Wolf. The two females collided in midair, and Rhonda sank her canine fangs into the woman's collarbone. The woman cried out, dropping her sword, and Rhonda tasted hot blood. The Blade clattered on the floor a moment before the two figures crashed beside it. Rhonda tore flesh and meat from the right side of the woman's collarbone and gobbled it, smacking her lips.

The woman staggered to her feet and attempted to escape the space Rhonda's chains allowed her to reach, but Rhonda dove forward and snapped at the Achilles tendon of the woman's left leg, bringing her down. The woman screamed, and Rhonda shredded her other Achilles tendon with her claw. The woman tried to pull herself away using her only good limb, her left arm. Rhonda snared one of her wounded ankles and dragged her closer. The woman continued to scream, her fingers clawing at the floor. Rhonda leapt onto her back, sank her teeth into her neck, and shredded her buttocks and the backs of her legs with her rear claws. The blood between her toes felt good.

Straddling the woman, Rhonda rolled her over so they faced each other. The woman reached up to claw at Rhonda's face, but Rhonda snapped her jaws down over her fingers. She felt her teeth chewing through flesh and bone, then felt the fingers floating in the blood pooling on her tongue. The woman pulled her arm back and gasped at what remained of her hand: a thumb and four stumps for fingers, each spewing blood.

Rhonda spat out the severed fingers in a torrent of blood. Then she seized the woman's head and unwrapped the bandage around it, like a child unwrapping a holiday present. The woman twisted her head away, as if trying to hide her features. Rhonda turned the head around, staring at the grisly mass that had once been a human face. One of her fellow Wolves had certainly done a number on the assassin. If her vocal cords had not Changed with the rest of her, she would have laughed to taunt the woman. Instead, she seized the woman by the throat and stood, raising her victim like a doll. She hurled her against a wall within her reach—

*For Jason!*

The woman winced and appeared to be fighting not to lose consciousness. Unable to stand with her Achilles tendons severed, she collapsed.

Roaring through blood-slicked teeth, Rhonda threw

the woman into the adjacent wall, her body making a wet smacking sound.

*For my parents!*

The woman sank to the floor. "Just kill me . . ."

Leaping before the woman, Rhonda dragged her upright once more. She sank the fingers of her front claw into the glistening red wound around the woman's collarbone, then jerked them down, tearing flesh and fabric all the way to the woman's stomach, producing a protracted and agonized scream from the woman.

*For me, you bitch!*

Then Rhonda became violent.

Mace entered the house, turned on the dining room lights, and tossed his keys on the table. He hung up his jacket, stepped out of his shoes, and walked into Patty's bedroom, where the toddler slept undisturbed. He stood at the crib for a moment, listening to his daughter's regular breathing. Hearing a footstep in the hall, he saw a shadow fall over them, and he turned to see Cheryl standing in the light, wearing a silver-blue nightgown.

"You should be asleep," he said.

"Do you think I don't worry about you the way I used to when you go out? I liked it better when you were in the K-9 Unit. I saw you on the news just now. It's like Beirut. This whole city's going to be in a panic."

Unable to discuss any details, Mace put his arms around her and held her tight.

Looking up, she kissed him, then led him to bed.

Michael made his way into the brick warehouse complex and unlocked the steel door next to the loading bay. Inside, he peeled off his cap, then his duster, and waited for Angelo and Valeria to arrive. Henri's death weighed on his shoulders like a giant rock.

*And then there were four*, he thought.

His colleagues entered with shell-shocked expressions. Valeria's eyes appeared watery.

"Tudoro arrives tomorrow," he said. "Hopefully with reinforcements. He'll have instructions for us. Until then, let's all get some sleep."

Reaching into his duster, Angelo took out Henri's Blade of Salvation. "First, let's hang this in Henri's honor."

Michael closed and locked the door, then followed Angelo and Valeria to the freight elevator and then to the dining room on the second floor. Angelo hung Henri's Blade on the wall under Myles's.

*Two dead*, Michael thought.

Valeria sucked in her breath. "Oh . . . God."

Moving beside her, Michael followed her gaze to the security monitor on the wall. On the left side of the screen, they saw the muscular and furry back and shoulders of Rhonda, sitting on the floor of her cell in wolf form, the straw on the floor behind her caked in blood.

Picking up a remote control from the counter, Michael aimed it at the monitor and panned the camera in the cell left, framing the image so they saw the werewolf sitting cross-legged, her fur red with blood, chewing on a human leg that had been stripped of its skin. Organs and other body parts lay on the floor like scattered jigsaw puzzle pieces, with what appeared to be intestines piled in the corner.

Valeria covered her mouth. "Eun . . ."

The werewolf looked up at the camera, staring at them through the lens, her snout covered with blood.

"She knows we're watching her," Angelo said. "She saw or heard the camera move."

The werewolf rose, glowering at her captors. She glanced around the cell for something, then moved out of frame. A moment later, she returned with Eun's head dangling by its hair in her claw.

"Mother of mercy," Valeria said.

The werewolf appeared to cradle Eun's head for a moment, but she was really just repositioning it in her claw. Then she approached the camera, as close as her chains would allow her to go. Pulling back her arm, she hurled the head at the camera, dislodging it in a shower of blood. When the camera struck the floor, the image on the monitor went dark.

# CHAPTER TWENTY-EIGHT

**S**hortly after 6:00 AM, Angelo steered a silver SUV into Newark Liberty International Airport. After a long and largely sleepless night spent thinking about the deaths of Henri and Eun, he had waited at the warehouse until Father Tudoro called to say his flight had landed.

Twenty minutes later, coasting past the airport's ground transportation area, he scanned the walkways for his mentor. An elderly priest was not hard to spot, and he saw the gray-haired man soon enough. Pulling over to the curb, he got out and walked over to the smiling man. They clasped hands and spoke in Italian.

"It's good to see you, Father."

"And you, Angelo. I'm anxious to hear the details of your work here."

Angelo's heart sank. Despite his pleasure at seeing his

father figure, he had hoped the Brotherhood's apprentices would be with him. Masking his disappointment, he took the priest's large rolling suitcase and loaded it into the hatch of the SUV, then helped Tudoro into the backseat.

"You've been making headlines," Tudoro said in a non-judgmental tone once the vehicle had started moving.

"It's hard not to attract attention in a city like New York, Father."

"Agreed. Despite what the newspapers say, we're not terrorists. This is a war. Slow down up ahead, please."

Puzzled, Angelo slowed down. At a crosswalk ahead, a man with a backpack stood at the curb. He almost didn't recognize him with his beard: Reddick, Michael's apprentice. His spirits lifted.

"I should have brought the passenger van." Smiling, Angelo popped the hatch, and Reddick loaded his backpack into the hatch and climbed into the backseat.

"Ciao," Reddick said.

"Ciao. I never thought I'd be so happy to see your skinny little ass."

"I can't wait to fight beside you, brother."

*Just don't get yourself killed*, Angelo thought as he shifted the SUV into gear.

At a bus station on the outskirts of the airport, Tudoro pointed out another man, this one wearing a bandanna. Angelo recognized Colum, Henri's French-Canadian apprentice. He pulled over to the curb and popped the hatch again, and Colum loaded his suitcase into the back and got up front.

"Bonjour," Colum said to the other passengers.

"Bonjour," Tudoro and Reddick said.

"Now we have to switch back to English," Angelo said. "It was nice while it lasted. Colum, Reddick, what have you heard?"

Colum glanced at Tudoro. "Only that the Beasts killed Myles."

*They don't know about Henri or Eun yet.*

"We can bring everyone up to speed at your headquarters," Tudoro said.

Angelo nodded. "*Si.*"

Mace awoke to Cheryl stroking his face. Sitting on his edge of the bed, she had already dressed and made herself up for work.

"What time do you want to get up? Anna's here."

Mace glanced at the clock—6:30 AM. It felt earlier. "How late is she working? There are labor laws, even for nannies."

"Her mother's taking care of Patty tonight."

"I'll get up now. Technically, I'm supposed to work a swing shift, but after last night—and since I'm leaving early to be at your interview . . ."

Cheryl kissed him. "Last night was wonderful. Thank you." Standing, she walked to the doorway.

"You look great," he said. "I'll see you later."

Smiling, she left.

Mace got out of bed and stretched his arms, legs, and lower back.

Sniper came into the room, wagging his tail.

"No running today, buddy." He rotated his bad arm in its socket. *My broken-down body is holding up pretty well so far.*

He had taken a shower after making love to Cheryl only a few hours earlier, so all he did now was splash water over his hair before dressing in a navy-blue suit.

Anna spoon-fed Patty when he came into the dining area.

"Good morning, Anna."

"Good morning, Captain. It's a big night for Mrs. Mace!"

With an exaggerated frown, Mace kissed Patty on the forehead. "Do you hear that? Mama has a big night."

"Mama!"

"Thank you and your mother both for the long day."

Anna smiled. "It's no problem. We love her. She's an angel."

"Have a good day." He tapped the tip of Patty's nose. "Be a good girl."

While waiting at a light on the drive into Manhattan, he experienced déjà vu. At least a dozen military vehicles rolled into the street ahead of him: jeeps, Humvees, and troop transport trucks. The National Guard. His cell phone rang in its hands-free cradle, and he pressed it. Jim Mint's name flashed on the display.

"Well, well, if it isn't the keeper of the brass ring."

"Tony, please tell me you're making progress."

"Yesterday was only our first full day. What do you expect, a miracle? Give me a break."

"I'm under a lot of pressure here. That explosion last night turned the department upside down. A lot of other agencies and departments are breathing down my neck, and none of them are producing results. You're the only ace I have up my sleeve."

"That's kind of you to say. I see the governor's made a few calls."

"They're all over the city. The last thing we need is for these bastards to turn and run like everyone *thinks* the Manhattan Werewolf did."

"I don't know what they're going to do. But when you pull out guns this big, guys with swords are bound to consider their options."

"Have you got anything at all?"

"Give me until lunch for an update, okay?"

"What time do you eat?"

"One o'clock."

"Make it noon." The line went dead.

Angelo drove the SUV into the warehouse complex parking lot.

"Are all of these vehicles ours?" Tudoro said.

"Yes. They were paid for with cash, using aliases." Angelo switched off the engine and got out.

Colum and Reddick helped Tudoro out, and Angelo led them to the door by the loading bay.

Colum looked at the darkened windows around them. "Are these other buildings empty?"

"Yes. There are plenty of complexes like this around here, thanks to the economy." Angelo unlocked the door and took them inside.

"This place is huge," Reddick said. "And cold."

"It would cost a fortune to heat the whole building. We use space heaters on the second floor."

They boarded the freight elevator, and Angelo threw the lever. As they ascended to the second floor, Angelo felt Tudoro avoiding his eyes. When they reached their destination, Angelo pulled the gate up and led his colleagues into the complex. In the dining room, he found Michael and Valeria sitting with a tall man with thinning hair.

"Loreti!" Angelo could not help but smile at the sight of his own apprentice.

The Argentinean rose and embraced his teacher. "I'm glad to find you well."

Angelo made a noncommittal expression. "These are difficult times."

Michael and Valeria stood and approached Tudoro.

"Welcome, Father." Michael shook his hand.

Valeria hugged the old man. "It's good to see you."

Watching Tudoro pat Valeria's back, Angelo felt a twinge of jealousy, which caused guilt to well up inside him. Discounting the apprentices, Valeria was the youngest member of the group, and he knew the priest felt protective of her.

Michael shook hands with Reddick and Colum.

"I'm keeping Scioli in Rome," Tudoro said. "He and I have a great deal of work to do as soon as I get back. I'm flying out again in two days."

"You're leaving so soon?" Valeria said.

Tudoro offered a patient smile. "Of course, child. This is no social visit."

Valeria bowed her head. "I apologize. My emotions . . ."

Tudoro rubbed her arm, then moved to the security monitor. Rhonda lay unconscious on the floor, her nude body on full display. "Has she spoken yet?"

"Nothing of consequence," Michael said. "I don't think she will, either."

The priest faced him. "Then find another use for her or kill her."

"I plan to do both."

Tudoro gave him an approving nod, then moved over to the wall where three Blades of Salvation had been mounted for display. "It's time you shared your news with everyone."

Michael motioned to the tables. "Sit down, please."

The priest and his soldiers sat at the two tables.

Michael remained standing. "We've inflicted casualties, but we've suffered as well. Eight beasts are dead, but so are three brothers. Myles was killed in the second battle. Henri was fatally wounded, and we had to leave him in the vehicle we destroyed last night. While we were out, our captive murdered Eun."

The newcomers glanced at the screen, and Tudoro gestured to the table. "Sit down, Michael."

Angelo watched Michael sit opposite the priest.

"You've told us what you know. Now let me tell you what I've already shared with Reddick, Colum, Loreti, and Scioli. Monsignor Delecarte has suffered a stroke and is at death's door."

Angelo stiffened and saw Michael and Valeria do the same.

"The monsignor was not just our spiritual leader; he was also our treasurer. I don't think I need to specify where the funds came from that have kept the Brotherhood active for the last five decades. Monsignor Delecarte had hoped to bring me into a position where I would one day succeed him. Alas, politics have prevented that from happening, and now we're out of time. With the economy's collapse, we've lost most of our savings. Upon his death, Monsignor Delecarte's revenues and possessions will go to the church."

"We're broke?" Michael said.

"I'm afraid so."

"What about those rich men and women who contributed to our cause in the past?"

"They're all based in Europe. We were too successful in purging the continent of these unholy beasts. None of our friends seem to care what happens in the Americas."

The disbelieving look on Michael's face mirrored how Angelo felt.

"Are you shutting us down?"

Tudoro shook his head. "No. At least, not yet. But the clock is ticking."

"How long?"

"I'm still trying to secure funds. I haven't given up, but this is an expensive operation—intelligence, transportation, expenses, the modest sums we've banked for each of you . . ."

Michael lowered his voice. "How long, Father?"

"You have maybe one month to wrap up your assignment here, if that's what you choose to do, then another month to go underground."

*Eight weeks*, Angelo thought. "And what will we do then? We've trained for this our whole lives. We don't know how to do anything else."

"All good soldiers face the same predicament," Tudoro said. "I will of course find work for everyone in this room, either with the church or with one of our satellite organizations. Safe work out of the public eye. Consider it an early retirement."

"I will not spend my days gardening on church property while this country is home to our enemy," Michael said. "I pledged my life to our cause."

"I appreciate that," Tudoro said. "But we have to be realistic. There is a time for everything, and the time has come for the Brotherhood to become dormant, perhaps to rise again another day."

"What about the money intended for Myles, Henri, and Eun? That could keep us going for a while."

"That money was placed in numbered Swiss bank accounts, just like yours. And just like you, each of them changed their passwords. That money is lost, never to be recovered."

"The Brotherhood's existed for centuries. I can't believe it will come to an end because of money."

"Michael, other than myself, you're the oldest person here—too old to be so naïve regarding finances. Perhaps I'll succeed in finding another benefactor one day. If that happens, I'll issue the call for each of you to return to service. In the meantime, you must carry on with your lives. It's not too late for you to marry and have children."

"Will we keep our swords?"

Tudoro seemed to think on the question. "I'll allow you to keep your Blades, but only on the condition that upon your deaths, they'll be returned to a secret foundation for safekeeping."

Michael smiled. "This secret foundation will remain in operation, but you can't continue to fund the war?"

"There are always secret foundations and men to run them."

"Forgive me, Father," Valeria said, "but why now? If you'd told us this even a week earlier, Myles, Henri, and Eun would still be alive."

"A week ago, Monsignor Delecarte was in good health," Tudoro said. "A week ago, there was no reason to believe that the months of planning for this operation were in jeopardy."

"Bureaucracies," Michael said with contempt.

"You're correct. Bureaucracies run the world. They rise and they fall, just like the Roman Empire. And men like you and I do as we're told." Tudoro looked around the table. "I didn't expect any of you to take this news well. Colum, Reddick, and Loreti agreed to come here to provide you with necessary support for this operation."

"We've trained for this too," Reddick said.

"I'd regret it for the rest of my life if I never got the chance to face our enemy," Colum said.

Angelo glanced at Loreti, who nodded.

"So you have your reinforcements," Tudoro said. "But under the circumstances, I feel compelled to allow you the chance to determine your own fates, something soldiers are rarely afforded. Do you continue this battle until it can be fought no more, or do you wish to shut down now? I'll think no less of you if that's the case."

Rising, Michael turned to each of his fellows. "Thanks to Father Tudoro, I was raised with one goal in life: to slay the beasts who roam this earth. I've done that with relish and dedication, and I've risen through the ranks. I still have plenty of fight left in me. I'm not ready to lay down my sword and retire to the country. I say we fight. That bitch in there may not have provided us with the information we wanted, but we know who Gabriel and Raphael Domini are—*what* they are. There's still work to be done and comrades to be avenged."

"Aye," Angelo said. He looked at Valeria, expecting her to be indecisive.

"I made a vow to Father Tudoro," she said in a slow cadence. "I intend to keep it."

Michael turned to the newcomers. "We have three Blades on the wall and three apprentices who wish to serve our cause. Stand up if you'll wield these holy weapons with honor."

Angelo felt pride swell his chest when Loreti rose first, followed by Colum and Reddick at almost the same time. Michael removed Myles's Blade and presented it to Loreti with both hands, then gave Henri's Blade to Colum and Eun's to Reddick. Each apprentice admired his silver weapon.

"Welcome to the Brotherhood of Torquemada," Michael said.

# CHAPTER TWENTY-NINE

Emerging from Starbucks with a tall latte, Cheryl stopped and watched a pair of National Guards with M-16s climb out of a troop transport truck across the street and take up positions near the corner. She had seen other weekend warriors stationed around the neighborhood.

"It looks familiar, doesn't it?"

She turned at the sound of the voice. A paunchy middle-aged man with blond hair stood a few feet away. He wore a brown shirt open at the neck and a tan corduroy sports jacket beneath a gray wool coat, a maroon scarf hanging around his neck. She knew him: Carl Rice, the author of *Rodrigo Gomez: Tracking the Full Moon Killer* and *The Wolf Is Loose: The True Story of the Manhattan Werewolf*. His hair appeared disheveled, but she gave him the benefit of the doubt that this was due to the wind rather than poor grooming.

"Hello, Carl. Yes, it does."

"Two years ago. How time flies."

"Fancy just bumping into you on the street like this on the day I'm scheduled to interview Rodrigo Gomez."

"Congratulations on landing that choice assignment, by the way." He shook a cigarette loose from a pack and lit it. "He won't talk to me anymore."

"Imagine that."

"Yeah." He offered her an amused smile, then a cigarette.

"No, thank you."

"How did you pull it off?"

"He asked for me."

Carl exhaled smoke. "It just fell into your lap?"

"I prefer to think that Rodrigo appreciated my coverage of his exploits and trial."

"As opposed to my coverage?"

Now it was Cheryl's turn to smile. "You sensationalized everything."

Not only did Carl smile, but his eyes twinkled. "And I made a killing."

"Congratulations. It was nice seeing you again. I think I mean that." She headed in the direction of the studio.

Carl fell into step beside her. "So how did you like the movie?"

"It was entertaining—for fiction."

"You know how they exaggerate everything for TV."

"Your book exaggerated everything too."

"Connie Roberts made you look like a babe, though, didn't she?"

"I bet no one has ever called you charming."

"No, I don't think they have. I've been called a lot of other things, though."

Cheryl sipped her latte. "I'm sure."

"How's your husband?"

"Why do you ask?"

"I saw him on TV last night at the scene of that car explosion. Last I knew, he was walking the doggies at Floyd Bennett Field. It's weird to see him back in action, especially since the stiff in that vehicle may have been tied to the group that abducted Rhonda Wilson and toasted those two houses."

"I hadn't heard that."

"It's almost like they pulled Tony out of storage for some big case that only he has insight into. It's a great angle after the Manhattan Werewolf debacle. You know, redemption and all that. People love it when a former hero makes a comeback."

"He'll always be my hero. I think he'll always be yours too. I bet you'd love to write another book with him in the lead role."

"Well, he did kind of let me down in the last one, but let's get back to Rodrigo Gomez. Can you get me into Sing Sing tonight?"

Cheryl felt amused. "Why on God's green earth would I try?"

"For old times' sake?"

"We never had old times. All I've ever done was turn down your interview requests."

"*The Wolf Is Loose* sold well, but the development of the movie is stalled. The studio execs say it needs a third act, and no one can decide what that should be. One yutz they hired to write the screenplay included a real werewolf, and another had your husband solving the case instead of getting yanked from it. Hollywood's crazy like that. Anyway, I need to make a living."

"I thought you made a bundle off those books, plus the TV rights to *Tracking the Full Moon Killer*."

"Hey, I've got alimony to pay."

"You were married? I'm impressed."

Carl raised two fingers and wiggled them. "Both times it was love at first sight over tequila."

"You *are* charming. I'm sure the tabloids will welcome you back into their fold with open arms."

"Can I be honest with you? I don't want to do that. It would be a step down. But if you can get me into that interview tonight, just as an observer—"

Cheryl stopped and faced him. "What? You'll write a book about it?"

"Okay, hear me out. A new book, tying Rodrigo Gomez and the Manhattan Werewolf together."

"I don't see the connection."

"Why, Cheryl, your husband is the connection."

She cocked her head. "I'm flattered by your sudden reappearance in my life and your interest in me and my career and my husband and his career, but this conversation is over. I hope you enjoy my interview." She resumed her trek.

Carl appeared at her side again. "Okay, forget about

getting me in. A guy's got to try, right? How about asking Rodrigo one question—*one question!*—on my behalf? You don't even have to give me credit. I just want to know the answer, and so will you when you hear the question."

Cheryl stopped. "What question?"

"Ask Rodrigo why it was that your husband paid him a visit when he was in the heat of the Manhattan Werewolf case. What was so important that Tony Mace needed to see the Full Moon Killer when he was hunting the Manhattan Werewolf? It was on your husband's last day in homicide before they suspended him and yanked him off the case. *There's* your connection."

He might have still been talking, but she had tuned him out. If Tony had interviewed Gomez in connection with the Manhattan Werewolf, why had he kept it a secret from her?

The entire task force sat around the conference room table. Landry, Shelly, and Norton worked from laptops, and Mace sat at the end of the table closest to the conference room door, facing the PowerPoint presentation screen. Digital video footage with a date and time stamp showed a man descending concrete stairs.

"Candice obtained this security cam footage from the Thirty-third Street PATH station." Controlling the image from his laptop, Landry froze the picture. "See the long coat?" He zoomed in on the man's feet. "He's also wearing combat boots." He tabbed up to a close-up of the man.

"And his nose is bandaged. The time was twenty-four minutes before that SUV exploded."

Landry struck a key, and the image switched to a man and a woman walking down another flight of steps. The man had his arm around the woman. "Same station, different stairway, five minutes later. These two are both wearing long coats too, similar to the first man's, but not identical." He zoomed in on the man's feet. "The man is wearing combat boots." He tabbed over to the woman's feet. "And so is the woman."

"Why wear long coats?" Candice said. "Besides the obvious answer—the weather—the other one is to carry around swords without anyone seeing them."

Mace turned to Willy. "Do you recognize any of them?"

Willy frowned. "I wish I could say yes, but the lights were off. All I had was a little flashlight, and they were wearing night vision goggles. The coats look right, and maybe if the woman's hair was in a ponytail . . ."

"We're circulating screen captures to law enforcement and antiterrorist agencies around the globe," Landry said. The image showed the first man standing alone at the far end of a train platform. "Here's the first man." Another image showed the man and the woman chatting at another end of the platform near stairs. "And here's our happy couple." The image switched back to the man. "The man with the bandaged nose boards the train." From the second angle, the couple boarded the train as well. "And so does the couple. Different cars, same train."

The image changed to that of the train pulling into another platform. "Here we are in Newark, New Jersey. Same train." The couple got off the train. "There's our couple." The man with the bandaged nose walked in the same direction. "And there's our independent operator." Another view showed all three people exiting the station.

"We're trying to find additional surveillance footage in Newark to point us in a more specific direction," Shelly said.

The image on the screen changed to a street view. "This footage was taken a block away from the PATH station on Thirty-third Street in Manhattan," Willy said. He zoomed in on a silver SUV parked between two vehicles. "That's our SUV." Three figures garbed in long dark coats got out, their features difficult to discern. "And here's our trio." The figures walked away, leaving the frame. The footage sped up, then slowed down. Willy zoomed out again. "Half an hour later . . ." A fireball consumed the vehicle and caused the image to flare.

"Good work," Mace said. "Newark seems like the place to be. But what part of Newark? As far as we know, they've driven a vehicle for every one of their missions. That means they passed through tollbooths."

"Do you want us to start looking for churches in Newark?" Norton said.

"No, I don't think so. They need a place where they can keep vehicles, a place that accommodates at least four people, who come and go as they please, with plenty of ordinance. Presumably, somewhere they can keep Rhonda Wilson captive without anyone knowing it."

"A warehouse," Willy said. "Or an abandoned building."

"Outer Newark's lousy with both," Candice said.

"Let's get everyone a map of Newark and its surrounding areas," Mace said.

An enlarged fingerprint filled the screen.

"This is the print Hector lifted off the hand at the scene," Landry said. "We're running it through international databases."

"Maybe I can expedite that search," Norton said in a frosty tone.

"That would be helpful." Landry turned to Mace. "A secretary from the Vatican got back to me. According to him, Monsignor Delecarte purchased that broken half of the Blade of Salvation from Terrence Glenzer two years ago. It was a personal purchase and wasn't made on behalf of the Vatican. But when Delecarte dies, all his property becomes the property of the church—and he just suffered a severe stroke. At the moment, he can't communicate."

Mace grunted. "Was your contact able to confirm if that Blade is still in Delecarte's possession?"

"No, he didn't have an inventory."

"What else?"

No one spoke up.

"Okay. Willy and Karol, I want you to go back to the funeral home and keep an eye on it. With Raphael lying low, Gabriel is still the Torquemadans' only target that we know about. Now that the governor's called in the National Guard again, we'll see how that impacts our investigation."

As everyone cleared out, Mace went into his office and closed the door. Sitting at his desk, he took out his cell phone.

Riding alone in the backseat of Micah's taxi, Gabriel felt his cell phone vibrating. Checking the phone's display, he saw Mace's name.

"This is Gabriel," he said into the phone.

"You pulled a disappearing act on me last night."

"It was a necessary precaution. I need to keep my location a secret and can't afford to be followed."

In the front seat, Micah glanced at Gabriel in the rearview mirror, then returned his attention to the road.

"Tell your people they're wasting their time in Manhattan," Mace said. "We have strong evidence that suggests the Torquemadans are holed up in New Jersey, possibly Newark. There are at least three more besides the guy who turned to toast last night."

Gabriel raised his eyebrows. "Thank you for the information."

"I gave it to you in good faith. If you find them, call me."

"I can't promise cooperation from anyone but myself."

"Understood."

Gabriel hung up on Mace. Scratching one thigh, he called Raphael.

"What is it?" Raphael sounded tense.

"Where are you?"

"Where do you think? I'm hunting the enemy."

"What if I told you the Torquemadans aren't in Manhattan?"

Raphael paused. "I'd tell you to consider the source of your information carefully."

"And if I narrowed your search perimeter?"

"Why would you do that?"

"I want them caught as badly as you do. I just don't want the whole pack exposed and endangered in the process."

"Where are they?"

Gabriel looked out the window at the buildings they passed. "Swear to me that if you find them based on my information, you'll contact me with their exact location and allow me to try my method first."

"We could lose them . . ."

"I know you won't allow that to happen. You're only to get involved if there's no other option."

Gabriel heard Raphael draw in his breath and exhale. "All right, I swear."

"They're in Jersey. Start your search in Newark."

Raphael wasted no time hanging up on him.

"Can I say something?" Micah said.

"*Please.*" *You're the only confidant I have at the moment.*

"I've already heard mutterings about this situation with Raphael. I don't like it. He's calling everyone to join him. I don't know if anyone's agreed, but the pack can't afford to fracture right now."

Gabriel sighed. "You're afraid divisions will form because Wolves perceive me as being weak."

"Let's just say there's a feeling out there that Raphael's doing something while you're running in circles. If he finds the Torquemadans and kills them, you're handing him the victory he needs to challenge your leadership."

*He's not there yet, even with Elias coaxing him along.*

"Thank you for your candor. Raphael's still my brother. He's served me well. I have faith in his loyalty."

"I hope you're right," Micah said without conviction. "I've got your back no matter what."

"I appreciate that." Gabriel's phone vibrated, and he saw that he had received a text from Karol Williams: *Start looking in Newark.* He closed his hands around the phone. Mace's entire team must have known the general vicinity of the Torquemadans' base. At least he knew Mace wasn't trying to distract him with a wild-goose chase.

# CHAPTER THIRTY

**M**"om, when will we be there?"

Melissa looked over her shoulder at Damien. "Soon, if we don't get lost."

"We're not getting lost," Arick said behind the wheel.

Gareth sat up and blinked. "Wow."

Deep forest unspoiled on either side of the highway.

*It's so beautiful*, Melissa thought. She and Arick had spelled each other at the wheel, stopping for meals, bathroom breaks, and an occasional view of the Ontario, Canada, scenery.

"Are you guys hungry?" she said.

"We just ate," Gareth said. "That's what made me nap."

"She wants you to nap again," Damien said.

A sign appeared in the distance.

"Hudson Bay," Arick said. "We should be only ten minutes away."

And then what? Melissa wondered. How long would she and the boys have to stay with Angela before Gabriel summoned them home?

Arick got off at an exit and took a side road on the left. The trees grew denser.

"Mom, does Aunt Angela have cable?" Damien said.

"I don't know. I don't even know if she has a television."

*"What?"* the boys said in unison.

"How are we going to play our video games?" Gareth said.

"Be glad you brought your handheld games," Arick said. "But I hope you brought a lot of batteries."

Damien slapped his forehead. "I never want to leave New York again . . ."

"It's beautiful here," Melissa said. "This will be good for both of you; I can feel it."

Arick slowed to a stop. A wooden gate for a driveway had been left open with a piece of paper tied to it. "Wait here." He got out, untied the string around the paper, read the note, and returned to the car.

"What does the note say?" Melissa said.

"To shut the gate." He pulled forward, got out, swung the gate closed, latched it, and got back in.

"Why did you have to do that?" Gareth said.

"Because Aunt Angela likes her privacy," Melissa said as the car rolled forward.

Melissa had always liked Angela, even though she disapproved of her breaking the pack's rules and mating with the human John Stalk. She had found Angela's unofficial excommunication from the pack a harsh punishment, though she understood why Angus and then Gabriel had found it necessary to be harder on their own blood than they would have been on unrelated pack members; appearances meant everything in politics. After Stalk had been murdered by a rogue Wolf, Angela had turned her back on the pack and its rules. Now Melissa had to impose on her to take them in.

*For the safety of the children*, she thought.

The road grew steep, and they moved uphill. The boys looked around in wonder.

"Does Aunt Angela own *all* this land?" Damien said.

"I don't know," Melissa said.

A cabin appeared at the top of the hill. Then another and another after that. When they reached the top, she counted six in all.

"Some kind of closed down camp," Arick said. "There's smoke rising from that chimney."

He drove them toward the farthest cabin. A black truck sat parked in the dirt driveway. They got out, and Melissa peered at the blue haze in the distance, rising from the lake beyond the trees.

The cabin's front door opened, and a woman stepped out. She wore hiking boots, faded blue jeans, and a red flannel shirt, her dark hair short.

"Looking for me?" Angela said.

Standing outside the loading bay, Valeria watched Angelo drive off in the SUV with Tudoro beside him. "I don't think I'll ever see him again."

"You mean you didn't buy his story about summoning us to duty again?" Michael said.

"I don't know." She turned to him. "What do you have planned? Even if we had more time, law enforcement agencies have got to be closing in on us."

"You're right. It's different here than it is in Italy, France, or Germany. Everything in New York is so . . . concentrated. It may have been a mistake for Tudoro to send us here just because this is where the largest pack roams."

"What will we do?"

"I'm not going to leave the status quo in place. We need to make a big move, something that will expose the beasts for what they are. Then the Americans can fight them while we regroup."

"I'm nervous about fighting with the apprentices," Valeria said.

"They aren't apprentices anymore. And don't forget you were one not long ago."

"They haven't seen any action before, and there are three of them. One half of our number . . ."

"I know. We'll have to pair up with them."

A droning sound overhead caused them to look up. A helicopter soared in the distance, a searchlight sweeping the area.

"Let's park the vehicles in less conspicuous places," Michael said.

Rhonda sat in the corner of her cell, flexing the muscles that had grown back in her severed arm. Every time she assumed

Wolf Shape and the longer she remained in that form, the more her stump grew. She wondered how long it would be before the Torquemadans noticed. They had not visited her since the night before when they had tranquilized her and removed the body parts of the woman she had killed and her Blade of Salvation. Perhaps they feared her now.

*Good.*

She wanted to kill them all, and she hoped she got her chance, but she suspected time was running out for her, and she wondered how her enemies would seek to destroy her. She had enjoyed killing the woman and feasting on her. Her belly remained full, so she did not care that they hadn't fed her yet today.

Hopefully she would feed again soon enough . . .

Mace studied a map of Newark when Landry entered.

"Tony, can you step into the conference room? Shelly and Norton have something on that print."

Mace rose and followed Landry into the conference room, where Candice waited with the federal agents. The face of a black man with a shaved head filled the screen.

"Meet Henrique Marcellus," Norton said. "The owner of the hand you found last night and presumably the corpse that burned in the explosion. Mr. Marcellus was twenty-eight. He was born in Saint-Gaultier, a village in France. When he was seven, his parents died of drug overdoses on the same night—bad heroin. Henrique was made a ward of the church, which placed him in a foster home until he was old enough for boarding school. After graduating high school, he went largely off the grid: no additional education, no jobs . . . but a lot of traveling. He spent a great deal of time in Rome, France, and Greece. He arrived here three weeks ago . . . and hasn't turned up since."

"His story seems similar to Pedro Fillipe's," Mace said. "Run a comparison check on them."

"We already did," Shelly said. "The priest who placed Marcellus in foster care and boarding school was named Jonas Tudoro. He also placed Fillipe with *his* foster parents and boarding school."

"What else?"

"Tudoro has an extensive travel history. He's some sort of floating ambassador for the Vatican . . . assigned to Monsignor Delecarte."

"Can we find out how many other orphans Tudoro placed with foster families and in boarding schools?"

"We're already working on it," Candice said.

"And we'll keep digging," Norton said.

Mace glanced at his watch. It was already almost 4:00 PM.

*Only four more hours until Cheryl's interview*, he thought.

# CHAPTER THIRTY-ONE

Willy sat watching the funeral home from the passenger seat of Karol's SUV, which Karol had parked closer than they had been the day before. A thick man in a leather jacket exited the business, and a few minutes later a woman in a purple coat entered. People had visited Gabriel inside one at a time, staying for less than half an hour. Karol identified each person to Willy as a member of the council for the Greater Pack of New York City: Wolves.

"Why is he meeting with them one-on-one? It's taking all day."

"I don't know. I'm not a council member, and I'm not Gabriel's confidante."

*No, you're just his spy,* Willy thought.

"I imagine he's reassuring them. Word on the grapevine is that Raphael's got his eyes on the seat at the head of the table."

"Like the mafia."

"Only we're not criminals."

"What about babies?"

"What about them?"

"Could I get you pregnant?"

"It's possible but unlikely—as long as I'm human when we mate."

Willy grunted. "You'd better always *be* human when we do it. A surprise like that could traumatize me for life. There are laws against that kind of thing too. So, how would the baby come out looking? Normal?"

"If you mean like you, then yes. I was born in human form, like my mother before me and her mother before her. It's my natural state, so any cubs I birth will appear human. That's one of the reasons why we have laws against interspecies procreation: we're an endangered species, so our women are supposed to produce Wolves. As unlikely as it is that you and I could produce, it's even less likely that a child of ours will be able to Change."

"I'm sorry to disappoint you."

She slid her hand onto his leg. "You can't help it that you're only human."

"Yeah, I'm just as God made me. What about you? Do you believe in heaven?"

Karol looked at him. "I'm an atheist. Does that bother you?"

"No, I can deal. Are all of your people going to hell?"

She smiled. "Do all of your people believe the same thing?"

"No."

"The most common religion among my people—I'm

talking about American Wolves—is that there's a spirit world and a grand creator. We don't believe we're created in the creator's image because he *has* no image. Many of us believe that we're descended from gods, we'll be reunited with our ancestors when we pass on, and we'll be treated like gods when we arrive."

"Wow, talk about a superiority complex."

"The Indians worshipped us. That sort of thing can go to your head."

"I could buy you as a goddess."

"Thank you."

"Why don't you follow that religion if it's so common?"

"My parents believe it. So does my sister. I guess every family has a dissenting member."

"What makes you so special?"

"I guess because I think I'm *not* special."

"Lady, you turned into a werewolf and saved my life from another werewolf. That makes you the most unique person I've ever met."

Karol looked at the funeral home. "I've been Changing ever since I got my first period. It was a pretty scary time. I'm no different from any other female of my species. If we were gods, we wouldn't have to hide among your people. If the European Wolves were gods, they'd still be alive today. And if a creator exists, why would he allow us to face genocide?"

Willy sighed. "Those are deep thoughts."

"My people are vanishing. All of us face fertility issues. It's a matter of evolution."

"And if you have my baby?"

"It will be one more step toward our eventual disappearance."

"You're dour, you know that? I'm talking about a little baby, the most beautiful thing in the world."

"I'd love to have your baby. If I do, I'll be happy. But a baby from you would likely continue your species, not mine, if we can produce one at all."

Willy's cell phone went off. He checked the phone's display, then took the call. "What is it, Ken?"

"Get downtown right away. Synful Reading just blew up."

"*Ay, caramba.* Copy that." Hanging up, he turned to Karol. "Put on your siren, kid. It looks like another brick-and-mortar bookstore went down for the count."

Karol's expression slackened. "Synful Reading?"

"Yeah."

She picked up her magnetized strobe light and rolled down her window, then hesitated.

"What's wrong? Let's roll."

"What if it's a setup? We go to a crime scene where we can't do anything anyway, and the Brotherhood marches in here and takes out Gabriel."

Willy glanced at the funeral home. "Shit."

Setting down the strobe, Karol took out her cell phone.

"Now what are you doing?"

"I'm warning Gabriel."

"The hell you are."

"It's not violating protocol to tell the man his bookstore just blew up."

Willy watched her face grow concerned as she waited for Gabriel to answer.

"Come on; come on."

Then the ground shook, and the windows and glass doors of the funeral home shattered.

"Get down!" Willy threw himself over Karol, shielding her from the blast. He pulled the lever between the seat and the door, and the seat dropped into the reclining position. Unable to see the explosion, Willy heard a deafening roar. The alarm in the SUV went off even before its windows shattered and debris rained down on the vehicle, denting it and shaking it from side to side. Outside, other alarms went off, a cacophony of electronic screams that drowned out the shrieks of men and women. Within seconds, brownish-gray smoke enveloped the SUV.

Warden Strand and two uniformed corrections officers led Cheryl, Colleen, Stan, Ryan, Paul, and Alex down a windowless corridor of the prison. They passed other guards holding rifles and numerous security cameras before Strand punched a code into a keypad and unlocked a door.

"After you," the man said.

Although the warden had waived several security precautions in giving them the VIP treatment, Cheryl still found the experience unsettling. She thought the thick walls and steel bars of Sing Sing were far more oppressive than she had ever imagined.

*Maximum security*, she reminded herself.

They entered a wide room with a low ceiling. A single table with two chairs occupied the center of the room, with two more tables pushed against the walls. A Plexiglas window five feet high stretched from one end of the far wall to the other, offering a view of a room with several unoccupied chairs. A shudder ran down Cheryl's arms as she realized where they stood.

"This is where they kept the electric chair until '72," Strand said. "Six hundred and fourteen people were executed here, including Julius and Ethel Rosenberg. Did you know New York was the first state to use an electric chair?"

"No, I didn't," Cheryl said.

"We rank third in the nation in terms of the highest number of executions since 1608. I bet you can guess who ranks first."

"Don't mess with Texas," Colleen said.

"Fifty years ago, this interview would have been impossible."

Cheryl looked through the viewing window. "What's Gomez like as an inmate, Warden?"

"This is a maximum security prison, so there's no such thing as a model prisoner. They're all worse than animals. Gomez is no different in that respect. In other ways . . . well, he's more disturbing. He's a small man, but it's safe to say the other inmates are frightened of him. He keeps to himself and reads a lot, but the others give him a wide berth. He's been involved in many incidents during the time he's been here, usually because someone challenged him. If there's a Wild West mentality here, he's the meanest gunslinger we have."

"Will you repeat that on camera?" Colleen said.

"I'd be happy to."

*He probably rehearsed that*, Cheryl thought. Still, Colleen knew to keep him enthused. "Is there a room I can use to make myself up?"

"There's a small office down the hall. The guards will have to escort you."

"That's fine."

The sound of the old RKO radio signal filled the room, and Colleen answered her phone. "What? You've got to be fucking kidding me. Have we got both locations covered? . . . All right, let me know when we have it on the air. I'll watch it on my phone." She faced Cheryl. "Two separate explosions in Manhattan: the Synful Reading bookstore and the Domini Funeral Home."

"Oh, shit." Cheryl took out her cell phone.

Candice drove her SUV out of the Fifth Precinct parking lot with its strobes flashing and siren wailing. Sitting beside her, Mace called Cheryl, who answered on the first ring.

"Are you all right?" she said. "I was just calling you."

"I'm fine. I take it you found out." He had to shout to be heard over the siren.

"Just now. Was anyone hurt?"

"I don't have any details yet. I'm heading to the bookstore now."

"This is insane. What fucking country do we live in?"

"Take it easy. You've probably already guessed, but there's no way I can make it out there."

A pause. "That's okay. I didn't want you here anyway."

"Is Warden Strand with you, by any chance?"

"Yes, he is."

"Put him on, please." Mace heard Cheryl say something away from the phone.

A moment later, Warden Strand came on. "Yes, Captain Mace?"

"Warden, I assume you'll be present when my wife interviews Gomez?"

"I'll be watching from the adjacent viewing room, but I'll have two armed guards in here, and Gomez will be secured to his chair."

"Make it four armed guards."

"As you wish."

"I know Gomez better than anyone." *Maybe better than he knows himself.* "He's a sick fuck, and he's full of surprises. I want you to tell your men that if he makes one wrong move, they're to shoot him in the head."

A moment of silence followed. "If Mrs. Mace is in any danger, we'll follow protocol—"

"*In the fucking head*, do you hear me?" Mace thought he heard Strand swallow.

"I understand."

"Put my wife back on."

A moment later, Cheryl got on the line. "Yes?"

"You're in good hands, so don't be nervous. I want you to do me one favor, though: if Gomez tries anything at all— I don't care if he wants to scare you or if he just sneezes— get the hell away from him as fast as you can. It's imperative that the guards have a clear shot at him."

"But don't be nervous, right?"

"Right."

"I love you."

"I love you too. Avoid Lower Manhattan and Midtown when you go home. Traffic will be a nightmare." Mace shut his phone down. In the distance, black smoke rose into the sky.

"Your wife's a brave lady," Candice said.

"I know it."

"I sure wouldn't want to be in a room with Gomez, even surrounded by guards with orders to shoot to kill."

Candice didn't know that Rodrigo Gomez was a closet Wolf, and Mace couldn't help but think of the night Janus Farel killed Patty.

Sirens grew louder, and soon Candice turned onto St. Mark's Place, and Mace saw police cars and fire engines. Traffic slowed to a standstill.

"Take the sidewalk," Mace said.

Candice searched for an opening. "I can't get up there until we reach an intersection."

"Then I'll get out here." Mace opened the door and hopped out. Stepping onto the sidewalk, he broke into a light jog. When he reached a gathering of uniformed POs, he showed them his ID and kept moving. Car alarms rang around the street as firefighters blasted the burning buildings on either side of the fire where Synful Reading had stood with water from their hoses. Smoke billowed out of the rubble that had once been the small storefront where Mace had first encountered Angela Domini.

"The windows are blown out of buildings on both sides of the street," a male voice said behind Mace.

Turning, he saw Shelly and Norton. *You two made good time.*

"Probably C-4, maybe on a timer," Shelly said.

Mace looked up and down the street. POs held civilians back, and people with grime-smeared faces wept as an ambulance crept forward. "I want you two to stay here. Landry's back at base, and Candice is making her way over. She and I need to get to the funeral parlor and check on Diega and Williams. Let's regroup at base."

Norton surveyed the destruction. Somewhere behind them, a child cried. "Whatever you say, Captain."

Mace climbed into Candice's SUV, which had made little progress. "I'm glad I didn't wait in here."

"What's it like?" Candice said.

"No apparent casualties. Let's get over to the other scene."

"Oh, this is going to be fun."

As Candice pulled out of her lane and maneuvered into the opposite direction, Mace saw two National Guard jeeps heading their way. Forty minutes later, when they reached East Thirty-third Street, he saw that the neighborhood had been cordoned off by olive-green troop transport trucks.

"What should I do?" Candice said.

"Double-park here. This time we're both walking."

As they went up Thirty-third Street, Mace felt a chill, and it wasn't from the weather. Memories of past terrorist attacks on the city lingered in his memory. *We've got to stop these guys soon.*

A mixture of a dozen POs and National Guards stood at the wooden barricades that had been erected near the explosion scene. Mace noted four fire engines, four ambulances, two troop transport trucks, two jeeps, and six police cars. Black smoke filled the sky, and light gray concrete and dust covered the street. All the vehicles that had been parked in the vicinity of the funeral home had suffered damage, and several that must have been moving on the street at the time of the explosion had crashed.

A gaping hole in the middle of the block, where the funeral parlor had stood, revealed the buildings on the other side of the block. The wall that had separated the courtyard now resembled the brick ruins left standing in Italy after World War II. Strobes from multiple emergency vehicles cast dizzying blue and red light over the scene from different angles.

As Mace and Candice passed an ambulance, Mace saw Willy sitting inside the back of the vehicle with his legs hanging over the edge. One of two paramedics administered oxygen to him, and Karol stood beside them.

Mace clasped Willy's shoulder. "Are you all right?"

Willy nodded.

"You should have seen him in action, Captain," Karol said. "He ran into the street, waving his little flashlight through the smoke, directing civilians away from the scene. He practically cleared the area single-handedly."

Willy pointed at Karol. "And you saved my ass again."

"What are partners for?"

Mace could not remember the first time that Karol had saved Willy's ass. "Does he need to go to the ER?"

"They should both get checked out," one of the paramedics said.

Willy shook his head. "I'm fine . . ."

"I'll take him," Karol said.

"Then that's the plan," Mace said. "Exactly what happened?"

"We got the call from Landry to head down to Synful Reading," Karol said. "But I wanted to notify Domini first. I was still waiting for him to answer the phone when the building exploded. Willy threw himself on top of me a second before my SUV's windows blew into the car. Who knows what would have happened to me."

Mace studied Willy's sweat-soaked features. "Good work, Lieutenant."

Willy nodded his humble thanks.

"What about Gabriel?"

With a dazed expression, Karol shook her head. "He never made it out."

*Damn it,* Mace thought.

# CHAPTER THIRTY-TWO

When Mace and Candice entered the task force squad room, covered head to toe in dust and grime, Shelly and Norton looked up from their desks. Both FBI agents had changed into more casual attire, and Mace wanted to do the same.

Landry came out of his office. "Karol called from the ER. Willy's being examined now."

Mace checked his watch. It was 7:45 PM. "Give us ten minutes to clean up, then let's meet in the conference room."

Mace went into his office and peeled off his jacket and tie. He reeked of the smell of burnt wood. In the men's room, he took off his shirt and scrubbed his face and arms with soap. He did not want to put his shirt back on, so he exited wearing his T-shirt.

Joining his team in the conference room, he turned on

the TV, which was already set to Manhattan Minute News, and muted the volume. On the screen, Michael O'Hear, a colleague of Cheryl's, addressed the camera from Thirty-third Street. Using a remote control, Mace verified that all the other channels were broadcasting coverage of the attacks as well. Images of smoky streets, destroyed cars and sidewalks, and National Guardsmen filled the screen. Mace returned to Manhattan Minute News, which showed Synful Reading burning.

"This is the biggest stotry in the world right now," Landry said. "Public Information has its hands full."

"Everyone has their hands full," Mace said.

"Shelly and I have been monitoring the transmissions and reports from other agencies," Norton said. "'No terror-ist group has claimed responsibility for the bombings' seems to be the mantra."

"I've seen the satellite photos," Shelly said. "Nothing suggests that a RPM was used at either site. Most likely, the explosives were planted in each location in advance."

*Jesus,* Mace thought. "That would mean your C-4—if that's what they used—was sitting in the bookstore all this time, and they planted some in the funeral parlor last night. In both instances, the explosives were right under our noses."

"No casualties have been reported, thank God," Landry said.

"Except for Gabriel," Mace said. "He was the target. If they wanted to kill civilians, they would have."

"Then why target Synful Reading? The store's been closed for days."

"It was a symbolic gesture," Shelly said. "Terrorists produce terror. The Brotherhood of Torquemada wanted to send a message to the Class Ls, and taking out Domini was only part of that message."

"They also want to keep law enforcement busy," Mace said. "Nothing distracts from existing investigations like bombings."

"You're right," Landry said. "Missing Persons has turned up no leads on Rhonda Wilson, and the rank and file are hot for blood because we've got cop killers running around out there."

Mace counted off points on his fingers. "They've created a panic. They've killed people the general public believes are civilians. They've killed cops. They've destroyed property. Their efforts have resulted in the governor sending in the National Guard. You would think they'd lie low for a few days, but if anything, they've only ramped up their efforts. They're sending a message to everyone in this city, not just the Class Ls, that they won't be deterred."

"There's no reason to believe they're aware this task force exists," Landry said. "As far as they're concerned, no one knows that the Brotherhood of Torquemada or the Class Ls exist."

"Except they know we had two detectives watching Gabriel last night. We stopped one of their operations. They must have realized Willy and Karol were back there today. Maybe they were sending a message to us by taking Gabriel out. The question is: What's their next move?"

Freshly coiffed and made up, Cheryl shook her hands. Ryan and Paul had set up their cameras on tripods and some lights on stands in the corners, and Alex manned a sound mixer at one of the tables. Two corrections officers with shotguns stood at attention on the side of the room where Cheryl intended to sit for the interview.

"I never thought I'd see the day you were nervous," Colleen said.

"I know I shouldn't be," Cheryl said. "I covered Gomez's killing spree and his trial. He was a big part of my life. This feels like the final chapter between us. I wonder if anyone will even watch with everything that's going on in the city."

"Don't worry about that. We don't control the news, no matter how hard we try. We're going to repeat this all week, so people *will* see it."

Strand entered the room with an armed guard. "Ms. Wanglund? It's time."

Colleen rubbed Cheryl's arm. "Honey, I'll be calling the shots from the next room. Don't worry about a thing. You'll do great."

Cheryl watched Colleen exit with Strand and the guard. A moment later, Colleen and Strand entered the viewing room on the other side of the glass and took their seats. Two monitors had been set up for Colleen, one for each camera. She put on a headset, and Cheryl saw her mouth moving, then heard a tiny transmitted voice in her ear: "Camera check."

"Camera one, check," Ryan said.

"Camera two, check," Paul said.

The guard who had escorted Colleen and Strand returned to the room and walked over to Alex, who stood with a wireless microphone in one hand.

"I'll be right back," Alex said. "I hope."

Cheryl watched the guard lead Alex through a steel door near the wide window. The door closed behind them with a clanging sound. Taking a deep breath, she sat at the metal table. From this vantage point, she saw her reflection in the window.

A minute later, Alex returned with the guard. "That is one creepy little fucker." Alex adjusted the wireless microphone on Cheryl's collar, then returned to his sound station.

The guard went into the corridor and closed the door.

Cheryl's stomach felt queasy. "Any new developments in the city?"

"There haven't been any more explosions, and I haven't had any reports of deaths yet," Colleen said.

"Thank God."

"I could live without seeing National Guards with machine guns everywhere."

The metal door swung open, and another guard entered the room, followed by a short man in an orange jumpsuit and another guard. As per Colleen's instructions, Paul panned his camera on its tripod, following Rodrigo Gomez to his seat.

Rodrigo's hair was long and greasy, and the fuzz that covered his chin and upper lip resembled thick black thread. His hands were cuffed before him, and a chain connected the cuffs to leg irons. The guards eased him into the chair, which Cheryl realized had been bolted to the floor. One guard handcuffed his wrists to the arms of the chair, and the other secured his ankles to the steel legs. The guards stood on either side of the viewing window with their shotguns lying over their arms. The whole time, Rodrigo stared at Cheryl.

Meeting his stare, Cheryl waited for Rodrigo to speak and tried not to look at his unibrow, which seemed bushier than it had at his trial.

Rodrigo glanced around the room at the guards and the crewmen, then over his shoulder at Colleen and Strand. Returning his attention to Cheryl, he spoke in a soft voice. "Well, well. Cheryl Mace. I guess it's just the two of us. But it was Cheryl Chimera back in the day, wasn't it?"

Cheryl relaxed a little. "Yes, it was."

"Where's Sheriff Mace?"

"All right, everyone, we're going live in five seconds," Cheryl heard Colleen say in her earpiece.

"Live in five," Ryan said.

"Just wait for me to speak," Cheryl said.

Rodrigo smiled, revealing crooked teeth. "Let's give the folks at home a good show."

"I'm sorry, but I have to watch this." Mace raised the volume on the TV as a wide shot of Sing Sing filled the screen and prerecorded audio of Cheryl introducing the special came over the speaker.

"We can watch it from our desks and keep working," Norton said in a diplomatic tone.

"I'll stay here if you don't mind," Landry said.

"Suit yourself," Mace said.

Seven minutes of documentary-style presentation detailed Rodrigo Gomez's killing spree and trial, including excerpts from Cheryl's news reports. The recap ended with footage of two corrections officers leading Gomez, chained, into a windowless room. The camera intercut the guards chaining Gomez to a chair with Cheryl watching from across the table.

"Now," Cheryl the narrator said as the camera zoomed into a close-up of Gomez, "I'll speak to Rodrigo Gomez, the Full Moon Killer, one-on-one in an exclusive Manhattan Minute News special conducted live from Sing Sing Correctional Facility."

When the camera cut back to Cheryl, the live feed kicked in.

*She looks nervous,* Mace thought.

"Rodrigo, you've been incarcerated for seven years," Cheryl said. "That works out to one year for each of the five women you murdered. Do you have any regrets?"

With a contemplative expression, Gomez drew in his breath and exhaled. "There's days when I wish I was on the outside, not locked up in here, so I guess you could say I regret that. But like I told your husband two years ago when he came to see me, I think it's a good thing that I'm in here and people on the outside are safe. Do I regret killing those broads?" A wide smile broke out across his face. "No, I had to do it. I had something inside me that I had to let out. When it finally came, it was like I came. I've never felt so free, so . . . *natural* in my life."

"Those women had family, friends, loved ones. You caused them immeasurable pain. Don't you feel bad about that?"

Gomez shrugged. "Do they feel bad about the pain in my life? A junkie for a mother with a creep boyfriend who raped my sister? I never asked for any of that."

"Do you blame your mother for what happened to you?"

"Nah. I understand it now. We were a lot alike. She dealt with it her way—crack—and I dealt with it mine."

"You mean murder."

"Murder, I don't know. Murder is when one human being kills another one, right? Unless it's during war or something. Well, I ain't human."

Mace sat up in his seat.

"What are you, then?"

Gomez leaned forward. "I'm a wolf, baby, a freaking werewolf, just like the Manhattan Werewolf. That's why Captain Anthony Mace came to see me: because he knew it too."

"Oh no," Landry said.

Mace glanced through the glass partition at Shelly and Norton, who both turned in their seats, their backs to him, to watch the interview on the TV mounted on the support column. He could tell Cheryl was fighting not to react.

"You . . . believe you're a werewolf?"

"Believe it? *I know it.* Just like I know there are thousands more like me across this great country of ours."

"How do you know that?"

Mace knew that Cheryl had to ask the obvious follow-up questions.

"Because another werewolf told me. See, there's an entire society out there that I never knew existed, a society that you and people like you don't even have a clue about. But I met this guy in here, and he recognized me for what I am. He knew exactly what I was going through. He understood my pain to a T, and he told me about the Greater Pack of New York City and smaller packs across the good old USA. He taught me how to get in touch with my inner self. Thank God for prison."

"So you and the Manhattan Werewolf were two of a kind?"

"You got it."

"Do you know what happened to him?"

Gomez hesitated. "I assume he's got to be dead. Your husband was gunning for him, right? I'm lucky he took me alive."

Mace covered his mouth with one hand.

"Let's talk about you, not my husband. I can talk to him anytime, but this is the only chance I may ever get to talk to you. Why did you request this interview?"

"Because the people out there have to know what's happening. This isn't about me, and it isn't about the Manhattan Werewolf. It's about werewolves *everywhere*. Your mailman could be one. Your sister could be one. Hell, you could even be one. Wouldn't that surprise Sheriff Mace?"

Cheryl looked even more uncomfortable. "What do these werewolves want?"

"How should I know? Don't you see? I didn't know I

was one of them until I got in here. I guess they want what everyone wants—more vacation time, more money, better behaved kids. I'll never know, because I'm never getting out of here. But I'll tell you this much: they're an endangered species, and they're getting more endangered every day. That's what's going on in the streets of New York right now. It's open season on werewolves. They're the ones getting killed by these terrorists."

"You mean the Lourdes and Wilson families?"

"Yeah, sure, them. Who do you think did that?"

"Why don't you tell me?"

"The Brotherhood of Torquemada. Look them up." Gomez stared straight at the camera. "They've been around for centuries. They wiped out the werewolves in Europe, and now they want to do the same thing here. This is all-out war."

"Holy shit," Landry said.

"The werewolf is out of the bag," Mace said.

His cell phone vibrated, and he checked its display: Jim Mint. Sighing, he took the call. "Yeah?"

"I take it you're watching TV right now," Mint said.

"Yes, I am."

"Have you violated your nondisclosure agreement?"

"No, I haven't discussed any of this with Cheryl, and I know Gomez insisted on not doing a preinterview with her. She had no idea what he had on his mind."

"Well, how the hell does he *know* all of this?"

"Maybe you should take him at face value."

"What, that he's a fucking werewolf?"

"We call them Class Ls around here."

"Jesus H., the shit is really going to hit the fan now. Gomez just blew the lid off everything and accused you of killing the Manhattan Werewolf."

"Let me call you back. I'm missing my show. We need to know what else Gomez says." Mace shut off his phone.

The camera cut back to Cheryl. "Can you prove to everyone who's watching right now that you're a werewolf?"

"You mean, like change right now on TV?"

"That's right. A picture is worth a thousand words, and a live broadcast is worth a thousand pictures. Prove to the audience that you're not just wasting their time with some Halloween story."

A slow smile spread across Gomez's features. "I can do that."

With trembling fingers, Mace looked up Warden Strand's phone number.

"But I'm not going to," Gomez said. "Turning into a werewolf on live TV would be stupid. I'd be signing my death warrant."

Mace's finger hovered above Send.

"When you stood trial, you claimed insanity as a defense, didn't you?" Cheryl said.

Gomez's smile faded. "Sure, I wanted to get off. Who wouldn't rather spend time in a loony bin than in a maximum security prison with a bunch of killers? I've got a heightened sense of smell. The animals in here stink."

"How do we know you're *not* crazy?"

"The court shrinks said I was sane. I stood trial, and now here I am."

Cheryl's voice tightened. "You butchered five women."

"*Butchered* is a strong word. I hunted them."

"And you ate parts of them. That's called cannibalism."

"I already told you I'm not human, so it wasn't cannibalism. It was one species of animal eating another. That's the natural order."

"And since you came to prison, you've been in numerous violent incidents, haven't you?"

"Who can blame me? I'm a caged animal."

"You bit off one man's nose and ate another man's fingers . . ."

Gomez moved as if he wanted to raise one hand to make a point and grew frustrated that his chains prevented him from doing so. "I see what you're trying to do, but it won't work. I'm not crazy. I'm a goddamned werewolf!"

"Don't they have staff psychiatrists here?"

Gomez's lips formed a snarl. "So what?"

"I think you need to get better acquainted with them."

Roaring, Gomez lunged at Cheryl, but the chains snapped him back. A reaction shot of Cheryl showed her eyes following movement to the left of Gomez. A reverse angle zoomed out to reveal two of the corrections officers aiming their shotguns at Gomez, who settled back with a snort, his hair disheveled.

"You bitch," he said. "You fucking bitch. If I ever get out of here, I swear I'll eat you alive."

Cheryl remained stoic. "You had the last word, Mr. Gomez. This interview is over. I doubt you'll ever be allowed to give another one. Thank you for your time."

Mace heard only silence over Cheryl's close-up, which meant that both microphones had been cut off. The picture shifted to B-roll footage of the exterior of the prison during daylight.

"She turned it around," Landry said with admiration in his voice.

*Good girl,* Mace thought.

# CHAPTER THIRTY-THREE

Cheryl watched the guards drag Gomez snarling out of the room. She waited until the door slammed shut before she rose on wobbling knees.

Ryan strode over to her and put one arm around her. "Are you okay?"

"Yes. That wasn't what I expected."

The door to the corridor burst open, and Colleen ran in, followed by Strand and the guard who had been waiting outside.

"Honey, I don't know what the hell that was, but you were dynamite."

"I didn't think it would get that crazy," Cheryl said. "I knew it would be sensational, but we just fed into the werewolf frenzy."

"Fed into it? We pushed it to a whole new level."

"I'm so sorry," Strand said.

"For what? You helped deliver gold to us."

Cheryl's cell phone vibrated, and she knew Tony was calling her. She took the phone out and pressed it to her ear. "I'm here."

"How do you feel?" Tony said.

"My hand is shaking."

"I bet it is."

"I never gave much thought to how it must have been for you when you arrested him."

"I had a gun in my hand. I felt fine."

"I'm glad I *didn't* have one in my hand."

"Do me a favor and get out of there, will you? Don't hang around to sign autographs."

"I'm leaving as soon as I can."

"You did well. I think you might have pulled my bacon out of the frying pan."

"I knew he'd bring you up, but—"

"Don't worry. Just be glad it's over. Now get home safely. I'll try to be waiting for you when you walk in."

"Okay." Cheryl hung up and looked at Colleen. "Can we please leave right now?"

Colleen cupped her hands over Cheryl's cheeks. "You bet your ass we can." She turned to Ryan. "We'll see you all back at the station. Warden, we're ready to take the express train out of here."

The prison gates rolled open, and Colleen drove her car

through them. "Whew, I don't ever want to set foot in there again," she said, glancing in the rearview mirror. "But it was worth it, wasn't it?"

"I guess so," Cheryl said.

"I detect a lack of enthusiasm."

"We didn't really get into any of the areas I wanted to explore."

"There was no way you could have expected him to go off on that tangent."

"He controlled the conversation, not me."

"You did what you had to and rolled with the punches. Besides, you grabbed him by the balls at the end and didn't let go. That's what people will remember."

"No, they'll remember that he claimed he was a werewolf and that my husband supposedly killed another werewolf."

"And an urban legend was born: Captain Anthony Mace, werewolf slayer. Do you think Tony will do a follow-up interview, or would that be too weird?"

Cheryl shook her head. "He won't do an interview with me or anyone else."

"Too bad. I remember when he was a media darling before he dropped off the map. This would be a great opportunity for him to make a comeback. Carl Rice made enough money off Tony's name. Maybe he should write his own book. You could write it together!"

"Tony's had enough of the limelight." *Maybe I have too.* "We didn't exactly fill the whole hour . . ."

"We've got plenty."

They drove through Ossining, then along the Hudson.

Colleen turned the radio on to a news station.

Cheryl saw her glancing into the rearview mirror. "Is something wrong?"

"The car behind us came out of nowhere, and it's moving fast."

Cheryl looked over her shoulder as the back window filled with light. Then Colleen's car screeched to a sudden stop, flinging Cheryl forward.

"What the hell?" Colleen said.

Cheryl saw a van idling in the street ahead of them, positioned perpendicular to the road and blocking their way. "Oh, my God."

Doors opened and closed, and silhouetted figures encircled the van from all sides.

Colleen activated the locks.

Cheryl's heart pounded in her chest. "Just get out of here. Run over them if you have to. Plow through that van!"

Colleen twisted the steering wheel to her left, but her window exploded in a shower of glass.

Cheryl recoiled, pressing herself against her door.

A figure wearing some sort of mask or goggles leaned in through Colleen's window and pressed a cloth over her mouth and nose. Colleen turned her panic-stricken eyes to Cheryl and reached toward her with an outstretched hand, fingers clawing air in desperation.

Cheryl grasped Colleen's hand, reassuring her despite the terror she felt.

Then the window behind her crashed apart, and gloved hands groped for her. She turned her head, evading the cloth she saw in one of her attacker's hands, but the figure jerked her head back and covered her mouth and nose with the wet rag. Colleen's eyelids fluttered and closed. Holding her breath and clawing at the arms of her attacker, Cheryl kicked out with her left leg, striking the steering wheel with her heel, and blasted the car horn.

Colleen pitched forward, and Cheryl had no choice but to suck in oxygen. The chemical in which the rag had been doused took immediate effect, burning her nostrils and clouding her mind. As she lost consciousness, she wondered who kept honking that damned car horn.

Karol pulled into the Fifth Precinct parking lot.

"You think we should stop by the office?" Willy said. The doctor at the ER had given him a clean bill of health.

"No. If we do, we'll never get out of there."

"Yeah, you're right. So your place or mine?"

"Neither. I'm exhausted. I need sleep. So do you."

"I'm tired but not *that* tired. My adrenaline's pumping."

"Save it for tomorrow. You're going to need it."

"Oh yeah?"

"For the *job*."

"All work and no play makes Detective Williams a dull werewolf."

"Look, if we're going to do this, you'd better get your terminology right. I'm a Wolf. We don't like to be called werewolves."

"Whatever you say." He leaned close for a kiss.

"Are you crazy? Not here, not now. Anyone could see us."

He sat back. "All right, be that way. We'll have this big secret romance. But someday the truth will come out. It always does."

"Good night."

"Good night." Willy exited the SUV, jogged across the lot, and got into his own vehicle. He noticed Karol hadn't left. Leaning forward, he saw her speaking on her phone.

*Interesting. With Gabriel dead, who could she be talking to?*

Karol drove away, and Willy started his engine.

Mace entered the house at 9:45 PM and loosened his tie. Anna sat at the dining room table, textbooks spread before her.

"I'm sorry I'm late," he said.

She smiled at him. "That's okay. I understand. I saw the news."

He pulled off his tie. "I thought your mother was going to relieve you?"

Anna closed her books. "She came up earlier. I didn't mind coming back. Patty's asleep."

"Great. We appreciate this."

"I also saw Mrs. Mace's interview. It was really disturbing."

"Wasn't it, though?" His cell phone vibrated, and he saw Candice's name on the display. "Excuse me." He pressed the phone against his ear. "Go, Candice."

"I just got a call from the police department in Ossining."

*Cheryl's been in a car accident,* he thought.

"Brace yourself: Cheryl's missing."

He felt as if someone had slammed him in the center of

his chest. "What do you mean?"

"The Manhattan Minute crew van discovered Colleen Wanglund's car parked on the side of a road with its windows broken and Wanglund inside. She appears to have been drugged. The first thing she did was ask what happened to Cheryl. Ossining PD is trying to put together a statement, but it looks like someone snatched your wife."

Feeling the blood rush from his head, Mace grabbed the back of a chair with his free hand to steady himself. "Where's the crime scene?"

Candice described the location. "Manhattan Missing Persons is there now. They want you to stay at your house in case someone calls about a ransom."

"There isn't going to be a ransom demand, just like there wasn't one for Rhonda Wilson. This is the Brotherhood's doing. Call Brooklyn PD and have them send four squad cars over here. I want one parked at each end of my street, stopping every vehicle and pedestrian that tries to come through. I want the other two in front of my house. Tell Landry to come here too. I need him to watch over my daughter and babysit the Missing Persons detectives."

"Landry's already on his way over. What about me? I want to help."

"The best thing you can do is monitor all relevant activity from there while you finish your shift."

"Okay, I'll stay in touch. You do the same thing."

"Right." Shutting off his phone, he turned to Anna. "I'm sorry, but I need you to stay here."

"Is Mrs. Mace all right?"

*She's going to hear about it on the news anyway.* "No. She's been abducted."

Anna scrunched up her face in fear. "By the Brotherhood of Torquemada?"

She had said she'd seen Cheryl's interview. "I don't know. The police are coming here. Everyone in the house will be safe. I won't leave until they arrive. Some detectives from Missing Persons are coming, and a friend of mine named Ken Landry. You can answer any questions they have, but don't speak to anyone else. Don't even answer the phone. Do what Ken says. If I need to speak to you, I'll call your cell phone."

"Yes, Captain."

Walking down the hall, Mace resisted the urge to scream or punch a wall. Years of holding leadership positions had taught him to control his emotions in front of other people, but this was too much. He went into Patty's room, flicked on the light, and stared at the sleeping toddler, so beautiful and precious. Lifting her into his arms, he cradled her.

"Don't worry. I'm going to bring your mother home."

Willy sat in his department issue SUV half a block away from Karol's building when his phone rang. He checked the display, expecting it to be Karol calling to ask him why he was staking out her building.

"The Brotherhood's snatched Cheryl," Candice said.

"Get the fuck out of here."

"They grabbed her in Ossining after her interview with Gomez. Mace is on the way to the scene. Don't call him. He'll let you know if he needs anything."

"What about Patty?"

"Landry's at his house with Missing Persons. Will you let Williams know?"

"Yeah, sure. Let me take care of that right now." He hung up and called Karol, who answered on the third ring.

"Are you calling to wish me a good night?" she said. "How romantic."

"Not exactly. Candice called. The Brotherhood snatched Mace's wife in Ossining after she interviewed Gomez."

"Oh, Christ. What can we do to help?"

"Just sit tight and get some of that much needed rest until Mace tells us differently."

"I hope she's okay."

"Yeah, me too. See you tomorrow." Willy closed his phone down and waited.

Only fifteen minutes passed before Karol exited the building, got into her SUV, and drove away.

Mace let Landry into the house. The lieutenant seemed flustered. "Thanks for coming."

"Don't mention it. Are you okay?"

Mace gestured to Anna sitting on the living room couch. She held Patty, who slept with her mouth open. "This is Anna Sanchez. She and her family live downstairs."

"Hello," Anna said.

"Pleased to meet you," Landry said. "The squad cars are in position downstairs."

Mace lowered his voice. "I'm trusting you to take care of everything here."

Landry opened one flap of his coat, revealing his Glock. Then he opened the other, revealing a shotgun. "Don't worry."

"Thanks." Mace offered his hand, which Landry shook.

He hurried out the door, and halfway down the stairs his cell phone vibrated. He took it out without slowing down. Glancing at the display, he ignored it. When he opened the door, the two POs stationed outside turned in his direction.

"If you need to get inside, buzz Lieutenant Landry on the second floor." Circling the house to the driveway, he saw the strobes of another RMP at the far end of the street. His cell phone vibrated again. He climbed into his SUV and backed out of the driveway. Five minutes later when the cell phone vibrated a third time, he took the call. "Mace."

"Where the hell have you been?" Mint said.

"I've been a little frazzled," Mace said.

"Let me rephrase that. Where the hell are you now?"

"I'm halfway to Ossining," he said, twisting the truth.

"Jesus, Tony, why? There's nothing you can do there."

"I need to keep moving. I can't just sit around the house waiting for a call I know isn't coming."

"You really think the Brotherhood grabbed Cheryl?"

"I know it."

"Why not the Class Ls? Gomez made their existence public."

"The last thing the Class Ls should want is more

publicity. Cheryl did a pretty damned good job discrediting everything Gomez said."

"I'll give you that. You were in hot water there for a minute."

*Thanks.*

"Where the hell does that leave the investigation?"

"I'm going to find my wife. When I do, I'll find the Brotherhood. It's that simple."

"If you're planning to ride around like the Lone Ranger, I hope you plan to have a Tonto with you."

"My team is standing by if I need them." For the first time since accepting his position as head of the task force, Mace felt comfortable with the idea of killing every member of the Brotherhood of Torquemada.

# CHAPTER THIRTY-FOUR

Cheryl awakened in darkness. Trying to move, she realized her hands were cuffed behind her back. She heard an engine and felt a vibrating metal floor, and occasionally a bump caused the vehicle to shake.

*Blindfolded,* she realized.

She remembered seeing the van ahead of Colleen's vehicle in the road, then men garbed in strange paramilitary uniforms surrounding the car.

*Colleen!* Was she alive or dead? Was she also in the van, if that's what this was? As badly as she wanted to know the answers, she decided to feign unconsciousness. The vehicle made a sharp turn, and she rocked from side to side.

"Right up to the door," a male voice said.

The vehicle seemed to turn around and back up. A moment later, the engine turned off and the back doors swung open, admitting frigid air.

"Come on. Get up," a different man said. "That chloroform should have worn off ten minutes ago. Don't make us drag you."

With reluctance, Cheryl managed to sit up. "It's hard to move with my hands cuffed."

Hands grabbed her biceps and hauled her to her feet. She heard the doors of another vehicle close.

"Walk forward."

She obeyed, and a hand held her head down, presumably to keep it from bumping the ceiling.

"Watch your step."

Cheryl did, setting foot on some kind of platform outside. The van doors closed behind her, and she shivered. A key turned in a lock, and a door swung open. She heard no traffic noise, no neighborhood voices.

*We're not in Manhattan anymore, Toto.*

The hands on her arms guided her inside. The door closed, and her captors moved her forward.

A concrete floor. Echoing footsteps. No heat.

*An abandoned building? A warehouse?*

"Colleen?"

"Stay quiet," another male voice said.

Cheryl tried to guess how many of them there were by the footsteps, but there were too many to separate. They stopped her, and she heard a rattling sound. Then they pushed her into a space with stuffy air and crowded around her, and she heard the rattling sound again.

*A freight elevator.*

The elevator descended, and she adjusted her feet for balance. "Where are you taking me?"

No one answered. The elevator stopped, the door rattled open, and her captors guided her out.

*Just one floor. The basement.*

More footsteps but no echo this time.

*Lower ceilings.*

The footsteps stopped, and the hands held her steady. A bolt slid into place, a door opened, and the hands guided her inside a room. Something moved ahead of her—something weighty and swift—a very large animal. She recoiled at the padded footsteps, her heart pounding. The hands held her arms straight down, and she heard the clinking of chain links before metal manacles snapped around her wrists and ankles.

Then Cheryl felt the blindfold around her head being untied, and sudden light filled her sight. She found herself staring at a wild animal: matted hair, blood-spattered flesh, squatting in filth. Hearing footsteps behind her, she spun to see a shadow dart through the doorway. A moment later, the door slammed shut, and she heard the bolt on the other side slide into locked position.

She turned back to the pitiful creature chained to the floor near the far wall. "Rhonda?"

Driving along the Hudson with his siren on, Mace couldn't help but remember when he had made this same drive two years earlier. During their private interview, Rodrigo Gomez had seemed repentant. Tonight the serial killer had tried to destroy Mace through implication.

A quarter of a mile ahead, Mace saw bright lights in the road, surrounded by dense trees on one side and the river on the other. Drawing nearer, he saw an ambulance, a fire truck, and two police cars, and within the glare of their strobes, several cars and a Manhattan Minute News van. He slowed to a stop, got out, and strode to the scene, the wind from the Hudson blowing his hair. Shelly and Norton stood with a pair of police officers, causing him to raise his eyebrows, and Colleen stood with Ryan and several crewmen by the ambulance. He stared at a sidelined vehicle with broken windows.

"Tony," Colleen said. "Thank Christ you're here. I'm so sorry. I tried to get away!"

Mace held her biceps but stopped short of embracing her. "It's okay. Tell me everything."

As Colleen recounted what had happened to her and Cheryl, Shelly and Norton joined the party. Mace listened in grim silence as Colleen described the same assailants that Willy had seen at the funeral home. There was no doubt in his mind that the Brotherhood of Torquemada had taken Cheryl, but for what purpose? Did they even know who he was, or had Cheryl simply caused too much of a stir in their eyes?

"I'm so, so sorry," Colleen said, tears streaming down her face.

"You have nothing to be sorry for. These men were trained killers. You're lucky to be alive."

Ryan's chest rose and fell. "If I'd been here—"

"Be glad you weren't. They'd have ended up killing you." Mace's cell phone vibrated, and he saw a familiar name on the display, which he ignored.

"You should be at home with your daughter," Norton said. "You can't be involved in this aspect of the investigation. You're too close to it now."

"I'm the only man for the job, remember?"

"That was before this. You're a liability to the operation. That you don't even see that shows how clouded your judgment is."

"What operation?" an Ossining PO said.

Mace felt himself growing hot. "I'm going home now."

"What about me?" Colleen said, sniffling.

"She needs to come to our station and make out a full report," the Ossining cop said.

Mace glanced at Norton.

"This is way too public for us to contain," she said.

Mace looked at Colleen. "I'm sorry." He turned to Ryan. "You'll wait for her, right?"

"Yeah, sure. Someone's got to arrange to have this car picked up anyway. None of us is going to drive it in this weather with no windows."

Mace turned on one heel and returned to his SUV. After turning the vehicle around and driving off, he called the number on his display screen.

"Hello?" a familiar voice said.

"You sound well for a dead man."

"I think you should meet me," Gabriel said. "We know where they're holed up."

"How do you know my name?" the blood-spattered young woman said.

"The whole city's looking for you," Cheryl said.

"Really?" Rhonda stood straight and placed one hand over her crotch and the other across her breasts.

"Don't bother. You don't have anything I haven't seen before. Why did they take your clothes?"

Rhonda's face twisted with rage. "Because they're animals."

"I can't argue with that."

"Are my parents really dead?"

Cheryl's heart sank. How had she come to be in this position? "I'm sorry, but yes."

Tears filled Rhonda's eyes. "I didn't want to believe it . . . I'm glad I killed one of them."

*Oh no.* "What do these men want with you?"

Rhonda just stared at her, as if unable to speak.

"Are these men the Brotherhood of Torquemada?"

"The one I killed was a woman."

*Oh, my Lord.* Cheryl studied the blood spatters all over Rhonda's body. "What happened to your arm?"

"They cut it off."

Cheryl's head throbbed. Jesus Christ, she wanted to get out of here! "How many of them are there?"

"I don't know. I've only seen four."

Cheryl looked around the cell for any means of escape but saw none. "You and Jason worked together at Synful Reading, which was owned by Gabriel and Raphael Domini.

Jason and both of your families were killed, and today Synful Reading and the Domini Funeral Home were blown up. Gabriel and Raphael are the targets, aren't they?"

Rhonda stared at Cheryl with hardened eyes, her lips twitching.

*This girl is making me nervous.*

"How do I know you're not one of them?"

Cheryl looked at the floor between them. "Are those buckets what I think they are?"

Rhonda nodded.

Cheryl walked over to the buckets, dragging her chains behind her. She unzipped her slacks, squatted over one bucket, and released her urine.

Rhonda turned her back to her. "At least it's just me in here. They used to have a camera on the wall, but I threw a head at it."

The sound of the urine was loud, and Cheryl shuddered. When she stopped and stood up, Rhonda turned around again.

"I'm sorry for your sake that they brought you here," Rhonda said. "But I'm happy to have company. Hey, don't I know you?"

Cheryl buttoned the flap on her slacks.

"You're that reporter for Manhattan Minute News. My mother used to watch you. Why do they want you?"

"I guess we'll know soon enough." Cheryl couldn't help but think about Patty and how much she wanted to see her grow up.

Mace's mind raced as he drove into Newark, the Manhattan skyline visible across the water. The Brotherhood of Torquemada had chosen as the locale for its base the largest city in New Jersey, eight miles west of Manhattan. New Jersey: the perfect place for werewolf slayers to hide and still have quick access to their hunting grounds.

He drove along dark streets surrounded by tall buildings, his GPS guiding him away from the city proper, through different wards and neighborhoods beyond the city's ports. He steered the SUV through a neighborhood that consisted almost entirely of abandoned buildings, then drove along a field to a low, flat building with a Cyclone fence that had been ruptured in several places. An SUV, the only vehicle in the parking lot, idled near a loading dock.

Mace pulled up a few rows behind the SUV and parked his own vehicle. He scanned the industrial terrain, then got out and approached the other SUV, glancing over his shoulder at the rusted metal around him. Wind blew loose signs against the fence. Reaching inside his coat, he squeezed the butt of his Glock and stopped a dozen feet away from the rear of the SUV, noting its New York license plates.

*Plates owned by the city,* he thought with growing interest.

The passenger door opened, and Gabriel got out. In the dim light from the ceiling dome, Mace could not make out the driver before Gabriel closed the door and walked over to him. He removed his hand from the Glock.

"I'm sorry your wife got dragged into this," Gabriel said.

"I should have been with her. The explosions at your properties interfered with my plans."

"They interfered with mine too."

"But they provided you with a cover so that the Brotherhood and my people would stop tailing you."

Gabriel made an exaggerated shrug. "Leadership trains you to turn bad situations to your advantage."

Mace nodded at the SUV. "Who's your chauffeur?"

Gabriel pounded on the SUV's hatch. The driver's door opened, and a female got out. She was silhouetted at first until she stepped into a pool of light from the streetlight beyond the fence.

Mace blinked in surprise. "Detective Williams."

Karol spoke in a low voice. "Captain."

He glanced at Gabriel, then back at her. "You're one of them."

"I'm a cop, but I'm a Wolf first."

"You planted her," Mace said to Gabriel.

"My father always encouraged our people to assimilate," Gabriel said. "When I became his advisor, I encouraged our young to take those measures a step further, to take on positions that afforded them access to different branches of government so they'd be in a position to protect our secret. Karol was one of the first Wolves to join the NYPD but not the only one. She did the rest herself, excelling at her work. You selected her to join your task force; she didn't select you."

It made perfect sense to Mace. *Survival of the species.*

"Everything I confided in you—"

"I already knew, thanks to Karol. Still, I appreciated your honesty."

Bright light illuminated Karol's features, and Mace heard a car engine. He turned to see another SUV pull into the parking lot. He could not see the driver through the glare of the headlights.

Whoever it was killed the engine. The door opened, and the overhead light illuminated Willy as he got out. The sound of the door closing echoed around the lot, and he walked over to Mace. "I'm looking for the Cheryl Mace rescue party," he said. "Mr. Domini, are you a ghost now?"

Karol closed her eyes, as if in pain.

Mace felt relieved to see Willy. "You followed me?"

"No." Karol opened her eyes. "He followed me."

"I told you when we started this, I'm not losing another partner," Willy said. "I saw you making a call on your phone back at the Oh-Five."

"Don't tell me you were jealous."

"No, I just wondered who you could be reporting to besides Gabriel, since we thought he was six feet under the funeral home."

Narrowing his eyes at Karol, Gabriel sniffed the air.

Karol raised her eyes to the sky and clawed air near her face. "All right, yes. We're together."

Gabriel and Mace looked at Willy.

"I guess this is what they mean when they say it's complicated," he said.

"You knew Williams was a Wolf *and* reporting to Gabriel?"

Now Willy raised his hands. "I'm wrestling with a few issues, okay? Nothing Karol or I have done has compromised the operation."

Gabriel stared at Karol.

"I'm sorry," she said. "I didn't mean for this to happen."

"I'm irresistible," Willy said.

"Fortunately for you both, we have much bigger problems to contend with," Gabriel said.

Mace looked from one face to another. "Does anyone else have any secrets he'd like to share?"

"You carried one around for a long time," Willy said. "A big, bad one."

"Not by choice." Mace turned to Gabriel. "Where's my wife?"

Gabriel nodded at the building behind them. "Follow me."

# CHAPTER THIRTY-FIVE

Sitting on the straw-covered floor, Cheryl tried to ignore the blood around her, but she found she had to close her eyes to do that.

"They're going to kill us," Rhonda said.

Cheryl opened her eyes. Rhonda sat with her back against the opposite wall.

"They'll probably kill me first, but your head is on the chopping block too."

"I haven't seen their faces," Cheryl said. "I couldn't possibly identify any of them." She felt guilty for weighing her odds of survival against Rhonda's.

"Michael has a bandage on his face because I bit his nose off. He's the leader. Henri is the black guy with the shaved head. He's the one who hacked my arm off. And there's a woman with a big nose and long hair. I don't know her name. If I had to guess, she's not entirely sold on whatever they're up to. They all have accents: Italian, French, whatever. Who knows? Maybe you can use this information after I'm gone."

Cheryl stared at her fellow captive. Rhonda was more girl than woman, and yet her eyes revealed the weariness of someone much older. Whatever she was, she had no doubt suffered considerable physical and emotional pain over the last few days. "Neither one of us is going to die."

"What makes you think so?"

*Because my husband is a cop* would have sounded silly. "You've been stuck in here, so you don't know what's going on out there. These people aren't just killers and kidnappers; they're terrorists. People are panicking. The governor brought the National Guard in, and every law enforcement agency you can think of is working overtime to find them. It's just a matter of time before they do."

Rhonda's lower lip quivered. "What makes you think we have any time?"

Cheryl sighed. *Just my luck: the biggest story of my life and I'm the subject, not the reporter.*

Gabriel led the party around the building, Mace and Willy carrying flashlights. No streetlights or work lights illuminated the far side of the property, and they found themselves on a train platform overlooking dense foliage.

"This was a depot years ago," Gabriel said. "It hasn't been used in decades."

Mace played his flashlight beam over the bare branches

of the trees rising from below. Through the trees, he saw a dull yellow rectangle a little more than a quarter of a mile away. "There?"

Gabriel nodded. "It's a small warehouse complex."

"What makes you think Cheryl is in there?"

"My brother and his crew tracked the Brotherhood there."

Mace looked around the surrounding territory. Besides a field of power towers, he saw no other buildings nearby. "This is a pretty isolated area. How did they do that?"

"Don't underestimate our sense of smell or Raphael's determination."

"Where is he?" Willy said.

"I ordered him to report to me if he located the Brotherhood and then stay away for twenty-four hours."

"And he just agreed to that?"

"I'm the leader of the pack, and he's loyal to me despite our differences over this situation. He has no choice but to respect my wishes, which are that you, not my people, take these killers down."

Willy glanced at Karol. "Oh, so Tony and me are on our own, huh?"

"No. I have a personal stake in this as well. Karol and I will help you. We know how to control ourselves."

"How do you propose we reach that warehouse without being seen?" Mace said.

Gabriel pointed at the trees. "These woods extend right to the edge of that property. We scouted it while waiting for you to arrive. We can get at least that far without being seen."

Karol jerked her head in the direction from which they'd come. "Someone else is here."

The four of them exchanged alarmed glances.

Willy shone his flashlight into the brush below. "I don't see anyone."

"It's Shelly and Norton," Karol said.

"Tell me you don't smell them from here."

"I told you," Gabriel said.

Willy looked at Mace. "We could hide under this platform."

"No. I don't want any accidental gunfire or anything. Besides, we can use the backup. Let's just wait here for them to find us."

"We could call Landry and Candice too."

Mace shook his head. "Landry's at my house. Candice is joining him when she gets off duty. That's where I want them."

"How did the Frisbees know we were here?"

"They were on the scene in Ossining. They must have followed me."

"Everyone's following someone."

A pair of flashlights appeared around the corner. Mace turned his flashlight on himself and waved.

"They don't know about Karol," Willy said in a low voice.

"We don't know what they know."

Moments later, Shelly and Norton became visible.

"Is this a private club, or can anyone walk in off the street?" Shelly said. He held a pump-action shotgun in one hand.

"We were just about to call you," Willy said.

"There was no need," Norton said.

"Let me congratulate you on your tailing prowess," Mace said.

"I don't want to insult you, but it wasn't difficult."

"I've got a lot on my mind."

"Understood."

Willy gestured at Shelly's shotgun. "That's some heavy artillery you've got there. Are you hunting bear or the Jersey Devil?"

"Call me paranoid, but when three members of the task force I'm part of rendezvous outside their jurisdiction only hours after a spouse is abducted by the quarry we're after, I come prepared."

"I guess it's lucky for us this does fit into your jurisdiction."

Norton looked through the trees at the warehouse complex in the distance. "Is that our objective?"

"Yes," Mace said.

Norton returned her attention to Gabriel. "How do you know?"

Gabriel maintained a poker face. "I received an anonymous tip."

"Then this is unconfirmed?"

"That's right," Mace said. "But Mr. Domini has faith in the information he received."

"Even though it came from an anonymous tipster?" Shelly said.

"Yes," Gabriel said.

Norton turned to Mace. "We never discussed a civilian joining us."

Gabriel stepped closer to them. "I can handle myself."

"Do you have a gun?"

"I don't need one."

"That's fascinating, but we have a vested interest in your survival."

Gabriel smiled. "If anything happens to me, I'm sure I'll wind up on a slab in Quantico."

"My wife's life is in danger," Mace said. "Gabriel's already scouted the terrain out there. He and I are leaving now. Any of you wants to accompany us is welcome. Gabriel?"

Gabriel stepped off the moss-covered platform and flattened brush with his landing. Mace leapt after him. A moment later, Willy joined them. He offered Karol his hand, but she ignored it and landed farther out than he did. Norton hopped down next, then Shelly. Karol took out her flashlight.

*For show,* Mace thought. Norton and Shelly had to know Gabriel was a Class L, but there was no reason to believe they suspected Karol was anything but a cop. "Aim your flashlights at the ground, and shield them with your free hand. Keep the chatter to a minimum."

"Walk two abreast," Norton said.

Gabriel and Mace proceeded, followed by Willy and Karol, with Shelly and Norton bringing up the rear.

Cheryl jumped to her feet when she heard the bolt on the other side of the door slide open. She noted that Rhonda remained seated.

*Her spirit's broken,* Cheryl thought, unable to blame her.

A man with a bandaged nose entered, followed by a younger man.

Michael. The leader.

A woman appeared behind them, carrying several window-sized pieces of poster board. Michael held a camera. The other man held a shotgun. The door remained open behind them.

Cheryl felt the back of her throat turn dry.

"My name is Michael, Mrs. Mace."

*He does intend to kill us, or he wouldn't even tell me that much.*

"I've been impressed by your reporting this past week. No one's ever implicated the Brotherhood of Torquemada in the media before."

"You'll have to thank Rodrigo Gomez for that." Her voice sounded hoarse.

"I'd sooner decapitate him." He glanced at Rhonda.

"What are you going to do with us?"

Michael raised the camera. He popped open the LCD screen on its side and trained the camera on her. "I'm going to give you an up close and personal view of what this war is all about and then a chance to report on it."

Cheryl's gaze darted to the poster boards in the woman's hands. "You mean you want me to read a prepared statement."

Michael made a slight nod. "It will be the truth."

"And then I suppose you're going to release me?"

Michael's smile seemed sympathetic. "I won't insult your intelligence by making promises we both know I can't keep."

Cheryl stared into the camera's lens. "Then you'd better shoot me now. I'm not reading a goddamned word, and my husband will be coming after me."

"Captain Mace? Rodrigo Gomez seemed impressed by him. But as Gomez admitted, he's a beast, and I'm a man. Are you certain I can't change your mind?"

"Positive. Maybe you should torture me like you did Rhonda."

"We don't torture human beings, and that would delay our departure." Michael turned to the woman but kept the camera on Cheryl. "Help the others load out of here. We'll take it from here."

The woman glanced at Rhonda, then Cheryl, and left.

"You don't need to read our statement. Your presence here now will be testimony enough."

Cheryl heard a beep from the camera as it started recording.

Michael panned to the other man and stepped back, creating a wider frame. "Do it."

Fearing the worst, Cheryl sucked in her breath and took a step back.

The man leaned his shotgun against the wall and moved forward. He took out what resembled a remote control. Michael panned over to Rhonda, who rose with a brave expression on her face, then back to the man, who pressed a button on the control. Rhonda screamed and fell, and Michael panned over to her as she flailed her arms on the floor, a crackling sound coming from the collar around her neck.

# CHAPTER THIRTY-SIX

**M**ace walked over rusty railroad tracks covered with overgrowth. "Watch your step."

They pushed the branches of bushes out of their way, and thorns whipped against their coats.

"Your hand is bleeding," Gabriel said.

"I wish you'd stop that."

A minute later, they reached a perfect square in the earth, each side ten feet long, surrounded by young trees. Mace aimed his flashlight inside the hole and illuminated the rotting carcass of a buck lying on a mound of dirt, leaves, and branches.

"This must have been some sort of inground trash receptacle," Gabriel said. "The deer was probably galloping through and didn't see the hole. Maybe it broke its neck, maybe just its legs."

"Let's keep moving."

Rhonda thrashed around on the floor like a wild animal.

Cheryl ran to help her, but the chains around her wrists yanked her back. "You son of a bitch!"

The man with the remote control stepped back.

Michael moved his camera closer to Rhonda. "Relax," he said to Cheryl. "That won't kill her. It's just an electric charge, like a Taser, designed to elicit a very specific reaction."

On the floor, Rhonda looked into Cheryl's eyes. Her eyes changed, the irises expanding until no whites showed, and the teeth in her screaming mouth quadrupled in length.

Cheryl felt her eyes and jaws widening in unison. *Oh, Jesus, no . . .*

The transformation happened quickly. Rhonda's nose and jaws extended, as if a creature living inside her body fought to be free. The fingers on her remaining hand extended, and at the same time each fingernail extended into something sharp looking, the result being that each finger appeared two inches longer than it had. Her ears became canine; her feet stretched into additional segments of her legs, the front balls becoming lupine paws. And her breasts flattened out, absorbed into her powerful torso as if their mass had been distributed to other parts of her body. Black fur spread over her from head to toe as the muscles in her limbs reconfigured themselves with great spasms.

Out of the corner of her eye, Cheryl saw Michael panning back and forth from Rhonda to her, presumably capturing her terrified reaction. She backed away from Rhonda even before the werewolf stood on its hind legs and snarled at their captors, and her back bumped against the wall. Cheryl believed every word that Gomez had uttered.

"Welcome to the real world," Michael said.

Rhonda howled.

"You and me are going to have some talking to do after this," Willy said to Karol as they followed Gabriel and Mace through the dense brush in the darkness.

"When this is over," Karol said.

"I mean, I'm dealing with some very legitimate trust issues."

"Not now."

"If nothing else, I expect my *partner* to tell me when—"

Mace stopped ahead of them, and Willy almost collided into him.

"I said to keep the chatter to a minimum."

"Sorry, Captain."

They resumed walking.

"Am I being unreasonable?" Willy said in a whisper.

"I can still hear you," Gabriel said.

Willy sighed. "Let's just discuss this when this is all over, all right?"

"Right," Karol said, sounding exasperated.

Then he heard what sounded like the howling of a wolf.

Michael aimed his camera at Cheryl. "Any last words?"

Horrified, Cheryl shook her head.

Michael panned over to Rhonda, then switched the camera off and closed its LCD screen. Turning to his companion, he raised the camera. "Let's go download this."

The man nodded, and Michael led him through the cell's open door and disappeared. The door slammed with a reverberating sense of finality, and its bolt slid into place.

They crouched in the high grass along the Cyclone fence, and Mace stared at the side of the brick complex. The basement windows had been boarded up, and those on the first floor had bars over them. Three of the windows on the third floor glowed yellow through the filthy glass, and a streetlight cast harsh shadows over the chipped bricks. Thick vines crept up the side to the roof.

Gabriel said, "In the front, there's a brick archway that leads through a short tunnel into the parking lot, which is enclosed by brick walls. The front doors to each warehouse are locked. I don't know about the rear doors, which face the parking lot. When I checked earlier, there were two vehicles parked in the lot, a van and an SUV."

"I see three lines of attack," Mace sad. "Gabriel and I will break in through that boarded window. Willy and Karol, climb those vines to the fire escape, then go through a third-floor window. Norton and Shelly, go in through the parking lot tunnel Gabriel just described."

Norton took off her coat, revealing a Kevlar vest, and Shelly did the same. Willy removed his coat, revealing Kevlar as well, and so did Mace and Karol.

"Paranoid minds think alike," Willy said.

Norton removed a headset from her coat pocket and put it on, adjusting the microphone. "Give Tony your headset."

Shelly took his headset from his coat pocket and handed it to Mace.

"Go to channel two," Norton said.

Mace adjusted the channel and put the headset on.

"What about us?" Willy said.

"We're covered." Karol put her headset on and fiddled with its settings.

"That figures," Willy said.

"Everyone make sure your cell phones are off," Mace said.

While the task force members checked their cell phones, Gabriel pulled off his socks and shoes.

"What the hell are you doing?" Shelly said. "Never mind. I don't want to know."

Mace looked around the isolated wooded area. "There's no one around for miles, which is probably why they chose this location. Once we're inside, this could take five minutes or five hours. Don't any of you take any chances with Cheryl's life. Let's go."

Even in bare feet, Gabriel scaled the fence first and dropped onto the grass on the other side. Karol followed him, then Mace and Norton. Willy waited for Shelly to make it over, then climbed the fence last. Mace tapped Gabriel on the arm, and they ran across the grass to the boarded-up basement window. Mace pressed his back against the bricks on one side of the window, and Gabriel imitated him on the other side.

Karol gripped the vines creeping up the wall and climbed to the fire escape. Willy grabbed the vine but tore it from the brick. On the fire escape, Karol turned and reached over the corroded railing. Seeing her outstretched hand, Gabriel interlaced the fingers of his hands and looked at Willy, who set one foot in the locked hands. Gabriel boosted Willy, who took Karol's hand, and Karol pulled him up onto the fire escape.

Turning his head, Mace watched Shelly and Norton run to the front of the building and disappear. Despite the burden of keeping everyone safe, he preferred working with a team to breaking into Janus Farel's brownstone alone. And it wasn't even raining.

In the dining room, Michael watched the footage he had shot of Cheryl and Rhonda on his laptop, with Angelo and Reddick beside him.

"No edits. Let them try to call this a fake, especially after they find their corpses." Michael unhooked the camera's cable from the laptop and shut the computer down. "We'll blast the video across the web and watch it go viral. By this time tomorrow, the entire world will believe what Gomez said about the beasts. It will be a Cheryl Mace double feature."

Angelo frowned.

"What?"

"We could have exposed them anytime we wanted, but we didn't."

"We were never in danger of being shut down before. This way, Tudoro's backers will continue to fund the war. If they don't, others will pick up our cause."

"I'm loyal to Tudoro," Reddick said.

"You need to be loyal to the Brotherhood. In the end, Tudoro's just another bureaucrat. Go find Colum and execute the prisoners."

"Why me?" Reddick said. "I don't really feel like killing two women."

"Only one of them is a woman. The other is a beast. And you need to make your bones. The rest of us have already spilled plenty of blood."

"We triggered your explosives as you ordered."

"As far as we know, no wolves were killed in those explosions. Gabriel Domini's carcass hasn't been discovered yet."

Sighing, Reddick crossed the dining room.

"Tell Valeria and Loreti to start on the ground floor."

Reddick waved to him with the back of his hand and left.

"Maybe we shouldn't kill the newswoman," Angelo said.

Michael raised his eyebrows.

"She's innocent as well as human. Her death will turn people against us."

"She's seen our faces."

"She has now, anyway."

"We have only one course of action." Michael closed the laptop and rose. "Do an idiot check and let's get out of here."

Nodding, Angelo left the room.

Michael looked around the space one last time. They had stripped everything they had used in the warehouse:

weapons, cameras, monitors, luxury items. He knew their fingerprints were everywhere, which was why he intended to burn the building on the way out. He packed his laptop into his shoulder bag, which he slung over one shoulder, and headed out.

With her Glock drawn, Norton preceded Shelly into the dark tunnel that led into the warehouse parking lot. The brick tunnel ran perhaps thirty feet in length and had a curved ceiling. They hurried through it, an SUV and a white cargo van coming into view in the square parking lot.

Norton took a step forward into the lot, then jumped back when a loading bay door opened and a woman with long black hair, streaked blonde, and a scruffy-looking man emerged from the building onto the concrete loading platform. They wore civilian clothes, not the combat fatigues Willy had described.

The woman hopped off the platform onto the asphalt, then walked to the van and climbed into the front seat. She started the engine and backed the vehicle up to the loading dock. The man opened the rear doors and started loading equipment cases and luggage into the van. The woman got out and trotted up the concrete steps and helped him.

"Looks like ordinance to me," Shelly said.

"Looks like they're running for the hills to me," Norton said.

Valeria closed the van doors, then she, Loreti, and Colum walked back inside the loading bay, and she closed the door. No sooner had they entered the adjacent corridor than they ran into Reddick.

"The video's good," Reddick said. "Colum, we have to do the prisoners."

"Now?" Colum said.

"That's what Michael says."

"Okay, let's get it over with."

"Valeria, Michael said for you and Loreti to start on the ground floor."

"Right," Valeria said.

Reddick and Colum moved in one direction and Valeria and Loreti in the other.

Mace watched Willy attempt to open the second-floor window closest to the fire escape. When it didn't budge, the lieutenant looked down and shook his head. Mace made a fist with one hand, and Willy nodded.

Norton's voice came over the speaker in his ear. "A man and a woman just loaded up a van and went back inside. We're guessing artillery and ammo in addition to luggage. We got here just in time. They're bugging out."

"Sit on those vehicles," Mace said. "We can't have them retrieving those weapons or making a run for it."

"Copy that. If they come outside, we'll be ready for them."

Mace turned to Gabriel.

"I heard," he said.

Looking up, Mace saw Karol filling Willy in.

"Okay, let's take them," Mace said.

Drawing his Glock, he kicked in the plywood over the basement window. Above, Willy used a flashlight to smash a windowpane, then reached inside, unlocked the window, and raised it. Mace took out his own flashlight, got down on his knees, and crawled backward through the window, dropping into darkness. He landed on a concrete floor, turned, and aimed his flashlight, its circle of light moving across old machinery. Gabriel landed behind him, and they made their way through the darkness.

Willy climbed through the window and hopped onto the hard tile floor, then helped Karol do the same. "Careful," he said, turning on his flashlight.

"You be careful," she said. "I don't need the light to see."

"You go with your bad self."

They moved between rows of old sewing machines.

"This place is like a museum," Karol said.

"Let's just hope we don't become featured exhibits."

Mace and Gabriel penetrated the gloomy interior of the basement, stepping on wet floors and passing junk piled to the ceiling.

"I bet you wish you had your shoes on now," Mace said.

Gabriel touched his arm. "Hold it. I smell something."

"No kidding. This place reeks of sewage and must."

"No. I smell a Wolf. It must be Rhonda. She's alive!"

Mace's heart beat faster. Then Cheryl was alive too. "Which way?"

Gabriel sniffed the air. "I'm not sure. You're right about the odors in here. They're interfering with my sense of smell. And there's no ventilation."

*Come on; come on,* Mace thought.

"Up ahead. Keep moving."

"Do you get the feeling we're purposefully being kept out of the action?" Shelly said.

"Maybe," Norton said.

"I don't like being sidelined, especially when I brought my big gun."

"If anything happens in there, you'll get to use it." She scanned the first-floor windows, all barred.

"What do you make of Domini?"

"He sure looks human to me."

"Yeah, I was thinking the same thing."

"It'll be a shame if we have to kill him."

# CHAPTER THIRTY-SEVEN

At the far end of the warehouse space, Valeria unscrewed the metal cap on the gasoline can and splashed the fuel on the floor and furniture. Loreti did the same twenty feet away from her. By the time Valeria saw Michael approaching them, the area reeked of gas. He carried a can of gasoline in each hand, and when he stopped before them, they each took one and resumed their work.

"It will be just another abandoned building blaze when the authorities arrive," Michael said, "with no evidence that we were ever here, except for two charred corpses in the basement, which may never be discovered."

"Where are we heading from here?" Valeria said.

"Kentucky. There's a small pack we can exterminate without drawing attention to ourselves."

"And then?"

"Virginia. Or Florida. Maybe Arkansas."

Valeria closed her eyes for a moment. "It will never end, will it?"

"This war's lasted hundreds of years, and we've never been closer to success."

*Some success,* Valeria thought. Myles, Henri, and Eun were all dead, and the Brotherhood had run out of money. Somehow she had envisioned a different life for herself, but she continued to pour gasoline.

Angelo checked each of the offices the Brotherhood had used as bedrooms and a larger room that had been used for training purposes. The replacement brothers had removed everything as instructed. He passed through the dining room once more and was about to press the call button for the elevator when he saw a flashlight beam moving along the wall of the darkened corridor ahead.

*Intruders.*

He backed up into the dining room and drew his Blade.

Hearing the bolt slide open again, Cheryl rose, convinced the time of their execution was at hand. The door opened, and two men stood there. A strange sound came out of her mouth, one she could not control.

Tony smiled. "Are you glad to see me?"

Tears filled her eyes, and she sobbed.

Tony crossed the room and took her into his arms.

"Gabriel?" Rhonda said.

Cheryl watched Gabriel Domini walk through the cell with a ring of keys in one hand.

"It's okay, Rhonda." He tried different keys in the manacle on Rhonda's wrist. "What happened to your arm?"

"Th-th-they—"

The manacle snapped open.

"They'll pay for that," Gabriel said.

Rhonda raised her stump. "It's growing back . . ."

"Shh." Gabriel unlocked the manacles around her ankles, then tossed the ring to Tony, who searched for the keys to Cheryl's manacles. Gabriel took off his shirt and held it out to Rhonda. She turned her back to everyone and slipped her arms into the sleeves.

When she turned around, tears streamed down her cheeks. "Muh-muh-my muh-muh-ther . . ."

Gabriel buttoned the shirt. "I know."

Cheryl watched the girl wipe snot from her nose on the palm of her hand, and then she looked at Tony as he freed her wrists and set to work on her ankles. "I knew you'd come."

He nodded at Gabriel. "His people found you."

*People*, she thought.

A loud noise came from the corridor.

"That's the elevator," Cheryl said. "It's around the corner."

Holding his Glock in both hands, Willy turned down the intersecting corridor. Karol moved beside him, her gun raised. A dozen closed doors stretched before them.

Willy stopped at a door opposite the freight elevator gate, his hand closing on the knob.

The freight elevator hummed to life on the other side of the wooden gate.

"Someone's coming," Karol said.

Turning his back to the door, Willy aimed at the freight elevator gate and moved to his left. Karol did the same, moving to her right. Willy ignored the sweat forming on his brow.

The freight elevator rose into view and stopped at their floor.

*Empty,* Willy thought. "I wonder who—"

The door to Willy's right opened, and a man stepped out and swung a sword deep into his neck.

After unlocking the manacles around Cheryl's ankles, Mace sprinted through the doorway so fast he slammed into the wall just as two men rounded the corridor, each carrying a sword. Their eyes widened at the sight of Mace, and they jumped back just as he triggered his Glock, the ensuing gunshot ricocheting off the wall.

Mace ran toward the corner, then dove to the floor, sliding out where the corridors intersected. The two men stood before the door to an elevator and a gate to a freight elevator, pounding each call button with frantic urgency.

"NYPD!"

They turned in Mace's direction.

"Drop those swords!"

The men charged to a door set in the corridor wall, and

Mace depressed the trigger of his semiautomatic. The Glock barked in his hands, spitting empty casings into the air, the reports coming in rapid succession.

The first man got through the door, but the gunfire stitched a semicircle of crimson in the second man's chest and he fell, his sword clattering beside him.

Mace sprang to his feet, ran to the door, and flung it open. He found himself staring into a murky stairway with concrete steps. A muzzle flashed above him, and a bullet ricocheted off the door, and he jumped back.

Gabriel ran down the corridor and scooped up the fallen Blade.

"The other one made it up the stairs." Mace kicked the corpse of the assassin over. The man had worn a scabbard for his Blade slung over his back.

Cheryl and Rhonda came around the corner and looked at the body on the floor.

"Take them back the way we came," Mace said to Gabriel.

"*You* take them back," Gabriel said.

Mace shook his head. "I'm the leader of this task force. I have people up there. You shouldn't even be here. We both got what we came for. Now get them to safety."

"No," Cheryl said. "You need each other. We can do it on our own. Just tell us the way."

"Rhonda can follow my scent out of here," Gabriel said. "My going along would be a pointless gesture."

"All right." Mace pressed his Glock into Cheryl's hand. "It's ready to fire, so be careful. You should have six shots left in that magazine. Don't get cute and try to shoot it with one hand, and don't lose it. I'm breaking a law just giving it to you."

"I love you," Cheryl said.

He kissed her. "I love you too."

Karol watched in disbelief as blood jetted out of the side of Willy's neck and he sank to his knees and toppled over. His head flopped at an unnatural angle, and she realized he had almost been decapitated. More blood sprayed out of the wound, and his glassy eyes stopped blinking.

*"No!"*

The man with the Blade of Salvation pivoted toward Karol, drawing his sword back to swing again.

Screaming, Karol fired her Glock repeatedly. The man danced, dropped his sword, and danced some more, the rounds tearing into his body keeping him erect. Then the slide on Karol's gun locked into place, and the man collapsed in a bloody heap on the floor.

With gun smoke lingering in the air, Karol dropped to her knees and cradled Willy in her arms. His head hung off his shoulders, and blood gurgled out of the gaping wound.

Touching her headset, Karol said, "Man down! Man down!"

Then she burst into tears.

Norton heard gunshots coming from the basement.

"We've engaged the enemy," she heard Mace say over

her headset.

Then she heard a continuous burst of gunfire coming from the second floor.

"Man down!" Karol said. "Man down!"

Norton and Shelly looked at each other.

"Cover me." Shelly ran across the parking lot with his shotgun gripped in both hands.

Norton stepped out of the tunnel too, sweeping the lot with her Glock.

Shelly climbed the concrete steps beside the parked van two at a time. He threw himself against the wall next to the door and counted to three, then stepped away from the door, aimed his shotgun, and blew off the knob.

Michael watched Valeria and Loreti douse the walls with gasoline. The fumes smelled good to him but not as good as they would smell after he had ignited them.

A series of bangs caused him to stiffen.

"Gunshots," Valeria said.

More gunfire, this time coming from upstairs, caused him to flinch.

"Where are the guns?" Michael said.

"In the van, where you told me to put them," Valeria said.

From another direction, the blast of a shotgun echoed.

Reaching behind him, Michael drew his Blade of Salvation. Discarding their gasoline cans, Valeria and Loreti drew their Blades as well. Poised to strike, they moved toward the opposite end of the warehouse.

The door for the basement stairway flew open, and Colum leapt out, gripping a .38 revolver. He slammed the door shut and pressed its button lock.

*At least he has a gun,* Michael thought.

"Cops," Colum said, wild-eyed.

Michael smiled. "Is that all?"

A wet thudding sound echoed in the stairway leading to the second floor. A bloody head rolled down the stairs and came to rest on the floor, and Angelo's lifeless eyes gazed at Michael.

A shadow fell on the wall as someone came down the stairs. The first thing Michael noticed about the black woman was her nude body. The second was the Blade she held in one hand, its tip aimed at the stairs ahead of her. Measuring each of the Torquemadans below, she moved with deliberation, her bare feet touching the stairs one at a time.

When she reached the floor, she drew back her sword. "Which one of you wants to be first?"

Colum aimed his revolver at the woman. "Drop that sword."

The woman looked at each human in turn. Then she dropped her Blade on the floor and raised her hands.

"Shoot her in the head," Michael said.

Colum aimed his revolver at the woman's head. Then the door behind him burst open.

Mace kicked the door open, and Gabriel leapt out of the stairwell with his sword pulled back. Mace followed, the door swinging shut behind him, and took in the scene: the assassin they had chased upstairs swung a revolver in their direction. Behind him, Karol stood naked with her hands raised.

*What the hell?*

Twenty-five feet away, three more assassins stood with their swords drawn, two men and a woman. Somewhere to his right, a shotgun exploded and the assassin holding the revolver flew off his feet, a gaping hole in his chest, and lay dead near Karol's feet.

"FBI!" Norton said as Shelly pumped his shotgun.

Seeing no way to stop a shotgun with a sword from twenty feet away, Valeria drew her tranq gun, aimed it, and squeezed its trigger. The gun made a gentle pop, and the male FBI agent clawed at his neck in surprise. Valeria holstered her tranq gun and heard Michael and Loreti draw theirs.

"I'm hit?" the bald man said in a strange tone. His female partner glanced at him, and he hit the floor hard, still holding the shotgun.

"Shelly!" The female FBI agent crouched beside her partner, but instead of checking to see if he was okay, she seized his shotgun with one hand. Rising, she holstered her Glock and aimed the shotgun, but Michael and Loreti fired their tranq guns, and their darts struck the woman's Kevlar vest. Dropping the shotgun, she pulled one dart out with ease, then struggled to jerk the other one free. It finally came out, and she stared at it before pitching forward unconscious.

"Form a triangle," Michael said.

Valeria took up position ten feet behind him on his left,

and Loreti took up a similar position on his right.

The three of them held their Blades ready for action.

"Willy's dead, Captain," Karol said.

Mace turned numb. Out of the corner of his eye, he saw Karol drop down on all fours, where he couldn't see her without taking his eyes off the assassins, and within seconds he heard a deep growl. When she rose again, Karol had turned into a Wolf that stood a full foot taller than her human form.

*Oh, Jesus.* He had hoped never to see anyone in Wolf Form again.

Gabriel handed his sword to Mace and pulled off his turtleneck.

"Not you too," Mace said.

"I told you I didn't need a gun. I don't need a sword, either." And then he growled.

Mace looked at the Wolf to his left and the Wolf to his right. Karol reminded him of the creature Angela Domini had transformed into, and Gabriel reminded him of the more powerful Wolf that Janus Farel had been.

The leader of the assassins, a man with a bandaged nose, cocked his head in the direction of the woman. "Take the man, Valeria."

Then he charged at Gabriel with a warrior's cry.

# CHAPTER THIRTY-EIGHT

Michael swung his Blade down at a forty-five-degree angle, slicing open the male beast's torso from its left shoulder to its right hip. The beast howled in pain. Michael spun in a complete circle, slicing the beast's stomach with a horizontal slash.

Loreti charged at the female beast. Before he could swing his Blade, she sprang at him, and the impact drove him to the floor with the monster on top of him. He felt long teeth tear his throat open, and hot blood scalded his esophagus. As he struggled to force the bitch off him, her front claws dug into his chest and her hind legs shredded his thighs. Then he felt a long tongue flicking against his own tongue, deep inside his throat, which triggered a gag reflex. He glimpsed bristly black fur, then only blackness.

Mace circled the woman called Valeria. He did not know how to fight with a sword, and his bad shoulder already throbbed just from holding the heavy weapon.

Valeria, on the other hand, seemed lithe and comfortable with her Blade, which was the same size as the one he held. She lunged at him and he stepped back, lunged again, and he stepped back again. Her eyes gleamed with bloodlust, and her lips formed a half smile. He had no doubt that he faced a trained killer. She lunged a third time, driving her Blade toward his face. He swung his Blade like a baseball bat with such ferocity that Valeria almost released her weapon, and she pirouetted to regain control of it.

*That's it!* He couldn't fence with her, but he could use his sword like a Louisville Slugger if she gave him half a chance.

Michael circled his beast, which snarled at him with fangs jutting out. The creature's eyes locked on his, and he sensed no fear from the monster despite the serious wounds he had inflicted on it. He feigned a blow, then another, causing the beast to flinch and reach out with his claws. Then he dropped low and spun on one ankle, slicing the beast's right thigh. The beast howled in pain, and Michael's adrenaline pumped.

Karol chewed through her assassin's neck until his head

came free, then she stood straddling his corpse, which she seized with her front claws and raised above her head. She hurled it at the floor with all her strength, shattering bones and pulverizing meat and causing blood to gush out of its neck stump. Raising her head to the high ceiling, she unleashed a defiant roar.

Valeria advanced on Mace with a flurry of swings, forcing him back. Her efforts grew more driven, more ferocious, and an overhead swing drove the tip of Mace's sword into a board on the floor. Seeing that she was seconds away from disarming him, he stomped on her Blade with his left foot and kicked her in the chest with his right. She flew back, releasing her sword, and landed on her back. Releasing his sword as well, Mace dove on top of her, but using both legs, she propelled him over her and sent him crashing to the concrete, where he grunted in pain.

Sensing his advantage, Michael pressed onward, attacking the male beast with a barrage of cuts with the expertise of a matador disabling a bull. He had trained for most of his adult life for this very task, and he felt empowered facing the leader of the beasts one-on-one. He did not know how Valeria and Loreti were faring, and he did not care. His entire life seemed to come down to this single confrontation.

A slice to the beast's left collarbone caused it to clutch the wound with its right claw. The werewolf barked at him in defiance. Feeling the moment was at hand, Michael swung his Blade like a helicopter rotor and prepared to deliver the decisive blow, which would decapitate the beast. Then he would make a trophy of its skull.

Sitting up with a groan, Mace saw Valeria running to where their swords lay with the elegance of a dancer. She seized her Blade, faced him, then picked up the other one. For a moment he thought she intended to hand him his sword in a gesture of fair play. Instead, she crossed her arms, holding one blade against each shoulder, and bowed her head, her face taut with concentration.

*Oh, shit*, he thought, getting to his feet.

She charged at him, swinging both Blades in circular patterns with the accuracy of a power tool.

Michael felt a sudden disconnect in his lower left leg, then the same sensation in his lower right leg. Agony lanced through both of his lower limbs, and he sank to his knees. Looking over his shoulder, he saw the female beast licking blood from her lupine teeth, and he knew the blood was his. Lowering his gaze, he saw that she had bitten his Achilles tendons, crippling him. Pain seized his right wrist as the male beast sank the claws of its left hand into his flesh so that blood poured out of five different points.

The beast plucked the Blade from his hand with its right claw and stood towering above him. The creature stared into his eyes, then raised the Blade over its head. Michael felt his mouth opening, and then he saw the Blade swinging toward him. He felt the Blade hack halfway through his neck, and he looked at the weapon's handle clutched in the beast's claw—recognized the head of the wolf carved into the pommel—and saw his blood, which he coughed out. A moment later, he saw nothing at all.

Valeria advanced on Mace with blinding speed. He staggered backward and slammed against a column, trapped. Her face contorted into a mask of rage as she bore down on him. He knew he would have to duck to his left or right, and the only chance he had to survive was if she did not anticipate his move. He feinted to his left, then dove to his right and rolled across the floor.

Spotting the Blade that Karol had discarded, he scrambled over the gory heap that remained of the male assassin she had killed and scooped it up. By the time he turned around with the sword raised in both hands, Valeria attacked him with a series of ruthless swings with both of her Blades. He tried to fend off her blows, but one of the Blades sank into his left shoulder—his *good* shoulder—and he cried out. His feet slipped in blood and flew out from under him, and he landed on his back. With an inhuman snarl on her lips, Valeria raised both Blades over her head and prepared to bring them down on him.

For an instant, Mace thought about Cheryl and Patty. Then he heard a pair of gunshots, and a crimson flower blossomed between Valeria's breasts. She froze, looked down at the wound, then let go of the Blades and toppled forward, landing on top of Mace. Rolling to one side, he shoved her off him, then looked from her glazed eyes to Cheryl, standing with Rhonda in the doorway Shelly and Norton had entered through. With his chest heaving and his heart pounding, he got to his feet.

Gabriel and Karol sat naked in human form on the floor near the headless corpse of Gabriel's opponent. Though human in appearance once more, Gabriel licked his many wounds like an animal. Rhonda went over to them and sank to her knees.

Mace staggered over to where Shelly and Norton lay on the floor. Norton's chest rose and fell with regularity, but Mace saw that Shelly was dead even before he checked for a pulse.

*Willy and Shelly,* he thought. *So much for everyone going home alive.*

Cheryl got down on one knee beside him, the gun smoking in her hand. "What happened?"

"They shot him with an animal tranquilizer. It must have been too much for him."

She nodded at Norton. "What about her?"

"Same thing but she managed to pull the darts out. She must have prevented as big of a dose from getting into her bloodstream. We still need to get her to a hospital." He looked at his wife. "I thought you were going to find your way out of here."

"We did find our way out. Then we found our way back in."

Mace caressed one side of her face. "Are you okay?"

"Yeah. Thanks for saving my life."

He wanted to laugh but couldn't. Too high of a price had been paid.

"Your shoulder looks bad," Cheryl said.

"Flesh wound." Taking his gun from her, he stood up. "Karol?"

Karol looked over at him.

"You're out of uniform. How about if you and Gabriel get dressed and we call 911? Norton and I need medical attention. It's too late for Shelly."

"Yes, Captain." Karol stood, and Rhonda helped Gabriel up.

Mace limped over to Gabriel. He wasn't even sure how he had hurt his leg. "Two years ago, I told your sister I needed to keep the Blade of Salvation I used to kill Janus Farel. I want you to take all of them with you tonight. Make sure they don't fall into the hands of fanatics again."

"Thank you," Gabriel said.

Mace offered his hand. "Thank you."

Gabriel shook his hand.

Mace walked over to the shoulder bag that the head assassin had dropped on the floor. Kneeling, he opened it and saw a laptop inside. He could only imagine what evidence it contained.

"Oh, my God," he heard Cheryl say. He saw that she had stopped trying to awaken Norton. Instead she looked at the doorway. Six immense black Wolves stood there on their hind legs.

Mace returned to Cheryl and helped her stand. The Wolves moved toward them. Gabriel stepped between them, and Karol and Rhonda joined him. Cheryl squeezed Mace's hand.

"Go home, Raphael," Gabriel said. "There's nothing left for you to do here."

The lead Wolf stepped ahead of the others and dropped to all fours. Seconds later, Raphael rose, naked. He glanced at Rhonda, then shifted his gaze back to Gabriel. "We did as you asked. We tracked down the Torquemadans, and I gave you this location so the police could take care of them." He looked at the corpses on the floor. "But you broke our laws. You helped the police. You showed them your true nature. So did Karol."

"I did what I believed was necessary," Gabriel said. "And I was right. They couldn't have done this without us. It would have been a slaughter."

"Now there are three humans who know our secret. One of them is a police captain, one is an FBI agent, and the other is a newscaster. We can't allow any of them to live."

Mace studied the five powerful-looking Wolves behind Raphael. Gabriel and Rhonda appeared as exhausted as he felt, and he doubted very much that his surviving team could fend off six Wolves.

"There will be no more killing tonight," Gabriel said. "These people are under my protection from tonight forward."

"Our *laws*—"

"Laws change as circumstances require. I make the laws. I'm the leader of the pack."

Raphael glared at his brother. "For now but maybe not for much longer."

Gabriel snorted. "Do you plan to challenge me?"

"Maybe. Or maybe I'll just start a new pack. I have plenty of support." He stared at Cheryl. "After her interview with Gomez, we have to be ready to face a new world. You're obviously not strong enough to do what needs to be done. I am."

"Elias has been filling your head with unhealthy thoughts. Don't let him do this. You're my brother. I love you."

Raphael took a deep breath. "I love you too, which is why it breaks my heart to see you so weak. We'll leave you to your humans. I wonder if they'll protect you tomorrow as you've protected them tonight. Take care of yourself. The next time we meet, things will be different."

Transforming into a Wolf, Raphael turned and bounded out of the warehouse, followed by his Wolf soldiers, their howls filling the night.

# CHAPTER THIRTY-NINE

Mace sat in Jim Mint's seventh-floor office at One Police Plaza. Outside, the first snowflakes of the year drifted to the city streets below.

"Incredible," Jim said. "Absolutely incredible. I honestly didn't think you could pull it off. How's your shoulder?"

"It hurts like bloody hell," Mace said.

"Stabbed with a sword." Jim shook his head. "And not just any sword, but a historic one belonging to some ancient secret society. It's too bad you lost them."

"One of the drawbacks of working with no backup. We needed medical attention fast. Rhonda Wilson appeared traumatized, I was in bad shape, and Norton could have died. I made the call to drive straight to an ER rather than wait for an ambulance. It never occurred to me that anyone would walk into that crime scene before Landry and Smalls could secure it and walk out with our silver swords."

Jim grunted. "Any theories as to who the thieves could have been?"

"That warehouse was abandoned. It could have been anyone—squatters, gang members. Maybe even a cop looking to make some extra money."

"What about Class Ls?"

Mace wanted to shrug, but he didn't have the shoulder for it. "Sure, I guess it could have been a Class L."

"Did you see any werewolves this time?"

Mace had anticipated this question. "No."

"I'm glad to hear it. It's a damned shame about Diega and Shelly. They'll each get a hero's funeral. They died in the line of duty while taking down a terrorist cell. This city owes them a debt."

"If we'd had a bigger unit . . ."

Jim raised one finger. "Don't second-guess yourself like that. It won't happen again."

"Oh?"

"If nothing else, the success of this operation proves the need for a task force like this, one that operates under the radar and gets things done. Especially after that interview Gomez gave your wife. You took care of the Brotherhood of Torquemada, but now we know what freaks are out there. Surely it's occurred to you that Gabriel and Raphael Domini could be Class Ls. Otherwise, why would the Brotherhood have gone after them? Rhonda Wilson, too. Someone has to keep an eye on these people, and I think you're the man for the job. What do you say? It will be a larger operation next time, with a full crew and all the backup you need."

Mace wanted to say no. He didn't want to run a task force anymore. He didn't want to deal with Wolves or the department. He just wanted to enjoy life with his wife and daughter. But he couldn't stop thinking about the standoff between Gabriel and Raphael, or shake the feeling that the bad blood between them meant bad things for New York City—his city. So he stared out the window at the falling snow and weighed his options.

*Only two more years until retirement,* he thought.

Sitting in the backseat of the town car, Father Tudoro watched JFK International Airport come into view. After everything that had happened the last few days, he had switched airports for his return to Rome. The last place on earth he wanted to be right now was Newark.

The elimination of the terrorist cell known as the Brotherhood of Torquemada had made front-page news around the world. Combined with the interview Cheryl Mace had conducted with Rodrigo Gomez and Michael's foolish abduction of her that same night, he knew there was no chance the Brotherhood would ever rise again, at least not in connection with the church. He felt bad about the Brotherhood members—especially Valeria—but they had known the risks when he enlisted them. At least he had provided their lives with direction.

Tudoro had devoted his life to the cause, and now he was through with werewolves, covert operations, and church politics. As soon as he returned to Rome, he intended to apply for a position at some remote church in a warm climate.

The town car pulled over to his airline, and the chauffeur removed his luggage from the trunk and helped him out. He paid the man, who wished him a good day, and collected his receipt. He did not notice the woman and five men in black suits and dark sunglasses until they intercepted him.

"Father Jonas Tudoro?" the woman said.

"Yes?" He hoped he didn't sound too surprised.

The woman showed him a federal badge. "I'm Special Agent Norton with the FBI, and these are my associates from the bureau, Homeland Security, and the CIA. We'd like you to come with us to answer some questions."

"What is this? I've done nothing wrong."

The woman smiled. "Really, Father? My late partner, Special Agent Shelly, would disagree with you if he was still alive. So would Detective Diega from NYPD and countless others."

"Who? I don't know what you're talking about."

Leaning close to him, the woman raised her sunglasses. "Michael kept records on his laptop, and we have that. We've checked your travel history against his notes on your meetings. You're the last living member of a very special, very secret organization, which we're very anxious to learn all about."

Tudoro gasped. "Am I under arrest?"

"Oh no, Father. We don't arrest enemy combatants of the United States. We just make them disappear."

"But you can't. I'm a priest."

Two of the men seized his arms, while another took custody of his luggage.

"I have friends in the Vatican!"

"Not anymore," Norton said.

Sipping his coffee, Mace watched the feds load Tudoro into a large black SUV with tinted windows and drive away. An identical SUV idled at the curb, waiting for Norton, who walked over to him.

Norton nodded at the Styrofoam cup in Mace's hand. "Is that coffee? I thought your doctor told you to cut out caffeine."

"Don't tell my wife."

"Your secret is safe with me, but you're getting up there. You have to start taking better care of yourself."

"I appreciate the concern." He sipped the coffee. "What will happen to Tudoro?"

"Aw, Tony. You know that's classified."

Mace thought about Willy. "Good. Sometimes it's better not to know."

"See you at the office tomorrow?"

Mace gave it some thought. He still hadn't given Jim Mint his answer. "Yeah. See you there."

"Good."

He watched her walk to her SUV, and then he walked to his. He had a unit to assemble.

# CARNAGE ROAD

## GREGORY LAMBERSON

# MEDALLION
P R E S S

Be in the know on the latest Medallion Press news by becoming a Medallion Press Insider!

<u>As an Insider you'll receive:</u>
· Our FREE expanded monthly newsletter, giving you more insight into Medallion Press
· Advanced press releases and breaking news
· Greater access to all your favorite Medallion authors

Joining is easy. Just visit our website at
<u>www.medallionmediagroup.com</u> and click on
*Super Cool E-blast* next to the social media buttons.

medallionmediagroup.com